After Cambridge and a stint on the *Evening Sentinel*, Stoke-on-Trent, Michael Toner worked for more than twenty years as a lobby correspondent at the House of Commons, where he wrote the Crossbencher column in the *Sunday Express* and later became the paper's Political Editor. Though he has now left full-time journalism to concentrate on novels, he still contributes regularly as a leader-writer on the *Daily Mail*.

Michael Toner lives near London with his two children. *Seeing the Light* is his first work of fiction.

SEEING THE LIGHT

MICHAEL TONER

POCKET
BOOKS

LONDON · SYDNEY · NEW YORK · TOKYO · SINGAPORE · TORONTO

First published in Great Britain by Simon & Schuster, 1997
This edition published by Pocket Books, 1998
An imprint of Simon & Schuster Ltd
A Viacom Company

Copyright © Michael Toner, 1997

The right of Michael Toner to be identified as author of this work has
been asserted in accordance with sections 77 and 78 of the Copyright
Designs and Patents Act 1988

Simon & Schuster Ltd
West Garden Place
Kendal Street
London
W2 2AQ

Simon & Schuster Australia
Sydney

A CIP catalogue record for this book is available from the British Library.

ISBN 0-671-85587-5

1 3 5 7 9 10 8 6 4 2

Printed and bound in Great Britain by Caledonian International Book
Manufacturing, Glasgow

In memory of Carol

CHAPTER

1

On the night that will change his life for ever, the Right Honourable George Gulliver sits on the platform at the Easthampton Corn Exchange, displaying all those subtle skills which marked him out years ago as a leader of men.

He leans attractively in his chair, jacket unbuttoned and legs crossed to reveal socks of startling magenta. Such touches of flamboyance are intended to confirm his reputation as a bit of a card, just as the charcoal grey of his suit establishes his seriousness and the stripe of his tie hints at a regimental past and therefore a patriotic heart. The tie in fact has no military significance. It was a birthday gift from his mistress and George likes to show it off as a kind of trophy, in the belief that his wife is too occupied with good works to notice.

As he poses in daring socks and reassuring suit he wears an expression that, like his tie, suggests hidden depths. Mostly it consists of a frown conveying rapt concentration, but from time to time he'll nod thoughtfully as though he'd just heard some profound insight or universal truth. It's all part of the election game, and George plays it with dedication.

When his turn comes to address the meeting, he'll spring gracefully to his feet and stride as far as he can go towards the edge of the platform without falling off. It's a trick he learned years ago from the old biddy who ran classes in public speaking for the Cambridge University Conservative Association. 'Narrow the angle as much as you can, dear,' she'd advised. 'Make the buggers look up at you.' It is a great satisfaction to George that the buggers always have.

He'll use no notes. The illusion of spontaneity is important in politics, and it is his secret ambition that one day the name of George Gulliver will be mentioned in the same breath as those of Aneurin Bevan and Winston Churchill, orators who could reduce an audience to tears or rouse it to cheers with words apparently spun off the top of the head. George is of course well aware that both Bevan and Churchill rehearsed their impromptu speeches for hours on end, and of late he's started doing the same, practising statesmanlike gestures in front of his dining-room mirror, though only while his wife is out of the house. Rosemary seems to have no understanding of the pressures Cabinet ministers must endure in the public interest.

There he'll stand then on this drizzly spring night, dominant, fluent, an inspiration to the rank-and-file supporters whose role in life is to cheer their champions on. With luck there will be a spot of heckling from the enemy troops and the old Gulliver one-two will swing into action. Zap! George has a talent for splattering socialist troublemakers, militant feminists, hunt saboteurs and the like all over the walls, to such effect that the 'Crossbencher' column in the *Sunday Express* recently described him as the Tiger of the Tory Shires. Tiger Gulliver. Though he affects to disdain such vulgar stuff, George dreams of achieving such headlines as THE TIGER SHOWS HIS CLAWS or TIGER MAULS THE LEFT, proof at last that he belongs to the select band of politicians recognisable by their nickname alone. Supermac. Tarzan. The Great She-Elephant.

It's a pity then that the voters of Easthampton have failed to measure up to the occasion. Though the local organisers have done their best, with plenty of blue bunting, photographs of a vigorously beaming Prime Minister and a large slogan asserting the urgent need to March Forward with the Conservatives, the atmosphere in the Corn Exchange is undeniably dispiriting, the consequence no doubt of a certain emptiness in the hall. Not to put too fine a point on it, only thirty-six voters have turned up to admire the Tiger in action. which means that the place is only ten per cent full, or to look at it another way, ninety per cent empty.

George is too accomplished a professional to take this as a personal slight. He can think of any number of reasons why even his fearful symmetry has failed to draw a crowd. The weather is unpleasant. England's footballers are engaged in a televised friendly international against the Germans, and blood is expected on Wembley's hallowed turf. Worse still, the Government is mired in a slough of unpopularity and has no idea at all how to climb out. It irritates him that the Prime Minister has so far neglected to ask his advice, but the moment surely cannot be long delayed. Easthampton, after all, is likely to be the Conservatives' ninth by-election defeat in a row and the PM needs all the help he can get.

It is some comfort to George that none of the blame can be laid at his door. It is not he who has cocked up the economy, as the Chancellor of the Exchequer undoubtedly has. Still less has he enraged the nation's pensioners by advising them to stop whingeing, which is how the Social Services Secretary has just distinguished herself. George does not make such mistakes. He runs a tight ship, loyally beats the party drum whenever the need arises. One day, he hopes, his selfless contribution to the cause will receive the recognition it deserves and propel him higher still in government, perhaps to the very top. But he can hardly dwell on that. He's sufficiently experienced to understand that ambition must be dressed in modesty.

In a couple of minutes he'll be on. Not a moment too soon, either, judging by the surly expressions on show round the hall. Most members of the audience seem to have succumbed to a collective regret that they didn't stay at home to watch England. No matter. George is confident he can liven them up. He's a tiger.

Beside him, the smart young pinstripe of a candidate begins beating the air for emphasis as he launches into his closing harangue; and if we pay proper attention we'll observe that

George is gathering his energies for the fray. He's buttoning his jacket, uncrossing his legs, sitting up. His nods are just a little more pronounced, his expression perhaps a shade more intent.

'The late President John Kennedy once told the American people not to ask what their country could do for them, but to ask rather what they could do for their country,' the pinstripe proclaims, his eyes glittering. This is a bold ploy to try on a miserable night in an empty English hall, and George is rather impressed. He has a soft spot for brute windbaggery.

'My declaration to the people of this constituency is that Jack Kennedy's words are as relevant today as ever they were.'

'Hear, hear,' booms George, encouraged by such cheek. Jack Kennedy, eh?

'Let the message go forth from this place,' bawls the candidate, who's clearly suffering a bad case of Kennedyitis. 'The tide has turned. The fight-back begins at this election. The eyes of the whole country will be on Easthampton next Thursday, and with your help and your votes I know we shall win.'

It is a brave effort, and George leads the applause with every appearance of enthusiasm, though the audience seems reluctant to join in. 'Well done, Simon,' he whispers. 'Well spoken. Excellent.' He is proud of his way with aspiring young politicians, and is rewarded by the flush of pleasure glowing on the youth's face. If ever the boy gets into Parliament he'll be a Gulliver supporter from the start. George believes in the virtue of long-term planning.

'Our next speaker of course needs no introduction,' announces the chairman as George essays a small and modest smile. It is one of the looks he has practised at home, and he can safely let the rest of the remarks wash over him as he runs through the outlines of his speech. Ten minutes or so on the iniquities of the Labour Party, five more on the resolute courage of the Government in insisting on unpopular policies and a final blast about the need to keep up our guard in a dangerous world. It should be more than adequate.

Since the television cameras have failed to turn up, almost

certainly a consequence of the left-wing conspiracy in broadcasting, it may not be worth slipping in a hint about the new export deal with Sahelia. Perhaps he'll save it for the by-election press conference in the morning, though on the other hand Jack Cartwright of the *Daily Despatch* is at the press table, alone and obviously bored. Jack has been useful in the past and George likes to look after his friends in the press. An exclusive for the *Despatch* should do no harm at all. It would not only be one in the eye for the Trade Minister, who'd love to claim the credit for himself: it might teach a lesson to all those media pinkoes who have chosen to be elsewhere tonight. Bloody BBC. Bloody ITN, come to that.

'Now there's one other reason why we're especially pleased to welcome George Gulliver to Easthampton,' declares the chairman. 'He's one of us. One of our own. Born and bred in our town.' He pauses as one or two of the party faithful try to start off a round of applause. George, who has a happy knack of responding even when he hasn't been listening, smiles at the rows of empty seats.

'It's a privilege, Secretary of State, to welcome you home,' the chairman hurries on. 'You may have left us many years ago, but I think you'll find that there's still such a thing as an old-fashioned Easthampton welcome. Ladies and gentlemen, please show your appreciation for the only local man who has ever sat in Cabinet, the Right Honourable George Gulliver, Secretary of State for Defence!'

It does not matter that few members of the audience seem to have any idea of what constitutes an old-fashioned Easthampton welcome or that the only people clapping with any conviction are those wearing the blue rosettes provided by Conservative Central Office, or that Jack Cartwright is unsuccessfully trying to stifle a yawn. George is up on his feet and out where he likes to be, at the front, narrowing the angle, making the buggers look up.

The clapping dies away. The silence builds, thickens. George waits. His performance won't start until he can sense the tension in the hall, feel it stretch bowstring tight. It is part of the Gulliver technique, and it never fails. He has them now, all thirty-six of them, in the hollow of his hand. It's not so difficult when you know how.

Later, much later, Cartwright will tell his friends in El Vino's that George Gulliver was on the very top of his form that night in his home town, socking it to 'em like one of the old-time greats. Like Aneurin Bevan maybe. Or Winston Churchill.

But by then such things will have ceased to matter.

A mile away from the Corn Exchange, in the dining-room of the Bull Hotel, Ms Monica Holroyd sipped the dregs of her coffee and regretted the impossibility of creating a scene.

That she was a woman more than capable of stamping her foot and sending for the manager should have been obvious even to the slovenly crew who manned the Bull, if not from the set of her jaw and the glint in her eye, then from the severity of her suit. In its sleek, dark simplicity it was an outfit that proclaimed its wearer as someone to be reckoned with, a don't-dare-give-me-any-shit kind of suit, the sort of display that in London would be recognised at once as an example of power-dressing, designed to make bank managers cringe and cabbies compete to do U-turns.

In the dining-room of the Bull it had no impact at all. Provincial oafs.

Though the place was all but deserted she had of course been shown to a table next to the kitchen, in deference to the good old English custom of never neglecting an opportunity of putting an unaccompanied woman in her place. It was treatment that in other circumstances would have inspired a deeply satisfying row, followed in short order by a grovelling apology from the manager and a move in triumph to a better spot. Monica liked to think such small victories mattered in the greater scheme of things, felt irritated that George's insistence on discretion (not to mention the presence of a couple of journalists haggling over their bill in the corner) had deflected her from the path of duty.

Throughout her meal – potage du jour from a tin, a piece of skate in black butter from the freezer – she'd endured the crash of pans, the rattle of plates and the surly comments of the chef to someone called Janet, who had apparently turned up late for duty. Janet, needless to say, suffered in silence, as women so often did. As Monica herself had been doing, if truth be told. No longer, though. Not for a second longer. Tonight she intended to smoke out George once and for all.

'More coffee, madam?' asked the waiter, who had somehow managed to creep up on her unobserved. He was an unprepossessing young man with a stain on his shirt and hair that could do with an oil change.

'Just the bill, thank you.'

'Certainly, madam. Everything all right for you, was it?'

No, you fool, it wasn't all right, and if you worked for me I'd fire you on the spot, thought Monica. 'Fine,' she said.

The waiter smirked and disappeared, returning a moment later bearing a side-plate, upon which rested the bill, carefully folded. Monica opened it and ran a cold eye down the figures, which rather to her surprise added up. She scribbled her signature and room number and handed it back to the waiter, who had been hovering throughout in a manner designed to demonstrate both his helpfulness and his expectation of an enormous tip. 'Thank you so much,' she said, in a voice that made it clear the man wouldn't get a penny piece if he stood there for a twelvemonth. It wasn't much of a victory, but until George arrived it would have to do.

Not that she was looking forward to the confrontation. She couldn't predict the outcome. It might be wiser if she got in her car now, right now, and drove back to London. The thought of him creeping along to her room with that look of furtive anticipation and a bulge in his trousers would keep her entertained all the way home.

It wouldn't do though. Not really. However diverting the prospect of a bewildered and detumescent minister stumbling forlornly round the hotel at midnight, Monica hadn't any serious intention of scuttling off home. It would solve nothing, might even allow George to enjoy playing the injured party. He tended to be rather good at that.

In her colder moments, Monica was occasionally tempted to blame herself. In three years she'd never complained – or not with any great force – at the indignities in serving as mistress to a public man. Not when he left her bed in the small hours to return to his wretched wife, or when he insisted on taking her down remote streets to interesting Italian restaurants where they always had candles stuck in Chianti bottles. Not even when he cancelled their assignations at the last minute pleading pressure of work, or when he rang unexpectedly at midnight begging permission to come round.

Uncomfortable to admit, but she'd allowed herself to be treated like a bimbo, though with none of the rewards of bimbodom, no jewels or furs or holidays in the sun. As far as romantic gestures went, George's horizons never stretched much further than Chanel No. 5.

Well, enough of that. There comes a time, if you're thirty something and restless and your biological clock is ticking and your lover shows not the slightest sign of acting on the promises he's whispered on your pillow, when temptation becomes irresistible. Monica had made up her mind. If she couldn't force a commitment now, she never would.

He'd telephoned when she was fast asleep, dead to the world in her solitary bed. 'I need to see you,' he'd muttered with the urgency usual whenever he felt the need for a quick legover.

In normal circumstances Monica, who had her own needs, would have switched immediately into her courtesan mode which involved a hint of heavy breathing and a husky assurance that she'd be waiting, darling, and don't be long. But for once she hadn't been cooperative. It was, after all, nearly three weeks since he'd bothered to get in touch. 'It's past midnight,' she'd found herself saying.

'I've been at the SBAC dinner.' George was the only man she'd ever met who could sound plaintive without quite toppling over the edge into self-pity.

'What?'

'The Society of British Aerospace Companies.' Even after three years of groaning in her bed he tended to take all her questions quite literally.

'Good meal was it?'

'Beef Wellington,' he'd told her, reliable as ever.

'I had poached egg on toast.'

'Don't think I've been enjoying myself.' George always grew irritable at the merest suggestion that his job was anything other than a burden, bravely borne. 'I just thought it would be nice if we got together.'

'Mmm. I know, darling. But I'm really very tired.'

'I've sent my driver home.' George was careful never to use his official car on unofficial business. 'Managed to give my detective the slip. I'll get a cab. I can be with you in twenty minutes.'

'Sorry, George. I really don't feel up to it. Not tonight.' It was the first time Monica had ever refused one of his proposals without a plausible reason and she'd found she was rather enjoying the experience.

George of course hadn't enjoyed it one bit. After a spot of pleading and several minutes to no avail on the subject of how much he loved her, needed her, had never in all his life known another like her, and really, darling, you know I mean it, he'd suggested somewhat sulkily that she might like to come up to Easthampton, where he was doing a by-election turn.

It was at that moment, yawning and in her nightie, that Monica had taken the decision. It popped into her mind fully formed, the product perhaps of a thousand small resentments filed away for future use. She understood the risks, of course, though they were far outweighed by the potential rewards: they sustained her all the way to her solitary dinner at the Bull Hotel.

She was in love after all, or as near as made no difference; and as everyone knows, a woman in love is entitled to fight ruthlessly for what she wants.

Monica snapped her handbag shut and stood up. The dining-room was empty now. Even the waiter had disappeared, though it was barely 9.30. There would be plenty of time for a leisurely bath and a change into the necessary combat-gear. Hardly a man in the world could easily resist arguments backed up by transparent silk, lacy suspender-belt and sheer stockings.

Full of resolve, she swept through the lobby and over to the Bull's ancient lift. George would be panic-stricken of course when she presented her ultimatum, but it couldn't be helped. No doubt he'd rant for a bit. Might possibly burst into tears. He'd see reason eventually though. Had to. She'd studied the script. True love always triumphs in the end, doesn't it?

'A large Bell's whisky for the Minister,' called the chairman above the hubbub. 'Splash of water. Plenty of ice. I'll have the usual. Simon? Dashing off home to that lovely wife of yours?'

'Well . . .' The pinstripe seemed torn for a moment between marital duty and political ambition. 'I did promise I'd be back early.' He caught George's eye. 'Maybe just a half.'

'Give Mr Fishlock a pint, Arthur,' the chairman told the barman. 'Have one yourself.' He was doing the bluff, man-of-the-people bit for all he was worth, and George suspected that any minute now he'd start laying down the law about where the Government was going wrong. They often did: the trick was to nod sympathetically and promise to convey the message to the PM. Nothing local chairmen liked better than the opportunity to boast to their dinner guests how they'd torn a strip off a Cabinet star.

'Watch out for Geoff Norridge,' Central Office had warned. 'Profits aren't too hot in the building fraternity. He'll almost certainly bitch about the economy. Stay sweet, though. Need his cash.'

In deference to Norridge's wealth, George beamed the special smile he reserved for such occasions, the one that crinkled the corners of his eyes and glowed with good cheer. 'This place takes me back,' he ventured. 'It's been a long time.'

In fact the Easthampton Conservative Club had changed remarkably little in thirty years, but for a new carpet in turd-brown and a couple of fruit machines in the corner. Old jossers in blazers still chanted the traditional mantras.

'What are you having?'

'Let me get them in.'

'No, no. My shout.'

'Sure?'

'Absolutely.'

'Just a half then.'

The Annigoni portrait of the Queen still hung over the bar, and the Karsh photograph of Winston Churchill scowled from the far wall with an expression suggesting he'd been offered the smallest of small brandies and presented with the bill. George raised his glass in tribute. 'Great days,' he said. 'Easthampton Young Conservatives. We were a lively bunch.'

'So I'm told.' Norridge wasn't bothering to sound interested.

'Used to meet here every Monday night. Set the world to rights. Seems a million years ago.'

In fact George would never forget the painful, unrequited lust which drove him into the arms of the party, to the bafflement of his Labour-voting parents. In his adolescent years the Young Conservatives were reputedly in the vanguard of sexual liberation; week after week he'd turn up at meetings awash in expectation, a single hoarded rubber johnny tucked securely in his wallet. Just as regularly he'd slink home after an evening of table tennis or a discussion of the national housing programme. It was, he supposed, his first political lesson in the gap between promise and performance.

'Never had time for that stuff,' growled Norridge, examining the ice which was all that remained in the bottom of his glass. 'Too busy starting up. Had to leave politics to chaps like you. Pity. Could have given you a run for your money, eh?' He favoured George with a look somewhere between a grin and a snarl to show that he might have been joking.

'Can I top you up, chairman?' asked Simon, who was clearly used to Norridge's habit of hurling his drink down at a single gulp.

'Thought you'd never ask,' said Norridge, winking at George, who had hardly touched his whisky. Even in a place like Easthampton, you couldn't be too careful.

'Minister?'

'I'll stick with what I've got, thanks,' George said. 'Papers to go through later on.' Hints of an immense workload never did any harm.

'He's a good lad really,' confided Norridge, when Simon was out of earshot at the bar. 'Bit wet behind the ears maybe. Under the thumb at home, I'm told.'

'I thought he did very well tonight,' said George in an effort to discourage any further confidences. The bar was filling up, every ear in the place straining to catch what he was saying. He smiled genially round the room to show he wasn't being standoffish. 'Could do with more like him.'

'Won't let herself be called Mrs Fishlock,' Norridge pressed on oblivious of the hint. 'Insists on using her maiden name. One of those. You know the sort. Can't get her to go campaigning either. Hates political meetings, apparently. Poor little bugger doesn't know whether he's coming or going.'

'He'll learn,' said George. 'No room for half measures in this business.' He'd long ago convinced himself this was true: it was absolution of a sort for the endless evenings away from home and the bedtime stories he'd never read to his children.

'Aye, well.' Norridge leaned forward, a sly glint in his eye. 'A quick word about this Sahelia business, eh? Before the lad gets back.'

'Mmm?' 'Course, he'd never started out with the intention of becoming an absentee husband and father. It had simply happened. The price of getting on. No need to feel guilty about it. None at all.

'Sahelia,' prompted Norridge. 'When will we know the details?'

George wrenched himself back to the business in hand. 'It'll be in the *Despatch* tomorrow.' He recalled how eagerly Jack Cartwright had scuttled off to find the nearest phone. 'Good news, too, for a change, eh? Six billion pounds' worth of trade. Maybe more. Thousands of jobs. No funny money either. All paid for in hard cash.'

'Be nice if some of it came to Easthampton.' The gleam in Norridge's eye was unmistakable. 'All these planes and tanks. Got to be serviced. Runways, garaging. Good business for somebody, I should think, what?'

'Very good business.' George tended to enjoy watching supplicants squirm; it proved that the pursuit of power was worth the effort. 'Naturally everything will have to go to tender.'

A conspiratorial expression stole across Norridge's face. He lowered his voice. 'I don't suppose . . .' He glanced round. 'I mean, not much prospect of a firm like mine getting a look-in, I suppose?'

'Oh, I don't know,' said George, who knew very well. 'If you've got the capacity and you came up with the right price you'd certainly stand a chance.' Out of the corner of his eye he could see Simon returning with a drink in his hand. Time to end the game. 'I've nothing to do with the nuts and bolts though. It'll all be in the hands of the Trade Department. And the Sahelians, of course.'

'Brandy and soda, Chairman.' Simon's return cut off any opportunity Norridge may have had to suggest a little greasing of the ministerial palm. 'Lots of ice.'

'Aye. Thanks, lad.' The chairman seemed almost relieved to have missed his opportunity, as though it had just occurred to him that an attempt to corrupt a Cabinet minister might not be the surest way to a knighthood.

'We were just talking about Sahelia.' George took another sip of his whisky. 'A bit of good news for your campaign, eh?'

'Tell the Minister about your wife, Simon,' Norridge instructed. Was there just a hint of malice in his tone? 'Mrs Fishlock's an expert on Sahelia.'

'Really?' George noticed that Simon was beginning to blush. 'Most people don't even know where the place is.'

'She spent a couple of years out there before we were married,' said Simon, who was clearly beginning to wish he'd gone home after all. 'She's a doctor you see.'

Ah, yes. George fancied he saw all right. British doctors who insisted on plying their trade in the armpits of the world were invariably of a type. Left-wingers. Bleeding hearts, forever demanding more handouts for their ne'er-do-well patients. Obvious now why Mrs Fishlock wouldn't be seen on a Conservative platform.

'Go on then, lad,' ordered Norridge. 'Tell him the rest of it. Got herself thrown out, didn't she?'

'It wasn't really her fault, Minister,' muttered Simon. 'She treated this local girl who'd been raped, cut about a bit. Bad state, apparently. Anyway it turned out the attacker was one of the Vizier's supporters. A Sheikh Yusuf. So nobody would

do anything about it, see? Didn't want to know. Lucind
complained to our ambassador. Wanted him to put som
pressure on. Bit naïve of course.' Simon put on a little gri
to show he was a man of the world. 'She got the answer you'
expect. Embassy warned her she was wasting her time. Tol
her not to make trouble.'

'Mmm,' said George, impressed. The story confirmed his hig
opinion of Her Britannic Majesty's Ambassador to Sahelia.

'Then the Government ordered her out. Just like that. By th
next plane. So I'm afraid she's not very happy with the Vizie
and his friends. Don't suppose she'll be too pleased if we sta
selling them tanks.'

'Bolshevik propaganda,' grumbled Norridge.'What about job
then, eh?' His glass was empty again.

'Come on, Geoff. Let's be fair.' The use of a first name a
the critical moment often flattered old codgers into behavin
themselves. 'Simon's got a point. I'm sure a lot of people feel th
same way.' George took some pleasure in his ability to soun
judicious.

'The thing is, Simon, we've taken account of the loca
situation. Told the Sahelians we won't sell them as muc
as a pair of combat boots until they start respecting huma
rights. Okay? You can defend the deal with a clear conscienc
It's not only good for Britain. It's good for the ordinary peopl
of Sahelia.'

This was, in fact, the line he'd been saving up for th
inevitable row at Westminster once news of the agreemen
became public, and it was instructive to observe the impac
Norridge nodded his head gravely, as though the question o
human rights had never been far from his mind. The Fishloc
boy fairly beamed in gratitude. It's always a relief for any youn
politician to be absolved of responsibility for making a mora
choice. Or most *old* politicians, come to that.

It hadn't been an easy arrangement, mind. George recalle
the look of incredulity on the ambassador's face when first h
raised the question of how the Vizier and his appalling gang o
thieves, thugs and sheep-shaggers might be persuaded to sig
up to civilised behaviour.

'You do understand, Secretary of State, that it's a different world out here?' James Dalton had warned. He was one of those leathery, sunburned types who'd spent a diplomatic lifetime trailing from one desperate posting to another, with not so much as an OBE to show for it. He had a pretty wife though. And a giggly teenage daughter with a brace on her teeth. 'Pack of heathens, out here. Cut your throat for the fun of it.'

George had fixed the man with a steady, statesmanlike gaze. 'Nevertheless . . .'

Since the fellow was nobody's fool and still dreamed no doubt of a mention in the Queen's Birthday Honours, he'd taken the hint without missing a beat. 'So long as you understand they wouldn't know a moral principle if they fell over one. They're not Muslims, see? Aren't Christian either. Far as we can tell, they worship their camels. Still, offer them the right kind of stuff and they'll sign anything. Join the Salvation Army at a pinch. Can't fob them off with second-hand goods, mind. They'll want our latest fighters. Radar. Missiles. Tanks. God knows what else.'

This was the kind of stuff to warm the cockles of any defence secretary's heart, never mind if Sahelia was a million square miles of fuck all. That it existed as an independent nation at all was due entirely to the fact that until the discovery of oil nobody else wanted the place. Since then, as George had warned his Cabinet colleagues, the Republic of Niger was to the west and the Republic of Chad to the east had both discovered historic links with their Sahelian brothers and had let it be known they were anxious to offer whatever protection might be required. Alarming news, eh? Britain to the rescue. George hadn't felt it necessary to advise his fellow ministers that neither Chad nor Niger was capable of knocking the cherry off a Bakewell tart.

'We'll need to stress the human-rights aspects though,' said Simon, breaking in on his reminiscences. 'Lucinda will take some convincing the Vizier and his chums won't just turn these weapons against their own people.'

'You can take my word for it,' said George, somewhat irritated the boy hadn't done so already. 'Socialists may make

a fuss, but we'll just have to prove them wrong, won't we?'
He switched on a reassuring smile and wondered whether he
hadn't been a mite rash in giving the story to Jack Cartwright.
If a loyal scout like young Fishlock felt uneasy, what might the
hobbledehoys in the press make of the deal? For a sudden,
alarming moment a headline flashed into his mind's eye: ARMS
FOR THE MONSTER. But no. He'd stressed the positive side, hadn't
he? Old Jack wouldn't let him down. Not Jack.

Trouble was, you couldn't tell the truth, or not much of
it. What nobody outside his Ministry knew was that not a
single tank sold to Sahelia, not a rocket or a warplane or an
artillery piece, would be in proper working order a year after
the last British adviser went home. That was the beauty of
the arrangement. Heat would fry the electronic systems. Sand
would clog and abrade every moving part. Without constant,
expert, high-tech maintenance the whole of the Vizier's shiny
new war machine would grind itself to a standstill in short
order, while HM Treasury pocketed Jimmy O' Goblins by the
bagful and walked off whistling. And if the Vizier wanted to
recover from the fiasco he'd have no option but to come
running to London with his dick in his hand, begging for help.
Neat, eh?

'One for the road, George?' asked Norridge. 'We'll be closing
the bar any minute.'

'No, it's my turn. What'll it be?' Wherever he went, George
made a point of standing his corner. It prevented talk of
cheapskatery. 'Simon? Can I top you up?'

'Thanks, but I really should be going,' said Simon. 'Anyway,
I'm driving.'

'One of the advantages of being a minister, eh George?' Like
many of his kind Norridge clearly enjoyed being on first-name
terms with his betters. 'Never having to drive yourself.'

George smiled dutifully and went to get Norridge his brandy
and soda. In fact his ministerial Rover wasn't remotely the perk
it was cracked up to be, especially if you were trying to conduct
a discreet liaison. Especially if your driver happened to be a
Methodist lay preacher.

Sometimes he dreamed of emerging from an official dinner

or a late-night sitting at the House to inform cheerful Charlie Roberts that he wouldn't be going directly home after all. No indeed. Urgent business of the trouser-dropping kind required his attention at a certain flat in Pimlico, so step on it, Charlie.

Impossible, of course. Monica might not understand his terror of Charlie, but then she'd never seen the gang of government drivers hanging around in Speakers' Court at Westminster, gossiping, smoking and no doubt tearing their respective ministers' reputations to shreds. In theory they all took pride in their loyalty and discretion, but George didn't believe in theory. Given an inkling of his master's extramural activities, he suspected Charlie would waste no time at all in telling all to the *News of the World*. It was a prospect to take the bloom off romance as efficiently as a mention of genital warts.

Well, at least the occasional by-election provided consolation. There were no red boxes on the campaign trail, no Cabinet papers to read, no personal detective lurking at his shoulder. On such excursions the local constabulary were assumed to be capable of protecting him. Best of all there was no Charlie Roberts, in deference to the rule that government vehicles and official drivers were never to be used for party political purposes. Tonight George could plunder Monica's pale flesh without the slightest fear of discovery. He'd even bought some Chanel No. 5 to celebrate. Her favourite.

Which was just about the last clear memory he had before everything changed and the universe turned upside down.

He'd paid for the drink. That much he could grasp. It had cost three pounds and a few pennies. He'd counted the money out exactly. It seemed strange afterwards that such a detail should stand out. Not much else did. Not much that made sense anyway.

There would have been further conversation with Norridge of course, and he must have said goodnight to young Fishlock. He'd probably shaken a few hands before leaving the club, because that was what he usually did when out campaigning. He liked to cheer up the troops. Give them something to boast about when they got home. All part of the Gulliver charm.

Then he'd been sitting in the passenger seat of the chairman's Jaguar XJ6. He had the vaguest recollection of leather and the smell of alcohol. Hadn't there been a pair of fluffy dice dangling in the rear window?

Apparently they'd raced at sixty-five along a stretch of dual carriageway. That much was in the papers. Maybe he'd wondered about Norridge's consumption of brandy. Or maybe in his eagerness to get to Monica at the Bull he hadn't wondered at all. The Easthampton police weren't likely to embarrass a Cabinet minister and the local Tory chairman with an invitation to blow into this little bag, please, if you don't mind, sir; and anyway lust is easily capable of defeating the demands of prudence (though as it turned out Norridge's blood–alcohol level was below the limit – just).

They never troubled George to give evidence at the inquest. He could remember nothing of the crash, after all. And what came afterwards could have no conceivable relevance to the business of the court.

There's a bang. A wrench at the core of his being. A dissolution. Perhaps there's some screaming. It's hard to be sure.

He's a little bewildered at first, though not uncomfortably so. It's only natural to feel bewildered when you find yourself floating without effort twenty feet above the surface of the earth, with no visible means of support.

Though he has a magnificent view of the proceedings it takes a moment or two before he can work out what has happened. Below on the carriageway, Norridge's car lies smashed and steaming against a concrete lamppost. Hanging out of the doors, two bodies lie bloodied and motionless. Both are plainly recognisable, despite their injuries.

Death is not a subject that George has ever cared to contemplate, though he long ago gave up smoking in the hope of postponing the evil hour. If pressed, he might have said that he wished to expire at the age of ninety-five, worn out by the demands of lechery, but in truth his secret wish is to live forever. It ought to be horrifying then to see himself sprawled by the wreckage, cut off in his prime, but in fact he feels nothing but a certain curiosity about his present state and perhaps the beginnings of a strange happiness.

Contrary to the physical evidence, he's warm and safe. Far beyond the drudge of flesh. It's going to be all right. Really. He can tell. There's nothing to worry about. Soon there will be other developments, and George is looking forward to them. He's read enough about out-of-body experiences (though until now without believing a word) to know that there should be light somewhere, celestial music to knock the Last Night of the Proms into a cocked hat and, in all probability, a tunnel or stairway leading to a higher plane where he'll be assured of a welcome better by far than anything on offer at the Easthampton Corn Exchange.

This is what it's all about. His contentment is growing. There's a glow around him now, a sense that all his life and striving were but a preparation for this moment. A modest tug on the bonds of earth and he'll drift on into another realm where he might at last be able to seek oratorical advice from Aneurin Bevan and Winston Churchill.

There's no sign of a stairway yet, no tunnel for that matter. But the glow is becoming encouragingly brighter, flooding round him and through him, shining on secrets he buried long ago, bathing them in light. Somewhat to his surprise, George is not in the least embarrassed, though that business years ago in Cairo with the hooker and the donkey was certainly nothing to boast about. There are, it seems, worse sins. He burns in a brief, fierce moment of regret for the pettiness and meanness of his earthly existence, then the moment passes. He is at peace again. Instinctively he knows he has been judged and absolved. He hasn't felt quite so happy since Black Dog in the *Mail on Sunday* tipped him as a future prime minister.

On the road below there are lights flashing now, police vehicles and an ambulance parked beside the wrecked Jaguar. Men in uniform are talking into radios. Others are crouched over the bodies. Though he can see everything down to the expression of shock on the rescuers' faces, George can hear nothing. Not a sound. He finds this mildly puzzling. There ought to be music somewhere.

What seems rather more puzzling is that there's no sign of Norridge hovering around, though his body is sprawled on the road as dead as mutton, the ambulanceman pulling a sheet over his head. The man's spirit must be nearby unless . . . George shies away from the thought. He has never believed in Hell, and in any case Norridge hasn't been such an unregenerate swine that he deserves to be dragged down below, without the option. Not really.

The activity round the wrecked Jaguar seems to grow more hectic by the minute. Another ambulance and a couple of extra police cars have turned up, not to mention a knot of morbid onlookers. Well, it's quite a sight, isn't it? Not one of your common or garden accidents at all. Should make satisfactory headlines in the last editions tomorrow morning, and George wonders what the obituaries will say about him. Tiger Gulliver perhaps. Even Rosemary wouldn't be able to curl her lip at that. As for Monica . . .

There's a pull. He doesn't like it much. He's slipping. Above he can hear the music at last, the sweetest he's ever heard. Better than Mozart, though Mozart is probably lurking around. Maybe that's him playing. It would be a grand thing to see Wolfgang Amadeus in action, but something's wrong. The music is fading. Below on the road there are men leaning over his body, men loosening his tie and shining penlights in his eyes. There's a mask on his face, an oxygen bottle beside it. There's a needle, plunging in. He feels it. Shit. He's sliding down. Struggling. He's fighting to stay there, stay in the light but the men have him on a stretcher. They're lifting him into the ambulance and he feels the pain of it. Oh, it bloody well hurts all right. Where the fuck has Mozart gone?

It is his last thought before the darkness comes.

CHAPTER

2

Mrs Rosemary Gulliver, pale in D-cup and sensible knickers, studied herself in an unkind mirror and sighed.

It was hard to remember the better times, when she'd definitely possessed a waist and the muscles were more or less taut, times when George could be relied upon to tumble around with her beneath the covers at least twice a week, sometimes quite enjoyably. All gone now. These days he came home late and tired and smelling of whisky to work on his red boxes into the small hours and sleep at last with never more than a peck on the cheek to reward her wakefulness. The penalties of middle age.

Sometimes she ashamedly caught herself envying her husband. The thing about George was that he actually became better looking as he grew older, his lines and creases and greying hair only adding to his attractiveness, while she . . . well. No choice but to make what she could out of brisk tweediness.

Turning away from her reflection, she peeled off her underclothes and reached for her nightgown, one of those ankle-length shrouds in pink winceyette which efficiently covered every bulge and blemish. It would never arouse George, but the alternatives were to sleep naked – unthinkable – or endure the creation in black silk which he'd bought years ago as a Valentine present. It had excited him once, to such an extent that he'd made love to her twice in one night, a feat unheard of since their honeymoon. She wondered what his reaction would be if she wore it now. Panic, probably.

Safely covered, Rosemary sat at the dressing-table for the nightly ritual with hairbrush and moisturising cream, a pink confection in a cut-glass bottle which promised that with regular application it could restore the bloom of youth. Rosemary was perfectly well aware that the promise was an overpriced lie, and the allegedly secret formula no more than a nod in tribute to her unscientific optimism. In fact the product might just as well have been petroleum jelly; but the jar was pretty, and one had to make an effort. Thank God her skin was still supple, not many lines or wrinkles yet, only a hint of crêpe in the neck. Though the stern leaflets of the Health Education Council might accuse her of being twenty pounds adrift of her ideal weight her features weren't too bad. Large eyes, rich dark hair, a pleasant smile. Pity it wasn't enough to revive the twinkle in her husband's eye.

There were some, Rosemary suspected, who wondered why George stayed. Half the ministers in Cabinet, after all, had changed wives in mid-career, swapping middle-aged partners for the young flesh of their secretaries; and provided the unwritten rules of discretion were observed, they usually got away with it. The risk, for most, was obviously worth taking. It was a fact of life that men didn't value wives for their character or their recipes for crabapple jelly. Firmness of breast and pertness of bottom were the requirements. A tendency to thrash around in bed and utter small yelps of delight at the appropriate moment didn't come amiss either, as George in a black moment had once pointed out. Determined to cooperate even at the risk of feeling foolish, Rosemary obliged on the very next occasion they made love, only to stop George in mid-thrust. 'You're faking,' he complained.

Well, no point moping. Twenty-four years of marriage, twin sons and a fiftieth birthday lurking on the not-too-distant horizon could never pass for sweet spring lamb, whatever

Miss Jane Fonda cared to say. It had been a long time since Rosemary felt it worthwhile to dig out the old videotape, lock the doors, draw the curtains and try yet again for the elusive burn.

The phone downstairs began ringing the moment she switched off her bedside light. It couldn't be George. Not at this hour. It wouldn't be the boys either. They knew she liked her sleep. She lay in the darkness waiting for it to stop, irritated with herself for forgetting to switch on the answering machine. It would only be some wretched political reporter in search of a ministerial opinion. Unlike some of his colleagues George could be amazingly affable to the press, even when roused from his bed. He was a man who worked hard on his popularity.

The ringing stopped at last and Rosemary settled down. Perhaps she should let George have a phone extension in the bedroom after all, she thought drowsily. He was always having to stumble downstairs in the middle of the night. It wasn't fair on him when he worked so hard, poor man. The phone rang again.

'Aargh!' grumbled Rosemary. She swallowed her irritation on the instant. It wasn't the family's private number that was making such a racket but the official red scrambler phone in George's study. She bolted awake, her heart thumping.

'It's John Hamilton here,' said the voice at the other end as she stood clutching the receiver in her winceyette and bare feet. 'Duty officer at the Ministry.' His tone suggested that there was bad news coming, as if he were a surgeon nerving himself to confess that he'd somehow managed to cut off the wrong leg.

'George is in Easthampton,' Rosemary said, feeling immediately foolish. Of course the Ministry knew where he was. It knew his movements every minute of the day. Including, in all probability, his bowel movements.

'You mustn't be alarmed,' said Hamilton as Rosemary felt her insides dissolve. 'I'm afraid your husband's been involved in an accident.'

'Is he hurt?' It was curious how she couldn't open her mouth without sounding inane. Of course he was hurt. People got hurt in accidents, didn't they? Sometimes . . . But Hamilton pressed on before she could articulate the thought.

'He's in Easthampton General. Broken bones, as far as we can tell. We think he's all right though. He was wearing his seat belt fortunately. They're examining him now. They rang us straight away, you see.'

'Yes. They would.' Of course they would. When a government minister was injured they'd naturally tell the duty officer at his Department, who would tell his principal private secretary, who would tell the official on night duty at No. 10, who would tell the Prime Minister, who would immediately look up the size of George's majority in *Vacher's Parliamentary Companion* and start worrying about the possibility of another by-election. Somewhere along the line, Rosemary supposed, there might have been a question raised about whether the wife had been informed, and a bit of perhaps we better had. 'I understand,' she said. 'I'll get straight up there.'

'We're placing a car at your disposal.' Hamilton seemed relieved that she'd taken the news so well. 'Charlie Roberts should be with you in half an hour.'

'No.' The thought of sweeping up to Easthampton in the back of an official Rover was unsettling, though Rosemary couldn't have said precisely why. 'Thank you, but I'll drive myself.'

'Ah. Well. It might be better . . .' Hamilton trailed off, worried no doubt at the possibility that she'd disintegrate into hysteric if crossed. 'You're certain?' he asked.

'Oh, yes. I'll get there quicker.'

'Right. I'll let them know you're on your way. Drive carefully, Mrs Gulliver. Try not to worry too much. I'm sure the Minister will be fine.'

Which was the kind of thing, she thought as she hung up, that people usually said when they weren't sure at all.

'Defence Minister George Gulliver is fighting for his life after a car smash which killed a top Tory official. Point, par,' Jack Cartwright muttered into the telephone.

Normally he would have bawled such exciting information down the line at the top of his voice, enunciating every syllable

vith Teutonic thoroughness; but even at 1 a.m. the casualty
obby at Easthampton General Infirmary was full of potential
avesdroppers or others who might be up to no good. Half a
lozen scrimshankers with hardly a single noticeable infirmity
oetween them sat slumped in the waiting-room. By the desk
 policeman with nothing better to do stood chatting to that
oloody cow of woman in the green uniform who obviously
new what was going on and equally obviously was determined
o keep the information to herself. Even Cartwright's most
ngaging grin had been unable to elicit more than a sniffy
uggestion that a statement for the press might well be made
available in due course. Still, there was no doubt that the local
chairman had bought it. The XJ6 was a total write-off, and the
umbulance paramedic hadn't disagreed with Jack's suggestion
hat Gulliver was on his last legs too.

Cartwright turned his back on the pack of malingerers and
oressed on. 'The crash happened late last night after Mr
Gulliver spoke at a packed meeting in the crucial Easthampton
oy-election. Point, par.

'He was a passenger in the Jaguar XJ6 driven by local
Chairman, cap C for chairman, Geoff with a G Norridge (I
spell, N-O-R-R-I-D-G-E; got that?), which veered out of control
and . . . hold on.' Cartwright spotted a plausible looking figure in
a white coat with a stethoscope dangling from his neck who was
ust emerging from the lift. 'Excuse me,' he called. 'Doctor!'

The man, who on closer inspection turned out to be little
nore than a youth, trudged over obligingly enough to where
Cartwright stood by the public payphones. He had a piece of
olastic pinned to his breast pocket which announced him as
Dr Peter Willey.

'I'm sorry to bother you, Doctor,' said Cartwright, putting on
a worried expression. 'I wonder if you could tell me how my
riend is? Mr Gulliver?'

Dr Willey frowned, which had the effect of making him look
even younger. 'You're not a member of the family?'

'We're very close. I was with him just before it happened.
'errible business.'

'I'm afraid you'll have to ask at the desk. I can't—'

'It's just that I'm talking to his wife now.' Cartwright gesture piteously towards the phone. 'She's very upset. I though perhaps . . .'

'Well, in that case . . .' The poor devil looked hollow-eye through lack of sleep. Heartrending. 'You can tell Mrs Gullive that her husband is comfortable. He's broken some ribs an his ankle and he's badly concussed, but there's nothing to ge alarmed about.'

'Comfortable?' If he hadn't been such a well-trained reporte Cartwright's face might have fallen. Never trust a bloody paramedic. Instead he nodded gravely and murmured some thing appropriate.

'He's had a lucky escape,' said Willey. 'Would you like m to . . .' He gestured at the phone in Cartwright's hand.

'No! Er, that is, I'll tell her myself if you don't mind. I think might be more reassuring. Very kind of you though.' He waite until Willey had retreated a safe distance, then resumed hi dictation.

'Change of story,' he whispered. 'Scrub all the fighting-for-lif stuff. OK? New intro. Defence Minister George Gulliver had miracle escape last night in a car smash which killed a top Tor official.'

He rattled through the rest of the yarn, which now include a resounding quote ('I don't know how any man could hav come out of that crash alive,' said Dr Peter Willey. 'It wa more than just a lucky escape. It was a miracle.') and hun up, thoroughly pleased with himself. The story would certainl make the front page in the last edition. With the stuff abou Sahelia, that made two tales from one by-election meetin not at all a bad night's work. Better still, there was no sig of the enemies yet. Jack blessed the instinct that had sen him to observe the Gulliver campaign instead of following th rest of the press herd to Easthampton Town Hall, where th leader of the Liberal Democrats had been speaking. By no his rivals would be working their way through the menu i the rather smart French restaurant they'd found, wonderin perhaps what was keeping young Cartwright. Poor bastard They wouldn't have the slightest inkling of the ferociou bollocking their newsdesks would certainly deliver in the morning.

All highly satisfactory. And it was nice to know that poor old George was still in the land of the living. It would have been damned inconvenient, Jack thought, to lose one of his very best ministerial contacts.

'I'll leave you to it then, Mrs Gulliver,' said Dr Willey. 'Are you quite sure you'll be all right?'

'I'm fine. Thank you.' Rosemary did her best to look appreciative. 'Really,' she added for emphasis.

'Good. Good.' Willey's eagerness to please was apparently boundless. In fact from the moment she'd introduced herself he'd fluttered anxiously round her, like a butler with a guilty secret. 'Just remember, your husband's in much better shape than he looks,' he added with rather more heartiness than was strictly necessary.

'I'll remember.' In fact George seemed remarkably healthy, all things considered. True, there was a large white bandage covering the top of his head, more bandages on his chest and a drip going into his arm, not to mention a small bag, half-filled with urine, nestling in a cradle beneath the bed; but on the whole there was nothing in his appearance to provoke alarm. Sleeping peacefully, she thought. For the first time that night Rosemary felt herself on the edge of tears. Odd. There really wasn't anything to cry about.

Willey wandered off at last and Rosemary sat at the bedside, squeezing George's hand. Once, when they were young, they'd held hands all the time. Happy days.

Somewhere in the distance a half-heard train whooshed over the town viaduct, the sound fading almost before it registered. Rosemary shivered. There had been noisier trains in Easthampton long ago. Years ago. Lying awake in the small spare room of the Gullivers' terraced house she'd heard the engines clanking and hissing past the bottom of the garden, just beyond the wooden fence, and wondered how anyone could possibly sleep through the racket. 'A question of having to,' was George's explanation. 'When you work hard for a living

like my parents you'll sleep through anything. Honest slumber
The working classes don't need to bother with pills.' Strangely
though, he'd refused to take advantage of the dreaming household. Not once on a premarital visit to the proud mum and da
had he ever ventured into her room after lights out. In fact h
seemed alarmed when she suggested one day that he migh
Such escapades, it turned out, were inappropriate to the famil
hearth.

What was appealing about him then was his vulnerability
Once, not long after they'd met, he told her of a secret fea
that someday he'd be found out: academic investigators woul
discover that his examination successes at school were th
consequence of a vast bureaucratic blunder and he'd b
plucked from the university and sent home to be apprentice
as a fitter at the Easthampton Engineering Company. 'Peasan
guilt,' he'd confessed, apparently joking. 'I walk up King'
Parade in the morning and look at the chapel and feel
shouldn't be here. It's all a dream. I'm just terrified I'll wak
up.' Rosemary could remember his words exactly. It was th
moment she thought she might love him.

It was only a few weeks afterwards that she allowed him t
take her virginity, encouraged by the evidence that he was a
nervous and inexperienced as she. The giveaway was the singl
rubber he insisted on carrying in his wallet at all times, a devic
that had nestled there undisturbed for so long that it had raise
an unmistakable ridge in the leather. Poor George. When th
time came at last for his rubber to see the light of day he'd bee
so overwhelmed that he'd spurted messily on her thigh befor
he could put the thing on, and had immediately collapse
in a babble of apologies. Not for his less than satisfactor
performance – she had after all no standard against whic
to measure it – but for his beastliness in seducing her i
the first place. It would have been unthinkably unkind t
point out that she hadn't as it turned out been seduced
was indeed as disappointingly intact as the day she'd bee
born; so she'd done the decent thing, kissed him and cuddle
him and whispered that it didn't matter. Really it didn't. Don
worry about it. She meant it, too. It seemed only natural whe

he started babbling that he loved her. Of course he loved her. She wouldn't have undressed for him otherwise.

Well, they'd been very young. And when you came right down to it they hadn't made such a bad marriage, had they? Not really. All things considered. Perhaps if he'd never been sucked into the hateful business of politics . . . But then, George wouldn't be George without his insecurities. She understood his desperation for fame and power and the trappings of success. They were his safeguard against being found out, weren't they?

'No,' said George, and for an uncomprehending moment Rosemary imagined that he was answering her unspoken thoughts. 'No,' he said again. He lay flat on his back, his eyes open and unfocused. Rosemary pushed the call button beside the bed and clasped his hand, rubbing it between her own.

'Darling,' she said. 'Darling, it's me. Rosemary.'

'Light,' said George. 'It's all light. Am I dead?'

'You're in hospital, George. In hospital. You're safe. You're going to be all right.' It seemed a suitable moment to start weeping, but before she could get going properly a nurse bustled in, followed in short order by Dr Willey, and they ushered her out into the corridor. She blew her nose on a tissue. It was true, then. He really was going to get well. He was waking up. There were tears rolling down her cheeks at last, but that was all right. The occasion was worth a few sniffles. Dear George. Fancy thinking he was dead.

Since we're rational folk, you and I, brought up to believe that there's no phenomenon in all this vasty universe so baffling that it's beyond the grasp of logic, we may comfortably suppose that there was nothing in the least mysterious or other-worldly in George's vision. It was the consequence of a bang on the head. As simple as that.

The simplicity wasn't so immediately apparent to George.

Eight days after the accident he lay bandaged and morose upon his hospital bed brooding on the meaning of life and worrying about his career. Ministers of the Crown do not have religious experiences. They tend to be members of the Church

of England. If they know what's good for them they turn up
for services only three times a year, at Christmas, Easter and
Remembrance Sunday, thereby avoiding the odium of being
thought devout.

From the moment he awoke to starched sheets, dressings
and the smells of medical progress, George understood that
for the sake of his reputation he'd better keep his mouth
shut and his mind occupied with practicalities. There was
no future at all in eschatological speculation. It could only
end in tears, and to no purpose. He had, after all, watched
quite enough television documentaries of the just-fancy-that
variety to understand that the earth was full of rum goings-on
with bugger-all explanation. There were islands in the South
Seas where the natives walked unscathed through pits of fire.
In South America, spiritual surgeons operated without benefit
of scalpel, wresting cancers bloodlessly from the bowel. An
Irish faith healer regularly turned the lame into contenders for
the world walking championships, merely by the laying on of
hands. Well, then. Measured against such performances a spot
of hallucination seemed hardly worth a mention.

'We're coming along nicely,' said Mr Hugill, as his finger
probed the back of George's neck. 'Does that hurt?'

'A little,' George lied. In fact it hurt quite a lot, but Mr Hugill
was one of those consultants who invited a stoic response.
Silver-haired and stern of face, he possessed a manner that
suggested that any patient in his care had better buckle to
and look sharp about it.

'Hmm,' he said. 'We'll need to keep the brace on for a couple
of weeks. Tricky things, whiplash injuries. Otherwise you've
done well. Very well.' He paused, allowing George to summon
up a grateful smile. 'I see no reason why we shouldn't allow
you home. Probably tomorrow, eh, Sister?'

'Now that's good news, isn't it, George?' chirped Sister Jenks,
who was small and bubbly and dark. 'Rosemary will be pleased.'

George muttered something appropriately appreciative and
wondered yet again why the entire nursing profession insisted
on a policy of such unrelenting mateyness. In eight days on his
back at Easthampton General Infirmary he'd never once been

called Minister, let alone Sir. Instead it was George this and George that, with sometimes a lovey or a ducks thrown in for good measure. Such familiarity might be a comfort to the riffraff on the public wards, but it was intensely irritating to a Secretary of State with a fully paid-up BUPA subscription and a personal letter of good wishes from the Prime Minister lying prominently on his bedside table.

'I must say, Sister, that you've all been absolutely marvellous. It's almost been a pleasure to be here,' he ventured. Such affirmations of gratitude, he'd learned, went a long way in the Health Service, and sure enough Jenks beamed prettily. Even Hugill permitted himself a thin smile.

'Look,' George went on. 'It's a bit of an imposition I know, but we'll probably have some photographers outside when I leave. It would be good if you could find time to come down with me. I'd like to shake your hands. Thank you publicly.' That one cheered them up even more. It was instructive to observe what the prospect of appearing on the box could do. George had no doubt that Hugill and Jenks would willingly abandon a wardful of patients on the point of death for the privilege of being seen shaking hands with a Tory Cabinet minister. Even if the pair of them had almost certainly voted Labour in the by-election, thereby helping to thwart young Fishlock in his parliamentary ambitions.

'We'll certainly do our best.' Hugill's eyes were gleaming. 'A bit of publicity for the NHS can't do any harm, can it?'

'Exactly,' said George. 'It all helps.' In fact a few pictures of a plucky minister being bidden a fond farewell by doctors and nurses as he set off to resume his onerous duties might well prove very helpful indeed. It should anyway be some compensation for his ordeal.

In other circumstances George might well have tried to avoid feeling sorry for himself. Cracked ribs, a broken ankle, bruises, cuts and concussion all seemed pretty small beer when compared with the fate of the unfortunate Norridge, whose ashes probably now reposed in an urn on his widow's mantelpiece. Even the indignities of bedpan and bottle beat the hell any day out of an undertaker's urn.

The trouble was, the trouble bloody well was, that he couldn quite guarantee, couldn't look in the mirror and swear, tha the Right Honourable George Gulliver was entirely, solidly an indisputably all there. To be sure, the reflection that glare back at him showed no obvious signs of dementia, no ma gleams or maniacal grins. On the other hand, normal citizen didn't float about outside their bodies listening to the celesti version of the London Philharmonic and wondering when Peter was going to make an appearance. Though he shied awa from it, the fear of lunacy danced around his mind.

He watched with what he hoped was an expression of cheer optimism as Hugill and Jenks bustled off, and closed his eye against the temptation to call them back and confess. That tru would be mad. He could envisage the pair of them cluckin comforting platitudes and then scuttling off to inform the colleagues that the Minister had gone bonkers. George had n more faith in the sanctity of the Hippocratic oath than he ha in the discretion of government drivers.

Come on, Gulliver, he instructed himself. Snap out of i You're not potty or off your trolley or having a breakdow You're a Minister of the Crown, and in good working order to Listen! There's your heart, pumping away, like billy-o, even you can't quite hear it. Diastole and systole. Tick tock. Soun as a bell. Your bladder is filling up perfectly satisfactorily, an to prove it, a nice young nurse will come along soon with cardboard bottle. She'll probably call you Georgie, but that's a right because your kidneys are doing whatever kidneys shoul and your liver is in one piece and you can see and hear wit perfect clarity. Let's not forget your old John Thomas eithe because it's a fine thick dick, a dick to be proud of, a dic which unlike Norridge's is uncremated and pink and ready fc action the moment an opportunity arises. Be grateful, Georg You'll be going home tomorrow, and if you've suffered a spc of the doolallies nobody will ever know.

George stirred. It was no good. However fiercely he wante to embrace the comforts of common sense, he couldn't hel himself. He remembered too well, knew in his bones tha somehow, if only for a microsecond, he'd broken what Rona

Reagan once bathetically described as the surly bonds of earth.

Daft? Of course it was daft. He clearly hadn't died. The paramedics would have noticed. But it took no effort to recall the ambulances clustered around the wrecked Jaguar or the blanket being pulled over Norridge's ruined face. He recollected the sensation of floating, his contentment in the growing light, the pain and regret as he was pulled down into the darkness of his own body. And there was the buggeration factor. It all seemed as real as the plaster cast on his ankle, and if it ever got out would surely be the end of him.

But it won't get out, he thought as he drifted into a doze. He'd be going home tomorrow, and that was that. No more worries. Rosemary would be there to pick him up. Good old Rosemary. A brick, that one. Truly. Visits every day. Grapes and oranges and bags of sympathy. Quite a comfort to discover that your wife still loves you after twenty-four years of marriage. Must be doing something right, he thought. Astonishing, really.

George slept.

'Give us a smile, Minister,' called the photographer with the straggly moustache. 'That's it! Lovely! Now a little kiss for the nurse, eh?'

A dozen flashbulbs popped satisfactorily as George bent to kiss Sister Jenks on her blushing cheek. 'Thanks once again for everything you've done, Sister,' he said loudly, for the benefit of the reporter from the Press Association. 'We've got a Health Service to be proud of.' Jenks murmured something about how she wished all her patients were as nice as him, and George beamed while the cameras clicked and whirred. For once the press office at the Ministry had managed not to bollocks things up, and if that wasn't worth smiling about he didn't know what was. Astonishing, how one could cheer up in the bright light of morning.

'I think that's about it, lads,' he announced. 'I'm still a bit shaky you know.' That one got a dutiful titter, but in fact several minutes of posing and grinning on the hospital steps had begun to induce a certain wobbliness in the knees which might lead to all kinds of embarrassment if not taken care of immediately. He reached out to grasp Rosemary's hand. 'Time to go, darling,' he said.

Clinging firmly on, he managed to reach the bottom of the steps without mishap and stood by the car while Charlie Roberts grinned and said something about how good it was to see you back on your feet, sir, while the cameramen took a few more snaps. Getting into the vehicle might be something of a problem, George thought, what with a neckbrace, strapped ribs, cracked ankle and a platoon of onlookers eager for the first sign of collywobbles. Best done swiftly, he decided, like ripping off a plaster. Dive in with a fixed grin and save the wincing for later.

'Have you anything to say about the position of the Prime Minister?' The question came from a whey-faced, long-haired reporter whose voice trembled with nervousness, as though he could scarcely credit his own temerity in addressing somebody so grand. George frowned. 'I don't think I understand what you're getting at,' he said, though out of the corner of his eye he noticed that the man from the PA was busily scribbling.

'Sir Peter Coleman says that the Tories will lose power unless there's a change of leadership.' Long-hair was sounding more confident now. 'He says you can't possibly win with the present Prime Minister.'

George shrugged, and immediately wished he hadn't. 'It's the first I've heard of it,' he said as the twinge subsided.

'He claims a lot of Tory MPs support him,' the man from the PA joined in, as it began to dawn on George that the media turnout might be inspired by a motive other than the desire to record his brave convalescence. 'There's talk of a leadership challenge.'

George did a spot of slow head-shaking of the more-in-sorrow-than-in-anger kind until he was sure the solitary television camera had captured his loyal reaction. 'Well,' he said, 'we all know Peter, don't we?'

The long-haired reporter seemed not to appreciate the quality of the put-down. 'So what are you saying about the

Prime Minister's position?' he demanded, his timidity obviously having evaporated in the thrill of the chase.

'The Prime Minister has the support of the Cabinet and the party. There's no question of it. And frankly, when the country is confronting such difficult problems, we don't need the distraction of this kind of tittle-tattle.' George caught the severe tone in his voice and mitigated it with a smile. 'And now, gentlemen, I really must let my wife take me home.'

He ducked with surprising ease into the back seat and gave a parting wave as Charlie let in the clutch and drove off. The pain in his neck and chest caught him only when he began to laugh, but it was worth it anyway.

'Are you all right?' Rosemary asked.

'Oh, I'm fine,' said George. 'Tip-top. Believe it or not I've never felt better.' And to Rosemary's uncomprehending pleasure he kept on smiling all the way home.

Monica was curled on her couch watching *News at Ten* when George appeared on the screen hand in hand with his wife. The pair of them were negotiating some stone steps and George seemed to be moving stiffly, as though in some discomfort, hanging on to Rosemary for support.

There was a close-up next, George burbling something about the Prime Minister, but Monica took little notice of his words. She was studying the way Rosemary looked at her husband and for the briefest of brief moments, a moment gone before it had fully registered, she felt something that might have been regret. Or even guilt.

Whatever the impulse was, assuming it existed at all, it had no place in Monica's plans. She switched off her set and made herself a cup of Ovaltine to help her sleep. It was a comforting drink, a reminder of years long ago, when all she took to bed was a teddy bear named Rupert. Curious how affecting a sip or a smell could be. Perhaps that explained why she finished her solitary evening sitting in the kitchenette clasping her cup and blinking as if to remove an obstruction in the eyes.

We'll leave her then in her dressing-gown and mules, a lonely lady but one quite capable of looking after herself, not given to snivelling. Look: she's snapped out of it already.

'You're mine,' Monica announced to the empty room. 'Bloody well mine.'

Well, we shall see.

CHAPTER

3

I'd like to begin, Mr Speaker,' said the Leader of Her Majesty's Opposition, 'by welcoming the Right Honourable gentleman the Member for Mowsbury back to the House.'

George grinned across the floor in acknowledgement as the Chamber erupted in a heartening growl of yah yahs, which by long tradition is the parliamentary way of saying 'Hear, hear.' It was a great comfort to be liked, and there was no mistaking the warmth glowing on the overcrowded benches. Even Dennis Skinner, the socialist Beast of Bolsover, managed to look benign. Up in the Press Gallery platoons of parliamentary sketch-writers bent busily over their notebooks and it was a fair bet that every man-jack of them intended to portray Gulliver's return as an example of the Commons at its best. They always did on such occasions. 'Nobody can doubt the genuine affection and regard in which the Defence Minister is held,' seemed an entirely reasonable prolepsis.

'The whole House will wish to join with me in wishing the Secretary for Defence a complete recovery from his injuries,' Paul Barton continued to another rumble of approval. 'I congratulate him on being the only member of the front bench opposite who has a cast-iron alibi for the economic and political shambles that this Government has perpetrated on

the British people in recent weeks.' This one inspired anothe
cheer from the Labour benches and George composed hi
expression into a half-humorous frown meant to convince th
watching television audience that he stood four-square behin
his Cabinet colleagues.

'Mr Speaker, isn't it clear that the Prime Minister is no
an insupportable embarrassment to this country?' Tradition
courtesies dispensed with, Barton clearly intended to wast
no further time before getting down to the enjoyable busines
of the day. 'We've seen the inflation figures. We've seen th
unemployment statistics. We've seen what's happened to ou
balance of trade.' The old oratorical rule of three seldom fai
and Barton paused for a moment, thereby giving his supporter
the opportunity to wave their order papers and chant 'Resig
Resign!' and allowing the Speaker his chance to leap to his fee
and bellow a demand for 'Order! Order!' Such stimulating stuf
George reflected, was what made the House of Commons th
finest deliberative assembly in the world.

'It is painfully clear, Mr Speaker,' Barton resumed when th
bawling had subsided, 'that the Prime Minister is incapable o
dealing with this crisis. He knows it. The country knows it. Eve
his own supporters know it. Can he tell us why he doesn't d
the honourable thing and resign?'

On the off chance that the television cameras might still b
pointed in his direction, George rolled his eyes to indicat
his disdain, though he couldn't help wondering how poor ol
Michael Poultney would deal with the question. Apparentl
you couldn't walk into the Smoking-Room these days withou
being buttonholed by some disgruntled backbencher wantin
to know what the hell was going on, eh? And when's th
Government going to get its finger out? Such concerns, in fac
had just surfaced in a *Sunday Times* poll claiming that a nea
majority of Tory MPs wanted the PM to go, a story that Georg
had read with mounting enthusiasm. 'Give 'em hell, Michae
he murmured as Poultney got to his feet and stood graspin
the Despatch Box as the Opposition benches erupted again.

'Order!' snapped the Speaker. 'The House must give th
Prime Minister a chance to answer.'

At that the Chamber subsided somewhat, though as usual
Dennis Skinner wouldn't be restrained. 'You've had it, chum,'
he jeered. 'They're sending you to the knacker's yard!'

Still a professional despite his troubles, Poultney seized
his chance. 'I believe they employ a number of skinners in
knackers' yards,' he retorted, inducing in the Tory ranks
such paroxysms of mirth that the Speaker was forced to
intervene again. There is nothing the House of Commons
enjoys so hugely as a feeble joke. 'I'm sorry to disappoint
the honourable gentleman, but to paraphrase the words of
Mark Twain, rumours of my resignation are premature. No,
Mr Speaker, I shall not resign. This Government not only has
a mandate: it has the policies to succeed and the will to
succeed. And succeed it will.' Upon which nearly four hundred
Conservative MPs, many of whom had confided to the *Sunday
Times* their fervent hope that the Prime Minister would resign
and preferably be quick about it, rose to their feet waving their
order papers in triumph.

It was odd, thought George later as he made his way out into
the Members' Lobby, how rapidly the mood at Westminster
could change. With one brief flash of his old form and a
tolerably decent speech afterwards, Poultney was back in
business. For the time being anyway. It might be wise to send
the man a note of congratulation.

'With a single bound the Prime Minister was free.' Jack
Cartwright, one of the regular gang of lobby correspondents
who made a practice of loitering outside the Chamber in the
hope of picking up titbits, came scuttling up the moment George
appeared. 'Good to see you back in action. You had us worried
here for a bit.'

'I had myself worried,' said George, allowing himself to be
steered into the corner behind Churchill's bronze statue.
The left toe of the figure gleamed gold, rubbed to bright-
ness by all those Tory MPs who touched it as a talisman
before entering the Chamber. 'I don't think the Prime Minister would ever have forgiven me if we'd had another by-
election.'

'Nah. It would have been all right,' said Cartwright genially.

'You've got a twenty-five thousand majority. Even your lo
couldn't lose Mowsbury.'

'So what do you make of it?' asked George, mildly irritate
at such poor taste. It was of course true that whenever
Member of Parliament suffered an illness or an accident the firs
question from colleagues was always, 'What's his majority?' Bu
it was bad form to rub it in.

'The PM?' asked Cartwright, who seemed unaware of an
offence. 'Not a bad performance. He's off the hook, I shoul
think, for the moment. Barring another disaster. Talking c
which—'

'Don't tell me,' George interrupted, throwing up his hands i
mock horror. 'You've found out that he's secretly being pai
by the CIA.'

'Not quite.' An odd expression stole across Cartwright'
face.

'Has the Chancellor been caught with his fingers in the til
The Home Secretary arrested for kerb-crawling perhaps?'

Cartwright wasn't playing the game. 'As a matter of fact it'
to do with you,' he said.

'Ah.' George might have felt a tremor of concern then but fo
the certainty that he was, for the moment fireproof. 'I've bee
out of action for a month,' he said.

'Sahelia?'

'What about Sahelia?'

Cartwright lowered his voice. 'We sent a man out to have
look. This was after we ran your story about the arms dea
The editor thought she'd run a nice little piece about th
Government's latest friend in Africa. We all thought it was ju
another of her barmy ideas.'

'Nothing barmy about it. Sahelia's important to us. Lots
jobs involved.' George frowned. 'What's the problem?'

'The problem is they turn out to be a bunch of psychopathi
savages.' Cartwright's expression took on the texture appr
priate to indignation. 'You should see the pictures. Enough t
turn your stomach. Look, come and sit down. I'll show yo
something.' He gestured George across the lobby towards th
green benches at the exit to the Ways and Means corridor.

'Now then,' he went on when they were seated in relative privacy. 'What do you make of that?' He pulled a small colour photograph from an inside pocket and passed it over.

'Good God,' said George.

The picture captured a victim in the instant of beheading. The body was still kneeling, the trunk toppling to the sand, blood spurting from its neck. Nearby a head, its face frozen in what looked like a smile but was almost certainly a grimace, rolled on the ground. In the background a throng of Sahelians seemed to be applauding. 'Good God,' George repeated.

'We've got dozens like that.' Cartwright's voice had dropped to a furtive whisper. 'You can't credit what's going on out there. Public executions. Floggings. Torture. Jails full of political prisoners. And you know what?' He glared at George with a look that might easily have been mistaken for moral outrage. 'The people doing it are being bribed and supported by British companies.'

George stared down at the photograph in his lap. The head's eyes stared back at him. 'I had no idea,' he muttered. In fact he'd advised the arms companies they needn't start bribing for months yet.

'According to the statements we've got, you knew all about it.' There was a coldness in Cartwright's tone that George didn't much care for. 'We've talked to missionaries, engineers, doctors, everybody you can think of. Locals as well as ex-pats. They all tell the same story. A terrorist regime propped up by British expertise.'

'This is bloody disgraceful,' George spat out with genuine bitterness. The incompetent bastards at the Foreign Office had presumably sat on their manicured hands for weeks while the ferret from the *Despatch* snouted around all over Sahelia without let or hindrance. Worse, they'd failed to warn of impending embarrassment, thereby leaving a senior Cabinet minister, to wit the Rt. Hon. George Gulliver, up to his neck in ordure. 'Bloody swine,' he said.

'You didn't know?' Cartwright seemed genuinely surprised.

'No I bloody didn't.'

'So what are you going to do about it?' demanded Cartwright,

who fortunately misunderstood the target of such forcefu
ministerial condemnation.

'Not for attribution, right?' George was rapidly devising a
way of extricating himself from what promised to be another
almighty shambles.

'Lobby terms,' Cartwright agreed.

Reassured that nothing he now said could be traced back
George began his exercise in damage-limitation. 'The key poin
of our agreement with Sahelia was that they should respect
basic human rights, OK? I insisted on that from the start
Apart from the moral point it made political sense.' It was
some comfort to observe Cartwright busily scribbling down
the case for the defence.

'Now then, the only way we could make the deal stick
was through British officials already in Sahelia. They're the
people who know the country. Their job was to report any
human-rights issues to London.'

'You're talking about the diplomatic service?' asked Cart
wright, still scribbling.

'And the Trade Department. Don't forget, some of their
officials are in Sahelia as well.' With a bit of luck, George
thought, he might stitch up two of his Cabinet colleagues for
the price of one.

'Nobody from your Department?' asked Cartwright, with
perhaps just a trace of suspicion.

'We won't be sending anybody until the first weapons are
ready to be delivered. All we've got out there at the momen
is the military attaché, and he hardly has time to leave the
embassy.'

A light of understanding was beginning to dawn in Cart
wright's eye. 'So although this is mainly a defence contract
the Foreign Office and the Trade Department are the key
players?'

'At this particular stage, yes.' George placed the last brick in
his defensive wall.

'And they're the ones who've turned a blind eye.' Cart
wright's pen was flying with satisfying vigour across the
paper.

'I'm sure that's not the case.' George was not about to risk over-egging the pudding. 'Perhaps they don't know what's happening.' He caught a sceptical glint in Cartwright's eye. 'Perhaps they've reported these incidents. We might have protested already. I just don't know. You have to remember, I've been out of it for weeks.' He reached over to grasp Cartwright's arm in a gesture of friendliness. 'When are you going to publish all this?'

'God knows. Next week, I hope.' For the first time the journalist looked somewhat shifty. 'Even our editor can't sit on this one.'

'I think I see.' George affected a note of puzzlement, though in fact he saw very well. Prudence Willow, editor of the *Despatch*, was a woman whose unpleasantness to her staff was exceeded only by her obsequiousness to those in power and her desperation to be created a Dame of the British Empire. The merest possibility that anything carried by her newspaper might embarrass those in a position to further her ambitions would certainly make her think twice. If not thrice.

'Well, thanks for your time,' Cartwright said, stuffing his notebook back in his pocket. 'It might be an idea if we had lunch sometime soon. Talk things over.'

'I'd like that.' George stood. 'Give my office a ring to fix up a date. Maybe we could make it a threesome, eh? Bring Prudence along. And Jack' – George put on his most sincere look – 'it's an important story. Needs to be told. If you want any help just let me know. I'll do what I can. On lobby terms.'

All in all, he thought as a grateful Cartwright shambled off, not a bad afternoon's work. If the Sahelia story did indeed break, both Lucas Brotherton the Foreign Secretary and Mark Hastings at Trade would be satisfactorily up to their ears in it. Unless of course either of them was nimble enough to pass on the blame. Thing was though, you could never predict how one of these scandals might turn out. Pleasurable though it might be to cut the balls off his rivals, it would be safer – much safer – if the photographs from Sahelia never saw the light of day. Lunch with the loathsome Willow ought to fix that, he thought. Another bloody chore.

He glanced over at the Members' message board. The light beside his name was illuminated, which usually meant that duty beckoned. Not always though. No, sir. This time there was a slip of paper in his pigeonhole, of the kind that in other circumstances might set the heart pumping and the loins tingling. 'Please ring ALH Advertising,' it urged. Monica, of course. The code for black lace and willing thighs. He sighed, regretful. If truth be told, he still felt rather too shaky for bedtime adventures.

George checked the time: 5.45. There was a meeting back at the Ministry in fifteen minutes, which meant he must make the call at once if he wanted to make suitably apologetic noises. No possibility of telephoning Monica from his office of course, since all his calls – including, he suspected, those made on his supposedly 'private' line – were monitored, a system that, while no doubt useful in the interests of sound government, had the irritating consequence of keeping him from the occasions of sin he so much enjoyed. Never mind. A bank of public payphones was handily situated below the Members' Lobby. There shouldn't be any problem about putting Monica off for a week or so – he was only just out of convalescence, after all. And she was an understanding lady, on the whole.

The great advantage of possessing a mistress, in George's opinion, was that it lent a certain sparkle to the otherwise dull routines of public life. There was nothing like a spot of therapeutic lechery to relax a busy man at the end of a difficult day; and, on this tenth night after his return to Westminster, relaxation was absolutely what he had in mind. Oh, yes. What he didn't want at this particular moment, thank you very much, what he really couldn't face, was an in-depth discussion about meaningful relationships.

He reached across the table to take Monica by the hand. Her eyes were unusually beady this evening and there may have been the merest hint of a quiver in her lips. If he was any judge at all, a scene was very much on the cards. Fortunately they were tucked away in a booth at the rear of the restaurant, at their favourite table. Far from prying eyes and wagging tongues.

'You know I love you, darling,' he murmured, in the hope of cheering her up.

The downside with mistresses was that sooner or later they tended to make demands. It was adultery's biggest disadvantage, and George could spot the warning signs a mile away. Usually they began with a whinge about spending more time together and how nice it would be if we could go away for the weekend, with a progression then to apparently casual questions about what's your wife like, and do you think she knows. To which the appropriate answers were that my wife's OK and of course she doesn't know but she'd find out pretty damn quick if we were daft enough to bunk off for the weekend.

Not, he believed, that there was any future in giving women the appropriate answers. Ever. Unlike men they had no common sense, no grasp of reality, no instinct for discretion. George suspected that in spite of his strictest instructions Monica had almost certainly blabbed about their affair to her friends. Women tended to do that kind of thing. It was another of their disadvantages.

He gave Monica's hand another squeeze to demonstrate his affection. 'You know how I feel about you,' he murmured.

'Do I?' It was obvious that in spite of his best endeavours she was winding herself up for a real heart-to-heart, and George suppressed a twinge of irritation. It was damned nearly midnight and he was no nearer getting between the sheets than when he'd walked into the place, over ninety minutes ago. Didn't she care that he had to make an early start in the morning? No, of course not. The woman could have no idea of the job he'd had getting rid of Charlie Roberts either. Or of the humiliation involved in informing his personal detective that he had a private engagement that night, so a little bit of discretion wouldn't come amiss, eh? Some ministers got on famously with their gun-toting guardians, invited them in for drinks or Sunday lunch and made them one of the family. Not George. He'd never felt comfortable with Dennis Sharman, never quite understood what was going on behind that impassive stare. The man would be out in the street somewhere, sitting slab-faced behind the wheel of his car, waiting. Keeping out of sight, which was just as well. Monica would be appalled if she knew that many of their trysts were logged in the police overtime book. You could only pray the bastards really were as discreet as they promised. Such were the penalties of power. Nobody appreciated the security restrictions that must be embraced by ministers on the Grade A protection list. In the public interest of course.

He did the old looking-into-her-eyes routine. 'You know how I feel,' he repeated, in the absolute certainty that she didn't. 'We'll have a last couple of brandies, eh?' With luck, another drink might do the trick. He called the waiter across and gave his order as Monica picked up her handbag and muttered something about going to the ladies'. 'Make them large ones,' he told the waiter. 'And I'll have the bill, too, if I may.' Anything to expedite matters and get back to Monica's flat, round the corner.

He looked at his watch: 11.55. Say fifteen minutes to finish the brandies and jolly the woman out of her mood. Five minutes or so to walk her home. That would be 12.15 or thereabouts. On the job by 12.35 at the earliest, given the business of kissing and stroking and all the rest of the preamble necessary to persuade her that she wasn't being taken for granted. Damn. With the best will in the world he wasn't going to be at his own front door before about 2.30 a.m., even assuming that Monica proved cooperative. And he had a breakfast meeting at eight with all the ministers and senior officials in the Department. Hell. For a moment, for the flicker of an eye, George sagged in anticipation of the tiredness he was inviting. Maybe he was growing too old for this kind of caper. In fact he almost regretted not being at home now, this minute, in bed beside Rosemary, with a cup of Horlicks and the certainty of seven hours' sleep. A man needed such innocent comforts. One of the other disadvantages in the mistress department was that you never got a cup of Horlicks.

Nonsense, of course. Probably the consequence of delayed shock. Probably. George tried to shake off his mood. One glimpse of Monica in wispy lace should be more than enough to confound all the arguments of middle age; one wriggle of the hips as she slid deliciously from her dress would abolish all thoughts of Horlicks. His stomach clenched in anticipation. A man needed those comforts too.

What nobody understands about government, he thought, is that there's so damned much of it and what's more so few ministers with the ability to make it work. Your ordinary voter, your man in the Clapham omnibus, simply couldn't begin to imagine the pressures. Even Rosemary hadn't a clue. 'You need more rest,' she'd pleaded when he'd insisted on returning to his post. 'They seem to be getting along perfectly well without you.' Huh. George swirled his brandy balloon and took a reflective sip. What did Rosemary know? Though the defence of the realm may have been conducted with unimpeachable smoothness in his absence, George had no doubt he was needed at the helm. Otherwise the nation's military affairs would be run by mere experts.

'We need to talk, George,' said Monica, sliding into her seat opposite. Her visit to the lavatory had clearly done nothing to improve her mood. The quiver might have vanished from her lips, but her jaw was set.

'Fair enough.' George rapidly revised his timetable. Needing to talk, in his experience, usually took half an hour at the very least, not counting injury time taken up by the sniffing into handkerchiefs which tended to accompany such exercises. It meant that he might not now manage to get back home before 3 a.m., unless he gave up all thoughts of a legover. 'What do you want to talk about?'

'Not here.' Monica stood abruptly. 'We should go,' she said.

'Don't you want your brandy?' asked George, recognising at once what a bloody silly question it was. Without waiting for an answer he picked up her glass and drained it in two throatscraping gulps. 'Let's be off then,' he gasped.

It was chill in the street, the wind blustering off the nearby Thames. Monica thrust her hands into her coat pockets and began stalking off, with George half a pace behind wondering whether he should attempt to take her arm. Perhaps not. It seemed best to let her get on with it. And, anyway, Dennis would be trailing along somewhere behind with the lethal bulge under his left armpit.

They walked in silence, George peering up at the lowering sky. It would be the devil's own job to get a taxi afterwards if it came on to rain. Perhaps it was just as well Dennis was on duty. A lift home wouldn't come amiss.

Monica's flat, softly lit, softly furnished, occupied the basement of a large, Victorian town house and was the kind of place George always associated with the word boudoir. It was necessary to take off one's shoes on entering, since the floors were carpeted in thick, impractical white. There were curtains in red velvet, deep couches, fat cushions, an ormolu clock. Through an arched alcove the kitchen gleamed. The door to the left was closed, though behind it, George knew, was a large double bed with frilled pillows. He wondered whether his head would rest on them tonight. Fifty-fifty, he reckoned.

He stood in stockinged feet while Monica busied herself in the kitchen with a coffee percolator. The small beginnings of a headache nagged behind his eyes. He regretted that last brandy. In fact he'd probably end up regretting the whole evening if things didn't start looking up soon. It was becoming clear that Monica had no intention of allowing him into her bed, or anyway not until she'd wrung his withers about whatever was bothering her. Not that there was any great mystery, if he was the judge. In the weeks between leaving hospital and returning to his duties, he'd phoned her only once, which in all probability would turn out to be just a marginal improvement on not phoning at all. Truth was, he hadn't felt like it, needed time to get over his strange experience. No doubt he should have foreseen the consequences. He wished now that he'd bought her a bottle of Chanel No. 5.

'Do sit down,' said Monica, returning with a tray of coffee things. 'You're making me uncomfortable, standing there.'

George did as he was told, sinking deep into her overstuffed sofa. Monica chose the single armchair opposite. Not the most hopeful sign. 'Tell me what's the matter, darling,' he said.

She sipped her coffee, eyeing him over the rim of her cup, taking her time. George resisted the temptation to look at his watch. 'You know what's the matter,' she said at last.

'Ah.' At this point he supposed, he ought to start babbling

guiltily about the pressure of work and how sorry he was not to have kept in touch. 'You're quite wrong,' he said. 'I don't know. I only know you're unhappy about something.'

She replaced her cup with a clatter. 'It's been ten weeks, George,' she said. 'We haven't seen each other for ten weeks.'

George sighed. There was an obvious answer to that one, but it would certainly make matters worse. 'Well, circumstances haven't been entirely normal, have they? I could have been killed.'

'Exactly.' Monica was getting into her stride now. 'You could have been killed and I wouldn't even have been allowed at your funeral.'

'Eh?' George was genuinely puzzled. 'What do you mean, not allowed?'

'It might have been a bit embarrassing for your family, don't you think?'

'Don't be silly,' said George. 'There would have been hundreds there. Nobody would have noticed. Even if they knew, which they don't.' It was, he realised immediately, quite the wrong thing to say.

'You didn't phone,' she snapped. 'I used to sit here night after night worrying about you and you didn't phone. You didn't even let me know where you were.'

'I was convalescing. In the country. You know that.'

Monica's lips trembled. 'I thought I meant something to you.'

'Darling.' George was well aware that there was only one possible response to that kind of complaint. He struggled up from the sofa and went to kneel beside Monica's armchair, resting his hand on her shoulder. 'You know what you mean to me,' he whispered. 'You know.' Beneath his hand he could feel the tension in her muscles begin to relax. The old routines never failed. 'Anyway, I did phone.'

'Once,' she snapped, her shoulder tightening up again as George scrambled to undo his error.

'I love you, Monica,' he said, stroking her hair.

She was silent then, so he continued stroking and began nuzzling her ear, a technique that seldom failed to get her into a receptive frame of mind. There might still be time for a quickie, if he played his cards right. 'I don't like to see you unhappy, lover,' he murmured, observing with some satisfaction that she was beginning to respond. Her breathing had altered subtly, and she turned her head so that he could kiss her on the mouth. 'I need you,' he whispered.

'Do you?' Her voice had taken on a tone of promising huskiness and George began calculating the timetable again. It couldn't be much past 12.45, so he should still be home before 3 a.m. His hand crept in a southerly direction to brush the slope of her breast. He kissed her again, straining awkwardly across the arm of her chair.

'I don't know how I'd manage without you,' he said after a bit, his nose and mouth caressing the particular spot on her neck, which, as he knew from past endeavours, usually yielded excellent results. 'I haven't been able to stop thinking about you.'

'Really?' She pulled away slightly, gazing seriously into his eyes. 'Do you mean that?'

'Yes. I do,' said George, pleased with the splendid progress he was making. His voice thickened with longing. 'I need you, Monica.'

'More than you need your wife?' It was a question she'd never asked before, and in other circumstances a small alarm might have sounded at the back of George's skull.

'Oh, yes,' he gasped. 'Much more.' Two months of unwonted fidelity is, after all, capable of undermining anyone's judgment. He stood, pulling Monica with him, and wrapped his arms around her. 'I can't imagine what it would be like without you,' he breathed.

'I want you to stay.' Her voice was whispered urgency, her body pressing into his. Delicious.

'Yes.' George wanted to stay too. For an hour at least. His fingers fumbled at the hooks on her dress.

'I hate it when you go home. Hate it.' She wriggled against him.

'I hate it too.' For some reason the third hook down wouldn't come undone.

'You'll stay then?' She looked up at him, her lips parted, so he did the gentlemanly thing and kissed her.

'For a bit, anyway,' he said. The third hook came undone at last.

She pulled away. 'No. I mean you'll stay tonight.' The huskiness in her voice, he noticed, seemed to have vanished.

'I've got to get back at *some* time. She's expecting me.' He made an attempt to pull her closer. 'We've got an hour or two.'

'An hour or two?' It was extraordinary how a pliant, yielding posture could be transformed in an instant to the consistency of pre-stressed concrete. 'Then it's back to your wife, is it? Back to her bed?'

'You know I don't sleep with her.' George was beginning to lose patience with all this. Dammit, it must be about 1 a.m. already. 'You're the woman I sleep with. You.' He took a step towards her. 'Let me take you to bed,' he said. 'I need you.'

'A quickie. Is that it?' She gave George a detumescing glare. 'You're just using me.'

'Oh, for God's sake,' he snarled. 'That's it. Let's just call it a night, shall we?' With luck, he thought, he wouldn't need to beg a favour from Sharman. At this hour he'd probably find a black cab without too much trouble. 'I'm really not in the mood for a fight.'

'So you're running away. I see.' She seemed dangerously calm, as though events were turning out precisely as she'd planned. 'We really need to talk,' she said.

Now that, thought George, was bloody typical of women. 'We've just had dinner together. We've done nothing but talk for the past couple of hours.' He could tell immediately from the look on her face that the argument wasn't going to wash.

'You say you love me.' Monica was beginning to sound like a prosecuting counsel down at the Old Bailey.

'Yes, I do.' In such confrontations, he believed, it was always best to keep one's answers short.

'You say you need me.'

'That's true too.'

'You're not happy at home.'

In fact George always tried to avoid talking to his mistresses about his domestic circumstances, but it was a reasonable deduction for Monica to make. 'I try to make the best of things,' he said, with a twinge of unease.

'But you meant all the things you said to me?' There was a trace of uncertainty in her voice now, but since George couldn't remember precisely what he might or might not have told her, and anyway was anxious to end the interrogation, he found himself nodding with what he hoped was an expression of sincerity.

'I meant every word,' he said, as a new expression – triumph perhaps? – glinted in Monica's eyes. His sense of unease grew stronger.

'So why don't you leave your wife? Move in with me?' It was the daftest question George had heard in a long time, but there seemed no doubt at all that Monica meant it seriously. 'Don't tell me it would damage your career. Half the Cabinet ended up marrying their mistresses.'

'Marrying?' This was a novelty, right enough. George was as certain as he could be that he'd never mentioned marriage, except perhaps on those odd occasions when in the transports of pleasure a man is liable to say anything.

'I want to know why you don't leave Rosemary. She doesn't love you, does she? You've told me so.'

'Ah.' Dimly George remembered that he might once have muttered something of the sort when making his first attempt to get inside Monica's knickers.

'I want you to tell her about us, George,' she pressed on relentlessly. 'There's no reason why we can't work things out in a civilised way.'

George's head was beginning to throb again. That last brandy had definitely been a mistake. 'It's not possible,' he said, though of course it was.

'If you won't tell her I will.' She announced the ultimatum without any apparent emotion. It was at this stage, George supposed, that he should start shouting and waving his arms about, but curiously he felt no sense of shock or even surprise, as though he'd been expecting such a threat all along, as though he had more important things on his mind. Perhaps the pain in his head had something to do with it. Strange, really. In fact the only surprising thing about that particular moment was the odd expression on Monica's face and the fact that she seemed to be saying something else to him, which was ever odder, because he couldn't hear a word.

The scene dissolves, but he's all right. There's no need to worry.

He's quite alone now, standing in this balmy glade amid flowers that look as though they belong on the cover of a seed catalogue. They're red and purple, blue and white, impossibly glossy. Rabbits hop around agreeably among the trees and in the branches there are larks singing. Or maybe nightingales. George doesn't know much about ornithology, but you don't need to be an expert to enjoy this kind of birdsong. It's perfect.

He is of course well aware that none of this is real. It's an offence against the laws of physics to suppose that any human being, far less a government minister with a busy department to run, can find himself transported in a nanosecond from his mistress's flat to a place that reminds him of Kew Gardens on a spring morning. Such things happen only in fairy tales. If he puts his mind to it he has no doubt at all that he can will himself back into Monica's company any time he likes. What's happening now is merely a bit of a brainstorm, though undeniably pleasant. The last time he saw colours like this was in one of those paintings by Douanier Rousseau. The *Sleeping Gipsy*, perhaps, though there's no sign of a lion. Well, there wouldn't be in such a place, would there? Nothing here hints of threat. It's a garden created for the recreation of souls, as Eden must have been. George blinks at the thought. He mustn't allow himself to be carried away. In a moment he'll close his eyes and concentrate on getting himself back to Pimlico and normality. But not yet. Not quite yet. There's a path meandering through the woods and it's only natural to see where it might lead. This is a bit of an adventure, after all, and there's nothing waiting back in the real world but Monica in a mood.

Breathing deeply of the scented air, George ambles beneath

the trees in the comfortable expectation that something out of the ordinary is about to happen. Why he should feel like this is anybody's guess. It's a curious sensation. There's something waiting up ahead sure enough, and, though he knows it's just part of the illusion, he's growing impatient to see what might turn up. It would be a pity if reality supervened now, before he learns the answer. He hurries on through the dappled sunlight – yes, it's sunny right enough, which is quite unusual, in the middle of the night – until at last the path opens out into a circular lawn of tight-sprung turf.

In the middle of this carpeted greenery, there's a gazebo in fluted ironwork and within it a pair of rustic chairs. On one of them a young man sits, though he rises gracefully to his feet as George hoves into view. He is, predictably enough, dressed in shining white. George, who is nobody's fool, has been half expecting such an apparition. The human mind may play tricks from time to time, but it tends to stick to a familiar script. Visions are invariably clad in white, aren't they?

Buoyed up by his grasp of what's going on, George strides across the grass to confront the stranger, noting as he approaches that the fellow is outstandingly handsome, with piercing blue eyes. Par for the course. You don't come across many hunchbacks when you have these experiences. No, sir. Angels never have wrinkles or spots. Nor do they suffer from halitosis. George knows that, just as surely as he knows there are no such things as angels.

'You're quite mistaken,' says the eidolon in a voice that of course is as fetching as his smile.

'I beg your pardon?' George never likes to be corrected, and is not about to take any lip from a youth got up in a toga.

'We do exist.' The stranger's smile has vanished, to be replaced by an expression that manages to be both stern and forgiving. 'Here I am. You must try not to be prejudiced by my raiment.'

Raiment? George has never used the word in his life, and it's somewhat off-putting that it should pop up in this dream. 'Are you reading my mind?' he asks suspiciously, which is a damned silly question since it's obvious that the entire situation amounts to nothing more than a conversation with himself.

'Your mind is transparent,' says the apparition, with what might have been a hint of smugness but for the fact that angels aren't allowed to be smug. 'But I assure you again that you're mistaken. I'm real. I exist. This is not a dream, George.'

'But I'm not really here. I know I'm not here. I'm in Pimlico.' George is not about to be pushed around by his own subconscious.

'Your body is at this moment in Pimlico, that's true. But your soul is here. With me. In this garden.' It's an ingenious argument, and for a moment George flounders. It isn't often that he loses a debating point. He recovers quickly, however. Years of training in the House of Commons, he believes, have made him a match for any angel. Or any archangel, come to that.

'Huh,' he says, to show that he's not impressed. 'If my body's in Pimlico and my soul's here it must mean I'm dead, right?' Oddly enough the thought does not perturb George in the least.

'The fact is, George,' says the apparition, who has plainly decided that the matey approach is best, 'this isn't a place exactly. It's a state. A different kind of reality. More real, in fact, than the world you know. You're simply being vouchsafed a glimpse of another dimension.'

'Huh.' George is beginning to repeat himself but he can't really help it. He can think of nothing very sensible to say, and in any case the apparition's use of 'vouchsafed' has thrown him off balance again. His confidence wavers. He must concentrate. This has gone on long enough. He can return to himself if he tries. Of course he can. He closes his eyes, wills himself back to normality. He blinks open. The gazebo is still there, the apparition gazing at him with what might have been a look of pity. The fear of madness tugs at George's sleeve. 'So why am I here then?' he asks.

'That's a question you should really ask yourself.'

'Now wait a minute,' says George, nettled. 'You dragged me here. There must be a reason.'

'On the contrary. This is where you want to be. Perhaps

you simply didn't realise it.' There's no doubt about it. The apparition seems mighty pleased with himself.

'Bollocks,' barks George in the tone that's reduced many a permanent under-secretary to a quivering wreck. 'I want to know what you're up to. Tell me why I'm here.'

'You know why. Your soul is telling you why.' The voice has darkened now and the face is changing its aspect, suddenly alarming in its intensity. There's a wind rising, and clouds rolling in a sky no longer blue. For the first time, fear coils in George's stomach. He steps backwards, unable to help himself. He shivers. His control has gone, overcome by dread. It is no longer absurd to think of this being as an angel. 'You know why,' the voice repeats as the darkness gathers; and, in a way he can't begin to articulate, George suspects that this might be true. He's swept by a fearful loneliness.

The angel has vanished, shivered into nothingness and the garden with him. No flowers now. No rabbits or trees or sun. This is the future, or what the future might be. Nothing but a wasteland. Only the wind and the howling and a soul shrinking in terror of the dark.

CHAPTER

4

'So Montgomery shakes his head in sympathy and says syphilis, eh? That's jolly bad luck, soldier. What's the treatment?'

'The lotion,' muttered George, abstracted. 'The lotion and the brush. What you do is take the brush, dip it in the lotion and wipe it on the affected parts.'

Sam Ruddock's face fell. 'You've heard it,' he accused. For a Parliamentary Private Secretary whose only role in life should have been to ingratiate himself with his ministerial boss, Sam could be remarkably quick to take umbrage.

'Only once or twice,' George grunted, regretting his flash of irritation almost at once. Sam was a good PPS, forever recounting new or newish jokes in the bars of Westminster and faithfully trotting back with the latest gossip in return. He was as accurate a barometer of mood in the party as any minister could wish for, and George hoped his services would turn out to be mightily useful when the time came. 'Sorry, mate,' he amended. 'One of those days.'

'Seem to remember these working breakfasts were your idea,' Sam grumbled. 'Bloody uncivilised, if you ask me.' He wandered off in search of a more appreciative audience.

If I can get through this without screaming, thought George, I can get through anything. He glanced around his office, where junior ministers, political advisers and officials, some clutching plates of scrambled egg, others munching croissants, stood in apparently cheery groups. None of them seemed to suspect anything amiss with their Secretary of State, which was bloody odd, since, at this particular juncture, the overwhelming weight of evidence suggested that the said Right Honourable gentleman was as nutty as a bowl of muesli.

'Looking forward to Russia, then?' Andrew Briggs, the Minister for Defence Procurement, boomed with unnecessary joviality.

'What do you think?' said George not missing a beat, somewhat to his own surprise. 'Especially with the new MiG, eh?'

'Cheeky buggers,' said Briggs.

'Can't blame them for trying, I suppose,' said George, who in fact rather did blame them. In desperation for Western currency the Russians had started dropping hints about the possibility of selling their new MiG 39, an all-singing, all-dancing supersonic stealth fighter at a knockdown price of fifteen million pounds a time, spares included. It was an unrepeatable offer, the best value-for-money deal any defence minister could contemplate. Any defence minister, that is, who didn't mind enraging the Americans, infuriating our European partners and driving twenty thousand aerospace workers into the grateful arms of the Labour Party.

'No way of handling it tactfully. You'll just have to give it to them straight. Tell them it's simply not on.' Like every other minister in the Department, Briggs understood that a primary aim of defence policy was to provide work for British manufacturers and secure votes in marginal constituencies.

'What about the promises in our manifesto?' George heard himself saying. 'We'll cut Government spending by getting maximum value for every pound of taxpayers' money. Remember?' Briggs, he noticed uncomfortably, had allowed a startled expression to appear on his face. It changed into an uncertain smile.

'It's a bit early in the morning for jokes like that isn't it?' he said.

'You're probably right,' George agreed hastily. For a wild,

lunatic moment he'd been on the verge of burbling something about the sanctity of manifesto pledges. He picked up the empty coffee cup from his desk and drained the cold dregs to cover his confusion. It seemed to help. Professionalism reasserted itself. 'Look, Andrew, glad to have this chance of a word,' he said. 'We might have a bit of a problem. On Sahelia.' Briggs, he was relieved to see, listened intently as he outlined the nastiness being planned by the *Daily Despatch*. 'So just put the word out, would you?' he concluded. 'On the quiet. Everybody's to keep their heads down for the moment. All the manufacturers. Our people. Everyone. OK?'

'Just what we needed,' said Briggs gloomily. 'Anyone else know about this?'

'Not as far as I know. And if I have anything to do with it they never will. I'll be having a word with Prudence Willow.'

'Give her a bloody damehood,' Briggs growled. 'She's made for it. Like Widow Twankey.'

'I'll recommend her for the Lords, if that's what it takes.'

Briggs pulled a face. 'Doesn't bear thinking about, does it? You're a rogue, George.' He was grinning now, and George grinned back in acknowledgement at what after all was intended as a compliment.

Some compliment, he thought as Briggs wandered off and the other guests began making their departures. Some bloody compliment, eh? It didn't feel like a compliment. It felt in fact as complimentary as a free ticket to a shysters' convention. For a brief moment the memory of last night's vision flashed across his mind and an unfamiliar sensation made itself felt. Remorse, perhaps?

Stop it, he instructed himself. Concentrate. You can't possibly be mad. Never mind last night. Look: here you are in your office, safe on the fifth floor of the Ministry of Defence main building, Whitehall, SW1. Solid as a rock. There's a pleasing Hockney on the wall. There's your Georgian desk, the most elegant in Whitehall. There's Nelson's bookcase against the far wall, and the dent in the bottom where Churchill once kicked it in a rage. Good old Winnie. He wasn't mad either, or not very. Look: there are your junior ministers off to their duties, loyal colleagues all, waving farewell. They haven't noticed anything wrong, have they? And here are the stewards, come to clear away the breakfast things. Smile at them, George. It's expected. Part of your charm. There! All's well. They're smiling back. Pity about their white coats.

George turned and stared through his window at the Embankment far below. Everything was as it should be. Pedestrians under their umbrellas scurried to work along the rain-slicked pavements. Red buses queued behind black cabs in the rush-hour snarl. A barge chugged rustily downriver, and away to the left a train snailed across the bridge to Charing Cross station. Wednesday morning, as ordinary as can be. Nothing mad in the atmosphere at all. Not a pink elephant to be seen. George closed his eyes. If he wasn't mad then the alternative was twice as terrifying.

Suppose for the sake of argument . . . No. Impossible. George had stopped believing in miracles at around the same time as discovering the disappointing facts about Father Christmas. There could be no miracles, or visions either, in this enlightened world. Of course not. Those who believed otherwise tended to be pubescent peasant girls in places conveniently far from civilisation. Lourdes. Knock. Fatima. George sniffed. He had his own views on Catholic superstition. It was surely no accident that you never heard tales of miraculous events from Methodists. No. Not from Baptists either, or Jews or Wee Frees, and certainly not from members of the Church of England.

Right, thought George. All right. He could safely do without the possibility of miracles, thanks very much. He was a Cambridge man, with a degree, what's more, in Moral Sciences. Class 2, Division 1. Respectable enough, academically. He could still, at a push, discourse on the way dear old Rene Descartes had overturned the medieval constructs of Thomas Aquinas. *Cogito ergo sum.* No need thereafter for the absolute, uncreated Mystery. If thought determined existence, God could be safely left out of it. The thing was to keep hold of reality. This window. Those raindrops. The rattle of plates on the stewards' trolley. They were real. A man could anchor his life to them. Wasn't there something called methodological solipsism which encouraged us to do precisely that? George couldn't be sure. It was, after all, nearly thirty years since he'd looked at a philosophical treatise.

The stewards left at last and George turned back to his desk. He still hadn't completed yesterday's red boxes and there were more overnight papers and documents spilling from his in-tray. A contract with Vickers for a new submarine. A memorandum on allowances for the Territorial Army. A brief on another redeployment in Cyprus. Reports on the trials of a new torpedo. Pages of statistics on service pensions. A provisional itinerary for the Russian trip. Nothing, thank God, requiring much concentration.

Working on autopilot, George began skimming. He'd need to initial most of the submissions in the ten minutes left before his Permanent Under Secretary, Sir Paul Bradley, poked a nose round the door. Bradley was never late, and far too shrewd to miss any sign of trouble. George scribbled dutifully on, doing his best not to imagine the raised Wykehamist eyebrows of his PUS if he were to learn of his Minister's predicament.

Predicament was the word, right enough. Confused though he undoubtedly was, George understood well enough that for the first time in his life he was helpless before the thrust of events. For all he knew there were platoons of angels or whatever you might care to call them lurking behind the nearest cloud just waiting their opportunity to pounce. Whether they were real or illusory was beside the point. Emissaries of God or the perverse product of an injured brain, they had the power to overwhelm his conscious mind and drag him off whether he liked it or not to never-never land, where no doubt they'd see to it that he was once again made painfully aware of his own shortcomings.

George stirred uneasily. For reasons he couldn't begin to fathom, he somehow knew there would be further visions before long. No question of hoping for the best. Whether he was ill or possessed, suffering a nervous breakdown or merely experiencing a particularly lurid example of the male menopause, he was mired in a personal crisis likely to get worse before it got better. In common prudence there should be no option but to submit himself to psychiatric examination before disgracing himself beyond recovery. That little episode with Andrew Briggs showed which way the wind was blowing. Frightening.

But not, it struck George, as frightening as the consequences of medical treatment. He stopped scribbling, appalled. One phone call was all it would take. He'd be in a private room at St Thomas's Hospital over the river in less time than it took to say 'Cabinet reshuffle', attended in all probability by nurses who would insist on calling him 'luvvie', not to mention consultants fascinated by the details of his potty-training. Perhaps there would be classes in raffia-work and afterwards, when he was cured, a gentle return to Westminster where he'd take his place on the unfamiliar back benches to the sympathy of colleagues who would thereafter avoid him.

George clutched the arms of his chair, his knuckles white. In the circumstances there seemed every excuse for leaping up and delivering a hefty kick to Nelson's bookcase, inflicting a dent to match Churchill's. It might well, he thought as the mood passed, be the only permanent mark he left in the Ministry. Absurd, of course. Inflicting further damage really would be a memorial to madness; and he wasn't mad, didn't feel mad. In fact it might be said that his assessment of the situation so far was proof positive of his sanity. Who after all could prove that his experience in the garden last night wasn't as real as that sideboard?

Well all right, he acknowledged. The entire membership of the Moral Sciences faculty at Cambridge, every man-jack of them, could no doubt make a fair stab at it. The point was, they hadn't been there, couldn't possibly appreciate the solidity of the thing. Could the human mind in a fit of the barks really contrive such detail?

Though the possibility that he might, in spite of all the evidence, be in full command of his senses ought to have been encouraging, George's spirits failed to lift. Madness could be cured after all, whereas the alternative . . . Visionaries were driven to make exhibitions of themselves, weren't they? What's more, like Joan of Arc and John the Baptist, they often came to a sticky end, burned or beheaded, if not defenestrated, broken on the wheel, hanged, drawn and quartered, shot full of arrows or fed to the lions.

'Deep in thought, Secretary of State?' True to form, Sir Paul Bradley's head appeared round the door, bang on time.

'Preoccupied with the welfare of the nation,' George replied, rather impressed with his own ability to snap out of it.

'I thought we'd begin with your itinerary for Russia, Secretary of State,' said Sir Paul, settling himself on the other side of the desk. 'You've been through the preliminary brief, I take it.'

'I'm not terribly happy about the arrangements for Ryazan,' George said, slipping smoothly into gear. 'Can't we persuade them to let us have more time there? I'd really like to have a look at their paratroop capability.' It was a relief to get down to work; and, as he progressed with his usual efficiency through the day's business with Sir Paul, Her Majesty's Secretary of State for Defence almost managed to convince himself that, as in all proper fairy stories, things would work out fine in the end.

Some way downriver, in the shadow of St Paul's, Monica Holroyd sat in her office and glared in undisguised grumpiness at the presentation laid out before her. The storyboard told the tale of a young man, his face aflame with zits, sitting alone in a disco while his carbuncle-free friends capered about the dancefloor. The spotty youth hung his head in shame. There's a flash of light. A roll of drums. Suddenly a heroic figure appears, beaming. He is clad in cape and scarlet leotard. This is Captain Clearskin, and he knows what to do with zits all right. He's in possession of a new scientific formula. One week's application, he promises, will sort out the trouble. The youth's pox-encrusted face lights up. He clutches the bottle with manic glee. The scene dissolves. Now the youth is handsome, his skin smooth as a baby's bottom. He is dancing with a blonde nymphet, and well on his way to a legover.

'No,' snarled Monica. 'No, no, no.'

'You don't like it then?' The creative man's shoulders drooped. 'I thought it was on target, actually.'

Monica resisted the temptation to start yelling and thumping her desk. One of the penalties of being a woman in a man's world was the impossibility of indulging in masculine behaviour without sounding shrill or hysterical. 'Just have another go at it, would you?' she suggested, as though the man might have any choice. Had she been in a better mood, she'd have added an 'All right, darling?' perhaps accompanied by a fluttered eyelash. But she wasn't inclined to massage any male ego right now. Not after last night.

She watched as Mr Creativity gathered his sketches and retreated. Through the frosted glass of her office door she could see his silhouette as he made the obligatory pause beside Tracey, her pneumatic secretary. No doubt he'd be complaining that madam was in a filthy mood this morning, and was she suffering from premenstrual tension, or what? Tracey, a girl who was a stranger to loyalty and a pushover for anything in trousers, would probably giggle. Monica suspected the consensus in the office these days was that madam needed someone to give her a good, hard rogering, preferably twice a night. That would make her a bit more human, wouldn't it?

She pressed the switch on her intercom. 'Could you rustle up a cup of coffee, please, Tracey?' she asked with just a hint of frost. 'Soon as you can.' It was a minor comfort to observe the silhouette on the other side of her door take the hint and depart, no doubt to inform everybody on the art floor that madam was best avoided for the foreseeable future.

Damn George Gulliver. Monica's fist clenched. How dare he? How did he bloody well dare? Even now, in the hard light of morning, it was difficult to believe the man had coldly turned his back on her, simply slipped on his shoes and walked out without apology and with only the most perfunctory word of farewell. He might as well have slapped her face.

No, she hadn't expected him to be thrilled. Few men enjoy the prospect of being pushed into a confrontation with their wives; and, since George lived in mortal dread of his indiscretions finding their way into the newspapers, it was only to be expected that he'd panic at her proposition. She'd been ready for that, worked out in detail how she'd soothe him while he wriggled. A kiss or two, a few whispered reassurances, a gentle squeeze of the balls and she'd have him slavering for bed before he could devise an excuse for resisting. The scenario had been worked out to the last throb of satisfied flesh, all contingencies taken into account. All except the one that actually occurred. She could still see the colour draining from his face and the strange glaze that crept into this eyes. Spooky. 'George?' she'd ventured. 'What's the matter?' But he'd given no sign that he heard. He simply stood frozen, staring intently at nothing, like one of those stone heads on Easter Island. Then he came to himself, shook his head from side to side, looked around with what might have been bewilderment and muttered an abrupt goodbye. Just like that. A panic-stricken cheat scuttling home to his wife.

'Nobody treats me like dirt,' she snarled.

'I'm sorry?' Tracey had somehow managed to tiptoe in while Monica's mind was otherwise engaged and was now staring nervously, a cup of coffee in her hand. Bosoms heaved beneath a restraining blouse. 'I haven't done anything wrong.'

'Thinking of something else. It's all right. Miles away.' Monica summoned up an efficient smile. 'A bit bogged down in something, that's all.'

'I'll leave you to it then,' Tracey simpered. She set down the coffee and swayed out, her tight-clad buttocks undulating like an Atlantic swell. She'd probably waste no time spreading the latest tale of madam's eccentricity; and it was the surest of sure-fire bets the men would lap it up. There wasn't one of them capable of resisting Tracey's curves and billows and baby-blue eyes.

Monica's jaw set. She wouldn't – couldn't – allow herself to become a Tracey, enjoyed and discarded like an inflatable doll.

She pulled a sheet of writing-paper from the rack and unscrewed the cap of her fountain pen. Bitchiness, she promised herself, had no part to play in what she was about to do. It was a matter of principle. She was a serious professional person, yes? Her name was picked out in gilt on the door. She had a secretary and a walnut desk. Like other partners she had her own drinks cabinet and a private washroom. The walls of her office were adorned with testaments to her achievements: the Hard Labour poster she'd helped create for the Tories at the last election; a framed newspaper article headed THE IMAGE MAKERS – THE CONSERVATIVES' SECRET WEAPON; a montage of clips from successful television commercials. Monica was proud of them all. They meant something, defined her professional worth. Well, then. Bitchiness obviously didn't come into it. She was incapable of betraying the self that fought so hard to win a name in gilt upon an office door.

She drew the sheet of paper closer, picked up her pen. It was, as her American colleagues might say, time to piss or get off the pot. She began to write. After the 'Dear George' bit it was really quite remarkable how fluently the words flowed.

'And what did the accused say then?'

Sergeant Bullock turned his stolid gaze upon the Bench. 'May I consult my notes, Your Worships?'

'Very well,' said Rosemary, wondering not for the first tine how the police would react if once, just for the hell of it, she said no.

The sergeant produced his notebook and began reading. 'He said, "It's a fair cop, guv'nor. You got me bang to rights. I know I done wrong. I'll come quietly." When I advised him that it was a serious matter he said, "Why don't we kiss and make up?"'

'A bit of a comedian,' growled the prosecuting solicitor. 'Can we take it he'd been drinking?'

'His breath did smell of alcohol, sir, and he was slurring his words. When we got him to the station he was sick. All over the reception area.' Sergeant Bullock completed his evidence in the unemotional tones of a man who hadn't been given the task of cleaning up.

Rosemary studied the figure slumped miserably in the dock. Samuel David Edwards, occupation teacher, charged with malicious damage, being drunk and disorderly and conduct likely. The man seemed close to collapse, though fortunately for him the press table was, as usual, empty. There would be no paragraph in the local paper to fascinate his pupils and blight his career.

'Yes, Mr Burden,' she said, as Edwards's defence solicitor rose to his feet.

'Your Worships, my client admits all the charges against him and wishes to apologise unreservedly for his behaviour,' Burden began. 'There are however some mitigating factors which the Bench should take into account before passing sentence.'

It was a familiar tale, one that with remarkably few variations Rosemary had heard a hundred times before. Respectable man falls out with his wife, discovers she's having an affair, starts drinking and decides to wreak a cuckold's vengeance, in this case by tearing the radio aerial off his rival's car. Rosemary made a note on her jotter. Presumably there was a phallic significance in Edwards's choice of target. It was a well-attested fact that men were obsessed with the length, thickness and durability of their cocks, called them by pet names, compared them anxiously in the showers, sought reassurance in the gratitude of women. She had no doubt what had been going through Edwards's mind as he stalked the adulterer's car and tore its quivering attachment from the roots.

'In the circumstances, your Worships, I do respectfully ask the court to consider my client's suffering,' said Burden, concluding his plea. It was an affecting performance, and in the dock Edwards seemed a little more perky. Rosemary wondered how he'd look when he received the legal bill.

She conferred briefly for form's sake with her two fellow magistrates, neither of whom was rash enough to challenge the decision she'd already made. In the circumstances a binding over to keep the peace and an order to reimburse his wife's lover was punishment enough. Even a social disciplinarian like George couldn't cavil at that; and anyway she couldn't help feeling a sneaking sympathy for what Edwards had done. Would George ever display such caveman passion if one day she went off the rails? Hardly. He'd probably just sulk for a bit before stamping off to find consolation elsewhere. If he noticed at all. Or cared.

There wasn't much point pretending. These days Rosemary hardly knew what to make of her husband. It wasn't just the usual business; he'd always worked himself to a standstill, always run after popularity and political approval. She'd always tried to make allowances for his insecurities and secret fears. Only this time it was very different. George just moped about the house, sat for hours locked in his own thoughts, looked at her with the eyes of a stranger. He wouldn't talk. Perhaps he couldn't. It seemed entirely possible that he was going through a mid-life crisis of the kind that persuades men of a certain age to make adolescent idiots of themselves. It would be comforting to think George too clever or cautious for such a caper; yet she could recall plenty of husbands who'd run off apparently in the hope of finding themselves, like cats chasing their own tails. It was the kind of thing men did. And there was no getting away from the Chanel No. 5 she'd found among his effects after the accident. She really ought to ask about the Chanel. George knew very well she used Paloma Picasso.

'Case number eighteen,' announced the clerk to the court.

'Very well.' Rosemary hauled herself back to her public responsibilities.

'Raymond George Snoddy,' intoned the clerk. 'You are charged that on the twentieth day of August in the Plough and Anchor public house you did assault James William Cox, causing actual bodily harm. How say you? Are you guilty or not guilty?'

The oaf in the dock grinned with what he presumably thought was defiance. Rosemary glared at him. Snoddy was a regular customer of the court, one of the army of young louts spawned (depending on one's point of view) by the decline in religious observance, the absence of conscription, the unlettered shambles of the state educational system or the impact of free-market capitalism. 'Not guilty,' he announced.

Rosemary did her best to concentrate as the evidence unfolded. It was important to remember that a human being stood in the dock, however unprepossessing his demeanour. Her personal unhappiness would have to wait. She'd go home when court was over and settle down to reread all the cards that had come in the morning post. There were quite a few. She'd display them on the mantelpiece where George couldn't miss them, placing her gift to him prominently in the middle.

It would be quite something to see the expression on his face when he came in.

She'd probably cry a little then. It was only to be expected. When a husband manages to forget a twenty-fifth wedding anniversary a wife is entitled to her tears.

CHAPTER

5

The tanks bludgeoned past in the howling dust. Five of them. Perhaps six. In the maelstrom of muck and noise it was hard to see, damned nearly impossible to think. An explosion nearby shook the earth. One of the tanks swung a squealing turret and fired before racing back into the murk. Crash! Crouching soldiers ran in its wake. There was a flash behind them, then a shock to buffet the skin and snatch the breath away.

'Noisy buggers,' said Jack Cartwright.

Overhead but not by much, implausibly low in fact, a heavy-bellied Antonov transport plane lumbered in, tiny figures dropping from its rear end. The spectacle reminded Jack of his family's pet goldfish, which seemed to spend most of its time crapping. He stared in alarm as the figures hurtled towards the ground. At the last moment, an instant before they were dashed to pieces, they pulled their ripcords. Parachutes bloomed above them. In seconds they were safely down, rolling on the ground, shrugging free of their harnesses. Two set up a heavy machine-gun, which immediately began jack-hammering into the gloom. Others charged forward in attack formation.

Jack repressed a yawn. The remains of this morning's hangover throbbed behind his eyes. For the look of it he pulled out his notebook and scribbled some words. 'Tanks,' he scrawled. 'Transport plane. Paras. Noise.' So what? Back in Annie's Bar, he thought, they'd be sinking the first pint of the day, lucky devils, finishing the Skeleton Crossword in the *Daily Express*, telling each other the latest jokes. 'What the fuck am I doing here?' he scrawled. Away in the distance a human voice screeched in the chaos of men and machines. The voice screeched again, perhaps uttering a command, perhaps expressing some private agony. Who knew? Who the fuck cared? A starshell arched through the haze. Whistles blew. The exercise was over.

'Oppressive, no?' said the man from the Ministry with the unpronounceable name. Most of the British press corps in Moscow knew him simply as Mrs Malaprop. He looked expectantly at Jack.

'Mmm,' he said. The man from the Ministry frowned and Jack did his best to adopt an expression that conveyed both enthusiasm and admiration. According to the boys at the embassy, the Russians tended to get upset if visitors didn't positively gasp in wonder at everything they saw. Thin-skinned bastards. 'Very good indeed,' he said. 'Very oppressive. You must be proud of them.'

The man from the Ministry perked up. 'Like your British Parachute Regiment,' he beamed. 'Special training. Bang, bang! Everybody dead as doorknobs!'

Jack had stopped listening. The paratroopers from the Antonov were lining up for inspection, and even from a distance it was possible to see that, in one particular at least, they weren't a bit like the hairy-arses from Aldershot. 'They're women,' he said. 'Bloody hell!'

The man from the Ministry was delighted. 'They can kill you with a single blow-job,' he announced. 'They know all tricks. In Russia woman and men are the same. No difference. Not like in England, no?'

'Not a bit like in England,' Jack agreed. Unless he was much mistaken, one of the female paras sported the most enormous tits. 'We're not as advanced in our thinking as you Russians,' he said. 'Nowhere near.' He clapped the man from the Ministry on the back. 'I'd very much like to talk to them. My readers would be most interested in their military skill.' Too right they would. Already a headline was forming in his mind: SECRETS OF RUSSIA'S KILLER BIMBOS. Not that the ghastly Willow would allow the slightest reference to bimbodom, but never mind. She'd leap at a story about women capable of killing men with a single blow-job; and it would salvage something from an otherwise useless trip. He might even make something on his expenses.

Quite why bloody Prudence had insisted on sending him to cover George Gulliver's Russian visit was anybody's guess. It couldn't possibly be because the Minister was giving her one, could it? No, Jack had more faith in George Gulliver's good taste. The Russian trip was probably just one of the lady's demented whims, like her reluctance to run the Sahelia story. It obviously hadn't dawned on her yet that Moscow's military capability was yesterday's news. The good old days of the cold war were long gone. Nobody gave a stuff any more about Russia's tanks and guns, or twitched in fear of instant nuclear annihilation. A shame really. All the fun had gone out of defence reporting.

Only a few years ago under the old Soviet regime a Western journalist caught anywhere near the paratroop training school at Ryazan would have been shot on sight as a capitalist spy. Anyone who managed to get a story or a picture out of the place would have become famous overnight, a media superstar, international reporter of the year. Now the buggers in Moscow rolled out the red carpet, invited you to take as many pictures as you'd like and looked offended if you didn't jump at the opportunity. In fact they weren't best pleased that only a couple of reporters had bothered to accompany the Defence Secretary on his present trip, and pretty scrubby reporters at that. The Russians had made it unsubtly clear that they'd never heard of Jack Cartwright, or of the *Daily Despatch* for that matter; and God alone knew what they made of the girl from George Gulliver's local paper, the *Mowsbury Gazette*.

Well, bollocks to the Russians. Bollocks to George Gulliver too, come to that. The man looked as miserable these days as a bridegroom with brewer's droop. In the three days since his official visit began he hadn't once taken the press aside for a confidential chat, hadn't bothered to offer more than a 'Good morning' when the opportunity arose. Even the lass from the *Mowsbury Gazette* was beginning to look unsettled, and no wonder. Jack himself hadn't succeeded in getting a line into his paper since the moment the British party had landed at Vnukovo Airport.'You ought to be down at Westminster, not pissing about over there,' the newsdesk had informed him last time he'd phoned in. 'Government's in one hell of a state.'

Up on the reviewing stand a pair of red-tabbed Russian generals began gesticulating towards the killer bimbos while George nodded, an expression of what could have been boredom on his face. Or even irritation. He said something that obviously affronted the generals. Their faces dropped in a pair of perfectly matched scowls. The whole platform party in fact seemed to be affected by a sudden attack of the glums, with the exception of the British military attaché, who was scribbling energetically in his notebook. It was a curious scene, not in the least what you'd expect in an occasion that was supposed to represent amity, cooperation and hands across the sea. Jack stood and began edging closer to the group, Mrs Malaprop trailing in his wake.

'And you really find them effective in a shooting situation?' George was asking, the tiniest edge of incredulity in his voice. Jack rather approved. There weren't many politicians nowadays who dared lay themselves open to a charge of male chauvinism.

'We talk to them. You will see,' growled Marshal Smirnov, the Russian Defence Minister, whose face reminded Jack inescapably of a King Edward potato.

'The Israelis found that women in the front line were more trouble than they're worth,' George continued, evidently unimpressed. 'If they're wounded the men insist on staying behind to look after them.' The Russians began muttering among themselves and one of the younger colonels in the party actually clenched his fist. Small wonder. The Secretary of State was hardly exhibiting the diplomatic *savoir-faire* for which Her Majesty's Government was renowned. Jack fumbled for his notebook. What in God's name was Gulliver playing at? 'Minister in row over Russia's beautiful killers,' he scrawled.

This was more like it. Perhaps even a front-page yarn if George kept it up. The boys from the embassy looked appalled, as well they might. One of them noticed Jack's interest and immediately adopted a poker face. The man wouldn't have lasted five minutes in one of the old Fleet Street seven-card stud schools, thought Jack.

'We are not Israelis. We are Russian,' snarled Marshal Smirnov. 'Here we fight for the rodina, for our homeland. Russian men. Russian women. No difference. Patriots.' It was evident that he wouldn't mind punching the snotty English Minister on the nose.

As the two men glared at each other there was a satisfactory bit of official to-ing and fro-ing in the background, clever young Englishmen and clever young Russians murmuring in each other's ears and no doubt agreeing that their respective masters were a pair of schmucks. Jack went on scribbling. A smoothie in an MCC tie whispered something to George. Another smoothie, though in a tie that looked as though it came from a scout jumble sale, muttered to Marshal Smirnov, presumably something along the lines of '*Pas devant les domestiques*'.

'We have women soldiers in Britain too,' said George after an embarrassing pause. 'But not paratroopers. Perhaps we're old-fashioned, eh?' He thrust out a hand. 'Shall we agree to disagree, Marshal?'

For a blissful moment it seemed that Smirnov might ignore the gesture. But to Jack's disappointment he managed to summon up a grin from somewhere and clasped George's hand. 'We talk to my soldiers,' he said.

Jack followed contentedly as the entire party, ministers, generals, embassy officials and hangers-on, strolled over to the lady paras, all of whom were now lined up fetchingly at attention. The Brünnhilde with big tits, he was pleased to see, had wisps of blonde hair escaping from beneath her beret. He pulled out the idiot-proof camera provided by the office. 'Just point the bloody thing and press the button,' the picture editor had advised. 'Can't possibly go wrong.' Jack pointed and pressed. A motor whirred reassuringly. Great stuff. He pressed again, capturing the girl smiling prettily at an undeniably grumpy George. Oh, Gulliver, he thought. Whatever happened to diplomacy?

Speculation on that matter could wait though. Jack snapped a few more pictures for good measure and as the official party moved on homed in on the blonde lady with the curves and a smile to make your heart lurch. As it turned out, she not only spoke passable English but possessed a collection of Rolling Stones records, which she sometimes played in her barracks. Better still, her name was Natasha – yes, it was one of those days when everything goes right – and as a bonus she happily explained that she knew how to decapitate her enemies with a cheese-wire. Jack was so pleased at the news, so busy scribbling down her thoughts on the rightful place of women in society, that for a few minutes at least he forgot to wonder what in God's name had got into the Rt. Hon. George Gulliver.

There was no doubt about it, thought George. The Russians might not possess a pisspot between them but they presented themselves with a certain style. A four-car motorcade with police outriders and a fine disdain for red lights might flatter any visitor into the belief that not everything run by Moscow was held together by string and superglue.

He gazed through the smoked-glass windows as the fields and villages purred past. At every crossroads a saluting policeman stood, the everyday traffic halted deferentially behind. George would have offered a lordly wave each time, but of course the point about a Zil limousine was that you couldn't see in. The Russians, for all their boasts about the new democracy, had never believed in allowing the riffraff an unsanctioned glimpse of their masters. Quite right too. Leather seats and fringed lamps, frosted vodka and an assortment of salty nibbles were best kept away from envious eyes. He slathered caviare on a cracker and swallowed it whole, following it with a slug of Stolichnaya. A pity the ministerial car pool back home didn't run to such comforts.

George sighed and poured himself one more glass. In other

circumstances three shots of vodka before noon might have seemed excessive; but today was for sightseeing after all, with a Zil all to himself and no official business but for a Kremlin reception and a farewell dinner at the embassy. Anyway, he needed it. Especially after reading Jack Cartwright's report in the *Despatch*, which the Ministry of Defence press office had thoughtfully faxed in its entirety. Helpful bastards. GULLIVER IN ROW OVER GIRL PARAS. We Wouldn't Have You In Our Man's Army. Exclusive. By Jack Cartwright. Thank you, Jack. Thank you very bloody much. 'Defence Minister George Gulliver stunned Russia's army chiefs last night by snubbing their feared women paratroopers' was Cartwright's version of events.

'In an extraordinary public outburst he rounded on Marshal Dmitri Smirnov, Moscow's top military commander, and said that women trained to kill with their bare hands should have no place in any army.'

There was plenty more in that vein, not to mention an interview with a beaming lady called Natasha who claimed that she could tear the balls off any British paratrooper you cared to name; and if the English Minister didn't believe her she'd be delighted to come over to Aldershot for a demonstration. To add insult to injury the *Despatch* leader column carried a lengthy rebuke under the headline MALE CHAUVINISM AND THE MINISTER; and the women's page, not to be outdone, was running a readership survey with the exhortation: Let's Hear It, Ladies! What do YOU think? It was a cringe-making mess; and, to make matters worse, Rosemary had refused to comment on her husband's indiscretion. No matter that she never talked to the press if she could help it: everyone would infer she was too timid to contradict an overbearing husband.

'Nobody to blame but yourself, matey,' muttered George, and gulped the remains of his vodka. The glow spread satisfyingly through his stomach and he wondered whether he should risk another. In his present mood he suspected he could drain the whole bottle and hardly notice. Woman trouble did that to a man. Why couldn't wives understand more and complain less, eh? One of nature's mysteries, that. Still, he'd sleepwalked right into the mess at home, hadn't he? Like a zombie. Silly bugger.

'Lots of post today,' Rosemary had purred as he poured himself a midnight drink. He'd gone straight through to his study, preoccupied with the Navy's demand for a new amphibious assault vessel.

'Mmm?' According to the Navy the country's ability to project its military power beyond the European theatre would be fatally undermined unless they got a new ship pronto. Three hundred million pounds plus some small change should do it. Not a chance, of course, even though it would mean a welcome order for the shipyards of the Tyne or Belfast.

'It's all on the mantelpiece. In the other room.' He should have cottoned on then of course, woken up to the catch in her voice. No good explaining afterwards that he was going through a difficult time, what with his mind being wrenched from its moorings and his mistress threatening to go ballistic and the Navy seeming to think that money grew on trees. He walked unsuspecting into the dining-room and froze. He knew immediately that he couldn't be forgiven, knew the moment he saw the cards set out in reproachful congratulation and the little package tied lovingly in a golden bow. Stricken, he turned. But Rosemary was already stamping up the stairs, throwing herself into their bedroom, locking the door behind her with a grisly click. He trudged after her with nothing to say. What can be said when a man's forgotten his own silver wedding?

That night he'd slept in the spare room. 'I don't want to hear it, George,' said Rosemary, red-eyed but composed, when he faced up to her in the morning. 'No more excuses.' She'd turned her back on him then, standing rigid with hurt until he crept away. He hadn't even been able to thank her for his Rolex, its back engraved in words of love.

Not the ideal preparation for a ministerial visit to Mother Russia, he thought, putting his empty glass away in its wooden container. Halfway down the road to a mental breakdown, a glacial marriage and – third cherry in a miserable jackpot – that deadly little letter from Monica Holroyd still awaiting an answer. No wonder he was making mistakes. In fact it was a bloody miracle he could function at all.

George could read the signs as well as the next man. After

he latest nonsense with Smirnov there couldn't be much doubt
hat he was losing his grip. The headlines confirmed it. Male
chauvinism and the Minister. How long would it take to live
hat one down? Too bloody long, that's how long. Sometimes
he was tempted to wonder whether the game was worth the
candle. What must it be like to live a private life in an ordinary
suburb, free of calculation and political necessity? He shook his
head. Too late now. Much. Besides, it was important to make a
mark in the world. Otherwise, what was the point?

'Sergiyev Posad!' announced his driver as the official motorcade swept to a halt in what seemed to be a giant municipal
car park packed with buses, lorries, coaches, charabancs,
vans, trucks and taxis. Sunday-morning crowds thronged past
as George stood blinking in the sun, impressed in spite of his
mood. Above him reared the walls and onion domes in gold
that had beckoned pilgrims for six hundred years, the Trinity-St
Sergius Monastery, heart of Holy Russia, soul of the Orthodox
tradition, a religious community that had survived generations
of repression to triumph at last in the new freedom.

'Not bad,' said George.

'Fourteenth century,' said the man from the embassy, somewhat grumpily. He'd been made to travel in the second car while
George rode in solitary state and his disapproval showed. 'Two
major cathedrals. Trinity and the Cathedral of the Assumption.
Fifteenth century and sixteenth century respectively. Some of
the finest icons in the world. And wait till you hear the music.
Personally, I think it knocks spots off the Kremlin. Magnificent,
isn't it?' He leaned forward, a glimmer of malice in his eye.
'There's a blob of caviare on your chin,' he whispered.

George got to work with a handkerchief, hoping the man
hadn't smelled the vodka on his breath. Wasn't it supposed
to be odourless? He couldn't remember, but maybe that last
drink hadn't been such a good idea. No doubt it was all part
of losing one's grip. In fact the fresh air seemed to be having
a strange effect on his equilibrium and he staggered slightly
before regaining his balance. 'We'd better get on, then,' he said.
'Can't keep the Metropolitan of Russia waiting, can we?'

Ignoring a suggestion that it might be more advisable, don't you think, Minister, to wait for the official welcoming party, George strode off. It was always sound practice to take the initiative and, besides, the exercise might clear his head. With a gaggle of escorts grumbling in his wake he allowed himself to be swept up in the human tide pouring through the great gates of the monastery, into a seething warren of squares and narrow streets, the pious thousands jamming every thoroughfare, pushing and jostling as though their salvation depended on it. As maybe it did.

As far as George could make out in the press, there seemed to be churches and chapels every few yards. Around the doors of each one a denser crowd surged, craning, stretching, wriggling in pious frenzy to get inside. Bells boomed. It was difficult to breathe. 'Gets worse every time,' bawled the man from the embassy, which was as near as he could politely get to I told you so. 'They actually queue up to pray at the tomb of St Sergius. Can you imagine this kind of carry-on at Westminster Abbey?'

'Hardly,' gasped George as he was thrust aside by a very fat lady who muttered to herself as she passed. Prayers, presumably. It cheered him no end when she in turn was shoved out of the way by a uniformed policeman who appeared from nowhere, snapped an arm-quivering salute and announced in perfect English that he was in charge of the Minister's security and how could he apologise enough for the unfortunate misunderstanding? Behind him, a platoon of large men with batons scowled at the churchgoers, who obligingly shrank away.

'No apologies necessary,' said George. 'Though to tell you the truth I never thought I'd be glad to see the KGB.'

Behind him the man from the embassy rolled his eyes undiplomatically to heaven. 'He's military intelligence,' he hissed. 'GRU, not KGB. And anyway, it's not the KGB any more. It's the FSB. It was all in the briefing paper. The army looks after you because you're the Defence Secretary.' There was a subtext in his tone which George didn't much care for. It suggested that the Minister had better pull himself together and look sharp about it.

At this stage a couple of priests or bishops or possibly archimandrites hove into view, all beards and black robes and objects that might have been upturned flowerpots (but presumably weren't) perched on their heads. There was a fair amount of grinning and handshaking and babbling in Russian until it was suggested that maybe it would be a good idea to get on if the Minister wanted to keep to his schedule; before he knew it George was being ushered past the gawping crowds and through the vast doors of Trinity Cathedral, into a blaze of candles and the swirl of incense. Into the sounds of heaven.

His heart lurched.

Below him on the Easthampton by-pass, Geoff Norridge's wrecked Jaguar lay mangled and steaming. The music was the same but not the same; nothing like, in fact and yet . . . similar. Yes. It touched the same nerve. The man from the embassy was whispering something about a Credo, but George hardly took it in. The voices throbbed, soared, echoed. No instruments. Just a choir of priests and monks, bass and baritone and tenor in impossible harmonies. Dissolve me into ecstasies, and bring all heaven before mine eyes. Old Milton knew what he was talking about all right. Dissolve. From the Latin *dissolvere*, to loosen, to melt. It's a fair description of George's state at this particular juncture. The singing overwhelms him, sweeping brain, blood and soul into another dimension. He's transported.

This is a rum business. At one level he's perfectly aware that it's Sunday morning and he's standing jammed with a thousand others, sweating shoulder to uncomfortable shoulder, unable to see a damned thing, nose and throat full of incense, the smell of candlewax, the sour tang of armpits. In other circumstances he'd be tempted to push for the nearest exit and a gulp of God's good air, but of course these aren't other circumstances. This is here and now, at another level of reality, where in defiance of the most elementary laws of optics he can see perfectly well through the congregation, through pillars and round corners. On the altar priests are celebrating the mass in crowns and glittering copes; to one side a choir of monks in black is pouring out its collective heart; icons glow on every wall. Look: there's an old codger mumbling his petitions in a far corner, crossing himself repeatedly and bowing before the representation of a sad-eyed Christ. Through some hitherto undiscovered inner ear George can not only catch every word the man is whispering but understand it too. 'Lord have mercy,' he's murmuring. 'Lord have mercy on a poor sinner.'

Whether George is undergoing a religious experience is at this stage difficult to determine. It can't have escaped our attention that he's not entirely sober. Not drunk, mind; there's no chance of an appearance by the Jolly Green Giant or for that matter pink elephants. Still, it's worth reminding ourselves that vodka, heat and tiredness may in combination induce sensations that have nothing at all to do with the Infinite Other. It might be wise to suspend judgement.

George, however, doesn't share our doubts. For the moment at least he's convinced beyond argument, beyond cold reason or the claims of philosophy, that he's in touch with objective reality. Questions about his sanity or his emotional stability simply don't arise. His mind is clear. He looks into the eyes of the icon and in that shattering instant understands with a terrible clarity, understands himself and the world and a universe of light. Perhaps such intensity can't last; but while it does he really has no choice but to slough off his old life. No regrets are possible. In this instant he knows what he must do.

'Time to move, Minister,' murmured the man from the embassy, touching his arm.

'Lead on, Macduff,' said George, who curiously found no difficulty in behaving as though nothing had happened. He allowed himself to be shepherded out of the cathedral, stood blinking in the sun like any other tourist. 'That was magnificent,' he breathed. 'Sublime.' His Russian hosts nodded and smiled, probably because that's what all Westerners said when they came to Sergiyev Posad. George smiled happily back. Everything was all right now. He knew it.

Perhaps it was this certainty that propelled him so easily through the rest of the day: lunch with the Metropolitan and a piety of prelates; an evening reception in the Kremlin, toasts and speeches carried off without a hitch; dinner at the embassy. If he was operating on autopilot it didn't show. He went to bed at last and slept without a dream.

*   *   *

In the morning he woke with his resolution undimmed.

There would of course be hell to pay. No avoiding it. Scenes in the House, long faces in Cabinet and in all probability press denunciations of the latest ministerial folly. The thing he planned wouldn't lightly be forgiven. Well, so be it. In his new certainty George could contemplate the likely eclipse of his career without flinching. He knew only that it was necessary to act. Decisively. Even recklessly. Hesitation now would be akin to blasphemy.

On the other side of the Moskva River the blank, red walls of the Kremlin glowered, as though resentful at the cheeky presence of the British Embassy in such close proximity. Stalin apparently used to work himself into a rage whenever he saw the Union Flag fluttering within spitting-distance. Poor old Joe. What kind of destiny awaited such a monster when they finally put the pennies on his eyes? Too late then for redemption. The world's tyrants no doubt convinced themselves that Catullus was spot on: all we face in the hereafter is eternal darkness, *una nox dormienda*. It must come as a considerable shock to find Old Nick grinning on the other side complete, for all anyone knew, with an army of imps, demons, succubi and horned goblins all jabbering in delight at the capture of another soul.

A timid knock on the door interrupted these Savanarolaesque speculations, which was perhaps just as well. Even in his (presumed) state of amazing grace, George appreciated the dangers of going over the top. A man could lose himself in zealotry. If he didn't watch it he might well end up rootling around for the Third Secret of Fatima or demanding the opening of Joanna Southcott's Box. 'Come in,' he called.

Jack Cartwright was clearly expecting a bollocking. He stood in the doorway wearing an expression that managed to be at once apologetic and truculent. 'It was a legitimate story, George,' he began. 'Absolutely accurate.'

'What'll you have to drink?' asked George genially.

Jack's expression relaxed. He closed the door behind him. 'Scotch if you've got it. Splash of water.'

'I don't mind telling you I've had no end of problems over your piece,' George announced, busying himself with the drinks. 'You made me look a complete Charlie. Say when.'

'When.'

'A five-star gold-plated nincompoop, in fact.'

'I didn't mean to—'

'Cheers, then.' George handed over a well-filled tumbler.

'Cheers.'

'Serves me right, mind. That's what you get when you let the reptiles loose, eh?'

'Ah. Well. You've got to understand . . .'

'Only doing your job, Jack. That's the bottom line, yes?' George took a long, satisfying pull at his whisky. 'If I may say so, you do it very well. Too well for comfort sometimes.' This was the kind of flattery all journalists loved, and George was half tempted to play the game out to the end, to the point where Cartwright began to feel so guilty that he'd vow something – anything – to restore the reputation of the man he'd wronged. It was an old trick; but of course George didn't need tricks any more. If the interview had the consequences he expected, he'd probably never need them again.

'Anyway, this isn't about your story,' he went on. 'It's something else. Something rather more important. I'll probably be sacked for what I'm going to say. Almost certainly, I should think.'

Jack's' eyed widened. He put down his glass and licked his lips. 'Can I take some notes?' he asked in a voice that strove unsuccessfully to be casual.

'I think you should,' said George. 'This is on the record. I want you to take down every word.' At the back of his mind a small voice muttered something uncomplimentary about politicians who insisted on making prats of themselves. George ignored it. 'Sahelia,' he began. 'I've been doing a lot of thinking about those pictures you showed me. I've decided that we've no moral choice but to pull out of the deal.'

Jack stopped scribbling. 'You're not serious?'

'Totally.'

'But you spent months putting it together.'

There you are, said the small voice of common sense. You're

behaving like an arsehole. No two ways about it. 'I was wrong,' said George.

'I've been in this game twenty years.' Jack's expression was tinged with suspicion. 'I've never heard a politician admit anything like that.'

'Well you're hearing it now. I was wrong. I thought the Sahelians would modify their behaviour. They haven't. I should have known better.' George could feel the irritability creeping into his words and paused until the moment passed. 'It's entirely my fault. Nobody else's.'

'Bloody hell,' said Jack. 'You're not blaming the Foreign Secretary?'

'I'm blaming myself.'

'Or the Trade Minister?'

'I've told you. It's my responsibility.' Why was it, he wondered, that his protestations had a hollow ring? Because you're behaving like an amateur, replied the small voice. Cartwright thinks you're off your head. He may not be far wrong at that. Still sure of yourself, are you?

'You must have raised all this in Cabinet,' Jack murmured almost to himself, evidently trying to make some sense of the situation. 'There must have been a hell of a row, right?'

'The Cabinet doesn't know yet. I only decided a few hours ago. They may disagree with me, of course. Could be over-ruled.'

There was a sudden silence in the room. Jack laid his pen carefully on the table and took a sip of his whisky. 'You're having me on,' he said at last.

'I've never been more serious in my life.'

Another silence. Jack drained his glass. 'You've just decided to change a major piece of Government policy,' he said. 'You've also decided to tell me before you tell the Cabinet. Is that the situation?'

'That's about the size of it.' George couldn't quite interpret the look in Cartwright's eye.

'Do you mind telling me why?'

Come on, matey, jeered the voice. Tell him about your brainstorm. 'I feel it's the right thing to do,' he said. 'We've all got to live by certain moral standards. Governments too. We can't just abandon them whenever it's convenient.' It was, he thought, pretty unconvincing stuff, though Jack was dutifully taking it all down.

'Still doesn't explain why you're going public. I mean, the proper thing to do is go to the Cabinet, isn't it? So why didn't you?'

'I fully intend to. The moment we're back in London.' You're dodging the question, George, nagged the voice. Why don't you admit the real reason? Admit you've been driven to it. Come on, Mr Morality. Tell the truth and shame the Devil.

But Jack was staring at him with what by now couldn't be mistaken for anything but bafflement. 'They'll crucify you,' he announced. 'They'll nail you to the Cross. No anaesthetics.'

'I don't suppose it will be easy,' agreed George. 'I certainly don't expect it to be.'

But Jack was aglow with the sudden light of understanding. 'My God,' he breathed. 'You cunning old . . . That's it! You want a row! You actually . . . Oh, yes. Clever. Bloody hell!'

'I beg you pardon?' said George, miffed.

'You're taking a bit of chance, mind,' said Jack. 'More than a bit, I'd say. Mounting this sort of challenge with the election so near.'

'I don't know what you're talking about,' snapped George, who didn't much appreciate being called cunning by an inky scribbler. Even if the description was apparently meant in admiration.

'Course you don't,' said Jack soothingly. 'Just thinking out loud. Bad habit. Sorry. Look, George, can we run through this again? From the top? We want to make sure we get it right, don't we?'

Indeed we do, thought George as he watched the reporter fill his notebook. After all, it was a bit late now to start wondering whether he'd got anything right at all.

Two thousand miles away, Rosemary made up her mind at last. She turned the key in the lock.

Still she hesitated. Once she opened that door she'd have

committed an irreversible breach of trust. Crossed the Rubicon.
Though George had never specifically forbidden her to look in
his safe, she knew perfectly well that it was off limits. He kept
his most confidential papers there. State secrets. The security
of the realm might depend on them. It would never occur
to him that they might be laid open to the attentions of a
prying wife.

Feeling cheap and tacky, she tugged gently at the handle. The
door opened half an inch. Still time to push it shut and return
the key to its hiding-place. It was undoubtedly the honourable
thing to do. The decent thing. She tugged the handle again.
The door opened wide. Rosemary stood appalled at what she'd
done. George's fault, though. Not hers.

It was an innocent mistake that inspired her to snoop,
or so Rosemary told herself. There were two buff enve-
lopes in the post that morning from the credit-card company
and she'd simply opened the wrong one. An easy error.
Understandable. Rosemary should have replaced George's
statement the moment she glimpsed it, since her own monthly
account usually contained only two or three entries. Still,
as she'd come so far ... And it was unintentional, wasn't
it?

She'd run an eye down the list. Petrol. Payments to the
Churchill Room at the Commons. Flowers bought the day after
their anniversary. A bill for sixty-three pounds, settled at the
Paradiso restaurant in Pimlico. Oh. That was one to make the
heart sink. She'd never heard of the place. Now she'd never
forget it. An outing at the Paradiso. It wasn't one of the places
George used for lunch. She knew them all. Dinner, then, with an
unknown guest. On the night George had returned in the small
hours, a stranger in her bed. What wife wouldn't investigate
further?

Rosemary swallowed her guilt and peered into the safe.
Folders with red-striped covers. Confidential. Most Secret.
Confidential. Confidential. Restricted. A white letter underneath them all. Heavy paper and a feminine hand. This is
your last chance to stop, Rosemary told herself. You don't
really want to know.

But of course she couldn't stop. She picked up the letter and stood by the open safe and read every revealing word. Right down to the flourish of Monica's signature at the end.

CHAPTER

6

The most convenient gentlemen's lavatory in 10 Downing Street waits to welcome the visitor just a few yards beyond the front step and the saluting policeman. You stride across the chequered floor of the entrance lobby into a carpeted hallway and there it is on the left, discreet behind its plain white door. There are four substantial urinals, a bank of washbasins and a cool-tiled wall against which many a grateful minister has rested a throbbing forehead.

On this difficult morning George stands in just such a position before shaking himself dry and zipping up his flies. From our unseen vantage-point we might assume that he's in the grip of a hangover or perhaps suffering a fit of nerves, but in both cases we'd be wrong. Not a drop of alcohol has passed his lips in twenty-four hours; and, though his forthcoming interview with the Prime Minister is certain to be a strain, George has achieved a state far beyond the reach of ordinary apprehension.

The truth is, he's managed to convince himself he doesn't give a damn. It's been quite an effort. He ought to be appalled by his own recklessness, riven by doubt and the fear of consequences. He's throwing away his entire career, abandoning the ambitions of a lifetime apparently without so much as a second glance. Still, he has the memory of Sergiyev Posad to keep him warm. There might even be a thrill of exhilaration in his heart. For perhaps the first time in his career he's being driven not by ambition, calculation or the demands of party, but by the impulse to do the right thing. That's encouraging, isn't it?

George splashed cold water on his face. In his long ministerial career he'd endured a number of bollockings and was experienced in all the right responses. An appearance of contrition, a touch of humility and a seeming determination to learn from his supposed mistakes usually put matters right.

Not this time though. Not bloody well this time.

He patted himself dry, squared his shoulders and after a couple of deep breaths set off along the corridor to the Cabinet Room in the wake of a smooth young aide. The man knocked on the double doors and George entered. Michael Poultney sat in the Prime Minister's chair at the centre of the long table, which journalists always described as coffin-shaped, though it wasn't really. Papers were strewn untidily around the PM's place and the Cabinet Secretary, Sir Roger de Courcy, was murmuring something in his ear. The two men glanced up as George walked in and Sir Roger said something about finishing this later, leaving the room with a cool nod in George's direction.

'Beautiful morning,' said George, taking his usual chair on the opposite side of the table.

Poultney seemed engrossed in the documents before him. He picked up his pen and made notes in the margins. George sat patiently, studying the portrait of Walpole that hung behind the PM. He understood the game.

'Well, George,' said the Prime Minister at last. 'I rather think you owe me an explanation.' The edge in his tone made it clear that he wasn't playing a game at all. 'I might have expected it of some people. Not you.'

'I can promise you it wasn't meant as an act of disloyalty,' said George. 'I really felt I had no choice.'

'Ah.' Poultney pursed his lips. 'You felt you had no choice.' His eyes flared in a moment of fury before the curtain dropped again. 'You've caused untold embarrassment to the Government, George. And to me.'

'Not my intention, Prime Minister.'

'I don't know what your intentions were.' The glare flickered again. 'Been reading the newspapers, I suppose?'

Oh, indeed. George had been reading the newspapers all right. GULLIVER CHALLENGES PREMIER was how the *Daily Express* saw it. GULLIVER IN POWER GRAB was the *Daily Mirror* version. THE VULTURES CLOSE IN, trumpeted the *Sun*. Every political editor in Fleet Street seemed convinced that George's motive in turning against the Sahelian deal was to get himself sacked from the Cabinet as a preliminary to challenging for the leadership. Cynical sods. Not one of them could give tuppence for the moral dimension. It was hurtful to discover that the men and women he'd cultivated for years – people with whom he'd lunched and joked and swapped confidences – were unanimous in their assessment of his motives. Even Jack Cartwright, who got a handwritten Christmas card every year, had informed his readers that overweening ambition was about to plunge the Tory Party into a bitter struggle for power.

'The tone of those reports is nothing to do with me, Prime Minister.' George would have assumed an expression of honest sincerity but for the fact that he was honestly sincere. 'I've no intention of standing against you. I give you my word on that.'

'Your word?' Poultney's tone suggested that George's word had rather less value than a cowpat.

'Absolutely.'

'You also gave your word to be bound by Cabinet decisions. Collective decisions, collective responsibility.' His tone was ice. A vein throbbed in his temple. 'You'll explain, please, why you thought it appropriate to spill your guts to the press.'

'There was no other moral choice.'

'Moral? Choice?' Poultney's glare was back, and on full wattage too. 'You're a Cabinet minister, not a fucking boy scout!'

An immense calm descended on George. He spoke soothingly, as though to a fractious child. 'I'm sorry you take that view, Prime Minister. There's such a thing as human decency,' he said. 'It's our duty not to abuse the privilege of power.'

Poultney's rage subsided, to be replaced by a look that might have been disgust. 'And of course you didn't think it necessary to bring your opinion to Cabinet.'

'I should have. It was unforgivable of me not to. I accept that.' George watched the expression on the Prime Minister's face change yet again. 'The truth is I was so overwhelmed by those pictures from Sahelia and the horror of what we proposed to do that I couldn't wait. I couldn't stop myself.' It was, after all, the truth of the matter. If not quite the whole truth.

'I see,' said the Prime Minister, contriving to sound as though he really could. 'Then presumably . . .'

George waited for a bit, but Poultney didn't continue. Odd. The man was seldom at a loss for words and certainly wasn't the kind to piss around with aposiopesis. 'You have my resignation, of course,' he said at last.

'Of course.' An immense sigh accompanied his words. 'Brought it with you, I suppose?'

George pulled an envelope from his inside pocket. 'I thought you'd like to see the wording.'

'Most considerate.' The Prime Minister opened the envelope and began reading the message that George had so pain-stakingly composed.

'You'll see I pledge my continuing support for the Government,' said George.

'The Conservative Party always admires loyalty,' Poultney observed. 'There's rather a lot here about the importance of moral choice, however.'

'I hope the whole party would agree on that, Prime Minister.'

'And of course you wouldn't dream of giving the impression that the Cabinet is a pack of rogues?'

George frowned. 'That's unfair, Prime Minister. It's not what I say at all.'

'Our enemies might read that meaning into it.'

It had of course long ago occurred to George that the price of his principles would be uncomfortably high. Still, it was disturbing to think the socialists would gain an ounce more advantage than was strictly necessary. 'Then I'll redraft it,' he said. 'Here and now if you like.'

'Oh, I hope that won't be necessary.' The Prime Minister seemed to make up his mind. 'Let's stop beating about the bush, George, shall we? We both know the mood of the party. You understand perfectly well I can't afford to let you resign. In the present climate it's impossible.'

George shrugged unhappily. 'I don't want to go. But—'

Poultney held up his hand. 'Spare me your protestations. What you've done is unforgivable. But I'm going to have to forgive you all the same. Let's just do what we can to limit the damage, shall we?' He fixed George with a long, cold stare. 'The line has to be that your little outburst in Moscow was made in the light of discussions you've had with me. I shall say that I regret the timing of your remarks but make it clear that they represent Government policy.' The rage flickered briefly in his eyes once more. 'I take it that won't offend your sense of honour?' His voice dripped with sarcasm.

George gaped. 'I'm not sure I see where this is leading.'

'I think you see very well. I shall make it clear that you're right about Sahelia. It may interest you to know the Foreign Office has built up quite a dossier in the past few months. It leaves us no choice. In fact I'll be announcing our decision in the House this afternoon. They've broken their undertakings and we can't possibly do business with them.' He ventured a savage smile. 'You've won, George. No need for resignations now, eh?'

George gaped. 'I don't understand,' he managed at last.

'Oh, I imagine you do,' said Poultney, who seemed almost genial now. 'Sahelia's becoming an embarrassment. Not because of your little stunt, either. We'd probably have pulled the plug on them anyway.'

For the first time in his life George understood how stout Cortez felt when he stared at the Pacific. Bloody marvellous. He gestured at his resignation note. 'So I don't have to . . .'

Poultney folded the paper and tucked it carefully away in a file. 'It'll be a souvenir,' he said. 'Something for the memoirs, maybe.'

'What can I say, Prime Minister? Thank you for being so understanding.'

'I understand more than you suppose. Mind, I want you sitting beside me this afternoon.' Poultney's tone left George in no doubt that he expected absolute obedience. 'And I want a solemn undertaking that you'll go through proper channels in future. No more solo initiatives, ever again.'

'No more solo initiatives,' George agreed. He thought of offering Poultney his hand but decided against it.

It was only as he crossed Whitehall on his walk back to the Ministry that the full magnitude of his triumph struck. He'd taken on a Prime Minister and won. He was still in office, more powerful than ever. It was beginning to dawn on him that, while virtue was certainly its own reward, there might well be ancillary benefits too.

Back upstairs in the Cabinet Room, Michael Poultney stared through the window across Horse Guards to the trees of St James's Park beyond. Sunlight glinted off a thousand windscreens. It was always a source of irritation to him that the Civil Service enjoyed parking rights in the historic Parade, their Vauxhalls and BMWs messing up what should have been one of the capital's most remarkable vistas. One day, when he had the time and the energy ... But he'd never nerve himself to do it. Many a prime minister had tried, only to be fought to a standstill by the mandarins of Whitehall. The civil service, he thought, could have given lessons to the Bourbon monarchs in the ruthlessness with which it defended its privileges.

Somewhere on the Mall a military band began thumping out a muffled beat. Music to stiffen the spine. In his mind's eye, the Prime Minister could see a company of grey-coated Guardsmen somewhere beyond the trees swinging bravely along en route to Buckingham Palace; gallant lads one and all, reminders of what the nation was before the weevils got to work. Before the pride faded and the flags of empire were hauled down. Often these days, when he was alone, Michael Poultney wondered how some of his predecessors – a Churchill, a Disraeli, a Palmerston or a Wellington – would have felt had any of them foreseen what a poor, pinched creature their country would become. He listened until the drums faded in the distance, then turned back into the room he'd worked so hard to reach and sacrificed so much to dominate. It didn't look especially impressive. A long table, twenty-two chairs in red leather, the portrait of Walpole peering down at his successor. Most boardrooms in the City would put it in the shade. But this was the heart of the nation nevertheless. The fortunes of continents were once decided here. He wouldn't give it up lightly; and never for a Judas like George Gulliver. Walpole would have understood.

Poultney picked up the telephone. 'Get me the Chief Whip,' he said.

Like every prime minister there has ever been, Poultney understood ambition in himself as deeply as he feared it in others. Power was more exciting than any mistress, more addictive than crack cocaine – though, as with crack, the fulfilment seldom matched the promise. Not, of course, that the Prime Minister had ever indulged; but he had read a number of official reports.

'It's not good,' he said as the Chief Whip came on the line. 'It looks as though you were right.'

'I always had him down as a shit,' said Alan Matthews. 'He's still on board though?'

'Can't tell for how long. He showed me his resignation letter. Kept going on about moral responsibility.'

'I warned you the bastard's out for blood.'

'I know what he's after. Even had the nerve to say he didn't plan to stand against me.'

There was a silence as Matthews digested this further evidence of George's treachery. 'He hasn't got the support,' he said at last.

'Have you any idea how many constituency visits he's done in the last year?'

'I know *exactly* how many.' Matthews sounded offended. 'He's spoken at eighteen annual dinners and three regional conferences, opened four summer fêtes and done the honours at all nine by-elections. He even turned up for the Scottish Young Conservatives. Said he just happened to be passing.'

'Busy little bee, isn't he?' There was a note of anxiety in Poultney's voice. 'We really ought to have seen this coming.'

'I'm still not convinced there's any immediate danger, Prime Minister.' Matthews was clearly doing his best to be patient, as all Chief Whips should be when confronted with a jittery master. 'If I know George, he won't make a move this year. He can't count on more than seventy votes. Top whack.'

'Seventy!' The word came out in a yelp.

'Top whack. The usual troublemakers. Peter Coleman and his crowd. But we've got the summer recess starting in a few weeks. Things should calm down then. Provided there's no more bad news of course.'

The remark was meant to be encouraging, but Poultney sensed the abyss yawning beneath his feet. 'You're saying we're in trouble.'

'I'm saying it's perfectly containable. All things being equal. And they are equal, aren't they, Prime Minister?'

Michael Poultney took a grip of himself. 'You understand the situation,' he said. 'There's no way we can avoid spending cuts. Don't need to tell you it's going to get rough.'

'Just before an election too,' said Matthews undiplomatically.

Poultney ignored the jibe. His Chief Whip had never made any secret of his contempt for the Chancellor of the Exchequer's handling of the economy. 'Any leverage to keep our Defence Secretary in line?' he asked.

'Only the rumour we talked about. Late nights in Pimlico. It'll be the usual story, I guess.'

'Pity it can't be young boys,' growled Poultney.

'Hardly George's style. No, if there's anything going on at all it'll be the traditional beast with two backs. Not enough for our purposes.'

Poultney felt a headache coming on. 'I'm counting on you, Alan.'

'I'm making enquiries, Prime Minister. If anything's there I'll find it.'

Poultney didn't doubt it. Few sins of the flesh or fingers in the till would escape Matthews's antennae. The whips knew of virtually every skeleton in every cupboard. Their legendary black book recorded the phone numbers of mistresses' flats, brothels, drinking dens, strip clubs, gambling hells, all the places that might be used for rest and recreation by the modern legislator. Even prime ministers were not immune: Michael Poultney sometimes wondered what Matthews and his colleagues might know of a certain young lady in Snaresbrook (though she was of course a long time ago).

He sat on alone long after the conversation ended, cracking his knuckles from time to time and staring malevolently into the middle distance.

No doubt he's planning such things as shall be the terrors of the earth. Look! There's a muscle writhing in his cheek and that vein is throbbing in his temple once more. This is a fierce fellow, no error, a man of power defending his corner; we should congratulate ourselves that we're not the object of his fearful passion.

No, that hapless creatures sits all unaware at his desk in the Ministry of Defence, a couple of hundred yards away. At the moment he's feeling rather pleased with life, and if we're sensible we'll leave him to it. George Gulliver is a grown-up politician after all. He's been round the track, knows how many beans make five and should have learned long ago that anyone challenging the position of the Prime Minister risks getting his dick caught in the mangle.

This tale isn't turning out quite as cheerily as we might have hoped, is it?

'The Princess Royal,' snarled Prudence Willow, 'is a personal friend of mine!'

Morning conference at the *Despatch* offices in Rotherhithe was taking its usual course. Not for the first time, Jack Cartwright congratulated himself on his singular ability to remain in the editor's good books. Unlike today's victim.

'Her office says she won't do it,' said the pictures editor miserably. 'There's no press access at all.'

'Fuck off!' screeched Willow, her bosom heaving. 'Who did you talk to? The fucking footman?'

'We were on to her press office all day yesterday.' The pictures editor seemed close to tears. 'It's a private party. They don't want any coverage at all. Nobody's getting in.'

'Did you mention my name?'

'Didn't do any good. They're adamant. No photographers.'

Willow glared round the room as her senior journalists fiddled with their pens and did their level best to avoid catching her eye. 'It's the biggest royal party of the year and we're not going to be there. I see. Fine.' Willow never used a rapier when a bludgeon would do. 'My fault. I should have fixed it up myself. Like I do everything else round here.'

'We did our best,' protested the pictures editor feebly. His colleagues cringed. Everybody was aware that the poor devil had been frantically trying to find an answer until nearly midnight, just as they knew the problem was incapable of solution. One of Willow's malevolent techniques was to set her staff impossible tasks and throw a tantrum when they failed. It was always a mistake to protest.

'Your best isn't good enough, is it?' hissed the relentless termagant. 'Maybe you should start thinking about your position here. What else have you got on the schedule?'

'Well, there's some good—'

'Skip it. I've lost interest in the picture desk.' Her expression shifted in an instant from savagery to sweetness. 'What's happening on the political front?' Her eyelashes fluttered.

'I've got lunch today with the Financial Secretary,' said Jack, giving her one of his twinkles in return. 'With a bit of luck I should get something on spending cuts. And the Prime Minister's problems, of course.'

Willow beamed. 'I may have something for you on that,' she said. 'Stay behind for a word after conference, would you?' Her smile switched off. 'What's the sports department got to say for itself?' she snapped.

And that, thought Jack contentedly, is as glorious an example as you'll ever see of the benefits to be had in befriending a woman like Prudence. It didn't take much. A bit of buttering up, a respectfully appreciative eye on the latest hairdo and a very occasional murmur in the ear about who was being disloyal behind her back were the guarantee of a secure and civilised life. Some might call it toadying, though in fact it was nothing but elementary politics. How else could one earn a decent pay rise every year and expenses that went through on the nod? It always amazed him that his colleagues couldn't learn the lesson, silly sods. Only that morning, the features editor had observed, rather too loudly, that bloody Willow had probably sold her soul to the devil. It couldn't take long before that little gem found its way to Prudence's office.

The daughter of Beelzebub drummed her fingers as conference ended and her subdued underlings departed. 'Sometimes I wonder,' she said when the door closed behind them. 'Bloody useless, the lot of them.'

'Mm,' said Jack, warily. One had to be careful about agreeing too readily when Prudence blackguarded her staff. Otherwise she'd trot through the newsroom dropping more ordure in her wake than a herd of New Forest ponies. Jack Cartwright thinks you're all bloody useless. Jack Cartwright wonders what the fuck you do all day. Jack Cartwright reckons you're a bunch of bloody amateurs. In the matter of keeping her subordinates divided, confused and off balance Prudence Willow could have given tips to Caligula. 'I suppose they do their best,' Jack ventured.

But Prudence had something else on her mind. 'You're a friend of George Gulliver's, aren't you?' she demanded.

'Well . . . we get on all right,' Jack temporised, wondering what was coming next.

'He's a menace. A treacherous bastard.' She leaned across to rest her hand on Jack's knee.

'I know he hasn't got a loyal bone in his body,' Jack agreed, confident now that he knew the way the wind was blowing.

'I'm talking in strictest confidence now, Jack.'

'You think he's going for the leadership.' Jack wondered whether he should cover Prudence's hand with his own and decided against it. Too high a risk for the moment. 'I've got to say, Prudence, that's not the impression he gives me.'

She removed her hand at last. 'I was at Number Ten last night. Gulliver's planning to stand all right. Poultney's convinced.'

'That's a hell of a story if we can stand it up, Prudence.' Jack put on an appropriately enthusiastic look, though he knew perfectly well that George Gulliver would never take the risk.

Not after his last escapade. 'Can we write it?' Course we bloody well can't, he thought. You're making it up.

'Not yet. Not quite yet. We've got to pull together on this one,' Prudence said earnestly. 'The way things are going we could be looking at disaster. Complete catastrophe. A Labour Government.'

'Mm,' said Jack, before hurriedly adopting an expression as worried as Willow's own.

'So I want us to play it carefully to begin with,' she went on, evidently satisfied with Jack's commitment. 'Let's get the evidence. Talk to backbenchers. Take Peter Coleman out to lunch. He'll spill the beans if anyone will. I want facts. I want dates. I want the names of the plotters. I want what they had for lunch. I want it all. Understand? Especially the dirt. Dig it up. I hear he might be fucking around. Check it out.'

'Absolutely,' enthused Jack, his heart sinking. He was as certain as he could be that there was no leadership plot, no evidence of dirt and no story either. Well, life as a political journalist is never easy. 'Stand on me,' he said, with a confidence he didn't feel. 'If there's anything going on I'll find out.'

He watched her smile, wondered once again if his instincts were right. And if so, how long it would be before he'd have to risk his winkle between those carmined, carnivorous lips.

No!

George starts bolt upright, heart hammering, chest heaving. Sweating. Darkness smothers him. For a terrified moment he cowers in a wasteland. Then there's the rough familiarity of blanket, the drape of reassuring sheet. Nearby a clock glows green, its numerals slipping silently from 4.09 to 4.10. No grisly underworld this, but home. He's home in the spare bedroom and all's well, or as well as things can be when you've been made to sleep alone. A nightmare, that's all. Nothing to worry about. A bad dream merely. Even his shout might have been imagined. Listen! There's nobody stirring in the house. Rosemary would have come if he'd shouted. Of course she would. Reliable Rosemary. She is reliable, isn't she? In spite of everything. He sits on the side of his bed, shivering. Worrying.

He padded to the bathroom, pausing for a moment outside what the estate agent years ago had described as the master bedroom. No master enjoyed its comforts now. No mistress either. Just a middle-aged wife whose soft snores were just audible through the oaken door. Once or twice in the last couple of nights he'd thought of creeping in, snuggling quietly beside her and trusting to the sleepy instincts of her flesh. Impossible of course. He'd get nothing there but the cold curl of a lip. Anyway she'd almost certainly locked herself in.

Sighing, he shuffled onwards to relieve himself, taking careful aim at the side of the lavatory pan, just above the flush level. The design of his crapper, low-slung in fancy peach, was a recurring irritant. Point Percy straight at the water and the sound effects rivalled the Ribbon Falls, bouncing from pan to tiled walls and echoing through the rest of the house. Aim him at the side and the stream tended to disintegrate into a fine spray, droplets settling like dew on the carpet. In the business of avoiding either consequence it was essential to direct the jet precisely, with steady hand and resolute eye, striking the porcelain just so, at just such an angle. It wasn't an easy task at the best of times, and certainly not in the dark watches of the night when your soul has just been through the shredder. In the circumstances, he thought, it was a tribute to his character that he'd bothered to make the effort.

George could see no point in returning to bed. He'd never sleep now. He ducked his head under the cold tap, shuddering at the shock, and thought about a cup of tea. It might help. Tea in the kitchen, where all shadows would be banished in the clean wash of neon. An opportunity to sort himself out. And to wonder what he'd done to deserve such a shot across the bows.

It's the darkness that's so fearful. It isn't any ordinary darkness. It's a heavy, coiling, slithering dark, dark that has never known a glimmer of light nor ever will, a dark that can be touched though not quite felt. There seems to be a smell to it too, a faint whiff of brimstone, though this is obviously absurd since George has no idea what brimstone smells like and in any case smells don't exist in dreams. But then maybe this isn't a dream at all. We don't dream about darkness, do we? QED. This is something different. Terrifying. Perhaps the darkness isn't an external phenomenon at all. Perhaps it's inside him like a tapeworm. No, that's a rotten analogy. It's worse than a tapeworm. He's steeped in darkness. It's in his bones and blood. It's sucking the life out of him. 'No!' he bawls. As well he might. What other response should we expect from a soul that finds itself in hell?

It was of course a warning. George had no doubt of that. He sat in the kitchen nursing his cooling dregs of tea, a twentieth-century Englishman sunk in medieval dread, the comforts of philosophy stripped from him. It didn't matter that his experiences were incapable of objective verification. The final reality couldn't be expressed in an equation or inferred from a line on a graph. He'd seen the horror, and that was sufficient. For reasons he couldn't understand he'd been offered a glimpse or several glimpses of . . . well, of the ultimate alternatives, he supposed.

It was becoming evident to George that reasonableness or fairness played little part in whatever the Almighty expected of him. Risking his career wasn't sufficient to earn a gold star on the celestial register: to qualify for Heavenly approval it was obviously necessary not merely to avoid evil but passionately to embrace good. Quite what such an embrace would entail he wasn't sure. He seemed to remember that the Gospels were full of stuff about turning the other cheek and giving all one's money away to the poor, though fortunately such advice wasn't to be taken literally. All the churches seemed agreed about that.

The first hint of dawn was filtering through the window by the time he finally managed to calm himself. On the apple tree in the garden a gang of sparrows began shouting the odds. George peered out, trying without success to identify their shapes in the grey morning light. According to the New Testament not one of them could drop off the perch without God taking note and presumably experiencing a twinge of regret while He was about it. A disturbing notion. If the same applied to turkeys it probably went a long way towards taking the shine off His Son's birthday. It struck George that such theological considerations must from now on be a significant – perhaps the central – factor in his life.

It wasn't an especially exhilarating discovery. George didn't much care for the stick element that seemed to have crept into a spiritual odyssey previously strewn with carrots. Still, he'd do his best anyway. There didn't seem to be much choice in the matter. In future he'd lose no opportunity to do good in the world. No need for vulgar display. He didn't feel it necessary to buy a tambourine and join the Toronto-blessed evangelicals who gathered at St Chad's on a Sunday, where by all accounts they clapped and spoke in tongues and occasionally rolled giggling around the aisles. George felt there were other demands on his talents. Sufficient to pursue his new course in the area he knew best.

Yet he couldn't help wondering whether the Good Lord in all His wisdom fully appreciated that, though the British political system is certainly resilient, it has never had to cope with a minister whose overriding purpose is to be good.

CHAPTER

7

Since Providence is a central element in this tale (unless we prefer the hypothesis that poor old George is off his rocker), it's reasonable to suppose that the appearance of Mrs Wendy Hilliard at this juncture is part of some vast if as yet unfathomable plan.

She turned up at George's constituency surgery the following Saturday, a small, stern lady with anger in her eyes and perhaps a touch of fear. It wouldn't be surprising. The very elderly are often afraid, with good reason. The distant possibility of a one hundredth birthday telegram from the monarch isn't much consolation for all the spent years; and rarely enough to brighten the endless days dozed in the interim at considerable expense and inconvenience to the state.

'Well now,' George said, with what he hoped was an encouraging smile. 'How can I be of assistance?' Like many Members of Parliament, he took some satisfaction in the help he was occasionally able to offer his constituents. Politics didn't always have to be about self-interest. The glow of a good deed, he always thought, could be as warming as a decent dinner.

'I want to know why I'm being persecuted,' snapped Mrs Hilliard, in a voice that sounded disconcertingly like the Queen's.

George's heart sank. In common with every other politician he was plagued by battalions of the confused and batty, men who were convinced that their neighbours were aliens from Mars, women who believed the entire resources of MI5 were devoted to bugging their bedrooms. The best response in such circumstances was to nod sympathetically, take copious notes and promise the information would be carefully investigated. People under threat from Venusian death rays also had votes.

'I hope you don't think I'm persecuting you,' he soothed.

'I mean precisely that.' The strange thing was, Mrs Hilliard didn't look in the least batty. Well, you could never tell.

'I promise I don't mean to.' He crinkled his forehead reassuringly.

'Don't patronise me, young man. I won't be patronised.' Her eyes glinted. 'Why is it, do you suppose, that people of my age are always treated like imbeciles?'

George shifted uncomfortably in his seat while Mrs Hilliard calmed down. It dawned on him that he might well be failing a rather important spiritual test here, achieving *nul points* on some divine scoresheet, rather in the manner of Norway in the early days of the Eurovision Song Contest. 'I owe you an apology,' he said at last. 'I'm here to help you if I can. I certainly didn't mean ... Well, you know.'

'I'm afraid I do know. So will you, if you live long enough. People don't care, you see.' She spoke in a matter-of-fact tone that brooked no argument.

'I care,' George protested. 'Really.' It had become important to him that she believe it. 'Perhaps you could tell me what the trouble is.'

'It's my husband,' said Wendy Hilliard. 'He's got Alzheimer's disease.'

George sighed. *Nul points* it would have to be. There was nothing he could do for Mrs Hilliard after all. It was one of the peculiarities of the welfare state that the care of Alzheimer's patients – indeed the care of any citizen thoughtless enough to grow old and helpless – wasn't covered by the National Health Service (though maybe it wasn't as peculiar as all that: obliging the wrinklies to fend for themselves saved the Chancellor of the Exchequer several billion pounds a year).

'He's in a home, of course,' Mrs Hilliard went on remorselessly. 'They wouldn't let me look after him, you see.'

George nodded in sympathy. He did see. In the advanced stages of the disease old man Hilliard would be as helpless as a baby, unable to think or communicate or tell the difference between night and day, his brain, personality and character destroyed. That was another reason, of course, why he could safely be discarded by the state: he didn't have a vote.

'I think I know what you're going to tell me,' he said gently. 'I suppose you've been paying to have him looked after.'

'It's nearly four years now. They've been charging me three hundred and fifty pounds a week. All our savings . . .' Her voice faltered. 'I never minded the money. Not at first.'

'And it's beginning to run out, I suppose.'

'It's the upkeep of the house, you see. Far too big for us, of course, only we've lived there all our lives. Now I shall have to sell it. The Social Services people say I should buy a sheltered flat instead. On the other side of town.'

'You don't think that's a possible solution?' George asked cautiously.

Wendy Hilliard glared at him. 'That's what I mean by persecution,' she said. 'We've paid taxes all our lives. Never claimed a penny back. I've spent nearly all our savings. Now I have to sell our house or they'll move my husband somewhere cheaper and probably very much nastier. And on top of that they want to shunt me off out of the way.'

George couldn't deny the truth of it. 'You can get financial assistance of course,' he muttered, though he knew the answer to that one too. There wouldn't be a penny piece for Mrs Hilliard until most of the possessions of a long lifetime were sold to the highest bidder. Her Majesty's Government would step in then, all right. She wouldn't be allowed to starve. In fact they'd even allow her to keep enough of her own money to ensure a decent burial.

'What I want to know is why you're not interested in helping people like us.' Mrs Hilliard's tone suggested that she genuinely wanted to know. 'This is the only time in our lives we've needed help and we can't get it. We tried to live by decent standards. We worked hard and people just sneer at us for it. There was one girl from the council . . .'

'I promise nobody sneers at you. Really, they don't.'

Wendy Hilliard wasn't impressed. 'She wanted to know why I needed such a big house.She said the garden was overgrown. I can't afford a gardener any more, you see. She just said I'd have to get used to doing without servants. I think she was enjoying it.'

'I'm truly sorry,' George said. 'You shouldn't have to put up with that.'

'No, I shouldn't. Nobody should. The country should never have been allowed to get into such a state. What I want to ask you, Mr Gulliver, is what do you propose to do about it?'

'Well, I . . .' George was uneasy about the turn the conversation was taking. He could hardly admit that the miseries surrounding old man Hilliard were the consequence of half-witted policy. Every year the Health Education Authority spent a king's ransom discouraging smoking, warning against the perils of drink and preaching the virtues of jogging. The outcome, predictably enough, was an army of pensioners who tended to die not decently of heart attacks or cancer but in the slow disintegration of dementia and double incontinence. It would be a livelier nation, George had often thought, if citizens drank their fill, smoked themselves to a standstill, contributed vast sums to the Exchequer in taxation and died considerably before they had a chance to become a burden to others or themselves. Death, after all, was no great shakes, though it wasn't an argument he could reasonably put to Mrs Hilliard. 'I could write to the Social Services Department, if you like,' he offered. 'Try to make sure their staff behave better.'

'No, no, no.' For a moment George thought she might stamp her foot. 'That isn't what I mean at all. I want to know what you're going to do about it, Mr Gulliver. You.'

George wasn't used to this kind of treatment from surgery supplicants and might have bristled but for his newfound appreciation of what life was all about. 'The rules are pretty specific, I'm afraid,' he said.

'Yes, but do you think they're right?'

'What I think doesn't matter, unfortunately.'

Wendy Hilliard gave him an old-fashioned look. 'You're a Cabinet minister,' she said. 'Of course it matters what you think.'

'Well . . . fair enough,' George conceded. 'I suppose I do have some influence. But the rules have been in operation a long time you know.'

'Do you think they're right?'

The old George would at this stage have given up, thanked the old bat for her opinions, promised to think about them and courteously but firmly shown her the door. But then the old George had never fully understood that some unseen presence might well be lurking at his shoulder taking notes and awarding marks out of ten. Never mind his musings about the inconvenience of an ageing population; his duty was to the living. 'No,' he found himself saying. 'I don't think they're right. I think you've every reason to be upset.' This was very much the new approach. Refreshing, really.

Mrs Hilliard evidently thought so too. Her expression brightened. 'Then you'll do something about it?'

George thought of the Chancellor, struggling to hold back a rising tide of debt. He thought of the Financial Secretary to the Treasury, already embarked on a frantic search for spending cuts. He thought of Michael Poultney's plea for greater budgetary discipline throughout Whitehall, and the uproar that would certainly ensue if any member of the Cabinet was irresponsible enough to kick over the traces. 'You mustn't get your hopes up,' he said. 'It's not easy to change these things.'

'Oh, I know it's too late for me,' said Wendy Hilliard. 'I'm eighty-three you know. Not much longer to go, is there? No, I'll do as I'm told. I'll sell up and when my husband dies I'll do away with myself. That'll be that.'

'You mustn't talk like that,' said George, shocked.

'Why ever not?' Mrs Hilliard asked. 'No children. No family.

Friends all dead. I've already borrowed against the house. I'll just be a burden, you see. Better off out of it.'

'But life is the most precious thing we have,' said George, rapidly revising his cavalier views about smoking, drinking and jogging. 'You can't just throw it away as if it's of no value.' He had no doubt now that he was being set some kind of test. It wasn't at all clear whether he was passing.

'The important thing is that others shouldn't have to suffer what I've been through,' said Wendy Hilliard as though she hadn't heard. 'That's why I've come. I've been reading good things about you in the newspapers, Mr Gulliver. I feel you're one of the few politicians who might be trusted. You will do something?'

A shadow of the wasteland fell across George's mind. His heart thumped. On the edge of his consciousness a harsh wind howled. 'I'll try,' he said. 'I can promise you I'll try.'

'You really must,' said Wendy Hilliard.

Though it was years since she'd been so gauche as to admit it, Rosemary always felt a thrill of excitement when preparing for a state dinner at Buckingham Palace.

A world of unmatched elegance beckoned in every embossed invitation: long gowns, white ties and royal smiles, footmen in red livery, marble columns and painted ceilings, dark pictures in frames of gilt. Who'd be a republican? When sipping champagne in the White Drawing Room it was possible for a while to forget the grubbiness of politics and the loathsomeness of politicians; in this setting Rosemary felt she was in the presence of History, and, as we all know, that's not grubby at all. On such occasions in fact she found it hard not to take pride in her husband, despite his dismal profession. He'd come a long way from his childhood streets and trains clanking in the night. Dinner at the Palace was a kind of benediction and offered other benefits too. After their excursions to Buck House he usually wanted to make love, and pretty enjoyable love at that. Nobody could persuade Rosemary there wasn't magic in the monarchy.

Until tonight. It would take some pretty remarkable magic to do its stuff this time. In fact it would take a miracle.

She knocked on the door of the spare bedroom and entered. George had just finished dressing and was admiring the effect in the mirror. He always looked handsome in full fig, the rat. 'Just thought you might want a hand with your tie,' she said.

Though they'd been coexisting in chill silence, her husband wasn't the kind of man to show surprise. He reacted as though the moment was nothing out of the ordinary. 'I think I've managed all by myself,' he said. 'For once.'

'So I see.' She looked him up and down. 'Very distinguished. Quite the world statesman.' It wasn't easy to keep her voice under control.

'You don't look so bad yourself. Toothsome.' George seemed genuinely appreciative, so she gave him a little twirl, as though everything was as it should be. She wore a full-length gown in pale yellow, with the diamond choker he'd bought in a mad moment of extravagance, and earrings that nearly matched. He kissed her cheek, as a loving husband ought.

'Paloma Picasso,' he murmured. 'Sexy stuff. And you've lost weight too.' He seemed about to slide an arm around her waist, so she moved away, careful to keep it casual. George presumably found Chanel No. 5 sexy too, she thought. But not on her.

'I've been on a bit of a diet.' She kept the tone light. 'Does it show?'

'You look marvellous. Lissom's the word.'

'Thank you, kind sir.' They looked at each other with apparent amiability. Rosemary wished life wasn't such a damned mess. 'We've got a few minutes before the car arrives,' she suggested. 'Shall we have a drink?'

It was almost like old times. They sat nursing glasses of cold wine and talked of the twins, who so seldom came home to visit, the scamps, and how the clematis, which straggled over the back door, really needed more support. She wondered whether George could get his personal detectives to fix up a bit of a trellis, but George laughed and said he'd be shot if he so much as asked. Really. Apparently the police were ferociously strict about such things. He told her the tale of how a predecessor at Defence had ordered his bodyguards to spend a day dipping sheep down on his farm. There was uproar over that one. The head of Special Branch had complained to the Cabinet Secretary who in turn summoned the Minister and gave him a bollocking to end all bollockings, a bollocking so severe it was still the talk of Whitehall. What did she think about that, then?

Rosemary couldn't help laughing. When in raconteur mode and firing on all four cylinders George was a difficult man to resist. By the time Charlie Roberts turned up in the Jaguar she was responding as though the *froideur* of past weeks had never been. It rather pleased her to carry it off so well.

George clearly imagined he was on a promise. There was no mistaking the glint of expectation in his eye or the general jolliness of his demeanour. Even the irritating presence of Detective-Sergeant Dennis Sharman, sitting taciturn on the front passenger seat, didn't seem to blight his mood. George pressed his thigh against hers as they rode up the Mall. Rosemary let him get on with it. In the circumstances she was probably behaving like a bitch. So what?

Presumably buoyed by lust and the relief of burdens shed, George sparkled all evening. He could be quite an operator when he set his mind to it, she thought. At dinner he even managed to charm the wife of the Argentinian ambassador with insights into the intricacies of high-goal polo (culled, Rosemary knew perfectly well, from a novel by Miss Jilly Cooper). No doubt about his impact on women, was there?

She pushed resentment to the back of her mind and concentrated on the man sitting next to her, a Northern industrialist who seemed gloomily baffled by the ranks of spoons, forks and knives laid out before him.

'I suppose you do this sort of thing all the time,' he muttered. 'Me, I'm just a working man.'

'Look at it this way,' she said, picking up the implements suitable for lobster in a Pernod and ginger sauce. 'Nothing's too good for the workers.'

'Happen so.' He followed her lead. 'Bit of an eye-opener though, first time.'

'I think we all get a kick out of it, if we're honest. However often we've been.'

'Glad I'm not the only one.' He forked an impossibly dainty morsel of lobster. 'Saw you talking to yon royal though. Quite a privilege that, I should think.' The poor man sounded wistful.

'Luck of the draw,' said Rosemary firmly. 'I think they talk to as many guests as they can.' Still, she thought, it certainly helps if you're a member of the Cabinet. Or a Cabinet wife. In other circumstances it would have crowned her evening when she and George were presented to the Duke of York.

'There's this old sea captain,' confided the sailor Prince, bluff in the uniform of the Service. He was the only member of the Royal Family who thought himself capable of cracking a joke. George, she noticed, immediately put on an expression that might have been mistaken for keen anticipation.

'He's been sailing the seven seas in this terrible rustbucket of a tramp steamer,' said Andrew. 'Leaked like a sieve. Every time the weather got up the crew was convinced it was going to sink.'

'Bit like your old minesweeper days, sir,' said George. 'Not very comfortable in a blow.'

'Oh, worse. Much worse,' grinned Andrew. 'This tub was really on its last legs. But, whenever it looked as though all was lost, the old captain used to go down to his cabin, unlock his sea-chest and look inside. Then he'd come back to the bridge full of confidence and steer the ship out of trouble.'

Rosemary couldn't resist it. 'The Government could do with a sea-chest like that,' she said.

'Ah.' George, she was pleased to see, looked a little put out. Andrew's grin widened.

'Oh dear,' fluttered Rosemary in a parody of wide-eyed innocence. 'Have I said the wrong thing?'

'I promise not to tell the Opposition,' said Andrew, glancing across the room to where Paul Barton was deep in conversation with the Apostolic Delegate from the Vatican. 'If George promises not to tell the Prime Minister. Anyway, the day came when the old sea captain finally died and was buried at sea. The crew in tears. All that. But no sooner had his body disappeared beneath the waves than a terrible storm blew up out of nowhere. The worst ever.' He paused for dramatic effect. George sipped his whisky. Behind the Prince a courtier talked to the Chancellor and his wife, obviously next in line to be presented.

'The waves crashed on the deck. The ship began to founder. The crew were panicking. And the first mate remembered what the old captain used to do in times of crisis.'

'The sea-chest,' said Rosemary obligingly.

'He went down to the captain's cabin and dragged it out from beneath the bunk. The key was in the lock. He opened it.' Another pause. There's no doubt about it, thought Rosemary. His Royal Highness could give Sam Ruddock lessons in how to spin things out.

'He turned the key. Opened the lid. Looked inside. Nothing. The chest was empty.'

'Oh,' said Rosemary. This wasn't the way the tale went when George told it.

'But wait!' Andrew held up a finger. 'Right at the bottom there was something after all. A piece of paper. The first mate picked it up.' Andrew's voice dropped. 'And there he read the great secret of safety at sea: port is to the left. And starboard . . .'

George cracked up manfully. 'Starboard . . .' he spluttered.

'Starboard is to the right!' Andrew finished, joining in the laughter. Rosemary giggled a little too, leaning in to George, clutching his arm. 'Wonderful,' she said. 'Starboard is to the right!' George carried on laughing for a bit, as though he hadn't heard the story a dozen times. 'I'll be sure to tell the First Lord of the Admiralty,' he said.

'No need,' said Andrew. 'I'm sure he knows.' The three of them fell about once more. It should have been quite the jolliest moment of a jolly evening and Rosemary almost regretted the let-down that had to come.

'Did you enjoy it?' George asked as they waited at the Palace portico for Charlie Roberts and the car. Other guests milled around in the high good humour usually induced by a royal banquet as their vehicles crept forward in the queue, Jaguars and Rovers, Mercedes and Rollers, the traditional carriages of the great and the good.

'I always do. Been looking forward to it for weeks.' She looked into his contented face and resisted the temptation to slap it.

In the car Dennis Sharman did his impression of a razor-sharp bodyguard, glaring keenly from side to side, to and fro, as though some desperate assassin might leap from behind the next bollard. Rosemary ignored him. She sometimes thought the terrorist threat to her husband amounted to little more than a job-creation scheme for Special Branch; what wife wouldn't resent the lurking presence of a flatfoot like Sharman? She closed her eyes as the Jaguar purred like a cream-fed cat, half listening as George chattered to Charlie about what the Queen was wearing, what Prince Andrew has said, and what they'd had for dinner. Charlie was fascinated by menus. In fact he often put Rosemary in mind of a small boy with his nose pressed against a sweetshop window. The tastes, smells and textures of luxury were, she supposed, rather frowned on in the fraternity of Methodist lay preachers, though probably not as much as other sensual delights. 'Asparagus vinaigrette,' said George. 'Lobster in some kind of fancy sauce. Bit of a lemony water ice thing. Rack of lamb. Poached pear and sorbet with a butterscotch sauce.'

'Cor!' said Charlie.

'Poor devil's probably going home to baked beans on toast,' murmured George as he unlocked their front door. 'Bit cruel really, getting him drooling like that.'

'He doesn't really need to be envious of us though,' said Rosemary, 'does he, George?' She didn't need to disguise the hostility now.

He blinked several times, a little habit he had when life wasn't working out according to expectations. 'Shall we have a nightcap?' he asked.

She looked at him with what she hoped were hard, button-bright eyes. 'I think you'd better,' she said. 'I don't need one.'

She watched him pour a measure of The Macallan and sink into his favourite armchair. He raised the glass in a silent toast and smiled as though he hadn't noticed anything amiss. She waited as he sipped his whisky. Marshalling his thoughts, no doubt. Probably thought she was still upset over the fiasco of their anniversary.

'Aren't you going to sit down?' he asked.

'I'd rather stand.'

'Ah.' He put his whisky down carefully.Rosemary took a deep breath.

'I think you'd better tell me about Monica,' she said.

Monica paid off her cab outside Westminster Abbey and looked nervously at the great Gothic façade of Parliament on the other side of the road. Most of it she knew was as false as a salesman's smile, built and rebuilt after fires and German bombs; but in the floodlit softness of a summer dusk the building seemed to glow with the power of centuries. She shivered in the evening warmth. Nerves. Away to her left, the bells of Big Ben chimed the quarter hour. She was absurdly early, no doubt also a consequence of nerves. Understandable though. This was a big moment.

She crossed the road to the spot where the bust of Oliver Cromwell glowered at the passing scene. To fill the idle moment she strolled along the pavement as far as New Palace Yard, where the statue of Richard the Lionheart, chainmailed and with sword aloft, challenged some unseen enemy. It was on this site, according to George, that Guy Fawkes had been hacked to pieces, hanged, drawn and quartered to the jeers of the ravening mob. Brute justice. No probation in those days. If you got on the wrong side of the men in power you were for the high jump, and no pleas in mitigation. She turned away, retracing her steps to St Stephen's Entrance. Still ten minutes early for her appointment, but perhaps he'd be early too. He'd sounded frantic on the phone.

The procedure for getting into the place was as cumbersome as ever. Metal detector, explosives detector, her handbag passed through the X-ray machine. Off to the side the shadows gathered in Westminster Hall, the only part of the entire Palace that dated unequivocally back to William Rufus. On the one previous occasion George had chanced his reputation to invite her into the House – in the middle of the summer recess, when it was unlikely they'd run into a familiar face – he'd walked her through the Hall, showing her the spot where Charles I had faced his accusers, one of the long line of state prisoners who'd heard their fate beneath the massive hammerbeams of that roof. William Wallace, broken by the savagery of his English enemies, Thomas More, brought down by a malevolent king, the Earl of Strafford, betrayed by another royal master. All crushed by the hideous strength of the state. The place was an uncomfortable reminder of what could happen when you got it wrong. Monica was in no doubt that she was facing her own kind of trial. She retrieved her handbag and walked ahead on clacking heels into St Stephen's Hall and the Central Lobby beyond.

He was already there, hollow-eyed on one of the green leather seats, his face set. He sprang to his feet as Monica approached. 'I thought we'd go for a drink,' he said. No greeting. He looked terrible, Monica thought. She wished she could give him a hug, a squeeze of sympathy. It wasn't possible of course. Not yet.

They walked unspeaking down the carpeted staircase to the dining-room corridor, past rooms full of cigar smoke and laughter, past the Strangers' Bar and out to the flagged terrace overlooking the Thames. The tables were crowded, politicians, officials and journalists taking advantage of the breeze whispering off the river; but George led her to a quieter spot at the clock-tower end and parked her on a free seat. 'I'll get the drinks,' he said, without asking what she wanted. He walked away, stiff-legged as though in pain.

Monica watched a pleasure boat chug by, the voice of the on-board guide wafting indistinctly over the water. Tourists lined the side. Cameras flashed. She looked away, wishing the butterflies would stop fluttering in her stomach. She lit a cigarette, irritated by her own apprehension. This was the heart-to-heart she'd been seeking since that night in the Bull, wasn't it? Why she'd written that brutal letter? So. Seize the opportunity. Now that Rosemary was satisfactorily out of the way George could devise no further excuses. A dignified separation ... a quiet divorce ... there need hardly be a ripple as the new Mrs Gulliver proceeded happily up the aisle. In fact a second marriage would be the making of him. No longer would the man be burdened with a partner who despised the political life and sat reproachful at home while her husband scrambled his way up the greasy pole. No indeed. Monica intended to throw herself body and soul into the game. She'd be a rock, an intimate adviser, a gracious and influential hostess. She'd give dinner parties, receptions, yield to the tantalising touch of power. The Right Honourable George Gulliver and Mrs Gulliver at home. Sir George and Lady Gulliver – come, now; the moment surely can't be long delayed – enjoy a night at the opera. Lord Gulliver of Mowsbury – for the moment Monica must be permitted her dreams – puts on the ermine to the applause of an admiring world. All was possible now.

Monica focused her attention on the needs of the moment. Her putative peer of the realm was threading his way towards her, a pint of beer in one hand and a glass of what looked like Pimms in the other. She wasn't in the mood for a Pimms, but no matter. Once George had beaten his breast for a bit she'd coax him into a better mood. They'd sit and talk and plan their future in a civilised way, while half the members of the 1922 Committee sat within hailing distance.

'This is the first time I've been on the terrace with you,' she remarked, accepting her drink. It *was* a bloody Pimms. 'You usually prefer somewhere more discreet.'

He sat heavily opposite her, slopping some of his beer. 'Running three-line whip. Probably be voting all night. No chance of getting away.' He tried a grin, which didn't quite come off. 'It'll be all right this once. Needed to talk, that's all.'

He looked so forlorn that Monica might have taken his hand. She bit her lip instead. The man was obviously in shock. 'I'm sorry. Truly.' He stared into his beer. 'You think it's my fault, don't you?' she said, feeling immediately foolish. Of course he thought it was her fault. It's always the woman's fault. The first rule in all sexual relationships.

'I don't blame you,' he muttered. 'Shouldn't have left your letter where Rosemary could find it. Crazy.' His head drooped. 'She was so dreadfully hurt.'

Monica rapidly revised her strategy. A George who couldn't share his guilt might become a George beyond her reach. 'Darling,' she said, 'I wish I hadn't written it. I was so upset. Angry. I wanted you to know how much you mean to me, that's all. If I'd known . . .' It seemed a good idea to leave the rest unspoken.

'Couldn't have come at a worse time, you see,' said George, sounding much too glum for Monica's liking. 'We'd been going through a bad patch anyway. Then she found your letter . . . Just packed her bags and went off to her sister's. Twenty-five years we've been married.'

Monica lowered her head in an attitude of remorse. 'Try not to hate me,' she whispered.

'Oh, I don't hate you. Never think that.' Manful resolution, it seemed, was the order of the day. 'Really. You mustn't feel too badly about all this. My fault, you see. Every bit of it. Believe me. Your letter didn't tell Rosemary anything that wasn't true, did it?'

'Not the point though,' said Monica, wondering what the devil had got into him. 'We should both have been more careful. My fault as much as yours.'

'You'd never have had to write if I hadn't walked out on you though. One thing leads on to the other. It all hangs together. Do you see?' He seemed genuinely to want an answer.

'I suppose so,' said Monica, who of course didn't see at all.

'My marriage. My responsibility. Can't get away with pretending otherwise. Maybe that's what it's all about.'

'Mm,' said Monica, not much appreciating George's approach. It seemed a good time to put her cards on the table. 'I love you,' she whispered. 'Want you.'

In any other circumstances George would have responded with a gleam in the eye and some murmured endearment of his own. This time though he just gave her a wan smile. 'So long as you know I'm not blaming you for anything,' he said.

'You forgive me, I suppose.' Monica caught the edge of irritation in her voice and fluttered her eyelashes to compensate.

'Yes,' George said. 'If there's anything to forgive I certainly do. It's expected, you see. As we forgive those who trespass against us.'

Monica didn't know what to make of that, so she took a sip of Pimms while she considered her next move. This was a new George Gulliver and no mistake, the stuffing knocked out of him, the old sexual chemistry no longer bubbling. There wasn't the hint of a twinkle in his eye now. 'You know I forgive you too, darling,' she offered. If George was in a St Francis of Assisi mood she certainly wasn't going to be outdone.

'Thank you for that,' he said seriously. 'I think I need all the forgiveness I can get.' He looked so lonely and lost that Monica was again tempted to squeeze his hand.

In for a penny, she thought. It seemed a suitable moment to go for the big one. 'Darling,' she breathed, 'we can't undo what's done. We have to accept it. Make the best of it if we can.' She looked him full in the eye.

George didn't pick up the hint. 'No way to make the best out of this one,' he said heavily.

Monica tried again. 'Would you like to stay with me tonight?' she asked softly. 'It would be wonderful, darling.'

George jerked as though he'd been stung. 'Oh, Lord,' he said. 'I'm sorry, Monica. I didn't mean . . .' Was the man blushing? 'You see I can't do that sort of thing any more. It's not you. I think you're beautiful. It's me. I mustn't. I simply can't.' He avoided her eye.

A burst of laughter erupted further along the terrace. Monica blinked, her world beginning to crumble. 'I've never been turned down before. It's quite an experience.' She lit another cigarette in the silence.

'Things have been happening to me,' George muttered at last. 'I can't explain them.'

'Try,' she snapped.

He seemed to make up his mind. 'Look, that night in your flat . . . It wasn't anything to do with you. It was me. I can't explain. I just had an attack of something. Conscience, I suppose you'd call it. I just felt what we were doing was wrong. Simple as that. I couldn't cope.' He sighed, shaking his head slowly from side to side in what might have been regret for such a cock-and-bull story but probably wasn't. Judging by the expression on his face the poor booby was in deadly earnest. Monica felt sick.

'Sounds to me as though you've got religion,' she said, not troubling to disguise her contempt.

'Maybe.' His tone left her in no doubt that he meant 'Yes.'

She inhaled deeply on her cigarette. 'When did all this happen?'

'The accident. Shook me up quite badly. I haven't been the same since. Nothing's been the same. Can't even do my work without . . .' he tailed off. 'I hoped you'd understand.'

'I see.' Maybe the man was having some kind of nervous breakdown. On the other hand the whole performance could just as easily be an unusually original attempt at a brush-off. 'It didn't stop you trying to take me to bed though, did it?'

'I'm sorry.' George managed to look even more miserable. 'I couldn't go through with it though.'

'Let me get this straight,' said Monica slowly, keeping her temper under control. 'You think our relationship is cheap and nasty. Is that it?'

'I think it's wrong. It's a betrayal of my wife.'

Monica stared, incredulous. 'Is that what you've decided? After all this time?'

'I'm sorry,' George whispered.

'So you don't love me at all,' Monica snarled, not bothering to keep her voice down. 'If you love me it can't be wrong, can it?'

'I like you very much,' muttered George.

'Oh, buster. Now we get the truth. You like me very much.' Monica felt a satisfying surge of outrage. 'Not quite what you've been telling me for three years, George, is it?'

'I know I've treated you badly. I wanted to explain . . .' His voice trailed unhappily off. He didn't look much of an advertisement for the rewards of virtue.

'So you admit you lied to me about your feelings,' said Monica with a kind of savage enjoyment. 'You never had the slightest intention of leaving your wife, did you?' George sat in silence. 'Did you?' she repeated.

'I've changed,' he said at last. 'Everything's changed.'

She sat bitter and seething, another mistress let down by a worthless lover, another gullible woman left to cry on a lonely pillow. At that moment she hated herself almost as much as she hated the faithless swine opposite. A hundred country-and-western songs could never have done justice to her frustrated rage. 'Oh no, George,' she said, grinding out her cigarette. 'Nothing's changed. It's the oldest bloody story in the book.'

'Not a happy pair of budgies, are they?' commented Jack Cartwright.

'A bit of trouble on the home front, by all accounts,' said the Chief Whip, leaning comfortably against the balustrade.

'Nah. Rosemary's as good as gold,' Cartwright said with the confidence lent by four pints of Federation Ale.

Alan Matthews lifted an eyebrow. 'If you say so.'

'Ah.' Cartwright drunk or sober knew a hint when he heard one. He leaned closer. 'I don't suppose you know . . .' He bobbed his head towards the pair sunk in conversation further along the terrace.

'Come on, Jack. The soul of discretion, me.'

'Idle curiosity, Alan. Lobby terms.'

'Wasting your time, matey. I think her name's Holroyd. Maureen? Monica? Something like that. Works for ALH Advertising. Did some work for us at the last election, you'll remember. Bloody expensive. All above board, see? Having another?'

'I'll pay a call while you're getting it,' said Jack.

The Chief Whip allowed an expression of mild distaste to creep across his features as Cartwright shambled off. Then he made his way under the striped awning of the terrace bar and ordered a fresh round of drinks.

'Down in the dumps, sir?' asked Sam, the Irish barman who made a profession of cheerfulness.

'Don't ever go into politics, Sam,' said Alan Matthews. 'It's the pits.' He smiled to show he didn't really mean it.

In the useful emptiness of the gents' Jack Cartwright scribbled in his notebook. Maureen/Monica Holroyd. ALH Advertising. Central Office. He underlined the names. Damned careless of George, allowing himself to be seen having such an obvious heart-to-heart, he thought. Silly bugger. Some politicians might get away with it, like the elderly peer who'd just returned from a Parliamentary trip to Canada boasting that he was the only member of the entire delegation to get his leg over. Old Bert's standing had improved tremendously with that tale. But George Gulliver? Never. Not in a million years. Any hint of indiscretion in that quarter couldn't be received with such indulgence. It would be shocking even in this age of tolerance, if only because it was so spectacularly out of character. George might like to cut a bit of a dash and was certainly an established favourite with the Tory ladies; but everyone knew that at heart he was a straitlaced family man, solid as a rock and ambitious to boot. The thought of such a character indulging in a bit of how's your father on the side was as unlikely as Dennis Skinner abandoning his socialist principles or unbending sufficiently to accept a drink from a journalist. Impossible in fact.

And yet, thought Jack as he rinsed his hands, George was out on the terrace this very minute in the company of a woman whose looks and body language (Cartwright was a keen student of women's magazines) suggested a far deeper intimacy than anything you'd expect from a mere constituent or family friend. The sight of the two of them wrapped in conversation brought to mind images of passion and pillows and sighs in the night; and in all his professional experience Cartwright had learned that you can always judge by appearances.

In character or out of it, George was certainly up to no good. Maybe it was something to do with the male menopause. Jack didn't know much about hormones apart from what he'd gleaned from the agony aunts; still, it seemed a fair bet that George's bizarre behaviour over the Sahelian arms deal might be part of some seismic shift in personality.

Never mind. It's an ill wind. Jack had a name now on which to hang Prudence Willow's suspicions. It should be more than enough to earn a bagful of brownie points and perhaps a decent pay rise too. He grinned at his image in the mirror. You're not just a pretty face, Jack my lad, he assured himself.

CHAPTER

8

There is, we are assured in the traditional tenets of Christian theology, a redemptive quality in human suffering: the most undignified affliction can in fact be a blessing, if bravely borne *ad maiorem Dei gloriam*. Warts and haemorrhoids, diarrhoea and dandruff may all be turned to the soul's advantage, provided one enjoys the gift of faith; and, since George Gulliver has more reason than most to hold fast in the flux, we must suppose that he'll not let adversity tread him down.

He doesn't look too chirpy now though, does he?

Look: he's hollow-eyed and pasty-faced. There's an odd jerkiness about him, as though sleepless nights and worried days have breached his bodily defences. He drums his fingers, shuffles his papers, refuses to meet his interlocutor's gaze. The strain's beginning to show, right enough, though not to the extent that anyone has yet felt moved to look up the size of his majority.

'I have to say your proposal would be a remarkable change of policy,' murmured the Permanent Under Secretary. 'Quite remarkable.'

George hunched unhappily in his chair as he caught the nuance in Sir Paul Bradley's tone. 'You mean the Department won't support me?'

A cold smile born of Winchester, Balliol and the civil service fast-track appeared briefly on Sir Paul's face. 'We operate under your direction, Secretary of State,' he responded, leaving the qualifying 'but' hanging unspoken in the air.

'It's just a discussion paper,' muttered George defensively.

'Ah.' Sir Paul removed his glasses and began polishing them carefully on his handkerchief. 'In the present circumstances it might be rather . . .' He paused, presumably to give the impression that he was searching for the right word. 'Rather a hostage to fortune, don't you think?'

'You know the Prime Minister's views,' said George, calling up his big gun. 'There's no chance at all of achieving real spending cuts unless we think the unthinkable.'

A less disciplined bureaucrat than Sir Paul might have raised an eyebrow at this point. The notion that a beleaguered PM might risk throwing the whole defence industry into uproar was the merest fantasy, suggesting that George Gulliver was pursuing some scallywag agenda of his own. The job of departmental ministers, as everyone knew, was to seek but not to find, to pursue economies ruthlessly without actually volunteering a single one. It was known as fighting your corner and the entire structure of Cabinet government depended on it. 'Even so, Secretary of State,' he murmured. 'The MiG thirty-nine . . .'

'The cheapest possible option for a new fighter.' George managed to sound satisfyingly firm in his heresy; he understood well enough that he'd no chance of achieving even the grudging acquiescence of his officials without a touch of the old *Ich kann nicht anders*. 'We'll save what? Seven billion?'

Sir Paul tried a bit of civil service meiosis. 'But you'll accept there are substantial problems?'

'I know I'm not going to win any popularity contest,' said George virtuously. 'But there's no other way of increasing our firepower and cutting costs at the same time. The fact is, the MiG's better than anything else we can come up with. If our European friends object it's just too bad.'

It was in the circumstances a respectable enough argument, if a trifle lacking in the moral grandeur department. Still, it was the best he could do. The very best. George hoped it was enough. Perhaps in some celestial gazebo there was at that moment a white-clad angel pursing his lips in disapproval at his timidity. It was a fair bet that the Heavenly hosts would have preferred him to come right out with it, thump the table and proclaim that all swords would henceforth be turned into ploughshares; but what did they know? George was fairly certain that none of the Cherubim, Seraphim, Powers or Principalities had the slightest idea what it was like to be Secretary of State for Defence.

'Even if we leave the European aspect to one side . . .' Sir Paul replaced his glasses. 'The political situation . . .' He lapsed into discreet silence.

'Oh, yes,' said George. 'There's always the political situation.' Of course it wasn't the European Union that mattered. Not to any red-blooded British minister. What mattered was the home-grown aerospace industry, and the thousands of voters who would scream betrayal and run snivelling to the Labour Party at the first hint of a deal with the Russians. Not to mention a Cabinet already twitching with the fear of losing office and looking for someone to blame. Most of his colleagues, George suspected, would be appalled at what they'd consider an exercise in unnecessary boat-rocking. Even if the outcome meant that more money would be available for the relief of old Mrs Hilliard and her kind. 'I'll just have to cross that bridge when we come to it, won't I?'

'Then if you really wish it, Secretary of State, we'll certainly have another look at the options.' Sir Paul rose to his feet. 'I take it we proceed with maximum discretion though. For the moment.'

Absolutely,' said George. 'This whole thing's only an idea.'

'I understand, Secretary of State,' Sir Paul said. And with another of his cold smiles he sauntered out. Another enemy made, thought George. They're lining up in armies.

He sighed. It was one of those long, weary exhalations you'll occasionally hear in a man who's plumbed the depths. Dark-night-of-the-soul stuff. It is, he thought, devilish hard to be good.

The memory of Wendy Hilliard still worried George, kept

him sleepless in the small hours. It wasn't the fact of her misfortune that nagged; hers was an unremarkable plight after all, just one misery in millions. Yet it was perfectly soluble. Her situation could be transformed at the stroke of a pen. Why then wasn't it?

Disturbing though it was to find himself asking the questions appropriate to his own pimply adolescence, George couldn't help himself. On all the available evidence God Himself thought they were the only questions worth asking; worse still He seemed to expect satisfactory answers.

George sighed again and began shuffling listlessly through the papers on his desk. In spite of the soul's torment the work of Her Majesty's Government had to go on.

We'll leave him there to his profitless mithering. He's functioning, after a fashion. It might be worse. If he knew how closely his enemies were stalking him or suspected the depth of their malice, he'd hardly be able to function at all.

'Damn!' muttered Rosemary Gulliver as the first fat raindrops smeared softly on the courthouse windows. She peered out at the boiling sky.

'Might make it to the car park if you run,' suggested Bert Hodges, her fellow magistrate. 'Then again you might not.'

'Haven't got an umbrella, either. And I've just had my hair done.' Rosemary felt like stamping her foot. 'Damn!' she said again.

'Weather forecast said it would rain,' said Bert, clutching his own brolly with some complacency. 'Always pays to watch the weather forecast.'

'I'll make a dash for it,' Rosemary decided. There was plainly little point in waiting for Bert Hodges to do the gentlemanly thing. She grabbed her bag and clattered down the stairs. Too late. By the time she reached the canopied doorway the rain was swirling across the road in curtains, the gutters already full and gurgling. A couple of young men huddled for shelter in the courthouse entrance. Thunder rumbled low in the distance. Hopeless. She'd have to beg Bert for his assistance after all. She turned to re-enter the building.

'Excuse me. It's Mrs Gulliver, isn't it?' asked one of the men. He had an open, cheery expression that was presumably intended to inspire confidence. Rosemary was immediately on her guard. Years as a Cabinet wife had taught her to spot a reporter at a hundred paces.

'Mm,' she said discouragingly, beginning to push at the swing doors.

'Dave Sweetman, the *Despatch*,' said the young man. 'I wonder if you'd mind—'

'I don't think so,' said Rosemary as the second young man pointed a camera at her. Firmness, she knew, was the only way to deal with such creatures. She turned her head away and stepped over the threshold.

'It's about the break-up of your marriage,' said Sweetman loudly.

The thing to do at this stage, as Rosemary knew very well, was to march back into court without a word and hide in her office until the pair of them had gone away; but of course in such circumstances nobody ever does the right thing. She turned back into the rain. 'I beg your pardon? What did you say?'

'We understand you've left your husband.' Sweetman held up a small tape recorder. 'Wonder if you'd like to comment?' A camera flashed behind him.

'I don't propose to say anything to you about my marriage. Or anything else,' Rosemary snapped. There was another flash. Lightning, this time.

'But you have left him?' Sweetman persisted.

'Go away,' said Rosemary. Through the doorway she could see Bert coming down the stairs in the company of a police inspector. She backed away. 'I don't want to talk to you.'

'Matter of public interest,' said Sweetman, holding his tape recorder under her nose. Rosemary glared at him in disgust, then turned on her heel and stalked off into the downpour.

'Bugger!' she heard Sweetman mutter, then he was trotting alongside. 'Anybody else involved?'

She walked on furiously, her new hairdo disintegrating in the wind and wet, her coat soaked. A passing car sent a sheet of water splashing across her shoes. She felt like screaming. 'Mrs Gulliver,' Sweetman tried again. 'I know it's difficult . . .' She stamped on, ignoring him, until at last he stopped. She could see the car park now. Sanctuary. She began to run. 'Does the name Holroyd ring a bell?' Sweetman shouted after her, but she was fumbling for her keys, scrabbling at the lock, wrenching the door open, diving inside to safety and warmth. Through the windscreen she could see Sweetman and the photographer apparently arguing with each other before scurrying off to find shelter. She sat trembling for a while as the rain drummed on the roof, then pulled down the vanity mirror and examined the wreckage of her hair. Rats' tails straggled lank and dripping across her face. In her own mind at least she looked old and lined and defeated. It took no great insight, she thought bitterly, to deduce why George might stray from his marriage bed.

She sat on for a while in sodden clothes and squelching shoes, engulfed in unfamiliar loneliness. Confrontation with the vile Sweetman was yet another reminder of the doors closing in her life, of options narrowing. Women in middle age, she thought, so often got it wrong. They were quite capable of abandoning home and husband out of principle, boredom or disgust without seriously considering the long-term consequences. Men never made that mistake; hardly a one of them was capable of jumping ship until they'd fixed up another berth. Hot and cold running sex, slippers by the fireside, roast dinners on Sunday. No regrets troubled their nights.

Perhaps she cried a little at this point. It seems a reasonable supposition, though it's impossible to be sure. Rosemary is a strong lady and we mustn't be unduly influenced by her present mood. Generally she's not much given to self-pity or weepiness; and in the swirl of the storm only an omnipotent observer could confidently determine whether the glisten on her cheeks is the product of raindrops or of tears.

'I don't propose to say anything to you about my marriage.' Rosemary's voice sounded tinnily through the speaker. 'Or anything else.'

Jack Cartwright sighed and switched the machine off. 'Not

good enough by itself, Prudence,' he said, just the required touch of regret in his tone. 'Maybe I should have approached her myself. Can't just go charging in with people like Rosemary Gulliver. Never works.' He twisted the knife a little further. 'Dave Sweetman obviously did his best though.'

Prudence Willow glowered behind her desk. 'You shouldn't be standing up for Sweetman. He's fronting up the Holroyd woman this afternoon. If he fucks up again . . .' She left the rest of the threat unspoken.

'Look, we'll just have to take a chance,' said Jack, satisfied now that whatever happened he was safely in the clear. 'I'll give Gulliver a ring. We'll just have to hope his wife hasn't tipped him off yet. You never know.'

'Think he'll cough?' On occasions like this, Willow tended to adopt the language of the streetwise reporter she had never been.

'I shouldn't think so. Not unless we've got rock-solid evidence. We daren't wait now though.'

'Do your best, Jack.'

If they hadn't been separated by three feet of polished mahogany, he thought, she'd probably be fondling his knee by this stage. 'Always, Prudence,' he said. 'You know that.'

Careful, matey, he thought as he made his way back to his desk. Would it cool Prudence off a bit if he introduced her to his wife? Or cool her off too much? Problems, problems. He pushed them to the back of his mind and flicked through his contacts book for George Gulliver's number.

There was the usual to-do in the Private Office, with some snotty bureaucrat wanting to know the purpose of his call. After some inconclusive sparring Jack succeeded in leaving a message for George to call back. 'It might be some time,' said the official prissily. 'The Secretary of State is rather tied up.'

'He'll want to talk to me,' said Jack confidently. And in fact George was on the line within minutes.

'Good of you to ring back,' Jack said. 'I'm afraid it's a bit of a nasty one though.'

'Story of my life these days,' said George, sounding unusually listless. 'Well, fire away then.'

'A personal matter. You won't like it very much.' Jack lowered his voice to a sympathetic murmur. 'This is a bit of a private tip-off. Prudence wants to run a piece in the paper tomorrow about the state of your marriage. I'm sorry.'

A pause. 'I see. The state of my marriage, eh?' George didn't sound indignant or surprised. A promising start.

'For God's sake don't mention to anybody that I've rung you,' Jack muttered, establishing his bona fides as the candid friend. 'I'm taking a chance here. I think she plans to spring it on you later today.'

'You're tipping me off for the sake of auld lang syne, are you?' No mistaking the trace of sarcasm in the voice. Suspicious bastard. 'You're a noble fellow, Jack.'

'Hey!' Jack's tone suggested good-natured embarrassment. 'Don't shoot the messenger. This isn't my story. Nothing to do with me. I'm just trying to help. OK?'

'Better get on with it then, hadn't you?' George snapped. Then he sighed, his tone markedly changing. 'All right, Jack. Point taken. Apologies, apologies. Got to be some trust in the world, hasn't there?'

'Right,' agreed Jack, relieved. 'So long as you appreciate I'm on your side. Now here's the situation. As far as I can make out, the boys on the gossip column have spoken to Rosemary. They're claiming she's left home. Walked out.' He pressed the button on the tape recorder that he'd attached to his earpiece.

'Really?' George's surprise was obvious. 'What did she actually say?'

'I haven't got the details.' Jack lied. 'It's one of those secret squirrel things at the moment. Officially, I'm not supposed to know a thing about it. I'm pretty sure they've got something on tape though.'

'What can they possibly have on tape?' The man seemed genuinely taken aback. 'Even if ... No. Never. Quite apart from anything else, it would be out of character. Completely. Rosemary's not the greatest admirer of the popular press, I'm afraid. No way she'd talk to any of your reporters, if she could help it.'

'Well, they seem pretty convinced.'

'Huh!' said George. 'I know Rosemary. '

Shitshitshit. This wasn't remotely the required response. You're saying there's nothing in it?'

'Come on, Jack. What do you think?'

Jack kept it light. 'Always ready to share your dark secrets,' he said. 'You can tell me, you know. Off the record, of course.'

A pause. 'I'm calling you from my office,' George said gently. 'No such thing as off the record. Remember?'

Jack grimaced in frustration. 'Might help if I can just establish that Rosemary hasn't left you,' he blurted.

'Why, Jack. You're beginning to sound like a proper little newshound. Got your notebook out, have you?'

Jack scowled into the mouthpiece. 'Sorry, George. Just trying to clear this up quietly, that's all.' Fuckaroo. He'd forgotten how sharp George could be.

'Then let's clear it up, shall we? Rosemary's visiting her sister for a few days. That's it. Does it all the time. They happen to be very close. Good enough?'

'Absolutely.' Jack masked his disappointment with all the heartiness he could muster.

'You're a good man, Jack. Appreciate your call. Must get together soon, eh?' And before Jack had time to try a last throw of the dice, before he could even hint that the name of a certain Monica Holroyd was being bandied about the office, George hung up.

If Monica had been made of feebler stuff she might have ended the political prospects of George Gulliver that very evening, ended them right there on the pavement outside her office.

It could have been easily done. A blush, a stammer, a careless word and the men from the *Despatch* would have been presented with all the confirmation needed to justify the headline already crafted for the diary by Willow's own hand: MINISTER AND THE MATTRESS GIRL. (Monica's agency had long ago handled the account for a particular brand of orthopaedic mattress.) Underneath, in letters only slightly smaller ran the legend: CABINET WIFE STORMS OUT. It was a grand tale altogether; and, though in this age of liberation not sufficiently damaging to force George out of office, it was quite enough to frustrate any hope of a leadership challenge.

Monica of course knew nothing of this as she emerged into the rush-hour crowds, any more than she knew that her office commissionaire had been offered ten pounds to point her out, or that Dave Sweetman would enter the transaction in his weekly expenses as twenty pounds. She stood peering up the road in search of a taxi quite unaware that anything was amiss until the photographer's camera flashed.

'Miss Holroyd?' asked an agreeable-looking young man. Behind him the photographer took another picture.

'Who wants to know?' She was tired, longing for home and a bath and the man was standing in the way, blocking her view of the traffic. The sky was dark with the promise of more rain.

'Dave Sweetman. The *Despatch*. Could I have a word?

A cab with its for-hire sign lit turned a distant corner. Monica waved a hopeful arm. 'Not convenient,' she said. The camera flashed again.

'It's about your relationship with the Defence Minister,' said Sweetman. 'If you could spare a minute.'

Monica glared at him. The cab had stopped further down the road, its light turned off as a passenger climbed in. 'My what?' she snapped.

'Our information is that Mrs Gulliver has left home. Because of your association with her husband.' Sweetman had a small tape recorder in his hand now and didn't look in the least agreeable. Passers-by were giving them curious looks. The cameraman took another picture.

Monica took a deep breath. In her affair with George she'd occasionally wondered how she might react if a reptile like Sweetman tried it on. 'You filthy little creep,' she hissed. 'What are you suggesting?'

'We're running the story tomorrow,' said Sweetman, unabashed. 'We thought you should have the opportunity to give your side.'

'Taxi!' shouted Monica as another lit cab hove into view.

'I really think . . .' Sweetman tailed off as Monica pushed past him to stand on the kerb. 'Miss Holroyd,' he called again. By now the cab was pulling up. 'Can you say anything about your affair with George Gulliver?' he called. A passer-by turned round, startled.

'How dare you?' Monica raged. 'What's your name again?'

'Dave Sweetman.' He was beginning to look somewhat shifty now, like a parson caught on a date with the choirmistress.

'Well, Dave Sweetman. I'll be on to the Press Complaints Commission first thing in the morning. See what they make of your behaviour. And if your poisonous rag lies about me or so much as mentions my name I'll be in touch with my lawyer sooner than you can say exemplary damages. Got it?' She scrambled into the cab. 'Just get me out of here,' she instructed the driver. She was damned if she was going to mention her address until she was well out of earshot.

'Bit of trouble, eh?' said the driver as the cab began to move off. Sweetman was scuttling along the pavement, managing for the moment to keep up. 'Is that a no comment?' he bawled.

Monica wound down the window. 'That's a piss off,' she snarled. The cab gathered speed, leaving Sweetman standing open-mouthed. Monica leaned back in her seat, shaking.

'You all right, love?' asked the driver.

'Fine. Thank you.' She turned away to stare out at the rush-hour crowds and the driver took the hint, lapsing into silence. Rosemary, thought Monica. It had to be Rosemary who'd dumped, though it didn't really fit with what she knew of the woman. Perhaps she'd let something slip. Accidentally. Or maybe the *Despatch* was just following up some rumour. She should probably never have met George on the terrace. Hell, it couldn't be that either. Guests went onto the terrace all the time. It meant nothing. But hadn't that little creep Sweetman threatened to run a story in the morning? Shit. Maybe he was bluffing. You couldn't trust anything said by a pig like that.

Monica desperately needed a cigarette. THANK YOU FOR NOT SMOKING said the sign in the back of the cab. To hell with that. She lit up, dragging the smoke down to the pit of her stomach. Better. If the driver complained she wouldn't give him a tip. Damn, she thought. Damn, damn, damn. They'd love this in the office. But the story surely wouldn't appear. Couldn't. There wasn't any evidence, was there? Not unless you counted that letter. A full confession and a signature to go with it. Bloody stupid. Still, they couldn't possibly have got hold of it. Rosemary wouldn't dream of publicising her humiliation. Never. She must have known something was going on, or sensed it anyway. But never said a word. Lots of women are like that. Stand by your man. Cling on. Wait till it all blows over. No, this didn't look like Rosemary's doing. Hard to believe that George could be the culprit either, even if the bastard seemed near to cracking up. Any muck on the front pages would devastate him.

Though such devastation would certainly serve the ends of justice as far as Monica was concerned, her own reputation clearly came first. She spent an anxious evening at home, trying without success to reach George at the Commons. Once she even rang his Private Office at the Ministry, only to hang up before some functionary could demand to know her business. Her behaviour, she realised, was becoming panicky, an insight that did nothing to lighten her mood. Independent women who are free to do as they please shouldn't be reduced to jelly so easily, should they?

Had she commanded our privileged overview, Monica's evening might have passed more placidly.

Over at the *Despatch* offices, an unhappy Dave Sweetman was agreeing with the night lawyer that maybe the headline MINISTER AND THE MATTRESS GIRL was a tad over the top, since the girl in question turned out to be a sharp and very articulate professional woman who seemed to be denying it all and was certainly threatening to sue. The sub-deck, CABINET WIFE STORMS OUT, didn't quite add up to the full shilling either, given that Rosemary Gulliver hadn't uttered a single word to confirm a separation. In fact the only solid piece of evidence in the entire tale came from Jack Cartwright's memo: the Minister's wife was innocently visiting her sister.

'We'll have to spike the fucking thing,' screeched Willow.

'Pity though,' said Dave Sweetman, unwisely.

'Yes, well you needn't bother coming in tomorrow if anyone else has got it,' she snarled. 'One fucking mention anywhere, and you're out.'

There were many the following morning who felt their burdens lifted as they read the daily papers. Dave Sweetman scoured every page of every publication to learn with some relief that he still had a job. Rosemary Gulliver locked herself in the lavatory and read the *Despatch* through twice before emerging pale but reassured. As for Monica Holroyd, her satisfaction was so apparent that the entire office began speculating on the possibility of a new lover.

What then of George? He was glad of course that Rosemary would be spared further hurt, grateful that Monica's reputation remained unsullied. Yet the circumstances of his escape disturbed him. He hadn't lied, exactly; but then neither had he quite told Jack Cartwright the whole truth. Perhaps it would have been better to admit his failings and take the consequences. On the other hand, newspapers like the *Despatch* were seldom easily diverted from the scent of scandal. Could it possibly be – he hardly dared wonder – that his character and career had been miraculously preserved, to serve some great if so far unexplained purpose?

Only time would tell.

CHAPTER

9

'Proper food,' enthused Sir Peter Coleman. 'None of your French muck, eh?'

'Can't beat it,' said Jack Cartwright. 'Only place in London you can get a decent treacle pudding.'

'My father first brought me here when I was about thirteen or so. Hasn't changed a bit.' Sir Peter dug into his roast beef. 'None of this cholesterol nonsense. Some places, they give you a plate with a little sliver of meat here, a spot of spinach over there and great empty spaces in between. Two bites and that's your lot. Give me Simpsons every time.'

'You're looking well on it,' teased Jack. He always felt envious of the way Coleman could demolish mountains of food without putting on an ounce.

'Clean living and a quiet conscience. That's the secret.' He leaned sideways to peer at Jack's thickening waistline. 'Oh dear,' he said.

'Wife's put me on a diet,' Jack confessed. 'I've got to lose at least a stone, or she says she'll take a lover.'

'Listen to some advice. Always keep the little lady happy. Pays dividends.'

'Easier said than done with a job like mine.' Jack refilled their wineglasses. 'Beginning to get me down, to tell the truth.'

'Willow?'

'None other. Her latest obsession is George Gulliver. She's convinced he's going for the leadership this year. God knows where she gets it from.'

Coleman carefully loaded a slather of beef, half a roast potato and a mound of cabbage onto his fork and piled the lot into his mouth. 'She's right,' he managed, indistinctly.

'Nah,' said Jack. 'I don't believe it. Not a shred of evidence.'

'You sure?'

'He hasn't been doing the rounds. You don't see him in the tea room. Or pushing the boat out in the smoking-room. He's got no organisation. Not making any speeches. As far as I can see he's just keeping his head down. Certainly not behaving like a man with his eye on the main chance.'

Coleman's plate was empty now. He picked up the remains of his bread roll and carefully mopped up his gravy. 'Take it from me. He's going for it.'

Jack grunted in apparent scepticism, not letting his interest appear too obvious. Coleman was quite probably the world's most indiscreet gossip, but he was no bullshitter.

'You won't have heard about the Russian MiGs, I shouldn't think.'

This was a new one on Jack. 'Go on,' he said.

'He's apparently toying with the idea of buying them for the RAF. So what does that tell you, eh?' He stared at Jack with innocent blue eyes.

'It tells me someone's pulling your leg. Winding you up. Got nothing to do with the leadership anyway.'

Coleman smiled. 'You're not thinking, Jack.'

'Thick as a docker's sandwich, me. Everyone knows that.' He leaned across the table and lowered his voice. 'You've got something, you old bugger.'

Coleman could never resist such an appeal to his superior knowledge. He looked around furtively. 'Right,' he muttered. 'This is gospel. Apparently, our friend George has ordered a study into RAF procurement with a view to purchasing from the Russians. OK? Now if he goes down that route it could save billions on the new fighter.'

'And create the biggest row since the Poll Tax,' Jack objected. 'If it's remotely true it'll cause uproar.'

Coleman shook his head. 'Forget that. The clever bit is what he wants to do with the savings. Put it into the health service. Pensions. Education. You name it. '

'Bloody hell.' Jack thought for a moment. 'Swords into ploughshares.'

'You're getting there.' Coleman looked pleased. 'Now let's just take it on a bit. We know there's a spending squeeze on. The budget this November is going to be horrendous. The party's terrified. There's not much more than twelve months to go before the election and we're running out of time. I don't like the way my seat's looking, I'll tell you that for nothing. None of us are happy. We're all in the same boat.'

'You're in the shit right enough,' Jack agreed.

'Wish you could persuade the Prime Minister. Man's got a death wish.' Coleman finished his wine. 'Do you think the *Despatch* could run to a spot of pudding?'

Jack summoned the sweet trolley and watched as Coleman made a great production over what he'd have, settling at last for a glob of gateau.

'With cream, sir?' asked the waiter.

'Certainly with cream,' growled Coleman. 'Not the same without cream.'

'Nothing for me, thanks,' said Jack, thinking of his avoirdupois. 'Just a couple of coffees and two very large Armagnacs.' He wondered whether Coleman genuinely appreciated the sheer megatonnage of his story. Russian fighters for the RAF? More money for hospitals? Fanbloodytastic.

He watched as the man's spoon rose and fell on a steadily diminishing mound of stickiness. 'What's he going to say about the unemployment argument?' he asked.

Coleman's spoon never faltered in its task. 'Joint venture,' he mumbled through a munchy mouthful. 'We'd build the engines here under licence. Do all the radar ourselves. Wings, maybe. Plenty of work.'

'Still be one hell of a row.'

Coleman sucked his spoon clean and looked regretfully at his empty plate. 'Which is why the Government can't possibly go for it. Too risky by half. But it's a bit of a stroke from George, eh? Isn't it just? The only minister to come up with an idea to stave off the worst cuts.' He shook his head admiringly. 'It won't do him any harm, Jack. No harm at all.'

'But he hasn't told you he's going for the leadership?'

'You know George. Always plays his cards close to the chest.'

'Not a man to take chances,' Jack pointed out.

'All points that way though.' Coleman held up a finger. 'One. He cuts up rough over Sahelia. Nearly gets himself sacked.' Another finger flicked up. 'Two. He's been acting bloody strange. Ask anybody. Obviously got something on his mind.'

'Three,' said Jack. 'If he really has asked for a study about the Russians—'

'No if about it. He has.'

Jack knew better than to ask how the man could be so certain. 'OK. Let's say there's a study. The Ministry of Defence can't be best pleased.'

Coleman looked at him unblinkingly. 'Don't ask my sources.'

'But they're upset?'

Coleman inclined his head a fraction. A bit late now to start playing Mr Discretion, thought Jack. Still, a nod's as good as a wink.

'There's only one reason why any minister would go out of his way to upset his own department. Is that what you're saying?'

'Oh, yes,' said Coleman. 'There's no doubt about it. By hook or by crook, dear old George is determined to make himself Prime Minister. And between you and me, quite a few of us will be going along for the ride.'

'Are you going to live with us forever, Auntie Rosemary?' asked little Amanda.

'I don't expect so, dear,' said Rosemary, wondering why all children other than one's own were so obnoxious.

'Daddy says you are,' chattered Amanda with what couldn't in all fairness have been malice. She was only six. 'Don't you, Daddy?'

'Ho, ho,' chuckled Tom Brownrigg unconvincingly.

'Daddy says you might stay for years and years,' Amanda babbled on. 'Daddy says you're like the man who came to dinner.'

'Don't bother your Auntie,' growled Tom, his face reddening.

'Go and play in the garden, dear, if you've finished your breakfast.' Tom's wife Alice looked helplessly at her sister. 'Kids,' she said.

'She's right though. I can't go imposing on you like this.' Something on the radio snagged Rosemary's attention.

'Thousands of panic-stricken refugees are fleeing the civil war which has erupted in the North African emirate of Sahelia,' declared the announcer.

'You can stay as long as you like, love,' soothed Tom Brownrigg, rather too obviously trying to recapture lost ground.

'We're glad to have you.' Alice seemed close to tears. 'Really. We're family.'

'. . . have been killed in clashes between rebel forces and troops loyal to the Vizier,' said the radio.

'No, I've made up my mind. It's not fair on you and Tom.' In truth Rosemary felt she'd explode if she had to put up with much more of the Brownriggs, family or not. And it wasn't just because they had a set of plaster ducks flying up the wall of what Tom insisted on calling the lounge.

'Reports from the capital suggest that the rebels are gaining in strength. Here's our Africa correspondent, John Patterson.'

'We want you to stay,' said Alice. 'Don't we, Tom?'

'It's up to Rosemary what she wants to do,' said Tom. 'Course, you're welcome to stay though.'

'. . . raises the question of whether a government traditionally friendly to Britain can survive,' said Patterson.

'I might have found the flat I'm looking for,' said Rosemary.

Alice looked even more upset. 'So the split-up's permanent?'

'Rosemary's business,' said Tom.

'. . . So far there are no reported casualties among the two hundred or more Britons, working to develop the Sahelian oilfield,' Patterson continued.

'I'll leave you two to sort it out,' said Tom. 'Get stuck into some weeding.' He seemed relieved to escape.

'The fighting began—' Patterson's report ended abruptly as Tom exercised his *droit de seigneur* by switching off the radio on his way out.

'Did you want it on?' asked Alice.

'I've got other things on my mind,' said Rosemary.

On Saturday mornings Monica usually slept late, seldom stirring much before nine, then soaking in her bath until the water cooled.

She never bothered with the morning news programmes. A little Vivaldi on the stereo went much better with the weekend mood. Afterwards she'd eat toast and honey, drink scalding black coffee and settle for a leisurely read of the *Independent*. A good little newspaper, the *Indy*, she always thought. None of your irresponsible guesswork there. Solid facts. Stolid writing. Just what the modern businesswoman needs.

The Governor of the Bank of England, she discovered, was urging caution over interest rates. The Government in India was about to call an election. In Strasbourg, the European Parliament had come up with a new proposal to reduce the democratic deficit in the Community by reducing the power of Westminster still further. Tribesmen in Sahelia were in open revolt against the regime of the Emir. It pleased Monica that she kept up with such things. They gave her the feeling she was on the inside track.

Which simply goes to show that in the middle of our communications revolution it's quite possible to be very well informed indeed, while suspecting nothing of the beastliness rootling and snuffling in the undergrowth outside your own front door.

George could claim no such innocence. From the moment Jack Cartwright phoned with an ill-concealed note of incredulity in his voice, he knew the game was up; the Prime Minister's revenge would be as savage as it was certain. George felt strangely calm. In the light of the few brief paragraphs he'd just read in his local paper, Michael Poultney's inevitable outrage hardly seemed to matter.

'When are you going with the story?' he asked, not really caring. Maybe exile to the back benches offered a solution. Of sorts.

'I'd like to do it Sunday for Monday, but I daren't wait,' Jack said. 'Too many people know about it already, if you take my meaning.'

'I can guess.' The boys at the Ministry obviously hadn't wasted a moment before spreading the word. In other circumstances George might have admired their ruthlessness. 'So it'll be tomorrow, yes?'

'Might be an idea to leave your phone off the hook.'

George sighed. With a story like this breaking on a Saturday morning, the sharks on the Sunday papers would lash themselves into a feeding frenzy. There would certainly be a mob seething on his doorstep by first light. 'Looks like a fun weekend,' he growled.

'Look, George. Willow's really gunning for you on this one.' Jack was beginning to sound embarrassed. 'The leader writer's under orders.'

'Oh?'

'Just wanted you to know it's nothing to do with me.'

'Rough?'

'Haven't seen the words.' Jack's voice dropped to a near whisper. 'Willow's raving about treachery. Lack of principles. You get the idea.'

It was the unfairness of the charge that stung. Oh yes, it bloody well did. 'I've told you. It's an exercise, that's all. Just trying to see if we can make some savings. Dammit, Jack, what's wrong with trying to get some figures together? At least let's establish the facts.' You're whining, he thought. Stop it.

'Hm,' said Jack, obviously unimpressed. 'Willow thinks it's all part of your leadership ambitions.'

George took a long moment to digest the accusation. 'She's wrong,' he managed at last. 'It's just a departmental study, that's all.'

'Not a very popular one though, is it?' Jack was beginning to sound like a hanging judge. 'Far as I can tell, your own Ministry is in uproar. We both know Michael Poultney will have a fit. It'll cause a hell of a row. You're the politician. What's Willow supposed to think? Come to that, what are any of us supposed to think?'

George swallowed his resentment. Moral principles, after all, are often misunderstood. 'You might give me credit for a bit of original thinking, Jack. Trying to save taxpayers' money.' You're whining again, Gulliver, he thought.

'So none of this has anything to do with the leadership?' Jack wasn't bothering to hide his scepticism.

'Absolutely not' said George firmly.

'You're ruling out a challenge?'

George hesitated. In all his sleepless speculations it had occurred to him once or twice that Providence might not be as unfathomable as everyone supposed. Perhaps he'd been chosen for some great service, his visions a necessary preparation to toughen the inner self, much as route marches across the Brecon Beacons hardened edges in the SAS. Of course he couldn't rule out a challenge. Wouldn't. 'A wise man never says never,' he told Jack.

The die, he thought somewhat portentously as he replaced the receiver, is cast. He wondered briefly which of his officials at the MoD had been suborned by Sir Paul Bradley to do the dirty. George hoped the culprit wasn't anyone from his Private Office. Not that it mattered. Betrayal was betrayal, however you looked at it.

He thought of Rosemary with a twinge of remorse and wished he could talk to her now, this minute. Not that she'd understand. Who could? She'd give him one of her I-hope-you-know-what-you're-doing looks, no doubt of it. But then there would be tea in a china pot and a squeeze of the hand and perhaps later an appeal for help with the *Guardian* crossword. It would be her way of saying, 'I'm on your side.' He missed her as he rattled round the house, missed her bulk in his bed, her common sense, her everyday presence.

Loneliness crept through him like a thief in a darkened house. He ached. Rosemary gone, Monica gone. His career gone, too, before the weekend was out. He had few friends to call on, no company but his red boxes and the ticking of his long-case clock. It might have been a cleaner end, he moped, if he'd died with Norridge on the Easthampton road.

Almost without thinking about it he found himself in his bedroom, throwing a couple of shirts, some pants and socks into a small leather valise. There was after all no point in passivity, enduring the weekend like a prisoner in dread of the hangman's knock. He'd drive north, find some windswept moor and spend the hours walking in the drizzle, driving the cobwebs away. Hoping for answers. The Prime Minister could wait. The Department too. They'd go berserk of course. Ministers never, under any circumstances, went off on their own without prior notification, without leaving contact numbers or informing Special Branch. To hell with all that. He'd be an ex-minister within forty-eight hours anyway; and if the United Kingdom should declare war in the interim, Her Majesty's forces would no doubt manage without the assistance of their Secretary of State.

Packed, fatalistic, a little light-headed, George strode to his garage. He'd hit the Friday evening rush hour on his journey, but it couldn't be helped. The thing was to get away. He swung the garage door open and stared at the emptiness within. Rosemary. Of course she'd taken the car. Fair enough when he had Cheerful Charlie to drive him everywhere. He sagged, forlorn with his bag and frustrated plans. Perhaps for a moment he panicked. Certainly he felt helpless. We must remember that George has been cosseted for years, his every waking moment shaped by his diary secretary, his every problem anticipated by the civil service machine, his every whim gratified on the instant. He's allowed an attack of anxiety. He's a minister with nobody to hold his hand.

George trudged back inside the house and sat as his clock ticked implacably on. After a while he searched through his desk for an address, then telephoned for a cab. He had an idea now where he ought to go. It wasn't to the moors.

He paid off his taxi under the fairytale turrets of St Pancras

Station and walked through to the main concourse. The time-table showed that his train would be departing in five minutes. It didn't surprise him. There was some purpose in all this, wasn't there? If he was indeed being propelled along a preor-dained path, there would be no unnecessary delays. He queued patiently for a ticket, then strolled back to Platform 5, where a guard was noisily slamming carriage doors. Whistles blew. An illuminated sign said OFF. A tardy passenger scuttled past, blowing heavily, and wrenched open the nearest door. George followed in more leisurely fashion. There was no hurry. It wouldn't leave without him. The train pulled smoothly away as he slammed the door behind him.

He sat in an almost empty first-class compartment as a quintet of gasholders slid past, then houses of dingy brick, back gardens, shops, flyovers in concrete and the long, jammed swathe of the M1, cars nose-to-tail in the weekend escape to hearth and home. Thousands of lives were going on out there through the window, thousands of citizens enduring or enjoying another evening nearer the grave with not so much as a passing thought for eternity. George rather envied them.

He closed his eyes, lulled into doziness by the rhythm of the tracks. Clackety-clack. You're getting the sack. You've put up a black. You'll never get back. He jerked awake to the green fields of Hertfordshire, blinking in confusion, uncertain for a second or two where he was or what in God's name he was doing without his red boxes or his officials or his detective. Then he remembered. He was travelling towards an answer. Or (in a colder light) running away. It was difficult to be sure. The miles unwound in the gathering dusk. George dozed again.

He woke scratchy and uncertain as the train pulled into Nottingham. Passengers stood, gathered their belongings, snapped hasps on briefcases. Men in suits, impatient for their waiting wives and children and the weekly trip to the supermarket. People who knew what was what and where they were going. George trailed along in their wake, half tempted to call his expedition off and take the next train back to London. Travelling hopefully is all very well; it's arrival that does the damage. He stood irresolute on the platform. It was obvious he should have phoned ahead. Made proper arrangements. A passenger brushed past without apology. George allowed himself to be swept along.

He surrendered his ticket at the barrier and wandered into the night. A line of taxis awaited but he turned away. He needed a drink. He crossed the road and began walking, loneliness seeping into his bones. This was idiotic, wasn't it? He should be at home now, right now, working on his papers, telephoning his allies, devising some way out of his predicament, making a fight of it. He wondered what his colleagues would think if they could see him now, tramping the streets like a derelict.

Perhaps, he speculated unhappily, this is how a nervous breakdown begins.

'We've crucified him,' exulted Prudence Willows. 'Nailed his hide to the wall.'

'Crucified the enemies too,' called the news editor through the hubbub. 'Poor sods don't know what's hit them. Well done, Jack!'

'The political department strikes again,' said Jack. 'Fair play to Prudence, though. She knew Gulliver was up to something.' He raised his glass in tribute. Willow beamed, flushed with triumph and champagne. Somewhere another bottle popped. Glasses clinked.

Pushing the boat out was hardly a usual part of Willow's regime; but then it wasn't often the *Despatch* hammered the opposition indisputably into the ground. The evidence lay in the first editions strewn around her office. GAS PRICE ROW, droned the *Daily Express*. GOVERNOR WARNS ON INTEREST RATES, yawned the *Guardian*. The enterprising *Sun* had added to the gaiety of the nation with TERROR OF THE WEREWOLF, but for once even the *Sun* was caught with its trousers down. STORM OVER RUSSIAN JETS, crowed the splash headline in the *Despatch*. 'TREACHEROUS' GULLIVER FACES SACK, shouted the strapline. Exclusive. By Jack Cartwright.

'Happy days,' said the features editor, refilling Jack's glass. 'Nice bit of brown-nosing to you know who.' He bobbed his head in Willow's direction.

Jack didn't bother replying. He was wondering whether the glint in Willow's eye amounted to an invitation. There could be a hell of a lot more at stake, he thought, than this year's pay rise. Wasn't the deputy editor retiring soon?

'Jack,' called Willow's secretary from the outer office. 'The newsdesk has put through a call for you. From Mr Gulliver.'

The room fell silent. Willow grinned. 'Take it on my desk, Jack,' said. 'Should be interesting.'

Jack put down his glass and – reluctantly – picked up the phone. It would be difficult talking to George with an audience hanging on every word. Especially as Gulliver was almost certainly expecting a sympathetic ear. 'Cartwright,' he barked. 'Hallo? George? Are you there?'

'Don't sound so fierce, Jack. Just wanted to know what you've done with the story.'

'Can't hear you,' lied Jack. 'If you can hear me, try again. Ring the editor's office direct. We're having a bit of a party.'

'You can't talk, then,' said George, catching on. He sounded rather less depressed than the circumstances warranted. 'If it's really bad, just hang up.'

'I'm hanging up now. Get back to me if you want a chat.' He replaced the receiver and shrugged. 'Couldn't make out a word he was saying.'

'Probably overcome with emotion,' giggled Willow. She raised her glass. 'Great story, Jack. Well done.' She looked him straight in the eye as the room burst into applause.

George pushed his way back to the bar and ordered another large whisky. Though the hotel lounge was full, he hadn't attracted the slightest attention. So much for power and fame, he thought. The tiger's on the loose and nobody notices. Why should they? They're all wrapped in their own concerns, all bobbing in the same current towards the same destination like so many pieces of driftwood. Discrete entities one and all. Touching, perhaps, from time to time but always floating apart.

'All right, sir?' asked the barmaid.

George realised he'd been frowning. 'Just thinking it's time to turn in,' he said. 'Long day.' He drained his whisky glass and smiled goodnight, feeling the tiredness wash over him. He trudged up to his room. Candlewick bedspread, scuffed carpet, a cheap wardrobe with a door that wouldn't close properly. A suitably dismal place to spend his last night as a member of Her Majesty's Government. He brushed his teeth, urinated, took off his clothes, folded his trousers carefully over the end of an upright chair, sat wearily on the bed. Tomorrow, he thought. Tomorrow I'll know what to do. He closed his eyes.

They dragged the first victim out babbling and crying into the noonday square. The crowds pushed forward, hissing. Spitting. The executioner grinned, a shocking gleam of white in dark skin and black burnous. 'Sahelian justice,' said the angel in white. 'Swift and terrible. Like the wrath of God.' The victim screamed. There was a puddle at his feet, the sudden stench of evacuated bowels. The crowds jeered. The executioner grabbed the man roughly by the hair, forcing him to his knees. Silence now. Only the incoherent moans of the condemned. George's heart thumped. What must it be like to know, know with absolute certainty, that in a matter of seconds your body would lie twitching and thrumming, blood spurting in gouts across the hot sand?

Slowly the executioner raised his sword. 'Aaah,' sighed the crowd. A hard heft down. A soft thump. The dead man's head rolling on the ground, eyes staring. Or was he dead? Did the brain go on living for seconds or minutes unable to grasp the shock? The crowd erupted in shrieks of delight, buffeting George in their excitement. A second victim was being dragged forth. A woman. George's heart lurched. Rosemary. The savages had Rosemary. 'Don't just stand there,' sneered the angel, looking supercilious. 'That's your wife.' George began pushing through the press, knowing it was hopeless. The headsman's sword glittered in the sun. 'Stop!' bawled George. 'I'm Her Britannic Majesty's Secretary of State for Defence and I order you to desist! Cease forthwith! There will be questions in the House!' The executioner laughed. A new Russian MiG was parked by the side of the square and George lunged for it. Shoot the bastards down, that was the thing to do. Michael Poultney stood in his way. 'Don't do it, George,' he ordered. 'We don't want a diplomatic incident.' George shoved him aside. 'Bugger diplomacy,' he snarled. 'Huh!' said Poultney, swinging a punch which caught him on the shoulder.

'What?' said George.

'I'm sorry, sir.' The chambermaid pulled her hand away, looking anxious. 'You were thrashing about a bit.'

George sat up, thick-headed, clutching the bedspread modestly to his chest. Sunlight streamed through a chink in the curtains. 'What time is it?'

'After eleven. I wouldn't have come in, only I heard you shouting.' She was a motherly soul, grey hair, plump cheeks, untroubled eyes. Which fortunately held no hint of recognition.

'Bad dream.' George felt gritty and unrested, his mouth dry. 'Is it really that late?'

'Should have the room cleaned by now. Thought I'd better give you a shake.' She twinkled. 'Hope you don't mind.'

'No. That's all right. My fault.' George tried to smile. 'Glad you did. Give me half an hour and I'll be out of here.'

He stood under a feeble shower until his head cleared. Then he brushed his teeth, shaved and dressed, every action accomplished with careful attention to detail. There! A perfect knot to the tie. A wipe of the shoes with the courtesy-cloth provided so thoughtfully by the management. He ran a comb through his hair. No hint of disintegration leered in the mirror. He walked downstairs and paid his bill in cash, a normal man about his everyday business. In control.

He strolled unhurried through the Saturday bustle, following the directions he'd been given the night before. RUSSIAN JETS SENSATION, yelled a placard outside a newsagent's shop. It was some comfort that he could buy the *Despatch* without a tremor, though the front page bubbled in venom and the opinion column inside amounted to his political obituary. 'George Gulliver's offence is not that he has stabbed his own Government in the back,' he read. 'His offence is to coldly place his own ambition above the needs of the nation. He has stabbed Britain in the back.' Now that split infinitive just had to be Willow's handiwork, thought George as he folded the paper and shoved it in his case. It struck him as odd that he felt no outrage, in fact no emotion at all, as though his feelings were protected by some providential shield. George shivered and began walking again.

The Roman Catholic Church of the Holy Family stood in soot-blackened Victorian Gothic just off the main road, a building of quite outstanding ugliness, all its proportions wrong by just enough of a margin to induce a curl in any stylist's lip. George pushed open a side door and peered through the gloom within. A dozen or so worshippers knelt hunched in the silent pews. Candles flickered beneath a simpering statue of the Virgin Mary. On the far side a red light glowed over a cur-tained cubicle, which George supposed was the confessional. A woman came out, genuflected before the altar and crossed herself. George stared at her, fascinated. What a comfort to believe in the possibility – no, the certainty – of forgiveness in the muttering of some priestly formula. But then, that was the thing about Romans. They were capable of accepting anything. In this land of atheists, agnostics, rationalists, humanists, sceptics, hedonists and mechanical engineers they might well be the only human beings who wouldn't immediately conclude that he was out of his skull. Why else would he have come?

He found the Parish House tucked behind the church. It was a modern box in brick with bow windows, a frosted glass door and a ding-dong bell. An elderly Volkswagen Beetle slouched in the driveway. George waited nervously. He'd come a long way in hope of . . . Well, he wasn't quite sure. Sympathy, perhaps?

'Yes?' The woman who answered was young, dark, pretty. The housekeeper? George had always supposed that such ladies tended to be stern, thin-lipped and in possession of a bus-pass.

'I'd like to see Father Davenport, please.' She was more of a girl than a woman, he thought. Barely into her twenties, with fetching legs and lips soft as cushions.

'Canon Davenport you mean?' Her voice was velvet. 'Is he expecting you?'

'I'm an old friend. From university days. Just passing,' said

George. Davenport a canon, eh? He wasn't entirely sure how promotions worked among the Papists, but it seemed clear his old friend was doing reasonably well. Not quite General Staff maybe, but certainly a colonel.

'You'd better come in.' She stood back, allowing George to enter. 'He's hearing confessions at the moment, but he should be finished soon. Through here.' She showed George into what he supposed was the Catholic equivalent of a dentists's waiting-room, carpet-tiled floor, upright chairs, a metal desk. 'Smile!' instructed a poster on the wall. 'My boss is a Jewish carpenter,' asserted another. A Celtic crucifix in bog-oak hung by the door. 'I'll leave you to it, then,' she said, showing her pearl-white teeth. No lipstick. Wide brown eyes with long, tremulous lashes. 'Do make yourself at home.'

George sat, wondering how Steve Davenport managed to keep his hands off her. If indeed he did. Celibacy, by all accounts, was a tradition more honoured in the breach than the observance these days, priests abandoning the Ministry in stampedes to search for the fulfilment that apparently could be provided only by a pair of willing thighs. If it was no longer impossible for cardinals to be caught in whorehouses or bishops to breed, then presumably a loose canon couldn't be ruled out.

On the other hand Steve in his Cambridge days had been . . . well, good. That was the only word George could summon up. Not pious, exactly. Not quite that. In fact he'd avoided all public manifestations of religious fervour so successfully that most of his colleagues thought him perfectly normal. (George discovered otherwise only after an unfortunate incident at Addenbrooke's Hospital. Young Davenport, it turned out, was in the habit of making surreptitious visits to the sick, and fell to discussing the need for European solidarity with a convalescing Old Contemptible. The fellow started up in his bed, bellowing incomprehensibly about the Jerries at Ypres, and died shortly thereafter of a stroke. 'Poor old sod was on his last legs anyway,' George had consoled. It seemed to help.)

Somewhere in the house there was a murmur of conversation. George got to his feet, a smile of greeting forming in anticipation. The door flew open.

'Good God!' said Canon Davenport.

'So I'm told.' George clasped him by the hand. 'Long time, Steve.'

'Twenty years if it's a day. George Gulliver! Well, well, well!' Throughout this welcome he pumped George's hand up and down with a manic enthusiasm that even in the context of an unexpected reunion seemed a little excessive. George disengaged at last, careful to keep smiling while he did so. This was obviously a household where friendliness was measured by the bucketful.

'Roz said it was an old friend just passing through. Course, I never guessed . . .' He seized George's hand again. 'Good to see you. Really marvellous.'

'Roz?'

'Sister Immaculata if you want to be formal about it. From the local convent. Helps me out in the parish.' The man beamed like a lighthouse.

'Ah.' George nodded as though the idea of a nun with legs wasn't in the least disturbing. 'Wondered if she might be your er . . .' No, he thought. Teasing obviously isn't appropriate. 'Your housekeeper,' he amended.

Canon Davenport's eyes widened. He released George's hand. 'Oh, my.' He chuckled uncertainly. 'Bit out of date, aren't we? Master's degree in sociology, see? Runs all our outreach projects. Totally committed. Drug abuse. Poverty. Homelessness. Alcohol problems. A lot of stress out there, George.' It was clearly a lecture he'd delivered more than once.

'Of course,' said George, rapidly adopting the expression he tended to use on visits to inner-city slums and hostels for unmarried mothers, the look that conveyed both sympathy and understanding in equal measure. 'I didn't mean . . .'

'Well, I know that. Course I do.' The Canon was all smiles again. For a moment it looked as though he might resume hand-pumping operations. 'It's really great to see you.'

George smiled back as genially as he knew how, wondering

what in God's name was the matter with his friend. 'Look, Steve,' he said with assumed heartiness. 'Thought I'd take you out for a pint. Long time since we had a drink together, eh?'

The Canon's face fell. 'Sorry, George. No can do. Thing is, I don't any more. Sets a bad example, you see. If you knew the problems round here . . .' He shook his head solemnly. 'Enough to put anyone off for life.'

'I suppose so.' George made a final effort. 'On the other hand I remember you could drink a yard of ale in twelve seconds flat. College champion.'

Plainly the wrong thing to say. The Canon looked embarrassed. 'We all do foolish things when we're young, don't we? Pub games. All that macho nonsense. Just a device to lure impressionable youngsters, you know. Exploitation. Roz did some research on it. Remarkable findings.'

George resisted a warm suggestion about what Roz might do with her findings and settled for a cup of tea. They sat in the kitchen and talked of other times. The Canon unbent enough to remember old Jasper, who climbed up King's College Chapel one night for a dare. George countered with the tale of old Sam, who blew up during finals and set fire to his exam paper, right there in the Senate House before rushing out, babbling. They ran through old Mike and old Eddie, old Pete and poor old Barney with non-specific urethritis who spent most of his days uncomfortably trying to pee.

'And then there's George Gulliver,' said the Canon finally, a new note creeping in. 'I was thinking about you only this morning.'

George sighed. 'Seen the papers, I suppose?'

'It was on the radio. All over the news. Remarkable.' The Canon peered into the bottom of his cup, as though fascinated by what the tealeaves might reveal. 'Must admit I was a little surprised. Always had high hopes of you, George. Always thought you were a good man.'

'I'm trying.'

The Canon raised his head, his gaze earnest. 'But all that money, eh? All those billions of pounds. Such a waste.'

I'm trying to *save* money,' said George, nettled.

The Canon made a face. 'Weapons of mass destruction,' he said. 'That's what it's all about. You're buying new planes while an awful lot of people go to bed hungry.'

The sensible thing to do at this point, thought George, was to make his excuses and leave. Take the next train back to London. Abandon all hope of finding an answer. 'I didn't just happen to drop in, Steve,' he said, wondering why he was bothering. 'I need some advice.'

'You know my advice, George. Sorry to get heavy and all that. Cut the defence budget. Forget these warplanes. Get rid of our nuclear weapons.' The Canon's eyes shone. 'Instead of buying more machines to kill people, we should give the world a moral lead. Could be our finest hour.'

The frightening thing, George thought, the truly cringe-making possibility, is that Davenport's barmy drivel might actually be The Message. Perhaps all along this was what the Deity had in mind. Was it possible? 'I'm not making myself clear,' he said after a pause. 'I actually wanted your spiritual advice.'

'Oh.' The Canon seemed genuinely astonished. 'I suppose that's one of the things I'm here for.'

'If you don't feel you want to . . .'

'No, no. That's all right. Please.' Steve's face seemed to have gone a deeper shade of pink. 'Thing is, most people make their own decisions nowadays. Autonomy of the individual conscience and all that. The internal forum. Can't say I'm used to people who actually . . . But I'll help if I can.' He perked up, as though he'd just remembered the terms of his job description. 'Makes a refreshing change.'

Feeling more discouraged than ever, George stumbled through his experiences since the crash, leaving out nothing but the existence of Monica and his separation from Rosemary. They were, after all, merely incidental to his predicament. He hardly dared look Davenport in the face.

'So you see, I don't know where I am,' he ended up. 'Doesn't make sense, does it? Here I am trying to do the decent thing and all I'm getting out of it is the sack. It's crazy. Or maybe *I'm* crazy.'

'Fascinating,' said the Canon. 'I've misjudged you, George. I apologise. Never believe what you hear on the news, eh?'

Quite what the news had to do with his predicament George couldn't fathom. 'I'm not sure I follow.'

'The planes. The Russian planes,' said the Canon with a touch of impatience. 'I understand now.'

George stared. 'Never mind the bloody planes. What about—'

'Ah. The vision thing. You mustn't worry about that.' The Canon waved a dismissive arm. 'You're certainly not going crazy. Happens all the time.'

'So I gather. But . . .' George felt vaguely let down.

'Course, it's not my field. Roz is the expert. Apparently something like twenty per cent of the population undergo your kind of experience at some stage in their lives. Often it's associated with physical or emotional trauma. It's some kind of psychological defence mechanism, you see. At moments of great stress the brain more or less shuts itself off. Well documented.' The Canon patted George's arm encouragingly. 'You're as sane as I am.'

George blinked. 'Is that it?'

'That's it. I can get Roz in if you like. I'm pretty sure she has access to some valuable fieldwork.'

'No!' George stood, appalled. 'Sorry. Didn't mean to shout. This has to be in strictest confidence, Steve. I'm in enough trouble as it is.'

'As you like,' the Canon seemed disappointed. 'Only an idea. It's just that there are some interesting features in your case. Your episodes after the crash for example. Now those are quite unusual. That feeling of desolation especially. Unless there's some personal crisis you haven't mentioned?' He raised an interrogative eyebrow.

'Nothing like that,' George lied. He felt sick. Was it possible he'd thrown his career away on an aberration, of the kind, moreover, that could be researched and documented by outreaching sociologists? No, it bloody well wasn't. 'You're convinced there's no other significance?'

'Well, now.' The Canon adopted a judicious pose. 'There are more things in Heaven and earth, eh? So I'm not saying it's impossible. It is however . . .' He hunted for the appropriate word. 'Unlikely. Yes, that's it. I think you'll find the Church nowadays takes a rather more detached view of such phenomena. On what you've told me I'd say you've got a case of quasi-schizophrenia. A mild one,' he added hurriedly as George's face dropped in dismay. 'With the emphasis on the quasi. In fact the effects seem to be quite beneficial, don't they? You're trying to behave in a moral fashion. That's good. Very good.'

But George was no longer paying attention. He thought of the red boxes in his safe at home, the endless messages that were certainly awaiting his return, the uproar in the Department if it was discovered he'd gone walkabout. 'I'd better be on my way, Steve,' he said as soon as he decently could. 'Things to do.' He swallowed the cold dregs of his tea. 'Lot of catching up.'

'It's been good to see you, George.' The Canon was still sounding rather heartier than circumstances demanded. 'And you're not to worry. OK? These things tend to pass quite quickly. It'll sort itself out. You'll see.'

'Course it will,' said George with an apparently confident smile. 'And thanks for your advice. Been a great help. Really.'

The Canon made a think-nothing-of-it gesture. 'I'll pray for you, George. You can count on it. Just stick to your guns, hear? And you know where to find me if you want me. Don't be such a stranger in future, eh?' He winked in what was presumably meant as a gesture of encouragement.

The trouble with Steve, thought George as he trudged to the railway station, is that he's turned into a berk. From the old Cockney rhyming slang. Berkeley Hunt. The point which seems to have successfully eluded the man's Catholic and canonical mind is that you can't stick to guns you haven't got.

Pretty soon now, probably within twenty-four hours in fact, George would almost certainly be reduced to the ranks, busted down to the lowest level of political life, forced to skulk on the back benches with all the other has-beens, wannabes, drunks, idlers and spear-carriers whose only claim to distinction is that they can call themselves Members of Parliament. It wouldn't matter then what he thought about Russian planes or anything else: he'd be fodder for the whips' office, valued for nothing but his vote. It was known to be the most depressing of truths that nobody was ever so emphatically ex as an ex-minister.

Curiously though, this bleak (if not entirely accurate) assessment didn't tread George down quite as heavily as we might suppose. As he made his way through the teeming streets his step lightened; his trudge became a walk and then a march. His head abandoned its droop. His shoulders snapped back in martial vigour. There's no obvious reason for such a change; it's as plain as ever that he's in the shit up to his eyebrows and sinking fast. Yet in the space of a hundred yards his burden has eased, lifted to such an extent that he's tempted to whistle like a hod-carrier on a tea break. There's no doubt about it: his perspective is changing. He feels himself retreating, stepping back from the scene, until the street seems as distant as a stage set viewed from the gods. He's a spectator now and the play must be unusually jolly because he's awash in happiness. In fact he can't help smiling, grinning like a Saturday night punter at the end of the pier show when the comedian comes on. It's a wonder there aren't any balloons, party favours or kiss-me-quick hats. Absurd. There's nothing for it but to rest on a convenient bench in an equally convenient park.

'Your friend is right about one thing,' says the Old Gentleman who (of course) happens to be sitting there and who (of course) must be given the courtesy of capital letters. 'This sort of occurrence is quite common.'

'Ten a penny,' says George, entering into the spirit of the thing. 'Apparently it's well documented.'

'He's a good man. Doing his best.' The Old Gentleman is wearing a suit that must have been cut in Savile Row and his tie is the salmon and cucumber of the Garrick Club. 'You mustn't be too hard on him. I'm afraid he simply reflects the temper of the times. The question you must ask yourself is whether his advice is valid. Mmm?'

Since he's feeling so inexplicably chirpy, George isn't capable of getting down to serious analysis. He knows in the deepest fibre of his being that this experience is as real as the bench on which he's sitting, just as he understands the scale of the privilege he's been granted. 'It's good of You to take the trouble,' he says. 'To come in person, I mean.'

The Old Fellow inclines his head in acknowledgement, perhaps a hint of amusement in his eyes. 'I'm glad you appreciate it,' He says.

'Very much.' George is aware that he's not displaying the awe and terror traditional on such occasions. 'I mean, I know You're good. Noted for it. Among other things.' He wonders whether he should emphasise the point by flinging himself to his knees.

'I think we can dispense with that,' says the Old Gentleman, evidently anxious to prevent George committing a social solecism. 'You'll get grass stains on your suit. Anyway, for the purposes of this interview I'm not in My *Rex Tremendae Majestatis* mode. You should regard this as an informal encounter. So. I repeat: do you think your friend's advice is valid?'

'Well of course it isn't,' says George, rather flattered that the conversation can be conducted man to man. 'You're here. QED.'

'Ah.' The Old Gentleman nods gravely. 'So on the evidence of eyes, ears and no doubt a certain euphoria you're prepared to agree that I exist.'

There's a hint of rebuke here and no mistake, thinks George, and it's jolly well not fair. 'You don't make it very easy,' he protests.

'Perhaps not.' The Old Gentleman sounds regretful. 'I must admit, many people seem somewhat sceptical. Bertrand Russell, now. Asked Me why I didn't provide better evidence for Myself. Quite brave, in the circumstances.'

'It's cancer,' explains George, anxious to be helpful. 'Earthquakes. Bluebottles. Beri-beri. All part of Your Creation. These things don't help.'

'One of the consequences of being ineffable,' the Old Gentleman points out with perhaps a hint of impatience. 'There's not the slightest point trying to explain. You just have to accept it.' He peers at George from beneath bushy white eyebrows.

'There's the ichneumon wasp, come to think of it,' says George, ever the combative debater. 'Ghastly little creature. Grows up inside other insects. Nibbles them away from the inside. Hard to understand why You made something like that.'

'Ah, yes. The ichneumon wasp.' The Old Gentleman nods as though conceding the point. 'They used to have great theological debates about that little creature, you know. Long before you were born. Strange thing was, they seldom worried about the tapeworm.' He sighed. 'Mind you, I've given up wondering about theologians. Sometimes I wish they'd give up wondering about Me.'

'Most people believe in You,' says George, trying to offer some comfort.

'Let there be light,' says the Old Gentleman. 'Simple enough, wasn't it? A proposition anyone could comprehend. These days it's all quarks and Higgs particles. Bosons. Hard to make head or tail of them, but a lot of people think they're more plausible than I am. Extraordinary.' He shakes his head in what looks like bewilderment but obviously can't be. 'Maybe I should have thrown in a few equations for good measure, eh?'

'I think most people like the Bible the way it is,' offers George.

'Most gratifying,' the Old Gentleman says dryly. 'It makes One feel One hasn't been entirely wasting One's time. Not that time is a concept that applies, you understand.'

'Absolutely,' agrees George. 'I do understand. In fact I see clearer now than ever before.'

'Really?' The Old Fellow raises His eyebrows in a swirl of wrinkles. 'If I may say so you've not shown much evidence of it so far.'

'It's different now.' George is uncomfortably aware that he's making excuses. 'The thing is, I know You're real. I know this isn't some kind of brainstorm. Makes all the difference.'

'Hmm. I wonder. It'll be easy enough to convince yourself in a day or two that this is all a hallucination. You'll have no indisputable evidence to the contrary. I'm not in the business of offering proof, George. If I allowed you to know, truly know beyond the possibility of doubt, you couldn't exist as a human being with free will. You'd be a slave, incapable of choice. Incapable of love too, as it happens, other than the kind of love a dog gives its master. So. You have to take the leap of faith. You. I can't do it for you.'

In the circumstances this seems a decidedly odd remark. 'So why have You picked me?' George wonders.

'Oh, but I haven't.' The Old Gentleman looks surprised, which is itself surprising in an omniscient being. 'At least not in the sense you mean. You picked Me.'

This is such an unlikely tale that in spite of his good cheer George is moved to utter a 'Huh!' before he remembers himself and blushes.

'Listen to me,' says the Old Gentleman sternly. 'I'm not in the habit of forcing Myself on anybody. Apart from anything else, it wouldn't be a fair contest. The fact is, you saw the possibilities for yourself. Light and shade. You made your choice when you imagined the wasteland. Whether you know it or not you've been searching for Me. Quite enthusiastically, as a matter of fact.'

'Still, all's well that ends well,' says George happily. 'Here You are at last.'

'As it happens I've always been here.' Is that a touch of *froideur* creeping into the Old Gentleman's voice?

'I only meant . . .' George stammers, disconcerted. 'It's just . . . I can see you.'

'Of course you can. And of course I'm an Englishman who belongs to the Garrick Club. You need metaphors, George.'

'Ah,' says George, somewhat put out.

'Course I could have shown up as Jehovah with a long white beard. Or as a burning bush.' It's a relief to George that the Old Gentleman seems to be chuckling. 'But you don't imagine Me that way.'

'So this is all in my mind?' George blurts in a lurch of dismay.

'Where else could it be?' The Old Gentleman reaches out and touches George's shoulder. The shock hammers through him. For a millisecond he blazes in a universe of light and love. Then the hand is withdrawn, leaving him drained and trembling. Yearning.

'Oh my God,' breathes George. 'Tell me what you want me to do.'

'There's no shopping list. I'm not a dictator, George. You must make your own choices. Free will, eh? That's the ticket. Understand yourself. Be true to yourself. It's harder than it sounds.'

This is disappointing stuff. George has read too many advice columns in too many magazine not to recognise a cop-out when he hears one. 'Can't You be a bit more specific?' he asks. But even as he speaks the Old Gentleman seems to be blurring before his eyes, the features fading. 'Wait!' George calls. 'I still don't know what You expect . . .'

But the Old Gentleman has become a mere disturbance in the air, nothing left now but the faintest sketch of a smile and a half-heard voice murmuring 'Ineffable, George, ineffable . . .'

He blinked in the afternoon sun. Over the way children shrieked on the park swings. A jogger puffed by, red-faced and sweating. Lovers strolled across the grass. He looked at his watch. Three o'clock precisely. Barely fifteen minutes since he'd left the Canon's house. Still plenty of time then to catch his train and face up to what was coming. Not that it mattered. He had a star to follow now.

Whoever designed these elegant little purses, thought Monica crossly, had no idea of the things a lady might require in the course of an evening out: keys, money, lipstick, a compact, tissues, a comb, cigarettes, a lighter. Together they conspired to make the velvet bulge like a camper's knapsack. Obviously the man responsible – yes, the designer would certainly be a man, probably some wimp called Jean-Paul – hadn't stopped to consider the impossibility of getting through a dinner date without conducting running repairs. He was probably a non-smoker too.

She crammed everything in somehow. Dabbed Chanel on throat and wrists. Ready. Her stomach fluttered pleasurably. Three long years since she'd embraced a new lover but tonight . . . Well, she would see. Stuart Hillmore, company lawyer at ALH Advertising and recently divorced, had been lunching her for months before making the strategic move to a dinner date. Perhaps he deserved the rewards of persistence.

He was a nice man, unlike . . . She pushed the thought away. Time for a glass of wine before her adventure.

She answered the doorbell smiling, a welcome that faded when she saw the stranger on her step. A tall man, stoutish, early middle age, eyes cold in a pink face.

'Miss Holroyd?' He held up a wallet containing an official-looking identity card. 'Sergeant Sharman. Special Branch. A moment of your time if I may.'

Puzzled, Monica gestured for him to enter and began to close the door before she thought better of it. 'Could I see your card again?'

After satisfying herself that the man was indeed a police officer and therefore entitled to her trust, she closed the door. Sharman meanwhile had walked further into the flat and was peering about with an air of unmistakable suspicion. 'So what can I do for you, Sergeant?' she asked, rather miffed by his cheek. At least the weather was dry, so he hadn't trampled muck into her carpet.

'Routine enquiry, madam. Do you have any idea of the whereabouts of Mr George Gulliver?' No doubt about it now. He was snuffling round the room like a pig after truffles. Monica felt a clutch of apprehension.

'George?' she blurted. 'What's happened?'

'Nothing's happened, madam,' said Sharman making a soothing gesture with his hands. 'We need to get hold of him rather urgently, that's all.'

'Oh,' said Monica foolishly as the implications of Sharman's presence began to dawn. 'Isn't he at home? Or in his constituency?'

Silly questions of course, as Sharman's look made only too clear. 'That's why we thought we'd check with you, madam,' he said. 'You haven't seen him then?'

A small bubble of outrage began forming somewhere behind Monica's breastbone. 'Why should you think I've seen him?' she demanded. The bubble was swelling quite noticeably now.

'Just checking his friends, acquaintances. That sort of thing.' Cold wasn't the word for Sharman's eyes after all, she decided. They were porcine. Full of lubricious speculation. 'Hasn't been here by any chance has he? Last night for example?' He raised his eyebrows in a way that hinted at something rather nasty.

'What do you mean?' Monica hissed, the bubble bursting.

'No need to take umbrage, madam,' said Sharman, unflustered. 'Just checking.'

'I want to know why you think he's been here.' Monica was close to stamping her foot.

'So you haven't seen him?' Sharman plodded on.

'No!' snarled Monica. 'I don't know where he is or what he's up to. And I don't understand why you should imagine otherwise.'

'Very well, madam.' Sharman's eyes lingered insolently on her breasts. 'If he turns up you'll tell him to get in touch with his office, won't you?'

Monica felt like slapping his face. 'I won't be seeing him. I haven't seen him in weeks.'

'I see, madam.' Sharman's expression made it clear he saw rather too much. 'But you will pass the message on, won't you? If the occasion arises.'

'I think you'd better leave.' Monica wasn't sure how long she could resist the temptation to scratch out those piggy eyes.

For some minutes after Sharman porked off into the night Monica sat seething. All that talk about the need for discretion, all the skulking in corners, all those furtive assignations were so much hypocritical bullshit. Bull. Shit. No getting away from it: she'd tamely allowed herself to be treated like some halfwitted teenage tramp. If the police knew about their relationship then the Ministry certainly knew. Probably the whole fucking Brigade of Guards knew. She understood now why that greasy newspaperman had dared to accost her in the street. She was fair game. A minister's bit on the side. A toy for George bloody Gulliver's male vanity who could be relied on to keep quiet while clubmen sniggered into their port. 'Bastards,' she snarled as her doorbell rang. 'Fucking bastards.'

Monica's date plays no further part in this narrative. He's done his duty simply by turning up. We'll leave him there on the lady's step, a nice chap looking forward to a pleasant evening in good company. It's all laid on: drinks at an amusing place he's only recently discovered, dinner at Mijanou, perhaps a spot of jazz at Ronnie Scott's. He has champagne on ice back at his flat in the Barbican, where later on he hopes to make good use of the packet of three nestling inside his pocket.

He'll never understand what he's done to provoke the fury approaching him on the other side of the door. Poor sod.

'There's Uncle George,' lisped Amanda.

'Hush, dear,' said Tom Brownrigg. 'We want to hear this.'

There was a confused babble on screen as journalists jostled in front of the camera. 'Mr Gulliver!' they shouted, thrusting their microphones forward.

'What are they doing?' Amanda wanted to know.

'They want to hear your Uncle George,' said Alice. 'And so do we, miss, if you don't mind.'

George was standing on the pavement outside 10 Downing Street. 'Have you resigned?' bawled the reporters. 'Have you a statement? Can we have a word? Minister?'

'Just get in the car, George,' muttered Rosemary, worried. There was something in his expression she couldn't fathom.

'. . . Perhaps not surprising if he chooses not to say anything at this time,' said the commentator. 'We haven't had a drama quite like this since Michael Heseltine stormed out of a Cabinet meeting.'

George was bending down, talking to his driver. Then he stood and crossed the road to the frantic mob, holding his hands up for silence.

'Don't do it,' muttered Rosemary.

'He's bloody well going to,' said Tom Brownrigg.

'Have you quit?' shouted an unseen reporter.

George smiled. 'The answer to that one is No. I haven't resigned.' He waited until the hubbub died away. 'I've been dismissed. I think you all know why.'

This one drove the pack wild. Cameras popped. Microphones jabbed in the air. Dozens of voices shouted. George waited patiently. 'The Prime Minister of course did me the courtesy of asking for my resignation in the normal way,' he said at last. 'In the circumstances, however, I told him that I was unwilling to take part in the traditional fiction. I'm afraid I left him no alternative.'

'Are you planning to challenge for the leadership?' gabbled the man from ITN almost before George had finished speaking.

George just grinned.

'He's enjoying it,' growled Tom Brownrigg.

'I don't think he is,' said Rosemary, uneasily. 'I've never seen him like this before.'

But George was speaking again. 'I'm afraid that's all, for the moment. With the Speaker's permission I hope to make a statement in the House this week. Thank you for your attention.' With a wave to the cameras he strode back across the street, ducked into his car and was driven away.

'Are you all right, Rosie?' asked Alice.

'. . . Extraordinary scenes then in Downing Street,' said the commentator. 'George Gulliver in apparently relaxed mood driving off to the back benches leaving the Government in turmoil and all sorts of questions unanswered. For Mr Michael Poultney the question now is whether he'll have to face a damaging leadership challenge in the autumn . . .'

'I have to go to him,' said Rosemary.

'Are you sure?' Alice squeezed her hand.

'Welcome to stay. You know that,' said Tom Brownrigg dutifully.

On the television screen the chairman of the 1922 Committee was assuring viewers that the Parliamentary party was in good heart. 'I think you'll find this is a bit of a nine-day wonder,' he predicted.

'He's my husband, isn't he?' said Rosemary.

CHAPTER

10

Buttock to buttock, thigh to thigh, squirming and squeezing, shifting and jostling, Honourable Members and Right Honourable Privy Counsellors snuggle hugger-mugger along the green leather benches, spill into the gangway, struggle for room at the Bar of the House, round the Speaker's Chair, in every cranny and corner. On such a day the Chamber makes no more concession to personal space than a tubful of fisherman's maggots; and if you've been a mite careless in your personal hygiene this is when you'll be found out. It will certainly serve you right, for this has been billed in the press as a Great Parliamentary Occasion, a moment for the history books and well worth a bath and precautionary brush of the teeth. Everybody who's anybody is here. Look: there's the Ambassador of Russia and the High Commissioner for New Zealand jammed together in the Distinguished Visitors' Gallery with the representatives of Pakistan, Venezuela, Israel, Pakistan, the United States and France, all come to enjoy the best free show in town. In the Strangers' Gallery they're packed tight as anchovies. Every desk in the Press Gallery is occupied too, a hundred notebooks open, a hundred pens poised. Doesn't take much prophetic skill to know what story we'll be reading on our front pages tomorrow morning, does it? No, sir. Some of the reporters here reckon there hasn't been such tension in the Commons since General Galtieri and the Argentinian junta walked into the Falklands. Well, such exaggeration isn't so surprising. July is traditionally the cruellest month in politics, and this event promises to be brutal for somebody.

The electronic clock flicks up to 3.42. This is it then. Chocks away.

'Mr George Gulliver!' bawled the Speaker. 'Personal statement!'

Not a sound. Not so much as an exhalation from those thousand crammed souls. For a frozen moment George believed he must suffer that dread, destructive silence with which the House of Commons crucifies its enemies. Then the growl began, a low surge of acknowledgement which rolled round the Chamber and washed over the surly ministerial benches. It wasn't support exactly. It didn't amount to a cheer. But it contained enough sympathy to let him know he wasn't being handed the Black Spot. Not yet anyway. George felt his nervousness drain away. He stood in his unfamiliar place below the gangway gazing round at the sea of suited bodies and pink faces, all of the buggers looking up. Just as he liked it. The Leader of the Opposition caught his eye and winked. Up in the Strangers' Gallery Rosemary leaned forward with a thumbs-up sign. It was going to be all right. Really. It was.

'Last week, Mr Speaker,' he began, 'a small item appeared in the local newspaper in my constituency, the *Mowsbury Gazette*. It was only three paragraphs tucked away inside, under the headline *RIVER TRAGEDY*. If I may I shall read it to the House.'

He held up the cutting. 'A body recovered from the River Ham has been identified as Mrs Wendy Hilliard, eighty-three, of Oak Drive residential home.

'Mrs Hilliard had been missing from the home for two days.

'Staff said she had been deeply upset by the death of her husband, Mr Harold Hilliard, eighty-four, and had vanished from her room shortly after being told. Police say they do not suspect foul play.'

The Chamber was deathly still.

'I accept, Mr Speaker, that the circumstances of Mrs Hilliard's death are now the subject of a coroner's court,' George continued. 'But when she came to see me not long ago she told me a story which I think the House has a right to hear and which she wanted to be heard. Certainly it has a bearing on my departure from the Government.'

Up in the Press Gallery the new Parliamentary sketch-writer for *The Times* regretfully scored a line through the phrases he'd prepared about Gulliver, Lilliput, Big Enders and Little Enders. It clearly wasn't going to be an occasion for flippancy. 'Hearts and flowers,' he scribbled, then crossed that out too.

From his vantage-point beside him Jack Cartwright studied the expressions on the Government front bench as George recounted Wendy Hilliard's experiences of social security regulations and her plan to kill herself. Most ministers were managing to remain impassive, though the Social Services Secretary was shaking her head slowly from side to side.

'I fully accept my share of the blame for her misery,' George continued quietly. 'She asked for my help. I was able to offer her none. In fact with my colleagues in Government I had already agreed in principle to a programme of spending cuts which could have no other outcome but to increase the stresses in our society and add to the burdens already borne by the old and the weak and the poor.'

Behind Jack Cartwright the man from the *Daily Express* let out a snort. 'Treacherous little shit,' he muttered.

'Gulliver, I charge thee,' whispered the well-read *Independent*. 'Fling away ambition. By that sin fell the angels.' He jotted the words down, pleased that he'd found a peg for his column.

'Maybe he means it,' suggested Jack.

'There could be fairies at the bottom of the garden,' retorted *The Times*, whose piece was falling handily into place.

VAULTING AMBITION

On the off-chance that the life of Tinkerbell might indeed be hanging in the balance, your sketch-writer is quite prepared to announce that he believes in fairies.

It's not difficult. Just close your eyes and concentrate. There! Can't you glimpse the little creatures dancing and skipping among the toadstools?

No doubt it was in hope of achieving such suspension of disbelief that our quondam Secretary of State for Defence set out to dazzle the Commons.

As performances go it was quite simply brilliant. Mr Gulliver's impersonation of a man racked with anguish for the sorrows of the world was so plausible that his audience may well have been moved to embrace not only fairies but ley-lines, horoscopes, the ancient wisdom of the Rosicrucians and the accuracy of Treasury forecasts.

Some parts of his statement were genuinely moving. His account of the sad death of a constituent and his appeal for a moral dimension in politics touched even the hardened old lags in the Press Gallery.

And yet, and yet – how shall we put this without giving gratuitous offence? – we're not talking Mother Teresa here. Until yesterday Mr Gulliver has managed to spend twenty years at Westminster without once departing from the grand old principle of *sauve qui peut*, never relenting in his castigation of idlers, welfare scroungers, trades unionists, feminists, homosexuals, social workers, liberals, socialists, pacifists, trendy clergymen, avant-garde thinkers, modern artists, the BBC, and the European Commission. It could only have been a matter of time before he got round to the Luton Girls' Choir.

None of this precludes a Damascene conversion. Yet even your Tinkerbell-fancying reporter must confess that his credulity stretches only so far . . .

Fortunately for George's feelings and the progress of this tale, the rest of the press will take a more charitable view. Perhaps it's merely a consequence of the Government's unpopularity. Or perhaps the speech has stuck a genuine chord. Whatever the reason, the disdain of the *Times* sketch-writer will find few echoes elsewhere, save in the snarls of Prudence Willow's *Despatch*.

But let's not stray too far into prochronism. George won't be reading the papers until breakfast tomorrow, will he? For now the praise, the criticism, the assessments and the opportunity are all in the future. He's more or less where we left him a couple of pages back: on his feet, approaching his peroration now, the House of Commons his to command.

'Mr Speaker I accept that hard and unpopular decisions are part of the process of government,' he declared. 'Ministers would betray the people they serve if they tamely followed the line of least resistance. But they are equally guilty if in the remoteness of power they too easily demand sacrifices in which they themselves will never share.'

'Hear, hear,' brayed someone on the Labour benches, incongruous as a drunk interrupting the enthronement of an Archbishop. George glared at him.

'It was for that reason I sought an alternative on the spending front and commissioned a study into the possibility of buying Russian fighter planes.

'It seemed to me that an initiative which might save up to twelve billion pounds – money which could protect our social welfare programme from the worst cuts – was worth examining. It was never my intention to embarrass the Prime Minister or my colleagues and if they feel any personal affront I apologise to them.' He glanced across at the front bench where Michael Poultney was engaging in some ostentatious impassivity.

'But, Mr Speaker, this is an issue which goes beyond personal feelings or even Cabinet solidarity. It involves a moral dimension in our affairs, a dimension which I have to say is in danger of being ignored.'

Poultney hunched forward in his place. The Chief Whip turned round with an expression of disgust. George looked him in the eye, unflinching.

'I return then to the back benches with no regrets save one,' he said. 'I spent many years in government believing that I was doing my duty by my country and my party. But only now, in the events of recent weeks and months, have I come to appreciate that duty, like patriotism, is not and can never be enough.'

Now I wonder what the Prime Minister will make of that, he thought, sitting down to what *The Times* report would describe, quite accurately, as a barrage of thunderous cheers, not all of which emanated from the Opposition benches.

The first bat emerged from its nest as usual on the dot of seven, darting into the gathering dusk. A moment later another followed, and another, till an explosion of black, squeaking shapes burst over the patio and flickered away across the valley.

'Definitely over fifty,' said George.

Rosemary shivered. 'Can't bear them. They're horrid. Ugh!'

'That's no way to talk about the Gulliver air force. Useful little creatures. Gobble up mosquitoes and creepy-crawlies. You can set your watch by them too.' George thought about putting an arm round her. Perhaps not, on the whole. Not yet. 'They're a protected species back home. Interfere with them in any way, my lass, and you'll end up behind bars.'

'Let's not think about home. It's probably raining right now. Umbrellas and macs and people shivering on the beach. Summer in England.'

'And all we've got to worry about is the next tropical storm, eh?' It wasn't an entirely accurate observation. 'I know what you mean, though,' he hurried on. 'Wouldn't be a bad life to spend your days beachcombing and your nights with a bottle of rum. And a good woman.' She gave him a little smile then. It seemed an appropriate moment to take her hand.

'Beautiful sunset,' she murmured, giving him a squeeze in return. They stood in silent appreciation as the flush faded from the western sky. Lights twinkled on a distant hillside.

I ought to do it now, thought George. This minute. His mouth was suddenly dry. He squeezed her hand again. In the garden below crickets trilled in noisy ecstasy. Rosemary moved encouragingly closer.

This was the bit that still managed to catch George off balance. Twenty-five years of marriage, twins, a menopause and a messy separation weren't quite the ingredients he'd have selected for a summer romance; yet – there could be no denying it – Rosemary these days managed to put on a pretty fair show with the materials available, responded to his advances as gamely as a bride. One night, in an apparent fit of enthusiasm, she'd even kissed his navel, a manoeuvre that encouraged George to dream that her lips might eventually travel further south, as recommended in all the best women's magazines. On this island, it seemed a plausible ambition. Peter Coleman had obviously known what he was talking about.

'My dear fellow, you must accept,' he'd insisted. 'The place is empty. You'll be on your own. All that Caribbean sun. All those tropic nights.' There might have been the suspicion of a wink. 'You'll be astonished at the difference it makes. You'll come back a new man.'

Well, perhaps he would, if the magic of the place did its stuff. He pulled Rosemary closer, kissing her softly on the cheek, running his fingertips down her spine.

'Mm,' she purred. 'We really ought to make a move, if you've booked that table for eight o'clock.' But she didn't pull away. They stood together, moving slightly against each other in comfortable familiarity. This is what it's all about, thought George. You'll never find a better moment. 'Darling,' he murmured.

'Mm?'

'Something I've got to tell you.'

Was there just the slightest stiffening in her shoulders? Hard to be sure. 'Do I really want to know?' she asked.

'Not a confession,' said George hastily. 'Nothing like that. It's not to do with . . . Well. What you're thinking. It's just . . . I need to get this off my chest.'

She sighed, stepping away from him. 'I knew there was something. You've been wanting to tell me ever since we got here.'

'Really?' George felt vaguely let down. 'Didn't know I was so transparent.'

'You've done a fair bit of staring into space, George.' Rosemary touched his arm. 'That day we went to Soufrière. For a while there, you seemed to fall into a trance. Weird. Could have stood on my head and you wouldn't have noticed.'

'Ah.' George hadn't taken to the volcanic springs at Soufrière. All that sulphurous air, all those bubbling pools and blackened earth, were too powerful a reminder for comfort. He'd found himself shivering, in spite of the heat. 'It was the accident,' he said. 'It all started with the accident.'

Rosemary may have murmured something then, but George was ploughing on, overriding her, stumbling over his words. There was a light, he said, and it made him feel . . . He couldn't think of a suitable description. It went beyond happiness. Exaltation, perhaps. That would do, though it was odd because he could see his body lying in the road. Not the kind of thing you'd normally take in your stride. Afterwards he'd almost convinced himself it was a brainstorm. Some kind of hallucination. Only it couldn't be. It was all real. That's the thing. It was real. Had to be. George was speaking faster now, staring into the dusk, hardly daring to look at his wife. There was a wasteland, he said. A bit like Soufrière, but then again, nothing like. Nothing like. It was then he began to understand. George's voice was shaking now, but he had to go on. All that desolation. Cold, dark emptiness. It came down to a matter of choice. What might happen if he turned away from it. Only he couldn't turn away. Impossible. George looked Rosemary in the face. She was staring at him, wide-eyed. There was this garden, he said. And an encounter in Nottingham. Ineffability in a Garrick Club tie.

'George,' Rosemary whispered.

'So now you know,' he said. 'Everything's changed. My whole life.' He straightened up, preparing for the worst. 'Probably think I'm mad, eh?' Apprehension coiled in his gut.

But Rosemary was rushing forward, throwing her arms around him, hugging him fiercely. 'Not mad,' she said. 'Never that. Not you, darling.'

'You don't think I've been seeing things?'

Rosemary clung on. 'I think you're seeing straight for the first time in years,' she said. Her eyes were bright with unshed tears. 'Should have told me sooner, though. Trusted me. I understand, George. I do.'

'More than I do,' he muttered.

'Just don't try and analyse it. Something's happened in your life. You've changed. That's what matters. Everything will be different now.'

'No doubt about that. You'll be amazed how different things will be.' George kissed his wife, giddy with relief.

It wasn't until much later that he began to wonder whether Rosemary had quite grasped the differences he had in mind.

Jack Cartwright stared fiercely at his empty screen and began again.

'Sacked Cabinet Minister George Gulliver is plotting spectacular revenge against the Prime Minister,' he tapped out, hammering the keys much harder than the designers ever intended. He paused to examine the paragraph. Definitely better. Much better. Just the right, authoritative stamp. All he needed now were a few facts to keep the adjectives apart.

'He plans to launch a leadership challenge at the Tory conference in Blackpool,' he bashed on. 'He stands no chance of winning. But a bitter contest threatens to tear the party apart oh bollocks . . .'

Jack rather prided himself on his muscular prose style. Staccato sentences. And short words. Make. An impact. He believed he could spot verbal infelicity a mile away. He erased the oh bollocks and then the bit about party apart. 'Threatens to split the party down the middle,' he substituted. Yes, he was taking off now. Flying. 'Top Cabinet Ministers . . .' Wait a minute. Wasn't that a touch tautologous? Sod it. *Despatch* readers liked this sort of thing. 'Top Cabinet Ministers are enraged at what they see as Mr Gulliver's treachery,' he wrote.

There! If that gutsy little intro wasn't a tribute to his professionalism and skill, Jack didn't know the meaning of the words. On a quiet news day, in the middle of the silly season, this was satisfactory stuff. More than satisfactory. Bloody good, in fact. It's a rare talent, making bricks without straw.

He riffled through his notebook, sifting the evidence, such as it was, for the prosecution. Item: Sir Peter Coleman, indiscreet as always, lets slip that he's lent the Gullivers his house in the West Indies. Item: Coleman also reveals that George has agreed to address a fringe meeting organised by the Millennium Group of MPs at the Conservative conference in Blackpool. Item: according to Prudence Willow, the Prime Minister is convinced that George is up to no good. What does it all mean? That's where professionalism comes in. This is another test of ingenuity. Add up the facts. Come to a conclusion. Don't dare call it lies. Speculation's the word. Intelligent speculation.

What irritated Jack, what sometimes pissed him off beyond measure, were the sneers of outsiders, civilians and other amateurs. Work for the *Despatch*, do you? Here's a curl of the lip, then. Here's a little moue of disapproval, the lift of a condescending eyebrow. Every wanker in town shares a certain view of Jack Cartwright and the popular press. Smart-arsed liberals, women in kaftans, men who wore sandals and drank home-made beer, the crew who worried about saving the fucking whale, concerned citizens awash in their lead-free petrol and elderflower wine. Even Pauline, who after twelve years of marriage ought to know better, wasn't on his side. Why don't you work for a respectable paper, Jack? By which, of course, she meant the poxy *Guardian* or the even poxier *Independent*, papers that paid a pittance and wouldn't recognise a proper story if it was inscribed in seventy-two-point Bodoni bold on the shithouse wall.

Since he was not by nature an introspective man, it never occurred to Jack that his occasional rages might have something to do with guilt. Why should it? He was a good operator. Everybody said so. A story-getter. He earned sixty-five thousand a year plus another eight grand on top in expenses. He had the private telephone number of every Cabinet member. The Prime Minister sent him a card, personally signed, every Christmas. Such were the rewards of success. How many others who'd left school at sixteen with a couple of O-levels could boast as much? Damn few. And that's a fact.

Feeling somewhat better, he focused once more on his story. 'Until now, there has been no real evidence that Mr Gulliver is planning a leadership coup. In the absence of a definite announcement, most Tory insiders assumed he would accept his relegation to the back benches, following his controversial plan to buy Russian warplanes,' he wrote.

'But it is now clear that he is using a free holiday at a secret Caribbean hideaway to plot against Mr Michael Poultney.

'Mr Gulliver is staying at a house owned by leading Tory rebel Sir Peter Coleman, who has made repeated demands for the Prime Minister to resign.

'Though Sir Peter will not be drawn on the details of a leadership challenge, he does not deny the possibility. "Let's just say that George needs time to think," he said.'

Good old Peter. He could never resist the opportunity to stir up a bit of mischief. Jack tapped on.

'In fact Mr Gulliver intends to announce his challenge in just five weeks, when he addresses a meeting organised by the influential Tory Millennium Group at the party conference in Blackpool.' Jack thought for a moment then erased 'influential'. No sense in over-egging the pudding. Everyone in the business knew that the Millenarians were a group of troublemakers and ne'er-do-wells united only by their inability to secure membership of any other political group. Jack pressed on.

'Friends say Mr Gulliver is so bitter about his treatment—' He paused. Suppose George made a fuss and demanded to know who these 'friends' were. No, that was all right. Lobby terms would cover that one nicely. Anyway, George these days was in such a peculiar mood that he didn't seem to care what was printed about him. Odd. Very. Serves him right then. Jack amended the sentence. 'Friends say he is so intensely bitter at losing his job that he is privately determined to do all he can to bring the Prime Minister down.' There. Argue your way out of that one, George. If it came to the pinch, Jack intended to claim that Gulliver had hinted as much in a private conversation. Wasn't there a scribble to that effect somewhere in his notebook? Well, there would be as soon as he could get round to it.

He taps stolidly on, a professional at the peak of his powers. It's unlikely that he's troubled by thoughts of betrayal. George Gulliver isn't a friend, exactly. He's a contact. Someone who uses people like Jack all the time, and can reasonably expect to be used in return. Symbiosis is the word for it. This is a game, that's all. At the fag end of August, when the entire Cabinet is still on holiday in Tuscany or the Algarve and there's nothing happening in the world, not even a royal scandal to fill the empty pages, a reporter needs to do a little ducking and diving. His readers expect it. His editor demands it. He has the mortgage to pay, the children to feed and a reputation to sustain. Jack Cartwright, the operator. He's only doing his job. He need feel no guilt or shame.

Besides, you never know. His story might turn out to be true.

'Oh to be in England,' muttered Rosemary as the rain blustered and bounced outside the arrivals hall. 'Makes you shiver just to look at it.'

'Plenty of cabs,' said George placidly. 'We'll be home in no time. Light a fire, eh?' He favoured her with one of his little twinkles. He'd been specialising in such looks ever since that night on the patio; and as always Rosemary couldn't help responding. It was lovely to see such a transformation in his character.

In her years on the magistrates' bench she'd usually been disappointed in her hopes of human redemption. The same parade of drunks, prostitutes, junkies and thieves appeared with depressing regularity in the dock, some defiant, some apparently contrite, some indifferent. Their demeanour hardly mattered. They paid their fines, saw their probation officers or served their time in jail only to turn up in court again and wearisomely again with no lessons learned or promises kept. Perhaps it was folly to expect otherwise; even George, she thought, probably hadn't changed his basic nature. He'd simply sloughed off the carapace that politics, power and ambition had made for him. Hadn't the real man always been there, underneath, just waiting to be set free?

'Come on,' she said briskly. 'Let's be brave. No point in hanging around in here.' She picked up her bag and strode into the Heathrow murk to join the queue for taxis, leaving George to follow with the heavy cases. In the old days this had been the point where he'd start fussing and grumbling, complaining about the lack of porters, fretting at the indignity of standing in line with the common herd. This time he just trudged good-naturedly through the rain. Rosemary grinned at him. All things were possible now.

'Want a hand, guv?' asked the cabbie when they reached the head of the queue, five sodden minutes later.

Her new George rose to the challenge like a champion. 'You're better off in the dry,' he replied without a trace of sarcasm. 'I can cope, thanks.' He ushered Rosemary into the back seat, pushing the suitcases in after her.

'Mr Gulliver, isn't it?' asked the cabbie, half turning in his seat as they pulled away. 'Just back from your holidays, eh? Very nice too.'

In earlier days, thought Rosemary, such familiarity might have provoked a dismissive grunt or maybe – depending on mood – a keep your eyes on the road, my good man. Instead George responded with a friendly smile. 'Good to be back,' he said. 'In spite of the weather.'

'Here,' said the cabbie. 'Don't suppose you've seen the papers where you've been, have you?'

'One of the nice things about going away.' George was fairly bursting with bonhomie.

'Reckon you ought to see this then.' To Rosemary's alarm the man began rummaging about on the floor, paying no attention to the road ahead. He surfaced after a long moment with a rolled-up newspaper, which he pushed back through the partition. 'Have a look at that,' he urged.

'Very kind of you,' said George with the kind of blokishness he usually reserved for election campaigns. 'Anything interesting?'

'You'll see,' said the cabbie, hunching over the wheel as though already regretting his gesture.

George unrolled the *Daily Despatch*. GULLIVER PUTS THE KNIFE IN, shrieked the headline. 'Oh dear,' he said.

Rosemary leaned over to read the story, biting her lip as she came to the bit about a free luxury holiday. Her heart began to pound. 'This is all wrong,' she protested. 'Isn't it?'

'It's certainly imaginative.' George didn't seem especially perturbed.

'This man Cartwright. I thought he was supposed to be a friend.' She was beginning to feel sick.

'Jack's got his problems. Mustn't blame him too much.'

Rosemary stared at her husband. At this point she needed the old George to make a farewell appearance. A few yelps of outrage and the promise of blood on the carpet would have made her feel better. 'This is all rubbish though,' she persisted. 'You haven't been plotting.' She peered at him anxiously. 'Have you?'

'Of course I haven't,' said George, waggling his eyebrows in the general direction of the cabbie's attentive shoulders. 'It's just a bit of wild speculation. We'll talk about it when we get home. OK?'

Rosemary stared out of the window, appalled.

'Not what you expected to come home to then, guv,' the cabbie called over his shoulder.

'You get used to nonsense like this in politics. Doesn't do to take it too seriously.' He reached over to touch Rosemary's arm. 'There are things we should talk about,' he murmured.

She pulled away without replying. All was clear now. George was still a politician with his eye on the main chance. There would be no graceful retirement, no seat in the House of Lords, no work in a worthwhile cause or quiet evenings at home. He was still in the horrid game. She felt disgusted with herself for imagining it might be otherwise.

They arrived home in silence. George paid off the taxi and humped the suitcases into the hall. A slew of letters and circulars lay on the mat. Rosemary picked them up and dumped them on the kitchen table. She filled the kettle while George pottered around, getting in her way. He cleared his throat. She wouldn't look at him.

'Glad to be back?' he asked, with a politician's cheeriness.

She found some teabags and dropped them into mugs. The kettle began to whistle. A thought struck her. 'Damn,' she said.

'What is it?' There was a professional inflexion in his tone, the kind one might expect in a social worker trying to calm a difficult client.

'No milk,' she said.

'I could nip out . . .' He trailed off. The local shops would have shut long ago.

'Doesn't matter. We've got evaporated.'

'So long as it's hot and wet.' He looked uncomfortable. 'Rosemary . . . We've got to talk.'

'Could you get the tin? On the top shelf in the larder.'

He sighed and did as he was told. They sat at the kitchen table. 'You're upset,' he said.

'Oh? Why should I be upset?' Rosemary immediately felt annoyed at herself for behaving so predictably. 'The newspaper story's all nonsense. You told me so.'

'I love you,' said George quietly. 'That's what matters.'

He's good at this, she thought. Very good. It would be so easy to believe every word. 'What matters is that you keep your promises. Things will be different, you said. Remember? Different.'

'Things *are* different!' He was almost pleading now. 'Only I didn't mean . . . I never said I'd just give up.'

'I don't want you to fight Poultney,' she said carefully, looking him straight in the eye. 'You probably wouldn't win anyway.'

'Oh, I know that. Probably finish me off in politics for good.' He favoured her with what she presumed was intended as a plucky smile. 'That ought to cheer you up, eh?'

Rosemary drank some tea to mask her anger. 'Will you give me some straight answers?'

'The truth, the whole truth and nothing but the truth.' Oddly, he sounded as though he meant it. Probably another politician's trick.

'All right. Tell me. Have you been making plans to go after Poultney?'

'No, I haven't. The paper's wildly wrong about that. Really.' His eyes flickered away. 'But . . .'

'But you're thinking about it. Yes?' She felt like hitting him. 'You've been thinking about it all the time. I really thought . . .' She wouldn't go on.

At least he had the grace to look uncomfortable. 'It's not what you think,' he said. 'This isn't about ambition. Nothing like that. It's just . . . I think I might not have any choice.'

She didn't care if her contempt showed. 'You really had me convinced. You know? I was beginning to hope we might have a normal life. Like other people. Not very bright of me, was it, George?' The one thing she absolutely wouldn't do was burst into tears. That could come later. When she was alone.

'You know what I've been through.' He was managing to sound aggrieved, as though he was the one being let down. 'I'm really not sure I'm in control, feel I'm being driven. Please believe me.'

Well, yes. Rosemary had no difficulty at all with that proposition. Why should she, when all George's experiences conveniently conspired to push him in the direction he intended to go anyway? 'I won't stand in your way then,' she said. 'Do what you like.' She took her mug over to the sink and rinsed it out. Even in the half-light she could see that the garden looked ragged and neglected and sorry for itself, weeds everywhere. She'd make a start on them in the morning, if the rain ever stopped.

CHAPTER

11

The most strenuous test of Christian goodwill ever devised, George decided, is undoubtedly Blackpool by night.

He perched uncomfortably on his seat as the tram clanged and squealed along the seafront. Beside him a fat lady squirmed in the vain search for space and ease, her thighs rubbing against his in unsought intimacy. He shrank away the best he could and stared in gloomy fascination through the window.

All the way along the clifftops, for mile after lurid mile, the famous illuminations winked and glittered, flashed in bulbs of red and green, white and blue, splashing, cascading, exploding in a frenzied parody of fun. Cartoon faces grinned maniacally from every lamppost. Postman Pat leered in his giant tableau and the Seven Dwarfs capered beside a simpering Snow White. 'Oooh! Look at that!' called someone as the Mad Hatter poured tea in an endless stream. The tram rumbled forward and stopped, more passengers piling aboard. Children shrieked. Mothers scolded and smacked. The tram clanged off again. On the road beside the tracks cars and coaches inched along, nose-to-tail, every vehicle packed with wide eyes and open mouths. It wasn't hard to imagine the conversation inside each one. 'Ooh!' they were saying. 'Look at that!'

George found it all embarrassingly tacky. He wasn't a snob,

or so he reassured himself. In fact of all the Cardinal Virtues humility was his favourite, the one he practised with Heepish zeal. In his reformed and therefore heroically humble nature he'd begrudge no family its innocent pleasure. But Blackpool illuminations! He closed his eyes against the vulgar glare, indulging himself in a little compassion for those who knew no better. Poor devils. Happy as sandboys with their candyfloss and kiss-me-quick hats. It took quite a leap of faith to accept that God loved and cared for each one of them with the same unfathomable passion He devoted to Conservative Party representatives in dinner-jackets and silk scarves. George did his best however. A man's a man for a' that, eh?

At the next stop he pushed his way out of the tram, shivering in the bluster of salt air. The evening crowds seethed past. He began walking with the flow, past cafés and chip shops, boarding-houses and holiday flats, tattooists' parlours, rock shops, fortune-tellers' booths, hotels with glassed lounges where residents, incurious as fish in an aquarium, ignored the passing throng. In the morning no doubt they'd send postcards bearing images of the Tower, the Golden Mile, the pier and donkeys on the beach. Having a great time. Wish you were here. Doing us a power of good.

There was, George (rather pompously) supposed, a political lesson in all this: if the British working class could be fobbed off with Blackpool it could be fobbed off with anything, patronised with lies, cozened by promises, bribed with its own money or sold for a pittance. He doubted whether a single holidaymaker in that passive multitude knew of his moral turmoil, or cared. Unlikely any would bother to mention the Conservative Party Conference in their postcards home; the battle-lines drawn in the Winter Gardens and the lobbies of the Imperial Hotel meant nothing to them. GULLIVER THROWS DOWN THE GAUNTLET, the headline bawled in the *Express* that morning. So what? said Blackpool. Jim Davidson is packing them in at the end-of-the-pier show ('howls of laughter' – *Lancashire Evening Post*) and that's quite enough excitement to be going on with. Well, fair enough. George did his best to be magnanimous. You could take censoriousness too far. For all anyone knew, there might be more virtue in Blackpool's simple pleasures than in an entire consistory of cardinals.

He crossed the tramlines to the foreshore and the slobbering sea, turning his back on the common folk with their homely joys and destinies obscure. There ought to be comfort in the westering darkness. Peace of a kind. Out there the winds blew and the waves heaved in perfect indifference. Shoals of cod and herring swam in scaly harmony. The earth rushed towards the dawn, spinning obligingly on its axis every twenty-three hours and fifty-six minutes. Cosmic clockwork. Sniff the briny then, Gulliver. Consider the lilies. Don't be a chump, like Ozymandias. A speech is only a speech, no great matter even if reputation and the future of the party depend on it. The fish won't care. Or the sleeping gulls.

George sighed. No point in pretending. When it came down to it there was nothing for him in the darkness but a confusion of wind and water. He wished . . . No, he couldn't think about Rosemary. Didn't dare. She talked of ambition gone mad, retreated to her room in silence when he resisted. He could see her patience fraying by the day, measure the degrees by which her resentment increased. He wondered unhappily why he couldn't simply give her what she wanted.

His new status as the party's chief troublemaker couldn't compensate. He missed his place in the inner circle. The hostility of former colleagues trod him down. He shrank from the humiliations that very probably lay ahead. In the Conservative Party there is nothing so low or so worthy of punishment as an unsuccessful challenge to the leader; yet step by step he felt himself pulled to the ruinous edge. He wondered sometimes whether the Old Gentleman in the Garrick Club tie sympathised with his plight. Probably not, on the whole. Eternal Truth might well be found in the still, small voice of conscience; it seemed equally happy to manifest itself in the snarls of war, the Crusader's cross and the kindling piled round a heretic's stake. Blood sacrifice. Presumably it all balanced out in the greater scheme of things, though George wished he'd had the presence of mind to ask whether in his case such drama was strictly necessary. The requirement of heroic endeavour seemed to him a little harsh; in a properly ordered universe, church every Sunday and a regular donation to Oxfam should be more than sufficient to earn any man a place in the Heavenly host.

He turned away from the shore and trudged back towards the lights. Over the road at the Imperial Hotel, the evening's parties would be well under way, sausages on sticks disappearing down a thousand throats, the bars roaring. In other circumstances he might have looked forward to the fray and the buzz of recognition that would certainly greet his appearance. Tonight he felt only depressed. A man self-consciously embracing the principles of decency, honour and goodness shouldn't in all fairness suffer near-universal condemnation as a ruthless shit.

Like most injustices in public life, George believed, it was all got up by the press. Ever since Jack Cartwright's squib in the *Despatch* the other papers had piled into the story with a frenzy directly related to the absence of genuine news. It had after all been an unusually placid summer: no scandals, no disasters, no embarrassments in the royal family, not so much as the hint of an inner-city riot. Nothing to report, in fact, but a spot of nastiness in faraway Sahelia. It was an opportunity ready-made for political editors back from their breaks in the Dordogne, Tuscany or the Costa Blanca and they seized it with enthusiasm. TORIES IN UPROAR, they proclaimed. GULLIVER READY TO POUNCE. George had hidden from them as best he could, refusing to answer the telephone, never leaving his house until he was sure the coast was clear, skulking like a burglar through unfamiliar streets; but of course his unavailability only stoked the fever. Why wouldn't he do the honourable thing then, asked the commentators, and rule himself out of a leadership contest? What did he mean by tying himself in with rebels like Peter Coleman? How come he was unavailable for interview? THE BACKSTAIRS PLOTTER, accused an unflattering profile in the *Daily Star*. At least, thought George, it would ensure a capacity audience for his speech to the Millenarians.

He could see the media pack slavering in the Imperial lobby as he queued to go through the security screen. Ever since the

IRA bombed the Grand Hotel in Brighton, Conservative conference representatives had been obliged to submit themselves to the necessary indignity of body searches, metal detectors, explosives checks, plastic passes and the cold scrutiny of policemen. Tonight George welcomed it all. It gave him time to collect his thoughts. He could see Jack Cartwright jostling beside a television crew from ITN, a fearsome ruck from the Press Association, a beefy young man from *The Times*, the clever young woman who represented the *FT*, and the entire gang from the popular tabloids. Microphones waved in the air. Lights glared in sudden dazzle. Bloody BBC. George passed through the metal detector, collected his coins and keys from the tray and smiled with apparent cheeriness towards the cameras. He took a deep breath and strolled into the scrum.

'Mr Gulliver—'

'Look this way, sir—'

'Can you tell us what—'

'Are you challenging Mr Poultney?'

'Can we have a comment? ... A quote? ... A word? Mr Gulliver! Is it true? What are your plans? Are you making an announcement?'

Shouting, shoving, sweaty with excitement, the Fourth Estate boiled in the ecstasy of the hunt as George stood trapped inside the door, quite unable to move further. Through the maul he could see the tall figure of Sir Peter Coleman grinning helplessly. Fellow Millenarians clustered behind him, some looking alarmed, others glowing in pleasure at the storm they'd helped unleash. George held up his hands in mock surrender, smiling as hard as he knew how. In such encounters with the press it was essential to appear relaxed and in good humour; one whiff of fear, one flash of irritation, and the hounds would tear their victim to pieces. You couldn't let them catch a glimpse of blood.

'It's a genuine pleasure,' he began in the accommodating silence, 'to discover so much interest in a lecture on Conservative philosophy.' It was a well-tried formula and drew the expected laugh. George in fact had insisted that his address to the Millenarians should be given the dullest title possible: Tradition, Challenge and Change: Towards a New Tory Synthesis. 'I shall be dealing,' he went on, 'with the way our principles have evolved from the days of Burke, Peel and Disraeli through to more modern influences like Oakeshott and Hayek, with some thoughts of my own on the future. Will that do you?' He grinned into the sea of faces surrounding him. None of the journalists, as far as he could tell, had taken down a single word.

'The leadership—' ventured one. George held up a hand to cut him off.

'Towards a new Tory synthesis,' he said firmly. 'That's my subject. I'll be delighted to see you in the audience. Now if you could just let me through . . .'

With a few growls of frustration they made way for him at last and still smiling in apparent enjoyment he sauntered over to Coleman and his fellow troublemakers. A few reporters tried to follow, no doubt in the hope of overhearing some indiscretion, but their way was blocked by a phalanx of Millenarian stewards. For a few brief moments George could allow his smile to drop.

'Bloody hell!' muttered Coleman, taking him by the arm. 'Hope you didn't mean all that synthesis stuff.'

'That's what the talk's called, Peter.' In fact in the last five minutes it had become perfectly clear to George that the possibility of putting off a decision was the merest fantasy. 'I am in blood stepp'd in so far,' he thought, 'that, should I wade no more, returning were as tedious as go o'er.' He felt an ache of regret for Rosemary, who would never understand.

'Troops are all fired up. You can't let them down now. We're ready.' Coleman was nearly hopping up and down in anxiety and (not for the first time) it struck George that the machinery of a leadership challenge was always driven more by brute ambition than the demands of principle. He wondered what reward Coleman expected for his assistance: promotion to Home Secretary, perhaps? The Foreign Office? It wasn't an inspiring thought, so he pushed it to the back of his mind. First things first. In any case the likelihood of a Gulliver victory was not great.

'I think it's piss-or-get-off-the-pot time,' he said. 'Death or glory.' The relief in Coleman's face was almost comic. There was a low mutter of appreciation from one or two of the perpetual backbenchers who'd been eavesdropping. No doubt they too dreamed of the ministerial cars and Right Honourable status so far denied their modest talents. George nodded at them, wondering why he felt no elation at the coming fight, imagining what Rosemary would say, worrying at his helplessness in the flow of events. He could smell disaster a mile off, cringed at the amateurism of Coleman and his crowd. He clung to a memory of the Old Gentleman, though in no expectation of protection from humiliation and ruin. 'Let's do it,' he said. 'Over the top.'

It was some comfort that he had no choice. Fear of failure, the demands of party loyalty, Rosemary's dismay and the sheer awfulness of his new allies couldn't deflect him now. He was marching to another drum. He squared his shoulders and followed Coleman into the crowded expectancy of the Lancaster Suite. Somebody started a round of applause which petered out almost before it had begun. There was some shuffling and coughing as Coleman began his opening remarks. George nodded in apparent geniality at the sea of staring faces. Many seemed hostile. A television light banged on. At the back of the room a gang of young twerps of the kind who infest every Conservative conference unfolded a banner. LOYALTY it proclaimed. The cameras swivelled to take the message in. George swallowed, wishing he'd brought some notes, trying to marshal his thoughts. '. . . My very great pleasure,' Coleman was saying, 'to welcome the Right Honourable George Gulliver.' He sat down to a dutiful clap. The cameras all swung back as George got to his feet. He gave a half-smile.

'I feel like Daniel in the lion's den,' he began, earning some self-conscious laughter.

'Traitor!' bawled a voice from the back. There was a bit of shushing then. Quite a few in the audience turned round to glare at the interrupter. George waited, feeling calmer.

'At the back of this room,' he said at last, 'some of our young friends are holding up a banner. It contains one word.

Loyalty.' There was a little snickering at this. 'It's entirely appropriate,' George went on as the room quietened. 'Because that's precisely what I'm going to talk about tonight. Loyalty.' He had them now, felt the adrenalin surging. Five hundred faces looked up at him, not so very hostile after all. Neutral perhaps. A little puzzled at his departure from the advertised topic. Interested anyway.

'I grew up in quite modest circumstances,' he said quietly. 'In an ordinary street. An ordinary town in middle England.' At the back he could see the troublemakers straining to hear. He hoped there would be no further problems from them. He lowered his voice a fraction more. 'We were not rich. Neither were we particularly poor. Like most citizens we lived ordinary lives.' He took a sip of water. 'Those of you who are old enough will remember what it was like. I want you to cling to that memory. Hold it fast. Then think of the things we have lost.'

George stepped from behind the table. He needed no barriers for this one. This ought to be a conversation between friends. 'We possess more things now than ever we dreamed of then,' he went on. 'We have more money. We're better housed and better fed. We are more widely travelled than ever before. We enjoy luxuries our parents never knew. And yet in the things that matter we are paupers. We have lost our faith. We have lost our pride.' He was almost whispering now. 'I truly think that in many ways we have lost our sense of national honour.'

'Bullshit,' the lady from the *Financial Times* muttered to herself; and to any detached or sophisticated observer the content of George's speech – had the room not been centrally heated one might more accurately have described it as a fireside chat – might indeed seem the stuff of ordure. But look: in this crowded room they aren't detached at all. On these uncomfortable chairs sit rows of people brought up on Avalon and Merrie England, men and women who have read of Bluff King Hal and believe every word, dreamers who think Richard I was an Englishman. These are representatives of the Conservative Party and – bless their romantic hearts – they're proud of their nation and its glorious past. They know about Drake's Drum and the roar of cannon at Waterloo; in their collective memory there's a Camelot and a King Alfred, a Wolfe scaling the Heights of Abraham, a Nelson sailing to victory over the filthy French. They're the people of Shakespeare, they are, and they beat Napoleon and Hitler good and proper. Money isn't their god. Really, it isn't. When you come right down to it, they're true blue. Guardians of a grand tradition. In the marrow of their bones they cling to a Britain that is Great not as a matter of geographical description but as a badge of moral worth.

Yes, there's the rub. That's why they're rapt and still, why they hardly notice the discomfort of aching backsides. Perched on unyielding chairs they share a deep, unspoken, barely acknowledged unease, guilt for a nation they inherited whole and which is now going to the dogs. For want of money the ancient glories have been packed away. The Royal Navy these days can muster only a handful of ships; there's nothing left of the old regiments but tattered banners and names carved in memorial stone; industry has lost its clamour, mines and shipyards all turned into garden centres (Refreshments. Kiddies' play area. A great outing for all the family); the hedgerows have been grubbed up and the green fields blotched in a rapeseed glare; the monarchy's uncertain, the Church of England an embarrassment, Parliament a poodle. Great Britain now is a province of Europe, diminished and unhappy. The Conservative representatives can't escape the mess they've made of their inheritance. George Gulliver is pushing their buttons tonight and doing it with palpable sincerity too. It's coming from the heart, unscripted. Of course they're responding. This is good stuff if you're in the frame of mind for it.

Think you're that much different? Don't kid yourselves. We all sang 'Land of Hope and Glory' when the fleet came home from the Falklands, didn't we? Lumps in our throats. Tears in the eye. Well then. Let's forget the smart-arsery. Never mind the lady from the *Financial Times*. George Gulliver means every word. You'd be impressed too. He's talking our language.

He took another sip of water and glanced at his watch. He'd been speaking for more than half an hour on the subject of loss: loss of faith in God and the principles of religion; loss of confidence in the law and the institutions of the state; loss of pride in the country; loss of hope for the future. The groundwork was done. Now his challenge could be issued: the solution is not in Westminster or Whitehall, not in society or the state, but in each of us. You. Me. The fault, dear Brutus, lies not in out stars but in ourselves.

Disturbing stuff. Impossible to guess how his audience might react. He took a deep breath.

The slow handclap was hardly audible at first. One trouble-maker, perhaps unsure of himself. Then another joined in. Another. Another. There was some hissing, a word whispered in rhythm. Members of the audience were twisting round, some shushing; but the slow clap was more insistent now, the word repeated and repeated in a soft snarl. 'Trai-tor,' it hissed. 'Trai-tor! Trai-tor! Trai-tor'!

George took a step backwards. He couldn't help himself. The audience was mumbling and squirming, mortally embarrassed; but the rhythm at the back of the room went on regardless. 'Trai-tor! Trai-tor!' Growing louder. Peter Coleman was on his feet, burbling ineffectually. Something about traditions of tolerance in the party. The claque ignored him. They're organised, thought George. This is all planned. A wave of red rage swept through him. He couldn't allow himself to be silenced by some gang of pimply adolescents. Wouldn't.

He didn't stop to think. He leapt forward, striding down the central aisle. Someone gasped. George barrelled onwards. The clapping faltered. Died. 'Trai-tor!' chanted one demonstrator before shrinking in his seat when he realised he was on his own. George stood in front of him, glaring. The room was still. His heart was thumping. Can't let go now, he thought. I can't.

'I began by talking of loyalty,' he whispered into the silence. There was the slightest shake in his voice. 'I must tell you that loyalty – loyalty to our country and to our deepest beliefs – now compels me to ask questions. I start with defence, the area I know best.' He turned his back on the troublemakers and began pacing in the silence towards where Peter Coleman was still standing, open-mouthed.

'I start with the absolute obligation of government to protect our people and our liberties with all the strength and resolution we can muster. Now then. Is it right to spend billions of pounds on a new weapons system when we can buy a cheaper and better alternative from abroad?'

'No!' said Sir Peter Coleman, rather too loudly. The audience seemed to relax. The demonstrators were still cowed. George swallowed.

'Is it right for a great nation like Britain to sell weapons to dictators who will certainly use them to slaughter their own people?'

'No!' Coleman again.

George swung round to confront the room. 'Is it right that the safety net of social welfare should become an expensively comfortable cushion for people who often don't need it?'

This time a couple of dozen members of the audience responded. 'No!' they growled. Scratch any group of Tories and you'll find an atavistic loathing of sturdy beggars.

George stood, grim-faced. The louts at the back still seemed shell-shocked. 'Very well. But is it right then for old people in genuine need to be deprived of help by this self-same system?'

This time the response was louder. Everybody had heard of the Hilliard case and no doubt feared for the consequences of their own mortality. 'No!' they bawled.

'Is it right merely to wring our hands while the crime rate goes up every year?'

There was a drumming of feet. 'No!'

'Should criminals – individuals – be made to take responsibility for their own actions?'

Applause now. 'Yes! Yes!' shouted the audience. One or two leapt to their feet.

'Are we satisfied with the quality of education our children receive in school?'

'No!'

'Do we believe that lessons in the mechanics of sex without any reference to responsibility or love are more important than religious or moral education?'

'No!' The room was roaring.

'Is it right that our taxation system should discriminate against married couples?'

'No!'

'Are we doing enough to preserve the integrity of family life?'

'No!' Three-quarters of the audience was on its feet by this time. Some were stamping and clapping, others cheering.

'Bloody hell,' muttered Jack Cartwright to his colleagues at the press table. 'First time I've ever seen the Christian eat the lions.'

George held up a hand for silence. 'One last question,' he said at last. 'Perhaps the most serious of all. Can we be satisfied, any of us, at what has happened to our country in the past few years? This isn't a question about our economy or our foreign policy or the state of the pound. It's about us. We as a people. It's a question about how we live our lives, how we relate to each other, how we measure up to the ideals we profess. This is our country. It's what we make it. So that's my question. Can we be happy with the job we've done? Any of us?'

For a long pause he stared into the crowd. This was the moment. One voice professing faith in the Prime Minister would break the spell. He half expected it. You simply don't ask representatives at a Tory conference to criticise in public the performance of their own Prime Minister and Government. Far less themselves. Still, this was a night for risks. 'Well?' he asked softly. 'In our hearts. Are we satisfied?'

Astonishingly, it was one of the young twerps at the back who answered first. 'I'm certainly not!' he called.

'Are we satisfied?' George roared.

Perhaps it was his unexpected shout that did it. 'No!' bawled the representatives. 'No! No!'

'What an old ham', hissed the lady from the *Financial Times*.

'That old ham', responded Cartwright, 'might just give our Prime Minister something to think about.'

'Huh!' said the lady reporter. But she scribbled as busily as any of her colleagues as George Gulliver smiled into the swelling applause.

*   *   *

'Jack!' Michael Poultney took Cartwright's hand and pumped it warmly up and down. 'Good of you to come.'

'Good of you to ask me, Prime Minister.' There wasn't a reptile alive who could resist a spot of flattery. Cartwright glowed.

'Always a pleasure, Jack.' Poultney was casually dressed in open-neck shirt and cotton slacks, an outfit intended to persuade the assembled political editors that this was a purely social occasion. 'Champagne's over there. Whisky. Whatever.'

'Nothing but the best for the scribbling classes, I see.'

'Absolutely,' the Prime Minister agreed, though his attention was already fixed on the BBC man who was next in line. 'Robin!' he enthused. 'Riveting piece by you on the six o'clock news, I thought. Bit severe, mind. We're not facing the end of the world, you know.' He allowed himself a brief frown. In the art of luring reporters in the right direction the Prime Minister understood the importance of a little vinegar mixed with the honey. Just sufficient to give his words a tang of sincerity. He replaced the frown with a look of amiability and murmured something about having a chat later on. From the corner of his eye he spied a group of latecomers hovering in the doorway: Trevor from the *Sun*, David from the *Mail* and Mike from ITN. That's everybody, he thought. The gang's all here. 'Trevor!' he boomed. 'Not ferreting out any more scandals, I hope!'

In one sense, the Prime Minister considered his annual conference reception for senior lobby journalists to be a damned nuisance. It always took place on the night before his wind-up speech, which meant he could never get on with any revisions until the pack had drunk him dry. On the other hand it offered a perfect opportunity to gauge the mood of the media and take corrective action, if need be. He wasn't in any doubt of the need this evening. The swinish Gulliver had seen to that. Poultney smiled to mask his rage. Give this lot another half an hour, he thought, and they'll be ready to pounce. Well, he'd be waiting for them.

In fact it took less than twenty minutes before the pack, at some unspoken signal, made its move. 'Fascinating conference,

Prime Minister,' ventured the man from the Liverpool *Daily Post*. Other journalists sidled up, anxious not to miss a word. No doubt they'd spent the day focusing the same obsessive interest on the wretched Gulliver: satellites, he thought, are drawn just as irresistibly to a dying star as to a blazing sun.

Poultney sipped his Tobermory. 'Reminds me of the old Chinese curse,' he replied easily. 'May you live in interesting times.' Obligingly, everybody chuckled. The journalists were in a circle around him now. There wasn't the slightest hint of a smile in their eyes.

'Brilliant speech last night though,' persisted the *Daily Post*. 'The way he handled that demo. Standing ovation at the end. Quite something.'

'Sorry to have missed it.' Poultney performed a little pantomime of regret. 'Especially the way he dealt with those hecklers.'

'He seems to think they were put up to it,' said the *Daily Mirror*, undiplomatic as ever. 'Someone senior in the party.'

'Not a chance.' Poultney was emphatic. 'A stunt like that would be bound to backfire. When he's on form, George can be quite something. A real crowd pleaser.'

'Maybe you should ask his advice about your speech tomorrow,' someone called. It sounded like Jack Cartwright. Poultney burst out laughing, one of the most difficult tricks in the business, when you don't feel like laughing at all. 'I don't think he's in a mood to be helpful,' he said, regretting it at once. Careful, he cautioned himself. Keep it light.

'You think it's a serious problem?' The man from ITN wasn't one to miss a nuance.

Poultney shrugged. Clearly an appearance of candour was called for. 'I can't pretend I enjoyed the headlines this morning. We've had a good conference, on the whole. I think party morale is improving. Obviously we want to build on that. A leadership contest can't help but be a distraction.'

'Course he claims a contest would be good for the party,' mused the *Daily Express*. One or two of the others groaned and rolled their eyes. 'Well, it's an argument,' protested the

Express defensively. 'Might give the Conservatives a chance to re-examine their principles.'

Poultney grinned. 'To quote the old Duke of Wellington, if you believe that you'll believe anything.' He shook his head. 'No, it won't be a help, and George knows it. The trouble is, he's gone too far now to back down. That's the sad thing. It's become a question of his own personal credibility. I know he claims he's only just made up his mind, but in fact . . .' He shook his head again, letting his words trail off.

'In fact?' prompted the BBC.

'Well . . .' Poultney allowed the pause to stretch, as though reluctant to pursue the point. 'I may be doing him an injustice, but I rather suspect his plans were made some time ago. At the time of the Sahelia business in fact.'

'Didn't he pledge his loyalty?' asked the woman from the *Financial Times*.

'Mmm,' Poultney agreed. No need to elaborate further. He swirled the whisky around in his glass and took another sip. 'I think what so many find a little irritating is this assumption that the rest of us in government don't share his moral concerns.' Poultney let out a small sigh. 'Hard to say so without sounding like a Pollyanna, but I think most of us probably agree with a lot of what he's saying. If it's not too pompous, I believe all of us should conduct ourselves according to certain basic standards. Doesn't matter whether we're government ministers or political journalists or whatever we are. We all try, don't we? Decency. Honour. Loyalty.' Rather than over-egg the pudding, Poultney stopped there. His audience could be relied on to do the rest.

'Are you saying he's a phoney?' asked Jack Cartwright.

'Wouldn't dream of it,' said Poultney, delighted. 'I've worked closely with him for many years. He's been a friend as well as a colleague. Now if he says he's been secretly agonising about our failings in government all this time, of course I want to believe him. It's one explanation for his recent behaviour, isn't it? So you mustn't ask me to call him a phoney, even on background terms. I'm certainly not going to be tempted into a slanging match. If we must have a leadership contest I hope it can at least be conducted in a civilised way.' And if that doesn't cut

that little fucker Gulliver off at the knees, he thought, I don't
know what will.

'You're not taking his attack personally then?' That was
Cartwright again.

'I've always liked George,' said Poultney as though such a
bloody stupid question deserved a serious answer. 'I'm not
going to challenge his sincerity. I'd like to think he's trying to
do what he thinks is right. If you ask him he may even feel the
same way about me.'

'I wouldn't count on it,' murmured the *Sun*.

Poultney shrugged. 'Then I'm sorry,' he said. Simple dignity
was always more effective than a bucket of abuse.

'Will he attract much support?' wondered ITN, breaking into
the admiring silence.

'Do you know, I've simply not thought about it.' Poultney
followed up this whopper with another spot of head-shaking.
'Look, we've got major economic issues to confront, real problems affecting real people. Unemployment. Inflation. Taxation.
They're not just words. They make a difference to millions of
families. You can never turn your back on those responsibilities. Certainly not for . . .' He allowed the words 'an arsehole
like George Gulliver' to linger unspoken.

'So you're not worried?' persisted ITN.

'Do I look like a man who's worried?' Poultney put a touch
of mock ruefulness into his voice. 'I'll tell you, the only
thing that's worrying me at the moment is I've got rather an
important speech to write for tomorrow. And I haven't even
started it yet.'

Had his audience been other than a bunch of hard-boiled
hacks, he told himself, they might at this point have burst
into applause, if not tears. Instead they took the hint, drained
their glasses and began muttering about how pleasant it had
all been and thank you very much, Prime Minister. For once
they seemed happy to turn their backs on the pleasures of free
alcohol; it was instructive, he thought, to observe the impact
of a damn good story on the habits of such seasoned topers.
Nothing was so important in their lives at this moment than
access to the nearest telephone. Sources close to the Prime

Minister last night launched a ferocious attack . . . No, that would do for *The Times* or the *Telegraph*, but Poultney fancied the *Sun* might write it more powerfully: Tory rebel George Gulliver was last night branded a phoney . . . a hypocrite . . . a treacherous skunk . . . When the last of the reptiles had gone the Prime Minister stood in his suite feeling almost cheerful.

'OK,' said the Chief Whip, tucking the telephone receiver under his chin. 'Read me the figures.'

He winced as his friend on the *Daily Express* newsdesk in London began speaking but wrote down the words carefully. 'Poultney thirty per cent, right? Gulliver fifty-two per cent. Don't knows and don't cares eighteen per cent. I see.' He drew a little doodle of a hanged man on his notepad. 'It's about what we'd expect in a poll at this stage. You always get a bit of novelty value with a leadership challenger. Won't last.'

Judging by the reaction at the other end, the assistant editor of the *Express* wasn't much impressed by this display of confidence. The Chief Whip tried again. 'Don't forget all this will be decided by members of the Parliamentary party,' he said. 'They're the ones who really know both men. On strictly background terms I can tell you that Gulliver won't get much more than about fifty. That's what I'll be telling the Prime Minister.'

The voice at the other end squawked for a bit. The Chief Whip waited patiently. 'Just to double-check,' he said at last 'The size of your sample is seven hundred and twenty, yes? All polled on the telephone today. Well, I'll admit you've got a bit of a story all right, but I wouldn't hit it too hard. A word to the wise, eh?' The Chief Whip dropped his voice to a confidential mutter. 'I promise you I've given you the right numbers. The Prime Minister is going to walk it, whatever your poll might say. You could look a bit of a chump if you're not careful.'

And that, he thought as he replaced the receiver after a little more to-ing and fro-ing, is what you call making the best of a bad job. Since all journalists are permanently terrified of making chumps of themselves there would certainly be a saving paragraph or two in the next morning's *Express* suggesting that the smart money was still riding on Michael Poultney.

The Chief Whip scowled. It wouldn't do. Never mind all the crap about not taking polls seriously. Thirty bloody per cent for the Prime Minister was a figure anyone could understand, especially Conservative backbenchers forced to face a General Election before they were many months older. Thirty per cent might inspire treachery just as effectively as thirty pieces of silver. For the first time the Chief Whip began to wonder whether there was the slightest possibility that George Gulliver might win after all.

The thought appalled him. Alan Matthews was by nature a loyalist, devoted to his party, committed to its leader. He'd watched Michael Poultney strive against unkind circumstance to keep the Government afloat and admired him for it. Another prime minister might have crumbled under the strain or cowered under the lash of unpopularity and public abuse. Poultney just stuck at it, dogged to the last. He deserved better than a stab in the back from a shyster like George Gulliver. The Chief Whip glared once more at the figures of the poll. Fifty-two per cent of the voters thought the little cocksucker should be in Downing Street, a reflection no doubt of public credulity. Higher moral standards be buggered. What would the punters think if their new hero was exposed for the adulterer, liar and all-round rotter he certainly was?

He drummed his fingers on the desk. In spite of the evidence on the files of Special Branch it wouldn't be easy. The press had already drawn a bit of a blank on the Pimlico love-nest presumably a consequence of the libel laws. Exposure wouldn't be pleasant either. The Chief Whip despised George Gulliver but rather liked Rosemary. He didn't enjoy the thought of subjecting her to humiliation in the outcome of some grubby little scandal.

Alan Matthews pushed the thought to the back of his mind. Distasteful necessity is after all a common duty for any chief whip; he couldn't possibly ignore the opportunity to impose such pressure on Gulliver's extramarital relationship that it might implode noisily, to the great advantage of party and nation. He recalled the obvious strains between George and his mistress as they'd hunched together that evening on the terrace. Yes, unpleasant though it was, his plan might work. It very well might. There would be no need to tell the Prime Minister all the details.

He looked at his watch. A quarter to midnight. Michael Poultney would still be up, working on his speech and probably in no mood for interruptions. The Chief Whip sighed. His task couldn't be avoided. Poultney needed to know about the poll. He picked up the telephone once more and dialled the suite along the corridor. 'I'm afraid it's not good news, Prime Minister.' he said.

Monica Holroyd bent over her desk, frowning in concentration at the sheet of paper before her. 'Tory Party: unique selling points,' she'd scribbled at the top. The space underneath was blank. After a while Monica picked up her pen again. Taxes, she wrote. Trustworthiness. Competence. She stared at the words for a few minutes, then crossed them all out. Her frown deepened. Experience, she wrote at last. The Government had bags of that right enough; but then so did every hooker who hung around Shepherd Market. Monica took up her pen once more and crossed out experience. Rain rattled against the windowpane.

Elsewhere in the building, she knew, some of the finest creative minds in the business were grappling in barely controlled frenzy with the same problem. This after all was a defining moment in the history of ALH Advertising. The big one. Winning the Conservative Party account for the second election running would propel the company and all who served it into the realms where the Saatchi brothers dwelt, to the gates of immortality. Monica shivered in delicious anticipation. Come what may she'd be ready for next week's brainstorming session; when the final submissions were hammered out in the ALH boardroom she intended to shine. All she needed was The Idea. A single thought could shake the world: the curves of a Coca-Cola bottle, the rivets on a pair of jeans, the mysterious recipe for Kentucky Fried Chicken. Somewhere in her files and folders and the tables of official statistics so carefully prepared by Conservative Central Office, the Idea was surely struggling to be born. Never mind outturns and throughputs, shortfalls and estimates. Ignore the public sector borrowing requirement. Dare to dream. Think of England.

Monica closed her eyes in concentration. She suspected that none of her colleagues was suffering a lack of inspiration. Young Jim Sandys could always be counted on to come up with something brilliant and Andy Pyatt was looking unusually pleased with himself these days. Her eyes fluttered open. She couldn't afford to be caught sucking her thumb when the time came.

Courage, she scrawled. Integrity. Huh. She struck a savage line through both words. What the Conservatives demanded and had every right to expect was a touch of the alchemist's art. A transformation of dross into pure gold.

Monica snatched up her paper, crumpled it into a ball and hurled it into the wastebasket. She took a fresh sheet and chewed the end of her pen, absorbed. Perhaps if she ... Her secretary's voice on the intercom interrupted her train of thought.

'The chairman wonders if you could step along to his office,' trilled Tracey in the singsong tones Monica always found so irritating. 'When you've got a moment.'

'On my way.' Presumably that meant more problems with the Captain Clearskin account. Monica bit her lip. They'd never got that campaign quite right. Well, she'd warned them. In this trade, fortunately, you could occasionally get away with an 'I told you so' if you played your cards right.

She did a quick repair job on her make-up and found the latest sales figures for Clearskin. Up less than two per cent in spite of three weeks on prime-time television and a run in the teen magazines. A poor outcome, but the chairman of ALH couldn't possibly blame her for that. Graham Anderson was a fair-minded man. On the whole. He'd read her memos. She stepped along the corridor to his office with a clear conscience. Fireproof. Nearly.

'You'd better tell me what the fuck's going on,' snarled

Anderson as she walked in. 'Come and sit down.' He led the way to a set of leather armchairs grouped round a low coffee table.

'One of those days, is it?' She'd long ago grown used to his rottweiler impersonation and prided herself on never cringing. Graham Anderson was a very red man: ginger hair, florid complexion, bow-tie in unvarying pink, flame-striped shirt and scarlet braces. Monica was often reminded of those baboons in the zoo who made a habit of baring their bright bottoms in shows of aggression. She smiled. Graham could be a sweetie underneath it all. 'We can pull Clearskin round, you know,' she said. 'It's no real problem.'

'Good. Good.' Anderson jumped up and strode to the window where he stood peering out into the October murk. 'Actually, that's not what I wanted to talk to you about,' he said, his back still turned. 'It's the Conservatives.' He swung round. 'What have you been up to, Monica?'

'I've been thinking, that's what I've been up to.' Monica didn't much care for the look in Anderson's eye. 'In fact I'm glad we've got this chance to talk.'

'Are you.' The tone was flat. It wasn't a question.

'The party's in a complete mess, right? Last week was a disaster. The worst conference in years.' Monica could see she wasn't getting through, but kept talking anyway. 'Parliament's back any day now and then we've got at least three weeks of a leadership fight. Seen the papers this morning? Daggers drawn. Tories in turmoil. The voters won't forget that in a hurry.'

'Monica—'

'No, let me finish. Seems to me we should forget any idea of a knocking campaign this time. It just won't wash. We've got to think positive. Build up Poultney. And we don't wait for the election. We should get on with it right away.' It dawned on Monica that she was wasting her time and she lapsed into silence. Something was dreadfully . . .

'What if Gulliver wins?' There was an edge in Anderson's voice.

'Not a chance.' Monica was beginning to feel uncomfortable.

'Anyway we could always build him up instead. It's the principle which matters.'

Anderson stared at her in silence. Monica could feel her heart thumping. 'You'd better tell me about it,' he said at last.

'Tell you what?' Damn. She could feel herself beginning to blush. Her mouth was dry.

Anderson sat down opposite her, leaning forward in his chair. 'I've just spent the morning at Central Office. Your name came up. In connection with a certain former minister. Yes?' His eyes were bright and hard. 'The same former minister, in fact, who's now challenging for the party leadership. Course, I didn't know what the fuck they were on about. Really impressed them, that did.'

'That's a private matter.' Monica spoke with a calm she didn't feel.

'Fuck off,' Anderson exploded. 'Is it fuck a private matter. Fuck me. Half the fucking Tory Party knows about it. Turns out I'm the only fucker in London who's been kept in the dark. Fuck.' Anderson (Oundle and Brasenose, Oxford) was afflicted with a rare form of nominal aphasia when excited: the only adjectives he could remember tended to begin with f.

Monica glared at him. 'I had a relationship with George Gulliver. It's over. Finished. That's it.' She stood up as though to leave.

Anderson jumped to his feet too. 'Why the fuck didn't you tell me?'

'None of your business, that's why.' Monica stood her ground. 'You're not my father confessor, Graham. Just back off, will you?' For a wild moment she thought of slapping his red face.

His shoulders sagged. 'All right,' he said. He seemed calmer now. 'So long as you know the score. They're terrified it will all come out. Great story, eh?' He gave her a bleak grin. 'I wish to God you'd told me.'

'It was supposed to be very discreet. I didn't tell anybody. Not a soul.'

'Pity your boyfriend didn't feel the same, isn't it?' He touched her awkwardly on the shoulder. 'Come on. Didn't mean to yell.

Might not be the end of the world. Just damned inconvenient, that's all.'

'Do you think I could have a very large whisky?' asked Monica. She folded her arms tight as Anderson poured a couple of tumblers. 'You'll want me off the account then,' she said.

'What I want's neither here nor there. It's a question of keeping your head down, isn't it? Last thing we need now is a complication like this.'

She took a long pull at her whisky. 'You telling me to resign?' It was curious that the drink didn't warm her in the least.

'Don't be bloody silly. Just stay away from politicians, that's all. Nothing but trouble.'

'What did they say this morning, exactly?' Monica was quite impressed with her own self-control.

Anderson avoided her eye. 'It was just a whisper. You know how twitchy people can get.'

'Mmm.' Monica finished her drink and put the glass carefully on a coaster. 'You got the impression that George has been talking out of turn did you?'

Anderson grimaced. 'You're a good operator, Monica. You don't need me to spell it out.'

'I want to be on this project, Graham. I need it.' She was concentrating on keeping her voice low and steady.

Anderson held up a thumb and forefinger, a millimetre apart. 'We're that close to getting the contract, Monica. We're nearly there. You know we can't risk it.'

Monica took a deep breath. 'At least tell me who put the boot in.'

He shrugged. 'Who knows how these things get out? You might have been seen together. Anything.'

'Was it George?'

Anderson refused to look at her. 'I've never spoken to the man in my life. You should know that.'

'He's still got friends at Central Office. He could have put the word out. Come on, Graham. You owe me this, at least.'

'Monica, I just don't know. Why would George want to dump on you anyway?'

'Oh, that's easy.' Monica couldn't keep the bitterness out of her expression. 'He's a bastard, that's why. Thinks I might embarrass him.' She thought of Sharman poking round her flat and bit her lip. 'Just think of it. Suppose he wins. Wouldn't want me around, would he? Too much of a risk. As though I'd—'

'You shouldn't get upset.' Anderson said uncomfortably. 'It's not necessarily him. He's not in the Cabinet any more and he's certainly not in the campaign team. You shouldn't jump to conclusions.'

'It sure as hell isn't me blabbing. Doesn't leave many other suspects, does it?'

'Come on. There ain't many secrets in this game. You know that.'

'I do now.'

Anderson fiddled with his whisky glass. 'I don't know what else to say.'

'Well.' Monica attempted a smile. 'I'd better get on.'

'Why don't you take the rest of the day off? Give yourself a bit of time.'

'No, thanks,' said Monica. 'I'd better see what we can do to rescue the Clearskin account, hadn't I?'

Anderson waited until the door closed safely behind her and let out a long, unhappy groan. Then he picked up his private telephone and dialled a number at the Commons.

'I've told her, Alan,' he said. He listened for a moment, his face a picture of disgust as the voice at the other end jabbered on. 'No, I didn't have to put the finger on Gulliver. She jumped to conclusions. Did it all by herself.' He waited until the voice at the other end stopped chuckling. 'Just so long as you don't forget our deal,' he said then. 'If we lose the account now . . .' Anderson's voice trailed off. There was nothing he could do if the Chief Whip ratted on the arrangement. 'OK, Alan,' he said after a while. 'I leave it all in your capable hands.'

Anderson hung up and sat slumped behind his desk, a fierce red man with most of the fight drained out of him. Like many a bright-arsed baboon, he'd run away when confronted with superior force; but one of the many differences between men and baboons is that the beasts have no sense of shame.

Monica returned to her office calmly enough. She smiled hallo at Jim Sandys, who passed her in the corridor. Then she collected a couple of messages from Tracey and sent her off to lunch. She sat in her executive chair, numb. After a while she took her jottings about the state of the Conservative Party and tore them into small pieces. Her rage threatened to overwhelm her but she breathed deeply, sucking the air into the last recesses of her lungs until the crisis passed. She lit a cigarette and smoked it to the tip, crushing the remains methodically in the ashtray.

She had no need to look up George's number at home. She could rattle it off as readily as her own, though of course in the interests of discretion she'd never before dialled it. Well, it hardly mattered now. Her hand was quite steady as she picked up the receiver. But for the coldness in her eye one might have assumed she was phoning for an appointment with her hairdresser.

Rosemary was making bread in the kitchen when the phone rang, kneading the dough rather too violently. The loaf would probably turn out with the texture of rubber but she didn't care. She seldom ate bread anyway and George would take but a single slice for the sake of politeness. She gave the dough another thump. Perhaps she wouldn't bother sticking it in the oven after all. There hardly seemed much point. Baking isn't necessarily as therapeutic as it's cracked up to be. She wiped her hands on a towel, taking her time. The phone rang on.

Wearily she wondered who it would be this time. In the past few days she'd been approached by no fewer than fourteen national newspapers, six magazines, three BBC television programmes, ITN, Radio Telefis Eireann and – for some unfathomable reason – the South China *Morning Post*, all begging for interviews, photographs, details of her personal life. She'd turned them all down without hesitation, though at a price. Already one or two columnists had started writing bitchy little pieces about her standoffishness. Perhaps in the end she'd have to submit. George's assurance that she need play no part in his mad venture was as worthless as all his other promises.

'Yes?' she said curtly. Rosemary resented the fact that she was being forced to grow ruder by the day. It was another consequence of George's damned selfishness.

'George Gulliver, please.' The voice at the other end was cold, brisk.

'Not here,' said Rosemary, just as coldly. 'I don't know where he is. You might try his campaign headquarters. Lord North Street.' Damn George. She didn't want to be his secretary. She rattled off his new number.

'Have you any idea when he'll be back, in case I can't get him? I need to talk to him rather urgently.'

Something in the woman's voice sent a shiver down Rosemary's spine. 'Who is this?' she asked.

'Just a personal call. I'm sorry to have bothered you.' The voice didn't sound sorry at all. 'I'll try him at the office.'

'Wait,' said Rosemary before the woman could hang up. 'I'll take a message.' Now what possessed her to say that?

'Doesn't matter. Really.'

Rosemary plunged. 'It's Monica, isn't it?' The silence at the other end confirmed her suspicion. 'Isn't it?' she repeated. Damn George, she thought again. More broken promises.

'This isn't what you think,' said Monica at last. 'I shouldn't have called. I'm sorry. Something's come up at work, that's all.'

'I'm sure my husband will be very interested,' snapped Rosemary and hung up. She walked back to her kitchen and sat at the table, dry-eyed. This is how a marriage ends, she thought. She stood and tipped the ball of dough into the swing-bin. Then she washed up her cooking-bowl and put the packet of flour back in the larder. The phone rang. For the sake of something to do, she went through to answer it.

'Please don't hang up, Mrs Gulliver,' said the woman. 'It's Monica Holroyd. It really isn't what you think.'

'Isn't it?' asked Rosemary flatly.

'It's all over between us,' said Monica. 'Long ago. I don't want you to imagine . . . Look, I need to talk to him about something else completely. That's all it is.'

'Well, you needn't worry. I'll tell him you called,' Rosemary found herself saying. 'Was there anything else?'

'Only that I'm sorry. If it's any consolation, he's let me down too. Quite badly actually. Professionally speaking, I mean.' There was no mistaking the bitterness in Monica's tone. 'I don't expect you to feel any sympathy for me. I obviously don't deserve it.'

Something prevented Rosemary delivering a crisp lecture on the price of infidelity. 'Are you all right?' she asked.

'Not really.' Monica seemed startled at such apparent kindliness. 'Pretty angry as a matter of fact. That's my only excuse. I'd never have tried to get him at home otherwise. I'm sure I'm the last person in the world you want ringing up.'

Rosemary blurted out her next line before she had time for second thoughts. 'Would you like to meet?'

There was a short silence. 'I'm not sure that's a good idea.'

All at once Rosemary could think of nothing she'd rather do than talk to the woman who had taken her husband to bed and suffered some heavy if unspecified penalty for it. 'I've got a feeling it might help us both,' she said.

CHAPTER

12

'You hoity-toity Eenglish snobs,' declaimed Sam Ruddock in an extraordinarily bad Italian accent. 'You never fair to we poor Sicilian boys. Whena I come to your cold country I am a poor boy and you treata me like sheet. But I worka hard. I beelda all dese ships, but do you call me Mario the boat-builder? No!' In the Gulliver campaign headquarters all activity had ceased, in anticipation of the punchline. George did his best to look genial. His old Parliamentary Private Secretary was doing wonders for morale, but Lord, he did go on.

'I spenda years putting up da houses. But do you Eenglish call me Mario the house-builder?'

'No!' chanted his admiring listeners. Somewhere at the back of the room a phone rang. A young helper answered it with commendable swiftness. George allowed himself to relax a little. His people had to let off steam somehow.

'Then I create a beeg fashion empire, but do you snobby Eenglish call me Mario the dressmaker?'

'No!' everybody answered.

'No!' agreed Sam. 'You call me sometink else. Just because I shagga one leetle sheep . . .'

The room erupted in laughter. 'There's our next European

Commissioner!' spluttered Peter Coleman. 'The only man in England who understands the sheep-meat regime!'

'Nah. Head of the diplomatic service. That's the proper use of my many talents,' said Sam. More phones rang.

'Back to work everybody,' announced George, grinning gamely. 'I think we've already got a head of the diplomatic service, Sam. Might be something going at the Ministry of Agriculture though.' It was curious, he thought, how everyone these days laughed enthusiastically at his feeblest jokes. No doubt if he became Prime Minister it would be like that all the time.

Campaign helpers returned to their desks. Sam's smile faded. He leaned forward to murmur in George's ear. 'You don't have to make any promises to me, lad,' he murmured. 'It's these other buggers you've got to worry about.'

'What are you telling me, Sam?' They were standing in a corner, conveniently away from inconvenient ears.

'You're off to a good start, George. Better than we could have expected.'

'But?'

Sam shrugged. 'I'm not teaching granny to suck eggs. You know the score. You're going to have to start handing out some sweeties. First rule in this game. Got to keep the troops happy.'

'Jobs for the boys, eh?' George leaned forward to whisper in Sam's ear. 'Some of this bunch couldn't run a raffle.'

Sam blinked. 'What's that got to do with the price of turnips? Don't get pious on us, George. You've got a lot of hungry supporters to feed.'

'It's a new kind of campaign, Sam. This is supposed to be about principles. Remember?'

Ruddock gave him an old-fashioned look. 'Only two ways to go, George. Win or lose. Up to you.'

'I hear what you say.' Underneath the knockabout Ruddock was a shrewd operator whose ear was seldom very far from the ground. It never paid to underestimate Sam. 'Thanks for mentioning it.'

'Not everyone's as nice as me and thee. It's a rough old trade we're in.'

Rough was the word for it right enough, thought George as Sam wandered off. There's nothing like a leadership campaign to draw the weevils out of the Parliamentary biscuit. On the other side of the room Peter Coleman was deep in conversation with Jimmy Farquhar, another perennial backbencher with ideas above his station. The man had simply turned up at battle HQ in Lord North Street that morning claiming an irresistible impulse to work himself to the bone in the Gulliver cause. He wasn't the only one: every day, in ones and furtive twos, Conservative MPs – invariably those who had failed to prosper under the Poultney regime – turned up with equally implausible claims of conversion. George welcomed them all with slaps on the back and expressions of undying gratitude. The new recruits might well be the discards of the Parliamentary party, the halt, the lame, the incompetent and the bitter, but they all had votes.

He might have sighed or pulled a face but for the importance of keeping up appearances. Instead he bustled importantly down the stairs to the cubby-hole off the kitchen which served as his personal office. He closed the door and squeezed into the chair behind his desk. In more spacious days, he supposed, the room would probably have been the butler's pantry or possibly a larder of some kind. (George was a little vague about the layout of grand Georgian town houses.) Sometimes when he sat here alone he wondered why old Lord Wharfe was being so remarkably generous in lending his splendid property. He hardly knew the man and didn't much like his character. Could it be true, as Peter Coleman insisted, that a month's rent-free accommodation handily round the corner from the Palace of Westminster had been offered with not the slightest expectation of reward? George recalled Wharfe's tight mouth and veiled eye; not the face of a man who'd dream of giving owt for nowt. It wasn't a happy image; but then as far as George was concerned this wasn't turning out to be an especially happy campaign.

Let's leave our hero for the moment to his fit of the vapours.

Don't worry. He's only going to spend the next few minutes feeling sorry for himself. We won't miss much. At this stage in our tale we really ought to discuss the double-dyed folly that leaves every Conservative prime minister vulnerable to challenge from the likes of George Gulliver. No, you shouldn't be tempted to skip this bit. It may not leave you any the wiser, but you'll probably be better informed. Right?

Right.

The thing about Michael Poultney's administration is that it enjoys a thumping majority in the House of Commons. More than four hundred pairs of Tory buttocks are entitled to squeeze against one another on the green Government benches. But here's the rub: of all those competitive arses fewer than ninety at any one time can occupy a ministerial chair. The rest must languish in unrewarded disappointment.

It's a certain recipe for trouble. Back home in their constituencies those backbenchers are important folk. They open garden fêtes. Voters seek their advice. Their names appear with pleasing frequency in local newspapers. *Sic transit.* On their return to Westminster they're bullied by the whips, patronised by ministerial superiors, ignored by most journalists (except on those occasions when they're found drunk in a gutter or caught in trouserless indiscretion). It's a sad contrast, the stuff of plots and summer intrigues on the terrace. It's a problem for any party leader, especially a leader who looks like losing the next General Election.

Sure, you can buy the malcontents off for a time with baubles, soothe them with knighthoods and committee chairmanships, parliamentary trips overseas and dinner invitations to No. 10; but sooner or later they'll grow tired of standing with their noses pressed against the windowpane. Yes, they will. It's in their nature. Look: most of them became politicians in the first place because their mums didn't love them or because they were unpopular at school. Desperate for recognition, they ache for power and the perks of office. Why not? They think they're talented folk with a lot to give. Really. All they ask is a chance to serve and perhaps the opportunity to get their own back.

Now since all this is perfectly plain to those whose business it is to understand these things, you might suppose that the Conservative Party would so arrange its affairs that the riffraff can't easily upset the established order. That's the commonsense assumption, right? But. But. This is politics, and common sense doesn't apply.

In fact a leadership challenge is simplicity itself. All George had to do was find himself a proposer and seconder (roles willingly embraced by Harry Arkwright – a former Home Secretary who has never forgiven Michael Poultney for dispensing with his services – and by Sir Peter Coleman, who has absolutely nothing to lose), and he was halfway there. Provided he could then attract signatures from a mere ten per cent of Conservative backbenchers – none of whose names would be publicly revealed – his challenge had to go forward. Never mind a General Election on the threatening horizon or the prospect of a party split from crown to crotch. The rules are blind to consequences. Madness, eh? There's a lot of it about.

We haven't yet plumbed the depths. Now that he's done the dirty and placed his name in nomination, George is in the driving-seat. He can win even if he loses. It's a better bet than Pascal's Wager. That's how the rules work. Should Michael Poultney fail to win a crushing victory in the first ballot he'll have to resign. Even Margaret Thatcher couldn't flout that convention. Poultney must not only win the support of fifty per cent of his parliamentary colleagues but – oh, here's the cunning bit – unless he's ahead of his nearest rival by a margin of at least 15 per cent, he must submit himself to the humiliation of a second ballot. In short it's a question of smashing his opponent to a bloodied pulp or losing all credibility.

It's a sight easier for George. He's the underdog. Should he put on a respectable show he'll not only force Poultney out but will certainly be the favourite contender in the second round. Others may scramble to put themselves forward at this stage of the game, but it'll be damned difficult to catch up.

You'd imagine then that George should be rather pleased with himself. His nomination papers are safely in. He's got a campaign headquarters that isn't costing him a penny. The press, the party and the public are all treating his challenge seriously. He ought to be on top of the world.

In fact he's anything but. If we return to the butler's pantry, we'll observe that he's much as we left him. Staring unhappily at nothing in particular. What's the matter, Tiger?

It's not supposed to be like this, thought George. That's what's the matter. It's getting out of control. We've got a building full of volunteers hitting the phones as though their lives depended on it, drawing up lists, making calculations. Who's with us? Who's against us? Who can be won over? The place is humming. It's a good atmosphere. Loads of camaraderie. Everyone here thinks they might conceivably be on a winner. The trouble is, there's not one of them with the faintest idea what this is all about. Not a soul. And I can't tell them.

The problem troubled George. His secret nagged like an abscessed tooth. He woke up to it, nursed it during his waking hours, took it uncomfortably to bed. In reckless moments he thought of confessing his visions, cringing for hours afterwards in anticipation of the derision that would certainly descend on him if he did any such thing. He simply didn't dare admit the truth, grew guiltier by the day at his sin of omission. Like any other political harlot - George these days wallowed in the apocalyptic – he was enlisting support on a false or incomplete prospectus. Oh dear.

He wouldn't think of Rosemary; concentrated instead on what the Almighty had to say. Do what you think is right. Not so simple an injunction as it sounded. Suppose what you think right is, in fact, wrong? Some lines from Chesterbelloc swam into his mind. Pale Ebenezer thought it wrong to fight. But Roaring Bill, who killed him, thought it right.

Unsettling stuff. It was becoming embarrassingly clear to George that most of his difficulties had arisen because of a certain economy with the truth. A failure adequately to explain himself. Cowardice, perhaps? Well, maybe there was a bit of that. Only a bit, mind. It was bloody hard to explain yourself when you were just stumbling from one piece of guesswork to the next. Joan of Arc never had this problem, did she?

No, sir. There wasn't much Garrick Club geniality about her Voices. Knock seven bells out of the English, my lass, and quick about it.

Plainly, what he needed now was another revelation. Unfortunately his spiritual experiences seemed to have one characteristic in common with London taxicabs: they were never around when he needed them.

In the absence of further guidance from above, George at last came to a decision. There could be no guarantee of a Government job for any of his supporters. He understood that it wasn't an especially clever decision, but necessary. The Good Lord might well have some rum ideas: it was hard to believe they could ever be quite so rum as to require the inclusion of Jimmy Farquhar and his kind on the Government front bench. That outcome, he thought gloomily, might prove a sterner test of faith than the existence of the ichneumon wasp.

Suited, sleek, ready for anything, Monica Holroyd stepped into the bar at the Royal Gardens Hotel. At this late-morning hour there was hardly a soul in the place. Certainly nobody she recognised. Good. She chose a table in the far corner and sat where she could keep an eye conveniently on the entrance. In the coming confrontation she required all the tactical advantage she could get.

She ordered a Perrier instead of the longed-for gin and tonic. Waited. Thought about a cigarette and pushed the temptation away. Instead she picked up the little packet of peanuts that had come with her drink and tried to tug it open. The shiny material – no doubt of the same kind used to reinforce the nosecones of intercontinental ballistic missiles – resisted. She tugged again, more violently this time. The packet split suddenly, spilling nuts over the table. Damn. She scooped them up and poured them into her ashtray. They lay there conspicuously, a certain giveaway. Not the sort of clutter you'd expect to find in the presence of a woman icily at ease with herself. After a bit she swapped her ashtray for a clean replacement from the next table.

For the sake of appearances, she tried to read her *Independent*. Things were getting nasty in Sahelia. There were shootings and bombings in the streets. The Vizier had declared martial law. In London the Foreign Office was urging British nationals to stay indoors. Monica's attention wandered. She sipped her Perrier, then thought to hell with it and lit a cigarette. Better. Important to keep calm.

Rosemary arrived on the stroke of noon, hovering in the entrance as though having second thoughts. She seemed smaller than her appearances on television suggested, though no less tweedy. Quite attractive though, in a dignified sort of way. Pleasant face. Not the look of a woman who'd come to gloat or make a scene. Monica raised a tentative arm and sat with stomach knotted as her enemy advanced. The two women stared at each other.

'Miss Holroyd,' said Rosemary at last. Neutral.

'Mrs Gulliver,' said Monica. She had to concentrate on restraining an instinctive social smile.

'Do you think I could sit down?'

'Yes. I mean of course. Do.' Stop babbling, thought Monica. Stay in control. 'Can I get you something to drink?'

'I'd rather like a glass of champagne. Not really suitable to the occasion, of course.'

'I don't suppose either of us are in the mood for celebration. Still . . .' Monica felt the need for something stronger than Perrier. 'Could we manage a bottle between us?'

'I don't suppose we'll be here long enough for a bottle.'

In the circumstances it was as gentle a put-down as could reasonably be hoped for. Monica managed to cover her vexation by summoning the waiter and ordering two glasses. She picked up her cigarettes. 'Do you smoke?'

'No. Thank you.' Rosemary waited until Monica had flicked her lighter. 'But you go ahead.'

Monica inhaled, tilting her head back to blow a long, steady stream of smoke into no man's land. Thirty-love to La Gulliver in the first minute of the match, she thought. But I can handle you. I will. They sat in silence until the waiter returned with the bubbles.

'Well now,' said Rosemary after taking a sip. 'I'm not really sure how we should begin.'

Monica caught what might have been an undertone of nervousness. Or maybe not. 'This is difficult for both of us,' she said, carefully. 'Not exactly an everyday occurrence, is it?'

'Quite.' Rosemary toyed with her glass. 'Just to get it out of the way, I haven't come here to make a fuss. Nothing like that.' She ventured a thin smile and sipped her champagne.

Monica felt she was about to be outdone in the magnanimity stakes, but couldn't help herself. Even if it did leave the score at forty-love. 'I actually wondered why you asked to see me,' she said, going on to the attack. 'I thought perhaps you wanted to inspect the damage.'

Rosemary put her glass on the table. 'Frankly, I'm not sure why I'm here. I thought . . .' She trailed off, obviously uncomfortable. 'You said something on the phone. About being let down.'

Monica wasn't troubling to keep score any longer. 'If it's any consolation to you, he's just about destroyed my career. Deliberately. Just a snap of the fingers.'

Rosemary seemed taken aback. 'It's no consolation,' she said. 'I think you'd better tell me.'

Monica hardly needed the invitation. She launched into an account of how George had destroyed her ambitions, not bothering to conceal her bitterness. 'So that's why I'm able to sit here in the middle of the day. Nothing much for me to do in the office these days, is there? All the time off I want.'

Rosemary flushed. 'Not George,' she said. Her voice carried no conviction. 'He's not like that. I don't think . . . Are you sure it was him?'

'Oh, yes. Oh, yes. Nobody else it could be.' Monica couldn't hold back her rage. 'Obviously I became an embarrassment.' She crushed out the remains of her cigarette. 'Probably think I got what I deserved.'

'No. No, I don't.' A new expression edged into Rosemary's eye. Pain, perhaps?

'I'm sorry,' Monica muttered, without knowing quite why she should apologise.

'Well I'm sorry too.' Rosemary took a gulp from her glass. 'Do you think I could have a cigarette after all?' She accepted a light and puffed inexpertly. 'I think I'm seeing things a little more clearly.' She leaned across the table. 'You're wearing Chanel No. 5,' she said.

'Used it for years.'

'I think I need some more champagne.' Rosemary signalled to the waiter. 'Chanel No. 5.' She stared Monica in the eye. 'How long were you and he . . .'

Monica looked away. 'Is that why you wanted to see me?'

'Not really. But I can't help wondering.'

'Sure you really want to know?'

Rosemary managed another of her smiles. 'A bit late for discretion, don't you think?'

'*Pas devant*,' said Monica as the waiter approached, soft-footed. 'We'd like two more glasses of champagne, please.' She waited until the man had left. 'A little over three years,' she murmured, absurdly embarrassed.

'Three years,' repeated Rosemary. She blinked several times.

'I thought he was in love with me.' Monica hated the defensive tone that had crept in.

'Did he ever say so?'

'I don't like saying this. But yes. He did.' Too right he did. Monica could remember every one of the words blurted ecstatically in her tumbled bed.

'I see.' Rosemary's voice shook a little. 'And of course you believed him.'

'I wanted to believe him. Right until the moment he walked out. Tried to claim he couldn't go on because his conscience was bothering him. Can you believe it? Conscience. Huh! After three years.'

Her words had a startling effect on Rosemary. She sat up straight, her expression intent. 'When was this, exactly?'

Monica frowned. 'Not long ago. A few weeks after his crash, I think. One minute everything was . . . you know. Next minute . . . Well. He dropped me. Just like that.'

'He said it was conscience?'

'Kept on and on about it.'

Rosemary seemed to deflate. Her face sagged. 'Just about the time he made up his mind to try for the party leadership.'

Monica nodded, wordless.

'And of course he immediately dumps you. Very unpleasantly too, judging by your letter.'

'Please believe me. I never meant those threats.' Monica had been wondering when the question of her letter would come up. 'I was in a state. I'd never have told you about . . . you know. Just wanted to give him a fright.' She had long ago convinced herself this was true. 'I wish I hadn't done it.'

'Just as well you did.' Rosemary seemed to pull herself together. 'We wouldn't be having this conversation otherwise, would we? I'm almost sorry you won't be there to see George's face when he finds out.'

'Reception committee,' said Jack Cartwright as the car pulled up at the black-barred security gates that guarded the entrance to Downing Street. It always astonished him that tourists had nothing better to do than hang around on the pavement waiting for a glimpse of the great and the good. There must be a good three dozen rubberneckers there, many in anoraks, all jostling for a better view. Some pointed cameras in his direction, presumably under the impression that anyone arriving in the back seat of a chauffeured limousine must be a man of consequence. Any minute now, he thought, Prudence Willow is going to give them a regal wave. Sure enough she leaned forward and raised a gracious arm, smiling prettily at the mob. One or two of the tourists waved back. Jack wound down his window. 'Prudence Willow and Jack Cartwright from the *Despatch*,' he told the constable on duty. 'To see the Prime Minister.'

The policeman consulted a clipboard and the great gates swung open. A modern version of the old castle drawbridge, thought Jack. So much for progress. We're still cowering behind our walls.

The car purred to the doorway of Number Ten while Willow examined her face in a little vanity-mirror. For once she looked pleased with life, presumably because of the gossipy morsel

Jack had just whispered in her ear. News that her own secretary was engaged in a spot of how's your father with the paper's deputy editor gave her the opportunity to do what she liked best, namely to devise suitable punishments. One up to me, Jack thought. Happy days.

The Prime Minister's press secretary, Phil Norris, was waiting in the lobby, a grin of welcome determinedly in place. Rumour had it that poor Phil was terrified of losing his job in the event of a Gulliver victory. Certainly he was going out of his way these days to help any newspaper supporting his leader, while (in defiance of all the rules of civil service impartiality) making difficulties for the rest. 'Prudence!' he enthused. 'Jack! Good to see you both! The PM's waiting in his office. We'll go straight on up, shall we?'

Jack, Prudence, Phil and the *Despatch*'s chief photographer Bill Robbins, who'd been obliged to arrive at Downing Street under his own working-class steam, crowded into the small lift. Robbins's job was to take flattering pictures of Willow deep in conversation with the Prime Minister while Jack skulked somewhere off-camera. *Despatch* Editor Prudence Willow discusses election prospects with Mr Michael Poultney. That kind of stuff. Jack's task was to ask pat-a-cake questions and write the report that would appear the next morning under Willow's name. MY VISION FOR BRITAIN. The Prime Minister talks exclusively to Prudence Willow. The usual bullshit. Jack didn't mind. There might be a deputy editor's job on offer any day now.

'So how's it going, Phil?' he asked.

'Never better. The old man's in great form. Keeping us all at it.' The grin never left his face. It struck Jack then that the rumours were probably true: dear old Phil obviously did have his doubts about the leadership contest, now less than a week away. Interesting. He tried a gentle probe.

'I'd say Gulliver's done himself a bit of good,' he ventured. 'Extraordinary development, wouldn't you say?' He didn't need to look at Prudence. He could sense the frown clouding her brow.

'A gimmick,' said Phil, still smiling gamely. 'You don't want to take these things too seriously, Jack.'

'Nobody's going to take it seriously,' Willow chipped in.

Nobody but the *Telegraph*, the *Independent*, the *Guardian* and the *Mail*, Jack thought, as the lift doors slid open. 'I'm sure you're both right,' he soothed. They all piled out into the corridor and Phil went ahead to knock on the Prime Minister's door.

'I don't want you going in with hobnailed boots,' Willow hissed.

'Trust me, Prudence. He'll expect to be asked.' Jack lowered his voice. 'This will be an interview you can be proud of.'

Willow relaxed. 'If you're sure . . .'

'I won't let you down,' said Jack confidently. 'I know what's required.' Behind Willow's back, Bill Robbins gave him a huge wink. Jack pretended not to notice. Phil Norris emerged from the Prime Minister's inner sanctum, beckoning them forward.

Poultney was sitting at his desk, his jacket off, apparently engrossed in paperwork. He leapt to his feet as they entered and advanced on Prudence with the eagerness of a lover, clasping her by the arms and leaning forward to plant kisses on both cheeks. Willow simpered, her eyes shining. Jack hung back while the pair of them buttered each other up for rather too long, then shook hands. Bill Robbins started unpacking his equipment, ignored by the others. It wouldn't bother Bill. He'd been ignored by better men than Michael Poultney in his time.

'Well now, Jack,' said the Prime Minister after a little more cooing and billing. 'I suppose we'd better get on with the old third degree, eh?' He gestured for Willow to sit on the sofa and plonked himself beside her, still in his shirtsleeves, the very image of a national leader stripped for action. Bill Robbins began taking his snaps.

'No bright lights or rubber truncheons, Prime Minister,' said Jack, switching on his tape recorder. 'I thought we'd start with one or two questions about the leadership contest, then move on to policy matters. If that's agreeable.'

Phil Norris interrupted. 'Just so long as it *is* a few questions, Jack. Remember the ground rules.'

'You see, I do have rather more important things on my mind

than these little local difficulties,' said the Prime Minister, giving his well-known impression of the world statesman.

'Absolutely,' agreed Jack. And I'm the rightful King of Ruritania. He smiled. 'What do you make of Mr Gulliver's latest announcement?'

'Which announcement are you thinking of?' Poultney raised a quizzical eyebrow. 'He seems to come out with so many.'

If Willow hadn't been sitting there with her sycophant's smirk, Jack might have raised an eyebrow of his own, just to show he wasn't in the mood to be fucked about. 'I was thinking of the story in this morning's papers,' he said patiently.

'Oh, that.' Poultney made a dismissive gesture. 'What should I say? Nothing to get especially excited about, I would have thought.'

'Seems to have made quite an impact,' Jack plodded on.

'I'll say one thing for you chaps. You're easily impressed.' He turned to Prudence. 'I thought the *Despatch* played it about right, if I may say so. Good judgement.'

Jack tried not to squirm while Willow did a bit more simpering. In fact she'd thrown the story away in a few grudging paragraphs on page four. Barmy. George Gulliver's statement that none of his supporters should expect an automatic reward in the event of victory was easily the liveliest development so far in an otherwise dull campaign. Wee Jimmy Farquhar, clearly under the impression that George's warning was aimed specifically at him, was running round telling anyone who'd listen that he'd never been so insulted in his life. 'Then it's time you were,' an unsympathetic colleague had snapped, to the delight of eavesdropping journalists. Peter Coleman was almost as distraught, buttonholing friends to see if they thought George's words applied to him. 'Course not, Peter,' everyone had answered, straight-faced. Uproarious stuff. Jack wondered whether the stunt might not win George more votes than it lost. Presumably Poultney wondered too.

Jack thought it was time to impress Willow with a display of political reliability. 'Frankly, I thought the *Telegraph* went a bit over the top this morning,' he said, pulling the paper from his briefcase and beginning to read. 'Mr Gulliver's démarche last night was as courageous as it was principled. Talent should be the only badge of admission to the Cabinet.' Jack did a bit of head-shaking to show what he thought of such nonsense. 'Huh,' he added for good measure.

The Prime Minister put his hands together in what could have been mistaken for an attitude of prayer. 'Frankly I hope anyone who aspires to sit in this office would take the same line as Mr Gulliver,' he began ponderously. 'There's no room in government for political payoffs or Buggins' turn. Any prime minister has a solemn duty to appoint ministers on the basis of ability.'

Jack couldn't help but admire the man's heroic disregard for the truth. 'Just another of Mr Gulliver's stunts,' he agreed, catching the smile of approval that spread over Willow's face.

On the Prime Minister's desk a phone buzzed. Phil Norris scuttled across the room to answer it.

'What about the campaign, then?' Jack asked, ignoring the interruption. 'Still on target to win?

'The Prime Minister's in a meeting,' muttered Norris.

'As you know, Alan Matthews is handling all that.' Poultney was sitting up straight now, frowning at his press secretary. 'I think you can say we're pretty confident . . .' His mind was clearly on other things.

'I see,' said Norris. 'Yes . . . If you'll just hold on.' He gestured across the room, waggling the phone in the air. 'Prime Minister?'

Jack rose. 'Should we . . . ?'

Norris looked grateful. 'If you wouldn't mind, Jack. Prudence.'

'Sorry about this,' said Poultney, taking the phone. 'Hallo?' he barked into the receiver.

Jack helped Bill Robbins gather up his equipment and they tiptoed out, followed by a reluctant Willow. 'What's going on?' she muttered as soon as the door closed behind them.

'Trouble,' said Jack. 'Something's up.' He leaned forward to murmur in her ear. 'Obviously serious. They'd never have interrupted an interview with you if it wasn't.'

Willow nodded, mollified. 'I think you're right,' she said.

They stood unspeaking for a minute or two, until Phil Norris emerged from the Prime Minister's study. He wasn't sporting a smile now.

He thrust a small tape recorder into Jack's hands. 'You left it in there,' he said. 'Still running.'

'Whoops!' said Jack, in a parody of innocence. 'Sorry, Phil. Accidental.'

'Sure, sure.' Phil's attention was obviously elsewhere. 'Look, I'm afraid we've got to scrub the interview. Perhaps we can reschedule it later on. OK?' He clearly didn't care whether it was OK or not.

'Can you tell us what's happening?' Willow demanded imperiously.

Phil Norris looked as though he was going to snap at her, then thought better of it. 'I suppose you'll know soon enough anyway,' he answered. 'We've just had some terrible news. From Sahelia.'

O tempora! And while we're about it, *O mores!* These are desperate days, no error.

Fat Germans run our world now. Non-smoking Americans and industrious Japanese are masters of our universe. Before we know it, planeloads of rich Chinamen will descend on us to jabber at Anne Hathaway's cottage or the Tower of London and we'll compete to sell them the traditional products of our native genius: pizza slices and Neapolitan ice cream, Big Macs and plastic representations of Hampton Court.

Never mind. We can still put on one hell of a show. Thatched cottages. Warm beer. Orderly queues. If they had a quaintness contest at the Olympics, we'd win the gold medal every time.

At 2.30 p.m. on each working parliamentary day, policemen snap to attention, helmets off. Badge Messengers, old servicemen all, stiffen the spine. Tourists fall silent, hushing their children. It's the proper thing to do. Mr Speaker's procession to the Chair is one of the few remaining glories of our land. Once, so it's said, an incautious backbencher chose this very moment to greet an old acquaintance. 'Neil!' he enthused. Whereupon a pair of American visitors humbly genuflected. Quite right too. We could do with more of it.

Here's the mace-bearer pacing in majestic tread, not looking the least bit silly in his black breeches and buckled shoes. Here's Mr Speaker himself, in full-bottomed wig and gown of black and gold, the traditions of centuries on his shoulders. Here's his train-bearer, solemn as a monk. This isn't the moment to chew gum or chatter, far less to point or take photographs. This is a glimpse of living history and it's little wonder if visitors sometimes feel a compulsion to grovel. This isn't any old politician we're watching. He may once have been known as Ray Tobin, the pigeon-fancying Labour Member for Sheffield Attercliffe; now he's become Mr Speaker Tobin, holder of an office that goes back to Thomas Hungerford, 1377, and we'd better not forget it. A cell underneath the clock tower awaits anyone reckless enough to affront his dignity.

Fortunately this Speaker, like many of his most distinguished predecessors, has neither eyes to see nor ears to hear, save as the House of Commons directs him.

'You little cockroach!' snarled George Gulliver, his words clearly audible in the Members' Lobby.

Credit where credit's due. Mr Speaker's step never faltered. Not the slightest tremor disturbed his features. He processed gravely through the lobby, through the double doors into the Chamber and out of sight. Only then did the policemen and Badge Messengers unbend, casting sly looks at each other and at the doorway of the Government Whip's Office in the corner. A couple of Labour MPs drifted casually in that direction, ears flapping.

But by now George had his temper more or less under control. Perhaps he understood that shouting at the Chief Whip wasn't getting him anywhere. He followed Alan Matthews through to the inner sanctum and relative privacy. 'Shouldn't have blown my top,' he muttered, taking a seat without being asked. It was as much of an apology as he could manage. 'Not the thing to do.'

'Certainly not when there's an audience just a few yards away,' said Matthews icily. 'You may not think discretion's worth bothering about, but I rather do. They probably heard that little outburst in the Chamber.'

And that's one of the most basic lessons in politics, thought George. Never lose your rag. 'Your behaviour's been somewhat provocative,' he grunted. 'More than somewhat.' It was, he recognised, a pretty feeble counterattack.

Matthews managed a plausible impression of astonishment, raising both eyebrows in conjunction with a spot of head-shaking. 'Really?' he drawled. 'Frankly I would have expected you to be grateful. What I did was for the protection of the party. And for your protection too, incidentally.'

'I suppose you'd like me to thank you.' George knew perfectly well he was being outmanoeuvred. 'You've ruined a woman's career. For no good reason.' This is all a huge mistake, he told himself. Crazy. Why don't I just get up and leave, right now? He sat on, miserable.

'For no good reason,' Matthews repeated slowly. He allowed the words to hang in the air for a bit. 'Do you really need me to spell it out?'

Well, no. George thought he could do without the Chief Whip's reasons, thank you very much. 'We both know why you did it,' he snapped, game to the last. 'To embarrass me, that's why.'

Matthews curled his lip in a show of disdain. 'I'm beginning to think you're beyond embarrassment. Beyond common sense, come to that. It may interest you to know that I've just been speaking to the party chairman. Quite a scene you made, apparently.'

'At least I discovered who's behind all this pettiness.'

'Damn you, George!' Matthews slammed a hand down on his desk. 'I've just about had enough. I don't care who you sleep with. But I do care if there's the slightest suggestion of a security risk. I care when all your little assignations are logged in the police overtime book. Public money, remember? And I bloody well care when the press start sniffing around. I'm not having it in an election year, old cock. That's it.' He leapt to his feet, scowling. All good chief whips know how to make an impact.

George didn't move. 'And I've told you my relationship with

Miss Holroyd is over,' he said, reasonably enough. 'Finished. I don't see her any more. There's no reason to push her out. She's not to blame for anything I'm doing.'

Matthews gave him a look of apparent bafflement. 'You haven't been listening to a bloody word I've said, have you? This was all meant to be an exercise in damage limitation. God alone knows what's going to happen now. After this morning's performance with the chairman, your little fling must be all round Central Office. I swear I don't know what's got into you, George. Have you got a death wish, or what?' He sounded as though he genuinely wanted to know.

George stood, defeated. Matthews was right of course. Running round London to complain at the way Monica had been treated wasn't the most obviously sensible stratagem. Apart from anything else, it carried a frighteningly high risk of exposure.

On the other hand . . .

He could still see the contempt in Rosemary's eyes. She'd cornered him at breakfast, formidable in dressing-gown and furry slippers, her face set. She'd talked of treachery and spite, of a man who could coldly sacrifice both his wife and his mistress in the name of ambition. He'd cowered under her tongue, cringed as she delivered a blow-by-blow account of her meeting with Monica. He'd hardly recognised the hypocrite she described, tried uselessly to protest. Afterwards he'd sat alone at the kitchen table, sick with shame and rage. Knowing he had no moral choice but to undo the damage if he could. Whatever the cost.

'All I'm trying to do is put things right,' he ventured.

But Alan Matthews, who naturally couldn't know the state of George's conscience or the anguish in his soul, was back in his seat, riffling through his papers. He didn't look up. 'So you had to pick today, did you?' His disgust was evident. 'Today of all days.'

'Don't know what you're talking about,' said George, who genuinely didn't.

Matthews could contain his loathing no longer. 'Just fuck off out of my office, will you?' he ordered.

*   *   *

'Private notice question!' bawled Speaker Tobin. 'Mr Paul Barton!'

For once there were no cheers from the Labour side as the Leader of the Opposition got to his feet, no jeers or sneers from the pale muleteers on the Government benches either. Only an anxious silence. With the exception of George Gulliver, sunk in his own misery, the whole House knew what was coming. The lunchtime news bulletins had been full of it.

Barton grasped the despatch box, his face serious. 'I rise to ask the Foreign Secretary a question of which I have given him private notice,' he said quietly. 'Namely if he will make a statement on today's events in Sahelia.'

Up in the Press Gallery, Jack Cartwright leaned forward to study the expression on the Foreign Secretary's face. Usually, old Lucas managed to look cheerfully cherubic whatever the circumstances, famously keeping his cool even when negotiating with the French. There wasn't much of the cherub about him this time, though. His eyes were harsh, his mouth grim.

'Shortly before dawn this morning, Mr Speaker,' Brotherton began, 'our embassy in Sahelia was attacked by a group of armed men whom we presume to be part of the rebellion against the lawful government.

'The terrorists succeeded in breaching the walls of the embassy compound and began what can only be described as a massacre. Nine members of staff were shot and killed. The victims were the First Secretary, the military attaché, four other British officials and three locally-recruited servants.

'Our Ambassador, Mr James Dalton, was seized by the terrorists and taken away apparently unharmed, together with Mrs Caroline Dalton and their fourteen-year-old daughter Jacqueline. We have no information as to their present whereabouts or why they have been kidnapped.' Brotherton paused in the deathly silence and took a sip of water. His hand seemed steady enough.

'Mr Speaker, I have to tell the House that we have virtually no further information on today's tragedy. Government in Sahelia appears totally to have broken down in the last twenty-four hours. The Vizier and most of his officials have abandoned the capital. All attempts by Her Majesty's Government to contact those in authority have so far failed, as have our attempts to get in touch with our embassy itself. We must assume that its communications links have been destroyed. What little information we do have is reaching us from other sources, which in the circumstances, as the House will appreciate, I shall not identify.' The green figures on the electronic clock flicked to 3.36. It was the only movement in the Chamber.

'Our priority now must be to secure the safety of those British citizens still living in Sahelia. The feasibility of an evacuation by air is now being studied as a matter of urgency. In the meantime we repeat our advice that all our people should stay in their homes and await further instructions.' Brotherton was gripping his notes tightly, his knuckles white.

'Mr Speaker, the whole House will wish to join with me in offering our profound sympathy to the relatives and friends of all those who have died . . .' Brotherton paused until the low growl of assent died away. He took another sip of water.

'He's got to give them more than that,' muttered Jack.

'You don't have to worry about Lucas. Just wait,' advised the man from *The Times*.

'Meanwhile I can tell the House that the Cabinet Office emergency committee is already in session,' Brotherton continued. 'Our Rapid Reaction Force has been placed on full alert.' He got a rumble of approval for that one. 'We are of course consulting with our allies and have called an emergency meeting of the Security Council . . .' He faltered at the groan of collective contempt that erupted on the Government benches.

'Send a gunboat!' shouted a Knight of the Shires.

'Sahelia's only a thousand miles from the sea,' observed *The Times*.

'Whatever can be done is being done,' Brotherton ploughed on. 'This outrage cannot—'

Jack felt a touch on his shoulder. 'Excuse me, Mr Cartwright,' murmured the Gallery Badge Messenger. 'Could you ring your office right away?'

'What, now?' Jack was incredulous.

'They said immediately.' The old boy was a decent sort and evidently concerned. 'Sounds like an emergency.'

'. . . All the resources at our command will be deployed,' Brotherton was saying firmly.

Jack left the Foreign Secretary to it, hastening up the Gallery steps to the exit in barely contained fury. To be interrupted in the middle of the year's biggest story was . . . For the moment he was stumped for a word. No doubt a suitable one would occur eventually. Savagely he punched out the numbers on his phone. 'Cartwright,' he barked as the newsdesk came on.

'Thank Christ,' said Jim Finney, the news editor. 'Prudence has gone ape. Where the fuck have you been?'

'Where have I been? Where the fuck have I been?' Jack was incandescent. 'I'll tell you where I've been, matey. I've been covering the story of the year, that's where I've been. Ever heard of Sahelia?'

'Never mind Sahelia. Prudence wants—'

'I know what Prudence wants,' said Jack warmly. 'She wants Sahelia. All over the front page. Don't forget I was with her at Number Ten.' In fact Willow had almost wet herself in the excitement of the slaughter, her eyes lighting up like the jackpot on a fruit machine. 'They've set up COBRA. The Rapid Reaction Force is on standby. Could be the biggest rescue operation since Dunkirk. So I'll get straight back on to it, like a good little reporter, right?'

'Wrong,' said Jim Finney.

Count to ten, Jack told himself. Take a deep breath. There! It feels better already. 'You're joking,' he said after a bit.

Jim Finney stayed silent at the other end.

'Fuck me gently,' muttered Jack.

'So if you're finally ready to listen, I'll get to the point.' Finney dropped his voice to a conspirator's whisper. 'Dave Sweetman's been sacked. Called in just now and ordered to clear his desk. It's really hit the fan, Jack. You'd better watch your back.'

'What are you telling me?' Jack yelped. Never mind Sweetman, D. What about Cartwright, J.? He was reasonably certain he'd done nothing recently to incur Willow's displeasure, though with that bloody woman you could never tell. His hand felt clammy on the receiver.

'Your friend Gulliver.' Finney was speaking urgently, his voice still low. 'Turns out he's got a bit on the side after all. What's more, he doesn't seem to care who knows it. There's been a huge punch-up at Tory Central Office. Ranting and raving because they've given his woman the push. A mega story, Jack. Half Fleet Street's down there already.'

Jack's stomach gave the kind of lurch he'd normally expect when running upstairs and stepping confidently on a tread that wasn't there. 'This is the tale we had weeks ago,' he said stupidly.

'But Dave Sweetman screwed up, didn't he? While we're on the subject, you didn't do too brilliantly, either. Now everybody's got the story and our leader's on the rampage.'

For a long, sick moment, Jack couldn't bring himself to speak. 'I told her the fucking story in the first place,' he managed at last. 'I can't be on the shit-list. Can I?'

Finney sighed. 'What do you think, Jack? You don't need me to draw you a picture.'

No, a picture wasn't necessary. Jack already had just the thing in the downstairs lavatory back home. Edvard Munch. *The Scream*. A morbid print, lines in a demented swirl, staring eyes, mouth gaping in a shriek of despair. Jack only kept it because of his constipation; when he sat straining of a morning it helped remind him that there's always somebody worse off. 'Does she want me back in the office?' he muttered.

'She wants you to find Gulliver. Drop everything else. Just get hold of the bastard and persuade him to talk. He's not at home and he's not in his campaign headquarters, so it's up to you. Forget Sahelia. We'll do that up in the office. Forget everything. All we want is your man.'

'Or else,' said Jack.

'You've got it in one. If anybody can do it you can.' Finney didn't sound especially convinced. 'By the way, what's COBRA?'

'What?'

'COBRA. You mentioned COBRA.'

'It's only the Cabinet Office briefing room, that's all,' said

Jack coldly. 'Where they do the crisis planning. Falklands war. The siege at the Iranian Embassy. Bang, bang. You're dead. They're not fucking about on Sahelia, Jim. Got to be our lead tomorrow.'

'Don't be an arsehole, Jack,' said Finney wearily. 'We both know what our lead's going to be.'

The gardens were bleak in an October chill, murk thickening by the minute. Away to the right, on the other side of iron railings, late-afternoon traffic grudged and growled along Millbank in a glare of lights. Off to the left, the Thames slopped unseen against its restraining wall. George shivered in the shadows. This is how it ends, he thought. Alone and cold on a wooden bench. Nothing left but Rosemary's contempt. A gust of wind flapped his jacket open. He shivered again. He wouldn't button himself up. There was justice of a sort in puckered skin and aching bones. This is how it ends.

He made no move to acknowledge the figure trudging towards him across the grass. Let the man come, if he must. It hardly mattered now. A dead leaf skittered along and lay at George's feet, trembling. He watched it idly as Jack Cartwright sat down beside him. There were no greetings.

'Thought I might find you here,' said Cartwright after a bit. 'You told me once. Remember? Favourite spot.' He huddled deeper in his overcoat. 'Not very nice in this weather though.' He accompanied the words with a mournful shake of the head. 'Suits the mood, eh?'

'Something like that,' muttered George, reluctantly.

'You look frozen,' Cartwright observed. 'Haven't been sitting here all afternoon, have you?'

George didn't answer. The leaf stirred beside his toecap, then tumbled away on the cusp of the wind until it was lost in the gathering dusk.

'You know why I'm here,' Cartwright pressed. 'We need to talk, George.'

'Do we?' For the first time he turned to look Cartwright full in the face.

'You know we do.' Was that a note of sympathy in his voice?

'The story's out, George. Everyone's got hold of it. At least if you . . .' He shrugged. 'I think the real question is why? What made you do it?'

Oh, yes. That was the question, right enough. Sixty-four thousand dollars' worth. George stood abruptly, wincing at the twinge in his knees. 'Let's have a look at the river,' he said, setting off without waiting for an answer. He moved stiffly, his toes numb. It was a relief to lean on the Embankment wall, though the stone was rough and chill. He stared at the dark waters and thought of his confrontation with Rosemary that morning, thought of Monica with her ambitions destroyed. Why shouldn't the truth be told, then? The damage was already done. He felt Cartwright's hand on his shoulder, presumably meant as a gesture of encouragement. The touch of a friend. 'All right, Jack,' he said. 'You'd better tell me what you've got.'

'It's not looking good. I'm sorry, George.' Cartwright's voice was low. 'Everybody knows you made a scene at Central Office this morning. And that you had a go at the Chief Whip.' He reached out and squeezed George's forearm. 'You weren't very discreet about your lady friend, either. Half London heard what you said. You must have known . . .' His voice trailed off.

'I didn't think I had a choice,' said George quietly.

Cartwright took his hand away and shook his head, incredulous. 'In the middle of a leadership contest?'

'Especially in a leadership contest,' snapped George.

Cartwright sighed. 'You wanted to know what we've got,' he said, his voice flat. 'All right. We've got a candidate for Prime Minister causing uproar over a woman who isn't his wife. Jobs for the girls. You needn't think Sahelia's going to knock this one off the front page. It'll be in every paper in the country tomorrow. I don't need to spell it out.'

'No.' George felt curiously calm. 'As a matter of fact I didn't even know about Sahelia until afterwards.'

'So tell me why. Has to be a reason.'

This is what it comes down to, thought George. A question of duty. Tell the truth and shame the Devil. It would be a kind of atonement. 'Get your notebook out,' he said.

*   *   *

'Fuck!' howled Graham Anderson. 'It's the fucking BBC!' He swung round to glare at Monica. 'Don't go near the fucking window,' he ordered.

Monica exhaled a stream of cigarette smoke and concentrated on keeping her panic at bay. 'How many does that make?' Damn. She couldn't keep the quaver out of her voice.

'Enough to clog the fucking pavement.' He darted a swift glance down at the street. 'Three television cameras. Fuck knows how many press photographers. Fucking monkeys.' He began pacing round the room like a caged beast. A baboon, perhaps.

'I suppose it's no use saying I'm sorry.' Monica felt close to tears but wouldn't give way. She took another pull at her cigarette.

Anderson slumped into his chair. 'A bit late now. I think you've been set up. I think we've all been set up.' He avoided her eye. 'Not your fault, lovey. Fucking politicians.'

Monica could bear anything but kindness. She blinked hard. It didn't work. She began rummaging around in her handbag for a tissue.

'Here.' Anderson awkwardly produced a clean handkerchief. 'Have a good cry if you want. I might even join you.'

Monica dabbed her eyes and blew her nose. 'We'll lose the account now, won't we?'

'That's the way it goes.' Anderson tried a smile. It came out as a grimace. 'We got caught in the middle, that's all. My fault as much as yours. Should have seen it coming.'

'You're being so sweet . . .' Monica cringed under the burden of her guilt. She had no doubt at all that her conversation with Rosemary Gulliver was the trigger for George's act of madness. 'There's no possible way it could be your fault,' she added.

'Ah well . . .' Anderson made a little gesture of waving her words aside, managing to look somewhat shifty while he did it. Strange. If she didn't know better, Monica might have thought he had something to hide. Dear, decent Graham. Always at his best in a crisis. She felt a rush of gratitude.

'Yes?' he barked into the phone, which had been ringing virtually non-stop all afternoon. 'I don't give a flying fuck what they say. No comment. Clear? No fucking comment. And make sure that door stays locked and bolted.' He slammed the receiver down. 'Fucking reptiles won't take no for an answer. Reduced the switchboard girls to hysterics.' He scowled malevolently. 'We've got to get you out of here.'

'I could just go and face up to them,' Monica offered, with a confidence she certainly didn't feel.

'That's the last thing you'll do.' Anderson hooked his thumbs decisively in his braces. 'Be like feeding time at the zoo. Not likely. Not fucking likely. This is George Gulliver's mess. Not yours.'

Monica couldn't help herself. She rushed up to Anderson and flung her arms around him. 'You're a nice man,' she blurted, her voice muffled in his chest. 'I never knew how nice.'

'Come on, Monica.' He disengaged gently, the look in his eye unfathomable. 'Let's get you out of here. Back of my car. Cover you up with a blanket, eh? Bastards won't know what's hit them.'

'They'll find out where I live.' Monica couldn't bear the thought of skulking terrified behind her own front door.

Anderson gave her a wink. 'You won't be there though, will you? Think about it. You're the prey. Give those fuckers out there half a chance and they'll tear you to bits. You can't go home. Not today. Not tomorrow. Not till all this has died down. So. Must be somebody you can stay with.'

Monica bit her lip. 'My mother, I suppose. At a pinch.'

'Then I'll take you there. Nobody will know about it but thee and me. All right?'

'All right.' It was hard to keep the tears back. 'I think you're the most chivalrous man I've ever met.'

'A real knight in shining armour,' Anderson muttered.

It was a strange modesty in a man, thought Monica, when a compliment made him look so uncomfortable. Attractive, though. Definitely.

Jack Cartwright couldn't restrain a long sigh of satisfaction. Despite the wind bullying off the Thames, he glowed to the cockles of his reporter's heart. Never mind the unpleasantness in Sahelia. This was the stuff. Sex and power. Villainy in high places and blood on the carpet. 'One hell of a story, George,' he enthused. 'Just one hell of a tale.'

'Glad I could be of service.'

A touch of the old Gulliver asperity there, no error. Never mind. Jack assembled his features into the solemnity appropriate to the moment. 'I think you've done the right thing,' he soothed. 'No, I'm sure of it. A lot of people will respect you for it. A lot.'

George didn't respond. He hunched over the parapet, staring at the river, his face unreadable. Perhaps he was toying with the idea of throwing himself in, though on the whole Jack hoped not. It might spoil his exclusive. 'Come on, George,' he murmured. 'You'll catch your death. Why don't we go and have a drink? Maybe a bite to eat.' He gave the man an encouraging clap on the shoulder. It was essential to keep him away from other journalists, for the next couple of hours at least.

'Poor company at the moment, I'm afraid.' George's voice was hardly audible. 'Go on. Off you go and file your report. I'll be fine.'

In situations like this, thought Jack, the trick is to be kindly but firm. Like an old-fashioned uncle. 'I'm getting you out of the cold,' he said briskly. 'Plenty of time to file once we've got ourselves settled down somewhere. Come on, George. Can't leave you like this.'

'Well . . .' George was shivering quite noticeably now. 'You're a good friend, Jack.'

'I hope so . . .' This was the moment for an apparently embarrassed grin. 'You'd do the same for me, eh? Come on.'

As things turned out, it was surprisingly easy to persuade George out of the gardens and into a passing cab. The poor sod seemed in a daze. Please God don't let him snap out of it. Not until the first edition's gone. 'Head for Bloomsbury,' Jack instructed the cabbie. He turned on the heater, which began blowing warm air noisily into the back. 'You'll feel better when you've got a couple of drinks inside you,' he said encouragingly.

'I'm not sure I'll ever feel better,' muttered George.

Jack performed a few sympathetic nods and began thinking about his story. Former Defence Secretary George Gulliver has sensationally accused the Prime Minister of mounting a dirty-tricks campaign . . . No, no. Pull yourself together, Jack. Tory leadership contender George Gulliver last night confessed to an illicit sexual relationship . . . Better. Much better. Exclusive statement to the *Despatch* . . . sensational allegations of dirty tricks by the Conservative high command . . . I've let everybody down, Mr Gulliver said with startling frankness . . . By the time the cab pulled up, Jack was ready to rock 'n' roll. The most vicious political in-fighting for decades . . . He glanced surreptitiously at his watch 5.30. Still plenty of time to remake the front page.

'Good pub, this,' he said, paying off the driver. 'Nice and quiet. Plus they do a great steak and chips. Just what we need.' He steered George inside and sat him down in a corner. 'I'd say a large whisky is in order.'

'Very large,' said George. At least he'd stopped shivering.

Jack went to the bar and bought a couple of trebles, with beer chasers for good measure. He carried them back to the table, together with a menu. 'Have a think about what you want to eat while I . . .' He gestured in the direction of the payphone.

'You go ahead.' George downed half his whisky at a single gulp. 'And Jack . . . thanks. Thanks for everything.'

After a spot of shrugging and hand-flapping, the traditional response of a good-natured friend, Jack went to the phone. He knew he'd have to be quick. In his present state of the glums, Gulliver was quite capable of wandering off and crying on the first shoulder that presented itself. 'Newsdesk?' he hissed. 'Jim? Listen, mate. You're not going to believe this . . .'

Rosemary cringed on the stairs, hardly daring to look. The shadow was still there. The doorbell rang again and the flap on the letterbox rattled. A note fluttered onto the mat. Through the stained-glass panels she could see the shadow moving at last. Metal-tipped shoes clacked on the front path. He was gone. For the moment anyway.

Keeping close to the wall, determined to betray no sign of

movement to the encircling mob, Rosemary edged forward and snatched up the paper lying there. It was just a scrap, torn from a notebook and folded. Too dark to read the message. She couldn't turn on the light. Sooner or later they'd probably go away. If. Out on the pathway she heard more movement, women's high heels this time. Click, click, click. Rosemary backed away. Why didn't the police stop such people? There was another shadow, slimmer this time. The doorbell rang again, insistent. Rosemary fled upstairs.

Through a chink in the bedroom curtains, she caught a glimpse of a policeman's helmet. Thank God. She leaned cautiously forward for a better view. Her heart sank. Far from moving the reptiles on, the bobby was just standing there, an indulgent grin on his face. Reporters, photographers and television camera crews milled about on the pavement, as though they owned it. Some of them had brought sandwiches. Rosemary shrank back. They must know she was here. Of course they did. She'd answered the telephone, hadn't she? Yes, and she'd been cowering inside ever since, sitting in the dark. Trapped in her own home, unable even to turn on the light.

There was a windowless boxroom right at the top of the house. She went inside, closed the door behind her and found the wall-switch. The note was addressed to Mr George Gulliver/Mrs Rosemary Gulliver. 'Our apologies for the scrum,' it read. 'In the circumstances you will understand why we're here. However if either of you would see us for just a very few minutes, we would undertake to go away and leave you alone.' It was signed by representatives of several newspapers including, she noted with disappointment, the *Guardian*. They're all as swinish as each other, she thought.

Downstairs, in the hallway, the phone began ringing. Rosemary found herself trembling. She'd never wanted this. Nothing like this. George must have known. She didn't understand. Didn't want to understand. He'd destroyed everything, roaring round London on some lunatic quest of his own. Downstairs the phone stopped, but the doorbell rang again. Rosemary sank to the floor, trying hard not to cry. After a while, the effort became much easier. She didn't need tears. All she had to do was think of her husband and how satisfying it would be to smack his selfish face.

After his third large whisky, George began feeling better. His demons had fled, or at any rate made a tactical withdrawal. No more rage. Somewhere in the mess there was probably a purpose, as there might well be purpose in the tapeworm or the ichneumon wasp. After all, he'd done the right thing, hadn't he, as per instructions? Tried to, anyway. Well, then. He managed to summon up a smile as Jack Cartwright returned to the table. 'I'm afraid I've been getting stuck in,' he said, gesturing at the empty glasses lined up before him.

'Sorry I've been so long.' Cartwright didn't look sorry at all. 'We must have the slowest copytakers in the world. Get you another? Or would you rather eat?'

'Not hungry.' George drained his glass. 'Tell you the truth, I feel like getting pleasantly squiffy. It's not every day you throw away the leadership. Deserves a bit of a celebration, don't you think?'

Cartwright gave him an old-fashioned look. 'Can I ask you something?' He leaned closer, dropping his voice. 'This isn't for publication. I just want to know. Tell me what you're up to.'

George frowned. 'You can be an irritating bugger, Jack. I've given you chapter and verse. That's it. A brave effort to save a damsel in distress.' He shrugged. 'Not the cleverest move in the world maybe, but that's the way it goes.'

Cartwright threw his hands up in mock surrender. 'If that's the way you want it.'

'Piss off, Jack. I'm telling you.' George stood up, nettled. 'I need another drink.' He went to the bar and ordered the round. Another large whisky for himself, a pint of bitter for Jack. He carried the drinks back to the table, not entirely steady on his feet. 'Didn't mean to snap,' he apologised. 'There's your answer, really. When I heard about Monica, I just flipped. Lost my temper, like a bloody fool. End of story.'

'How did you hear, exactly?' Cartwright had dropped his conspiratorial tone.

'Not important.' George certainly wasn't going into details of his painful scene with Rosemary. 'These things always get out. You know that.'

'Mm.' Cartwright drank some beer and put his mug down carefully on a cardboard drip-tray. 'Can I tell you what I think? Just between ourselves, I think you know exactly what you're doing. You heard Poultney and his friends were about to put the boot in, so you got your retaliation in first.'

George stared, open-mouthed. But for the glint in Cartwright's eye and the unpleasantness of the circumstances, he might have laughed. 'You're mad,' he managed at last.

'What did you have to lose? The story was going to get out anyway. Now you've muddied the water and made the Prime Minister look a complete shit. I don't think you've thrown away the leadership at all.' Cartwright picked up his beer and raised the mug in a mock toast. 'I'll tell you another thing. You're the hero of Sahelia. The only minister in the Government who wasn't taken in by that gang of camel-fanciers. You can't pretend you haven't thought about it.'

Something was happening to George. Something to do with tapeworms and the principle of purpose in the universe. He felt in the grip of influences beyond his understanding or control; and it didn't help that his head had started to ache. 'You're talking bollocks,' he said.

'This is me you're talking to, George. Remember?' Cartwright looked him straight in the eye. 'It's the only explanation which makes sense. That's my follow-up story tomorrow.' He finished his beer. 'Unless you can persuade me otherwise.'

'I was in a rage. Simple,' George muttered, dragging his eyes away from Jack's.

'Nah. Not you,' said Cartwright confidently. 'I've never known you do anything without a damn good reason. Don't forget, I've been watching you every step of the way. You're a planner.'

'My name's Gulliver. Not Macbeth.' George felt uncomfortable with the way the conversation was going. 'It's not anything like you imagine.'

'So tell me about it.'

George sat silent. It was hard to think in the cheery babble of the pub. Still, what was there to think about? Do the right thing. Just do it. Wasn't there something inherently dishonest in concealing the truth of his spiritual experiences? But still . . . 'This will have to be off the record,' he said.

'Sure.' Cartwright made a little cross on his lapel.

'I'm serious, Jack. Totally off the record. For now, anyway.'

Cartwright's expression changed. He picked up his notebook and made a great show of stowing it away in his briefcase. 'There you go,' he said. He leaned back with his eyes half closed, the traditional pose of the priest in the confessional.

Until the story finished, he hardly moved a muscle. Then he opened his eyes and touched George sympathetically on the arm. 'Thank you for telling me,' he said gently. 'Couldn't have been easy.'

'You're not tempted to send for the men in white coats?'

'There are more things in heaven and earth . . .' Cartwright murmured. 'Have you mentioned this to anyone else?'

'There's a Catholic priest I know. Rosemary, of course. That's all.'

'And?'

George sighed. 'The priest wasn't very impressed, as a matter of fact. Rosemary . . . Well. You know. She's a supportive lady.'

Cartwright's face betrayed nothing but kindly interest. 'But in your own mind you're quite sure . . .?'

'Took a hell of a lot of convincing.' George finished the remains of his fourth whisky. 'Even now . . . Come on, Jack. When something like this happens, of course you think the worst. Only it's real. I can't get away from it. Look: I saw four police cars at the accident. Two of them parked a fair way back. I couldn't possibly have spotted them unless . . .'

'Four,' said Cartwright, looking suitably impressed.

'Oh, yes. I checked afterwards. It was four.' In fact it had long ago occurred to George that he might have glimpsed those flashing lights when the paramedics lifted him into the ambulance; but then it was possible to contrive a rational explanation for anything, given sufficient ingenuity. 'I have to accept that somehow I've glimpsed another form of reality,'

he added firmly. 'Sooner or later I'll have to say so. Go
public.'

'Well.' Cartwright was a picture of doubt. 'You'll have to think
about it pretty carefully. And pick your moment. No talking out
of turn when you get home, eh?'

George was touched by his friend's evident concern. 'Why
should I?'

'You know . . . Under pressure and all that. Bound to be
reporters doorstepping your house.'

George blinked. 'They must know I'm not there.' The penny
dropped at last. 'Rosemary,' he blurted. 'I never thought . . .'
He scrambled to his feet. 'Got to get back.'

A brief shadow of annoyance crossed Cartwright's face. Then
he looked at his watch and his expression relaxed. 'Remember,
George. Don't tell them a thing.' He grinned. 'Apart from
anything else, you've taken a fair bit of drink. Just tell them
no comment. And don't let them get you in front of the TV
cameras, whatever you do.'

George squeezed Cartwright's arm. 'Thanks for everything.
You're a good man, Jack. Don't forget. Off the record. Absolutely.'

'You can trust me, George,' said Cartwright reassuringly. 'It's
what friends are for.'

He heaved a long sigh of satisfaction as George pushed his
way out of the pub. He glanced casually round. Nobody was
paying him the slightest attention. He reached down to his
open briefcase, moved his notebook and switched off the tape
recorder nestling underneath.

The box must have been thrown over the embassy gates
sometime during the night. It lay on the driveway, glittering
in the morning sun. From a distance, it seemed to be an old
biscuit tin. At this angle it was only possible to make out an
'ASS' on the lid. Assorted fancies, maybe. The Second Secretary
really didn't feel like getting any closer.

'What do you think?' whispered the head of the Consular Section. These days every British diplomat left alive in
Sahelia whispered. Perhaps it was a mark of respect for the

victims mouldering in their shallow grave on the embassy lawn.

'We can't just leave it,' said the Second Secretary, his voice equally low.

'Maybe we should send ...' The consul bit his lip and blushed. Her Britannic Majesty's representatives abroad pride themselves on leading by example. None of the junior staff could honourably be asked to risk their lives; and the military attaché, who might well have known all about bombs and booby traps, was lying two feet under the lawn.

'I'll have to go,' said the Second Secretary.

'Are you sure?' The consul was quite unable to keep the relief out of his voice.

The Second Secretary didn't answer. He picked up one of the gardener's long-handled hoes. The man who usually wielded it was dead too, lying in the earth with the military attaché and all the others. The Second Secretary couldn't bear to think about it. He tiptoed gingerly down the path towards the box. Yes. Assorted fancies. He held the hoe at arm's length, with the blade beside the box. A tentative push. The box moved easily. The Second Secretary swallowed hard. Surely that must mean no explosives? And if the thing had been hurled over the gate it couldn't be too sensitive. He gave the box another push. No resistance at all.

He glanced round. Consular Affairs had been joined by a couple of junior staffers. He waved them further back, feeling like a bloody fool. If you can keep your head when all about you are losing theirs ... you might stay alive, my son. He tiptoed up to the box and listened. No ticking. That was a good sign, wasn't it? Perhaps not. Perhaps it was when the ticking stopped that you should start worrying. He put his hand on the lid and gave a cautious jiggle. The thing felt empty. Almost. There was something inside. Not heavy. Breathing hard, he put his fingers under the rim of the lid and tugged. It came away. Suddenly. He reeled back in anticipation of ... Thank God. Nothing. Inside, there seemed to be some papers. He found a twig and prodded them. Again nothing. Just papers. He reached inside and pulled them out.

The ear was lying underneath. He saw at once that it was small and delicate. Unpierced. It had been hacked off the left side of the head. Her head. He had a vision of the ambassador's daughter, smiling and pretty and fourteen years old. Her name was Jacqueline and she wore a brace on her teeth. Then he was on his knees, retching and heaving his heart out, sobbing on the harsh Sahelian earth.

CHAPTER

13

'Shit!' snarled the new deputy editor of the *Daily Despatch* (twenty thousand a year extra, plus a personal secretary, an office with a rubber plant and a company car). The place was a fucking madhouse. Out of control. Still twenty minutes to go and the crush was already beyond bearing. It was hard to breathe. Impossible to move. Something jabbed against his back, but he couldn't turn to find out what. Grunting and pushing, sweating and swearing, the mob was turning the Committee Room Corridor into a fair approximation of the Black Hole of Calcutta. There was no chance of wriggling forward, to where the action would be. If he wasn't such a consummate professional, he might be tempted to bugger off to the bar.

But Jack Cartwright was morally incapable of buggering off anywhere. Out of the question. Never mind trodden toes, the smell of bodies, stale aftershave or the possibility – no, the likelihood – of being trampled. This was a moment of history. One for the memoirs. Besides, there was just the hint of a space by the wall. The recess of a window. The human frame can endure all kinds of contortion, if needs be. It was a matter of squirming in somehow. Anyhow. Jack twisted and shuffled side-ways, elbowing a photographer, ignoring the protest. Monkeys shouldn't be here anyway. This is the House of Commons, not the bloody Oscar ceremonies. No photography allowed. Pity the Serjeant-at-Arms doesn't enforce the rules. Place is going to the dogs.

Feeling somewhat more comfortable now he'd staked a territorial claim, Jack craned to see what was going on. Somewhere up ahead there was a disturbance in the crowd. As far as he could make out, some twerp was trying to push through. And getting nowhere, by the sound of it. He thought he recognised the raised voice of Jimmy Farquhar, MP. One of the silliest sods in Christendom. He caught a brief glimpse of a red and angry face bawling something about being impeded in his parliamentary duties. Arsehole. There was another flurry. Could Farquhar have thrown a punch? Difficult to be sure. There was a fair bit of yelling. Fists seemed to be clenched. Jack stood on tiptoe. There was always a chance this might turn out to be one of those knock-down, drag-out donnybrooks which so distinguish Parliamentary proceedings in places like Australia . . .

No, he could relax. There was a very large policeman, ploughing through like one of those nuclear-powered ice-breakers. Calming things down. Apologies all round, no doubt. An unfortunate misunderstanding. Pressures of the moment.

Jack leaned against the wall while the mob grumbled itself into some kind of order. Despite the regrettable absence of fisticuffs and the indignity of rucking with riffraff who didn't have a rubber plant or a personal secretary between them, he felt immensely pleased with himself. This maul was mostly his doing, after all; there could never have been such a media frenzy but for his interview with George Gulliver. Never. It set the leadership campaign off like a rocket. Whoosh! Light the blue touchpaper and retire sharpish. By universal consent he'd ignited the most impassioned debate on national morality in living memory. This wasn't a mere election any longer. It was a test of the British character. A penitent adulterer. Dirty work in high places. A wife betrayed. A mistress cruelly punished. Something for everyone, in fact. The *Sun* editorial that morning just about summed it up: 'The choice facing the Tory party today is between a cheating rat and a vindictive prat. It's almost enough to make us want to vote Labour.'

Well done, Jack. King of the Castle. Cock of the walk. No promotion could be more richly deserved. As soon as the leadership contest was over ... But there was something to savour in the delay, too. The gritted congratulations of rivals were almost as enjoyable as sex. Forced smiles and surreptitious glares, he loved them all. Popularity, in his opinion, was the mark of failure, the consolation claimed by obituarists and cycling correspondents. He took the envy and professional hatred of colleagues as a genuine if unintended compliment; they'd been well and truly shafted and resented it, poor dears. Jack wondered how they'd feel if they had the slightest inkling of the tape now locked securely in Prudence Willow's safe. Suicidal, probably. It was the tale that would hammer them all into the ground. The yarn of the decade. It was only a matter of timing now. Waiting. Gambling that George Gulliver would survive the first ballot. Pouncing when he seemed unstoppable.

If Jack had been a praying man, he might have appended a 'Please God' at this stage; but of course he didn't believe in God. Instead he stood on tiptoe again. There seemed to be a renewed buzz of anticipation in the air. The result couldn't be far away now. If he stretched, he could just see the door to Room 14, where the votes were being counted. For once, nobody had much of a clue as to the outcome. In all the uproar, few Conservative MPs had the stomach to declare openly for either the rat or the prat. Well, further speculation was pointless. At 6.30, on the dot, the chairman of the 1922 Committee would read the result to the assembled MPs. Afterwards he'd do it all over again for the slavering journalists. That was the theory anyway; but Jack was intent on the door. The moment it started to open, what civilised restraints still existed in the corridor would certainly break down. More than four hundred excited politicians would be fighting to get out while aggressive platoons of reporters, political editors, sketch-writers, broadcasters, pundits and hangers-on thundered down on them like

Cossacks in a pogrom. This was News. Capital N. Nature in the raw. Stoats and rabbits. Grab the first bastard who shows his face. Get the figures. Rush to the nearest phone. Who's going to be first on the airwaves, first on the wires?

Jack tensed. It was just on 6.30. Any second now . . . There! The first reaction. Muffled at this distance, but enough for a first impression. Half a cheer. Half a groan. Half a sigh. These things are quite possible in politics. The mob began heaving forward at the sound. Jack braced himself against the wall. His heart was racing. On the evidence so far, it seemed his gamble might come off.

They sent Sam Ruddock out first. Alan Matthews was just behind him. Impossible to read the expressions on their faces. Policemen were straining to clear a way for them. There was too much shouting and shoving for comfort. Flashbulbs popped. Ruddock and Matthews barged ahead, unspeaking. Ignoring each other. Ignoring the mob too, as well as they could. It was only to be expected: their job was to carry word of the result to their respective masters. They clearly didn't want to hang around. It didn't matter. Other politicians were venturing into the maelstrom. There was a fearsome scrimmage round the door, a babble of questions, notebooks and microphones waving in the air. From Jack's position it was hard to catch any answers.

The result was out though. He spotted the man from the Press Association, struggling back through the confusion. He was clutching a portable phone, stabbing the numbers as he moved until he found space at last. Room to think. He was shouting to make himself heard. Urgent snap, Jack heard him bawl. A burst of noise from Committee Room 14 almost drowned his voice. Jack pressed closer. The PA reporter was shouting figures into his mouthpiece. It was difficult to hear. Fortunately the figures were repeated, more clearly this time. Jack scribbled them down. It took a long moment before he grasped their meaning. Then he breathed a long sigh of relief.

Sam Ruddock burst in, not bothering to knock. One look at his face was enough. George's stomach turned over. His mouth was dry.

'It's all right, George,' said Sam. 'I told you it would be all right. Told you.' He was almost dancing with excitement. 'Read. Enjoy.' He slapped a sheet of paper down on the desk.

George swallowed hard and ran his eye down the figures:

> Michael Poultney 216
> George Gulliver 159
> Abstentions 28

For a moment he couldn't speak. First prize in the National Lottery. Or very nearly. By the merest whisker. He swallowed, willing himself to calm down. The numbers blurred. He blinked. What, tears? 'I never really expected . . .' His voice seemed to be coming from someone else. From a far distance.

'Congratulations, George.' Sam was exultant. 'You've done for him.' He began walking back and forth. Expansive. Gesturing. He was talking about second ballots and the chances of another contender entering the fight. George tried to concentrate. This was vindication, wasn't it? The Prime Minister was finished, Sam was saying. Mortally wounded. He might have achieved an absolute majority. But he'd failed to beat George by the magic margin: fifteen per cent.

'He'll fight it out to the bitter end!' George was nearly back in control. 'Whatever else Poultney might be, he's not a quitter.'

'Forget it.' Sam wouldn't allow anything to spoil the moment. 'Margaret Thatcher wasn't a quitter either. Didn't make a ha'porth of difference. She had to go. Fifty-two votes more than Heseltine in the first ballot, but it wasn't enough. She needed fifty-six.' He grinned. 'Nearly broke my heart at the time. Four lousy votes. Crazy system we've got, George. Except when it works in your favour.' He flopped on a chair, beaming.

'I owe you a lot, Sam. After all that's happened . . .' He made a face, embarrassed. They'd almost come to blows over the interview with Jack Cartwright.

'Nah. I got it wrong. Best thing you could have done, as it turns out.' Sam held up his hands in mock surrender. 'Got to hand it to you, matey. Hell of a risk, mind. Still, it'll be a long time before Alan Matthews pulls another of his little stunts.'

George tried to smile. Not for the first time, he wondered how Sam would react if he learned the truth. With pity, probably. Would you stand by me anyway, Sam? George couldn't pursue the thought. He watched Sam's mouth opening and closing as he talked of press conferences and policy statements and the need to do another canvass. How best to exploit the Poultney victory, which wasn't a victory at all. Essential planning. George heard every word without really listening. He couldn't help thinking of an icon in Sergiyev Posad and the weight of endless dark. Glimpses of Paradise, visions of Hell. He shivered.

'You all right?' Sam was looking curiously at him.

George pulled himself together. 'Probably need a few minutes on my own. Come to terms with it.' There's no clear purpose, he thought. No obvious direction or end. Only there must be. Somewhere.

'Don't be too long.' Sam got obligingly to his feet. 'I should think the entire Press Gallery is screaming for you by now.'

George sat on, alone. The phone on his desk rang and rang. He picked up the handpiece and cut the connection. Soon he'd have to face the world. Not yet though. Not quite yet. Sam's scrawled figures stared up at him: 216; 159; 28. At least that message was plain enough. A Prime Minister who failed to crush his opponent in the first round needn't expect a second chance. There was blood in the water, gobbets of flesh. The sharks would be circling already.

George stirred, uneasy. Others were paying a price too. Rosemary was gone, leaving nothing in the house but old clothes and a hurt silence. Monica was humiliated, her career in tatters. The reputation of Alan Matthews would never recover. Even Wendy Hilliard had been abandoned in the end to her despairing grave. Were they all ciphers then, in some greater scheme?

Enough. George stood abruptly. He strode to the wall mirror. Adjusted his tie. Brushed his hair. He needed to look presentable for the cameras. A Prime-Minister-in-waiting. This was no time for doubts.

He replaced the telephone handpiece on its cradle. It began ringing immediately. This time he answered. He was ready now.

'We ought to meet,' said the familiar voice at the other end. There were no preliminaries.

George concentrated on sounding matter-of-fact. It would be unforgivable to gloat. 'I'm at your disposal, Prime Minister,' he said carefully. 'Only you'll appreciate it's a bit difficult just at the moment.'

'I think in your own interests it ought to be sooner rather than later.'

'Really?' George tried not to let his interest show. 'Are you proposing to stand down?'

'I intend to fight and I expect to win.' The man was a professional, all right. He sounded much more confident than circumstances warranted.

'Then I'm not sure there's anything to talk about. Still . . .' George didn't want to appear graceless. 'I could see you tomorrow, if you like.'

'Tonight would be better.' For a man who'd just been kicked in the teeth by his own followers, Poultney seemed remarkably chipper. 'It's important, George.'

'Oh, yes?' said George, intrigued in spite of himself.

'Can we say eleven o'clock then? In my office here? I can promise you we'll be quite alone. And George – I think it would be best if you didn't mention this to anybody. You'll understand when we meet.' He rang off without another word.

'And goodbye to you, Prime Minister,' George muttered into the dead mouthpiece. He slammed the receiver down and wished he hadn't. There's something fishy here, he thought. Something not quite right. Sam Ruddock returned a minute later to find him still standing there, a look of uncertainty in his eye, like a sleepwalker who wakes to an unfamiliar place.

'There he goes again,' announced Mrs Laura Holroyd, in the voice she might use to describe an infestation of garden slugs.

Monica set the tray carefully down on the occasional table.

One mug of cocoa. One cup of tea. Two McVitie's digestive biscuits on a small china plate. On the television in the corner, George was saying how grateful he was to all his supporters and how he hoped they'd redouble their efforts now that victory was within grasp. She settled down unspeaking and began sipping her tea.

'Pleased with himself, isn't he?' said Mrs Holroyd remorselessly.

'Mm,' Monica agreed. The last thing she felt like at the moment was another dissection of George's personality, appearance, political prospects or moral turpitude. In fact she thought he seemed rather subdued. Surprisingly so, all things considered.

'I suppose he thinks he's got away with it.' Her mother was not easily deflected. 'Just listen to him.'

'Mm,' said Monica again. On screen George was acknowledging that, yes, his personal circumstances did sit somewhat uneasily with his appeal for higher standards in government but he hoped his failings would not invalidate his message. We all do things we bitterly regret. Only it's necessary to learn from them. The point is to keep trying.

'Humph!' sniffed Mrs Holroyd.

'Mm,' said Monica, trying to concentrate. There was something in George's demeanour that she couldn't quite pin down, though her mother's sighs and fidgets made it difficult to concentrate. He was adumbrating something about new beginnings, his words all but drowned by the rattle of cup on saucer.

Monica gave in. 'Why don't you turn it off, Mother, if it's upsetting you?'

Mrs Holroyd put down her drink and her biscuit and reached for the remote control. 'It takes more than that man to upset me,' she said. 'But if that's what you want . . .' She began fiddling with the buttons and the programme changed, cutting George off in mid-sentence. Clint Eastwood's face scowled from the screen. 'I always watch News at Ten though,' she added.

'Leave it on then, if that's what you want. I'm quite happy.' It was an effort not to let her irritation show. Mr Eastwood seemed to be involved in an altercation with a gang of roughnecks who'd made the mistake of being rude about his mule and if Monica was any judge there would certainly be gunplay before anyone was very much older.

'There's too much violence nowadays,' observed Mrs Holroyd placidly, as Clint explained to the unshaven baddies that his mule was a sensitive creature who wouldn't be happy without an apology. 'Sex. Bad language. I can hardly bear it sometimes. These young actresses. They just flaunt it. Then they wonder why standards are slipping.' She watched intently as the bullets began flying and half a dozen ill-mannered oafs paid the supreme penalty for their lack of courtesy towards mules. The slaughter seemed to meet with her approval. 'I just don't want you upset any more, dear. That's all.'

Monica snatched up the zapper and changed back to *News at Ten*. 'So that's Mr Gulliver in confident mood,' beamed the announcer. 'Meanwhile in the Prime Minister's camp there's a determination to fight on, in spite of tonight's disappointment. For the latest on that we go over to our Westminster studio.'

'I'm not upset,' said Monica. 'I've got over it now.' These days she could watch George perform without a twinge of regret for what might have been. Or only a small twinge. She reached across to squeeze her mother's hand. 'Really. All this will be over in a day or two. Soon as the election's settled. Then I'll be back at work. Off your hands.' It would, she thought guiltily, be a relief to get away from the cottage and her mother's unrelenting supportiveness.

'He seems a nice man,' said Mrs Holroyd, going off on one of her tangents. 'Your Mr Anderson. Not like some I could mention.' She did a little more humphing. 'At least he isn't married.'

'Mother . . .' Monica withdrew her hand, exasperated.

'I only said he seems a nice man.' Mrs Holroyd seemed hurt.

'Will you stop jumping to conclusions? He's my boss, that's all.'

'Rings you every day though, doesn't he?' Mrs Holroyd finished the last of her digestives. 'Won't tell anybody where you are. Anyone could see he's concerned. Your tea's getting cold, dear.'

'All right. He's a friend. He's been very good.' Monica could see she wasn't getting through. 'I've worked with him for years. We're just colleagues, that's all.'

'If you say so, dear,' said Mrs Holroyd placidly. 'None of my business anyway.'

'He wants me back because I'm so good at my job,' said Monica firmly. 'That's all there is to it.' But, as she picked up her magazine and pretended to read, she couldn't deny a flutter of anticipation at what the future might hold.

Big Ben was chiming a quarter past the hour as the taxi dropped him outside Old Palace Yard. He paid off the driver beneath the raised sword and resolute gaze of Richard I, a monarch forever prancing towards destiny. You may have been an old shyster, Your Majesty. thought George, and a bit of a bugger too, by all accounts. But you dreamed dreams.

He walked into the Palace of Westminster through Chancellor's Gate, acknowledging the policeman on duty with a wave. At this time of night, the Lords end of the building was deserted, its alleys and inner courts sunk in shadow, its walls pressing in, tons upon tons of glowering stone. In the silence his footsteps rang out and he made an effort to tread more softly. Like a conspirator. It seemed appropriate. Wasn't this passage into the House of Commons known as the Guy Fawkes route? Now there was another dreamer, only this time unrewarded with memorials in bronze, this time cursed by his countrymen, his name reviled for centuries. Poor, brave, barmy Fawkes, racked to pieces *per gradus ad ima* in revenge for the Gunpowder Plot, hanged until his face blackened and his eyes popped, cut down at the last gasp to have his balls torn off and his belly ripped, glistening entrails burned before his dying eyes, every torment lip-smackingly detailed in the Latin of the law. *Quod interiora sua extra ventrem suum capiantur ipsoque vivente comburentur* . . . On his scaffold the silly sod begged forgiveness of his slobbering king, his voice faint and unheard by the shrieking mob. George shivered. So perish all traitors, eh? Still, the man had been driven by a vision. had he not? A vision of sorts, anyway. Just suppose he'd succeeded. These days George tended to do rather a lot of supposing.

He pushed into the building through a side door. Here the lights were blazing; central heating overpowered his chill. His morbid musings evaporated as rapidly as they'd arisen. After a minute or two in the gentlemen's lavatory spent pulling himself together, focusing his mind on the business at hand, he made his way up to the Prime Minister's room behind the Commons chamber, passing nobody on the way but a solitary parliamentary official trudging along on some late errand of his own.

Michael Poultney, unusually, was alone and in shirtsleeves, his tie loosened. There was a bottle of Tobermory malt on his desk and a couple of glasses. He gestured George into an armchair and poured two large measures. 'Splash of water, if I remember,' he said.

'Fine.' George took his glass and raised it in a sort of salute. He thought the Prime Minister was for once showing the strain. There were definite bags under his eyes, a tiredness in his posture. In fact, the man looked a bit of a wreck. Well, perhaps it wasn't so surprising. 'Cheers,' he said, taking a sip. Ready for anything.

Poultney emptied half his own glass in a long gulp. The drink seemed to revive him. 'I should apologise for the hour,' he began, presumably in oblique rebuke for George's tardiness.

'Not at all.' George felt comfortably in control. 'Sorry I couldn't get here earlier. You can imagine what it's been like.'

'Oh, yes. I'm sure you've been busy.' What was remarkable about Poultney's tone was the complete absence of sarcasm, as though he simply couldn't be bothered. As though he had weightier things on his mind. Odd.

George put down his drink. 'As you pointed out, it's rather late, Prime Minister,' he said briskly, taking the initiative. 'Perhaps we'd better get on with it.'

A cold glint entered Poultney's eye. 'I'll give it to you straight, then,' he said. 'I'm asking you to withdraw, George. Preferably within the next twenty-four hours.' He held up a hand to forestall any interruption. 'There is a reason.' For a long moment, he sat in silence. Outside, a police siren hee-hawed around Parliament Square. At last he sighed. 'What I'm about to tell you is on Privy Council terms,' he went on. 'Not a word to anyone outside this room. For the next few hours at least.'

'I haven't forgotten the terms of the Privy Council Oath.' George was irritated at the man for labouring the point. But curious too.

'Of course.' Poultney was staring into his whisky as though some fabulous monster swam in its depths. 'I chaired a meeting of the Emergency Committee this afternoon,' he said quietly.

'COBRA?' George sat up. This wasn't what he'd expected. Not Sahelia. Not tonight.

'It's a nightmare,' Poultney was intense. 'An absolute bloody nightmare.' He drained his glass in a single swallow. 'I'll be making the announcement to the House tomorrow. We've ordered the Spearhead Battalion in. Two Para.' He glanced at his wristwatch. 'As of this moment, they're on their way.'

George stared, open-mouthed. Old Lucas Brotherton at the Foreign Office must have worked wonders, securing permission to overfly Egypt, Libya and Chad. No, more than wonders. Miracles.

'Orders are to seize the airport and hold it for forty-eight hours. Got to get our people out. Imperative.' The Prime Minister was clenching the glass. 'So. You can see. This isn't a time for distractions, George.'

'Hercules transports from Cyprus, I suppose.' George calculated the difficulties, ignoring the implications of Poultney's last remark. 'Extreme range though, even with mid-air refuelling. A hell of a risk if there's any local opposition.'

'There's a special forces unit already on the ground. Sneaked them in yesterday. It's feasible. Just about.'

George didn't much care for any of this. Could the Prime Minister be wrapping himself in the flag for purposes of his own? He stared suspiciously. 'You'd better tell me the rest of it.'

Poultney sighed again, a long exhalation that left no doubt that something was seriously wrong. 'It's bad. Worse than bad. We re-established contact with the embassy last night.

They've had a delivery. From the kidnappers. They cut off her ear, George. The ambassador's daughter. Cut it off and sent it to us.'

George sat frozen in shock. The Prime Minister was saying something about a biscuit tin, but he hardly heard. He was thinking of a pretty little girl with blonde hair. Her name was Jacqueline and she giggled rather a lot. He forced himself to concentrate.

'They're threatening to kill all of them,' Poultney was saying. 'The ambassador and his entire family.'

A wave of black rage swept through George. He breathed deep, waiting for the moment to pass. Emotion at such a time was only self-indulgence. 'What do the bastards want?'

'What *don't* they want?' snarled Poultney. 'Money. Arms. Recognition. Face-to-face negotiations. With a senior representative of the Government, if you please.'

'Otherwise . . . ?'

'Otherwise they'll not only kill the hostages but attack other British residents. They want our reply by six p.m. London time tomorrow.'

'Eighteen hours,' George whispered.

'Eighteen and a half.'

'Then for God's sake, man! Say yes. Stall them. String them along.' George was leaning forward now, glaring at the Prime Minister.

'They'll know our answer as soon as the troops start landing,' snapped Poultney, glowering right back. 'We can't negotiate with terrorists. You know that.'

'Look, Prime Minister.' George subsided, doing his best to keep his temper in check. 'I support your decision to send the paras in. We've no other choice. I'll say so publicly. Back you to the hilt. Only we've got to buy time.' He realised he was nearly shouting. 'For the sake of the little girl, at least,' he added, more quietly.

Poultney sagged. 'She's dead, George. They're all dead. As good as.'

'How can you know?' But of course George understood the pointlessness of the question. The Prime Minister was taking the realistic view, the only view consistent with national policy. No negotiations with terrorists. No risking of further lives. The ambassador and his wife and a girl with a brace on her teeth had to be abandoned. For the general good. For the good of the State.

'We haven't got the faintest idea where they're being held.' The Prime Minister was clearly trying to be patient. Perhaps he was rehearsing the announcement he'd be making to the Commons. 'We're not even sure who the kidnappers are. So.' He shrugged wearily. 'Since they've started cutting up the girl, we have to assume the worst. They're dead. Or they soon will be.'

'No question of a rescue operation?' muttered George.

The Prime Minister's silence was answer enough. 'The Emergency Committee took the view that we should concentrate on the evacuation,' he said at last. 'We can't keep our troops in for more than a day or two and we'll have to pull the SAS out with everyone else. We're certainly not leaving anyone behind to start negotiations. It would be an open invitation to another kidnapping.'

Yes. That was the right and sensible answer. There are times when no moral choice is possible. One must act from necessity. 'You have my full support, Prime Minister,' George announced formally. 'I'll do whatever I can to assist.'

'Will you, George?' asked Poultney softly. 'Will you really?'

'I hope my patriotism isn't in doubt.' George had to make a special effort to stay calm. The Prime Minister, after all, was under considerable strain.

'This is a moment of national crisis,' Poultney murmured. 'In the circumstances, I really think—'

'You think I should withdraw.' George completed the appeal. 'It won't wash, Prime Minister. You said yourself the troops would be out in a couple of days. This whole thing will be over before the next ballot.'

'It's a distraction!' Poultney thumped his desk. 'I can't . . . Dammit, George. Be reasonable.'

'I've pledged my full support. I promise you I won't do any campaigning until the troops are out. I'll make sure my people get the message. You'll have no distractions.' George summoned up a bleak smile. 'You'll probably win now, you know,' he said. 'I'm doing you a favour. The backbenchers will rally round. They always do at times like this. You'll see.'

Poultney wasn't convinced and made a great show of shaking his head. 'There are advantages, you know. I'd take you back into Cabinet immediately,' he said, a persuasive note creeping into his voice. 'If we lose the General Election I'll resign at once and support you as my successor. And if we win . . .' He did a spot of blinking then, as though to acknowledge the implausibility of such an outcome. 'If we win, I'll stand down within three years and put all my weight behind you. Come on, man. I can't say fairer than that.'

No indeed. It was, George acknowledged silently, a remarkable eirenicon. An entirely sane solution. It would cheer the party up no end. He sighed. 'I can't do it,' he said. 'I'm sorry, Prime Minister. I'm committed.'

'Humph!' Poultney sounded dismissive rather than surprised. 'It's not going to be as easy as you think. I'm warning you.'

'I don't think it's going to be easy at all,' George retorted. 'I know Sahelia's changed everything.'

'Well then. Why not follow your own logic?'

George shrugged. 'The situation may have changed. I haven't.'

'You bet the situation's changed, chum. And I'll tell you something else for nothing.' Poultney's eyes flared in sudden malice. 'I happen to know Lucas Brotherton's thinking of throwing his hat into the ring. If you don't call this contest off now, right now . . . He'll do it, you know. You can be stopped, George. By Lucas if not by me.'

'I dare say.' George was getting tired of this. 'All I can tell you is I won't pull out. Can't. I'm quite serious about bringing new standards into politics, you know.' There was, he realised, an unmistakeable pomposity in his words.

Poultney caught it too. 'Never mind splitting the party, eh? Never mind the damage. It was your fucking sense of morality which wrecked the arms deal with the Sahelians, wasn't it?'

'If you say so.' George remained calm. 'As I remember, you agreed with me.'

'Under duress, matey. Under duress,' growled Poultney. 'You didn't leave me much choice, hey? But I'll tell you a strange thing about that, shall I?'

George looked at his watch. 'It's getting rather late. So if you don't mind . . .'

'Oh, you'll want to hear this.' There was a savage expression on Poultney's face. 'Might have some bearing on your moral principles. You never know. See, now we're talking to our embassy again we've got some idea why this mess blew up in the first place. Turns out that some of the Vizier's many cousins thought he was losing his grip. They were just waiting their chance to shove a scimitar in his back. Know what persuaded them to make their move? Do You?'

'I've no idea.' But a worm of apprehension slithered in George's stomach.

'Have a guess. Go on. It's not hard.'

George could feel the pounding of his own heart. He stared at Poultney's red and angry face, unwilling to speak. Unwilling to hear.

'Only it's a bit of information we'd better keep to ourselves,' the Prime Minister pressed on relentlessly. 'I'm sure you know why.'

George swallowed. Somewhere, he sensed, a crack had appeared in the moral universe. 'Why, then?' he managed.

'Why? I would have thought that was obvious. It wouldn't do either of us much good, would it?'

The crack widened. 'What are you talking about?' George whispered. But he suspected. Oh God, he knew.

The arms deal, Poultney was saying. It inflicted utter humiliation on the Vizier and his counsellors, gave a green light to the conspirators, encouraged their butchery. There were bodies in the streets now, bodies black with flies. Bloated. Our fault, George. All that pain and terror. A girl with blonde hair and a brace and only one ear. We should have known. More to the point, you should have known. You. But you didn't think, did you, chum? Didn't calculate the consequences. Too

busy agonising, eh? Too busy pissing about with the ethical
dimension to worry about a few hundred dead tribesmen?

The bongs of Big Ben began chiming the midnight hour. The
room seemed to tilt. The air thickened. It was becoming difficult
to breathe. Shadows roiled in George's mind, smothering the
light. The Prime Minister's mouth was opening and closing but
the words seemed to be coming from a far distance, across
a widening chasm. There's something else, he was saying.
Something you should know. The kidnappers have named the
negotiator they want. It's you, chum. They want you.

It's all right. There's nothing amiss.

Look: the light burns steady, as it always did. There are no
shadows. The ground is firm beneath his feet. He can hear and
understand every word the Prime Minister is uttering. Well,
then. This is reality. He's suffered a shock, that's all. A dizzy
spell. Not in the least like the other times. Or rather . . . not
very like.

But there's something strange in this moment, isn't there?
Something not quite right. The Prime Minister is still sneering
about the ethical dimension, which is crazy. We had all this
some moments ago, didn't we? Yes, we did. The same words.
Exactly. Too busy agonising, were you? Too busy pissing
about . . . ? It strikes George then that Big Ben hasn't done
its stuff either: only one bong instead of twelve. It is midnight,
isn't it? He'd like to check the time on his wristwatch, but his
arm is heavy, incapable of movement.

It doesn't matter. Time will resume its normal course by
and by, that's certain. Just as soon as he's regained his
equilibrium. He's accepted the message. For of course this
must be a message, as potent as any.

But before he has time to consider consequences or wonder
what it might mean, the bongs of Big Ben echo through
the room.

'. . . Too busy pissing about with the ethical dimension to worry
about a few hundred dead tribesmen?' Poultney snarled. 'Well
here's something else you should know. You've obviously

made a big impression. See, the kidnappers have named the negotiator they want. It's you, chum. They want you.'

Oh, yes. It made sense all right. A pattern was emerging. 'I'll go,' said George. There was clearly no other choice. He felt strangely calm.

Poultney stared at him for a long moment, unspeaking.

'I'm serious,' George pressed. 'They know me over there. It's the obvious solution.'

The man's face crumpled in distaste. 'I don't think we can usefully go any further with this,' he said. 'I shall expect your full support when I make my statement tomorrow. There's nothing further to discuss.'

George sat on stubbornly, just managing to keep his temper under control. 'No publicity,' he said. 'I give you my word on that.'

'Your word?' The insult was unmistakable.

George ignored it. 'If there's the slightest chance of getting the ambassador and his family out, we have a moral duty—'

'Absolutely not!' Poultney's fist crashed on his desk. 'Enough. I don't know what game you think you're playing, but the answer's no.'

'Then you'd better explain why not, Prime Minister.'

'Why not?' For a moment Poultney seemed lost for words. 'Because we don't negotiate with terrorists, that's why not,' he got out at last. 'Because you'd have nothing to offer. Because you'd just become another hostage. A Prime Ministerial candidate! It's grotesque.'

'I'm willing to take that chance.' In fact it wasn't strictly true. The thought of surrendering himself to a gang of trigger-happy savages appalled him. 'I'll write you a note here and now. I'll say you've advised me strongly against it. Make it clear that if I'm taken hostage there can be no question of a ransom.'

'No,' said Poultney. 'Impossible.'

'I'd go in with one of the evacuation flights,' George pushed on, as though he hadn't heard. 'If all goes well, I could be back at the airport in a matter of hours.'

'No,' Poultney repeated. 'It's insane and the answer is no. How could you negotiate, when there's nothing to negotiate with? We're not handing over any money, so you can forget that. Weapons are out of the question. You'd be going empty handed.'

George pounced. 'I could offer them recognition. If they establish control over the territory, we'd apply the usual diplomatic rules wouldn't we? And following on from that, we'd resume technical aid as far as their oil is concerned.'

Poultney scowled. 'We don't negotiate with terrorists and we certainly don't negotiate under duress.'

'Fine. That's what I'd tell them. Release the hostages and win the war. Then we'll recognise them and give them all the aid they want.'

'Except our people are probably dead.'

'We don't know that.'

Poultney seemed to deflate. 'I've told you my decision,' he said wearily. 'For God's sake accept it, will you?'

For God's sake George could do no such thing. 'I'm afraid I must insist, Prime Minister,' he said firmly. 'I really don't feel there's any other decent choice.'

Poultney sat for a long moment, sunk in thought. 'You're in no position to insist on anything,' he muttered at last.

George didn't reply. They both knew otherwise. His offer had altered the equation. He could almost see the calculations flickering behind Poultney's eyes. Sooner or later, the terms of the kidnappers' demands would certainly become public; the argument had moved beyond the fate of the ambassador and his family. Political reputations hung in the balance now.

The Prime Minister stirred. 'The risks are too great,' he said.

George felt the grip of fear then. He knew he'd won. 'In the circumstances, I'm prepared to accept those risks. I'll write you a note to that effect. This is my decision.'

'There can't be any publicity. I'm not having this turned into a circus.'

'No grandstanding,' George agreed. 'I'll give you an undertaking on that as well.' This was what he should be doing, wasn't it? The right thing?

'You must understand.' Poultney was insistent. 'There can

be no question of a ransom. Not for the ambassador. Not for you. If things don't work out . . .'

'I'm on my own. In fact I'll put that in writing too.' George caught the puzzlement in Poultney's eye. If only you knew, he thought. This isn't bravery. I'm trapped, that's all. That's the curse of knowing. There's no room left for ordinary virtue.

Poultney was frowning. 'Only four days to the next ballot,' he said. 'You're prepared to abandon your campaign, just like that? You might not get back in time. You know that, don't you?'

'Oh, yes.' George had thought of that all right. 'It's fair to say I might very well not come back at all.'

Poultney nodded slowly, as though he understood. Then he stretched out an arm. For a brief but encouraging moment, George thought the man might be offering to shake hands in friendly tribute; but he was only sliding sheets of notepaper across the desk. 'You've got a letter to write,' growled the Prime Minister, in a way that wasn't friendly at all.

Norfolk Hotel,
Brighton.
Wednesday 19/11

Dear George,

You'll recognise the address, I dare say. Perhaps that's why I came here. In memory of happier times.

It's no good, George. I've had a lot of opportunity to think things through, this last week. I realise now I haven't been happy for years. In fact not since the boys were small. The strange thing is, I didn't really know it. Or maybe I did know, but persuaded myself it was all my fault.

What I'm trying to say is that this has nothing to do with your cheating, or not all that much. It's to do with me. I just don't think I want to be with you any more. I need to be free, George. Probably you do too. Divorce is the best way out for both of us.

We don't have to say anything yet. And of course we

SEEING THE LIGHT 269

*should do it quietly. Don't worry. I won't see a lawyer until
your election campaign is out of the way.*

*I hope you agree I shouldn't be the one to move out of our
house. You'll probably soon be living at Number Ten anyway.
If not, I'm sure you can find somewhere suitable at Dolphin
Square or the Barbican.*

*Let's not turn this into a nasty fight, George. For one thing,
we have to think of the twins; and we did mean something
to each other once, didn't we?*

*I'll phone you next week, after you know the result. In the
meantime, please don't try to get in touch. It won't do either
of us any good. Believe me.*

Rosemary fretted over how she should finish. A 'with love'
was obviously out of the question. 'Yours faithfully' was hardly
appropriate. In the end she just scribbled her signature, then
after a moment's thought added a PS. Good luck in the second
ballot, she wrote.

It wasn't until she'd dropped her letter into the hotel postbox,
actually seen the white oblong disappear beyond possibility of
recall, that she felt the tension flood out of her. There! It was
done. She felt absurdly relieved, as though a dreaded visit to her
doctor had ended in a smiling all-clear. For the first time in an age
– certainly since before her marriage – she'd seized control of her
life, as recommended in all the modern manifestos of personal
liberation. Nothing could chain her now. She was free. Open to life
in all its possibilities. It was a satisfying feeling. Truly, it was.

She looked forward to explaining it to George when any day
now he came charging down to Brighton, full of hope and
remorse, to reclaim her for his own.

'The risks are incalculable,' whispered the BBC man. 'Literally
incalculable.' He crouched flak-jacketed behind a rock and
stared resolutely into the night, as though in search of a
missing BAFTA award. 'Somewhere out there in the darkness,
an unknown enemy awaits. Hundreds, perhaps thousands of
rebels who may be poised to attack as I speak.'

'Wish they'd get on with it,' growled Jack Cartwright. He slouched on Prudence Willow's padded throne, his feet careless on her desk. While the harridan was unexpectedly away – embroiled, so it was rumoured, in fearsome embarrassment with the taxman – he was at the helm. Enjoyably in charge.

The BBC man was ploughing on with his impersonation of the plucky warrior. 'It is just two hours since men of the Parachute Regiment seized this remote airstrip in what many are already calling the most audacious rescue operation since Entebbe.' He gazed straight to camera, his face stern. 'Nothing less than an attempt to pluck hundreds of men, women and children to safety across thousands of miles of trackless desert.'

'Trackless desert be buggered,' sneered Jack. 'Worked with that guy on the old Sheffield *Star*. He was a tosser then and he's a tosser now.'

'Herrmph,' grunted the news editor in what might or might not have been agreement.

Jack eyed him suspiciously. There were times, he felt, when the deference owed to his new authority wasn't quite as evident as it might be. 'Not a shot fired so far,' he grumbled. 'He's going on like it's World War Three.'

'So he's a tosser.' Jim Finney shrugged. 'Still a hell of a story, Jack. Mission impossible.' On screen the BBC man was burbling something about the flood of refugees who should be turning up in the next few hours. 'Prudence was right, for once. No point running your story till all this is over. Be throwing it away.'

'Yeah, yeah. I know.' Jack glowered at the television, which was now showing a large transport plane lumbering to a heavy landing. An armoured reconnaissance vehicle appeared briefly in the background, then squealed out of view. 'Let's just hope all this crap really is over by the weekend, though. Eh? Be nice to hit Gulliver just before the ballot.'

Finney looked curious. 'I'll never know how you got him to fuck himself. I mean, he must have known. Your average politician might get away with a bit of shagging. Lying, fingers in the till, whatever. Joe Q. Public won't put up with religion, though. Voices. Visions. None of that.'

'Mm.' Jack thought of his story, already written and ready

to roll. GULLIVER: MY MESSAGES FROM GOD. 'He's fucked himself, right enough,' he said. On the screen in the corner a gun-toting paratroop officer was explaining that his men were ready for anything. Keen. Jack reached for his zapper and turned the set off.

'You don't feel sorry for him then?' Finney probed. 'Considering he's such a friend of yours.'

'He's a contact, not a friend.' Nobody could contradict this assertion, since Jack had wiped the tape of all George's appeals for confidentiality. 'If you must know, it's a pleasure to shoot him down. So.' He scowled. Time to exert a little editorial authority. 'Haven't you got any fucking work to do?'

'Whoops!' Finney held up his hands in mock surrender. 'Come back, Prudence. All is forgiven.'

'Bugger off,' said Jack. But he couldn't help grinning. He knew a genuine compliment when he heard one.

CHAPTER

14

George jerked awake to the roar of engines and a multitude of discomforts. In his dream he'd been trapped, lost in a maze of dead ends and nameless terrors. He blinked, confused. His backside was numb. His head ached. For a long moment he couldn't recognise where he was. Then his anxieties came flooding back. This was real. Here and now and bloody dangerous. Around him, in the half-light of the cavernous fuselage, men moved purposefully, checking weapons, tightening straps. Some crawled over chocked vehicles, intent on incomprehensible tasks.

'Ten minutes,' the RAF loadmaster bawled through George's ear-defenders. 'You OK?'

'Fine,' George shouted above the din, trying not to wince at the crick in his neck which had chosen this precise moment to make its presence felt.

The loadmaster was yelling something about the possibility of ground fire and how the pilot needed to throw the plane about a bit. George gave him a thumbs-up, smiling with the pluckiness the occasion seemed to demand. The RAF man slapped him on the shoulder and moved off. George leaned back against the metal skin of the aircraft, his mouth dry. On the benches that ran fore and aft along the fuselage, soldiers and airmen were now beginning to settle down for the final run, pulling the webbing of their seat-belts tight, bracing themselves. A squawk burst from the intercom, though George couldn't catch the words. Something about a bit of bumpiness. He swallowed hard. Even now, it was hard to grasp the enormity of what he was doing.

The Hercules wrenched violently to the left. Plunged. George's stomach leapt to his throat. The engines screamed. The plane seemed to be corkscrewing to the right now, throwing him forward against his webbing straps. He clutched them hard, knuckles white. The airframe shuddered, vibration running down his spine and into his knees. Across the aisle, a corporal with a hard-bitten face closed one eye in a slow wink. George tried to grin back, though he knew that any second now he might vomit shamingly over his own lap. There were no bags. He swallowed again, all other pains forgotten for the moment. Bile burned in his throat. The plane reared up and sank immediately. His gorge rose. You can't be sick, he told himself. Not in front of the smirking soldiery. You're a former Secretary of State for Defence. Emissary for good old HMG. A man of parts. Then there was a thump, which jarred him to the roots. A rumble of wheels. The plane bounced and banged along the ground, engines howling on a new note. George was sweating with the effort not to puke. But the loadmaster was on his feet now and the ramp at the rear of the Hercules was being lowered, though the aircraft was still moving. Men were already swarming round the jeeps and halftracks, removing chocks, loosening the restraining-webbing. Some of the vehicles were already coughing to life; and as the plane juddered to a halt they began edging back down the fuselage, down the ramp and out into the desert night.

George sat on, drained. I'm too old for this kind of caper, he thought. Knackered. Used up. All around, alarmingly youthful soldiers who didn't seem knackered at all were stamping, forming up in line, clattering down the ramp to shouted commands. A few waved half-heartedly in his direction. Most ignored him, as they'd ignored him throughout the long, noisy flight. Well, it was hard to blame them. He hardly fitted in.

After what seemed only a matter of moments, the giant aircraft was all but empty, its four engines whining to silence. George removed his ear-defenders, undid his buckles and struggled shakily to his feet. At least the urge to vomit seemed to have receded. He breathed deeply, relieved to be down in one piece. Good old Lockheed. The Hercules might be an ancient and inelegant old granny, but she was solid as a cement-mixer.

Up at the front of the aeroplane one of the pilots, another youth who might not yet have started shaving, poked his head into the compartment, grinning. 'Welcome to Sahelia, sir,' he called. 'Hope you weren't thrown about too much.'

'I've had worse flights on British Airways,' George lied. 'All except for cabin service.' His voice sounded steady enough. Curious, he thought, how the company of military men always brought out the gung-ho element. He stretched and wriggled his toes, feeling the circulation return.

'We kept it as gentle as possible,' confided the boy. 'There's no real ground threat, as far as we can tell. Don't seem to be any missiles, anyway. Maybe a rifleman or two, taking potshots.' He grinned even more broadly, as though he expected George to see the joke. 'Anyway, sir, we've just had word. There's a Major Carstairs coming on board to give you a briefing. You're to stay here until he arrives. Out of sight.' He eyed George, speculatively. 'Shouldn't be long.'

'Fine.' There was still no tremor in his voice, which was a comfort. He raised a hand in dismissal and turned away, striving to keep his movements casual. From now on, he thought, he'd have to seem in charge of events. No doubts or hesitations. He took a deep breath then, trying to ease the knot in his stomach. I'm not afraid, he told himself. It seemed to help.

Major Carstairs turned up minutes later, a lean, square-jawed para who loped energetically up the ramp and performed one of those quivering salutes with which men of action so often take the piss out of their political masters. Behind him trailed a plump young man who introduced himself as Jenkinson, Second Secretary at the Embassy. The man's handshake was flaccid, as though the last of his strength had leached from him.

'Right, gentlemen,' said George in what he hoped was a tone of brisk authority. 'Must we do it here?'

Carstairs wasn't impressed. Presumably he had views of his own about playing nursemaid to visiting politicians. 'My instructions are that you're to be kept out of sight. Sir.' The last word was clearly an afterthought. 'Terminal building's crawling with television people. Getting in the way.' Just like you, was the obvious if unspoken addendum.

It seemed to George that a gentle crack of the whip might be in order. 'I agreed with the Prime Minister that my visit should be confidential,' he said firmly. 'It's imperative the media don't know I'm here. So let's make the best of it, shall we?' He gestured to the benches bolted to the wall of the fuselage. 'I think we might at least sit down.' It was encouraging to observe the subtle change in the major's expression.

'Just to get things clear, sir,' said Carstairs, as the three of them tried without much success to make themselves comfortable. 'My instructions are that you're on your own. I can't give you any men and I can't let you have a vehicle. What I can do is let you have an escort as far as the embassy, but that's all. After that . . .' He shrugged. 'Sorry, sir.'

Well, thought George. At least you're saying sir as though you mean it. 'I appreciate the difficulty, Major,' he said. 'You've got problems enough without looking after me.' A little balm after the lash, in his experience, usually worked wonders. He turned to the diplomat without waiting to see how Carstairs responded. 'What's the latest on the ambassador?'

Jenkinson was slumped forlorn against a metal strut. 'Nothing new,' he muttered. 'Not since . . . Not since they sent their demands.' The man made an obvious effort to pull himself together. 'I think you're wasting your time, Secretary of State. They're almost certainly dead by now.'

'Wrong on both counts,' snapped George, rather more sharply than he'd intended. 'I'm no longer Secretary of State and the ambassador isn't dead. I'm certain of it.' He softened his tone. 'I promise you I wouldn't be within a thousand miles of this place if I didn't believe I could get him out. And his family. We've got a chance. Believe me.' Astonishing what a little bluster can do, he thought. This was good stuff.

Jenkinson blinked and straightened his back. 'Right. I'm sorry. Bit tired.' His expression perked up to something approximating what might be expected in an on-the-ball diplomat. 'Look, sir, we've given the kidnappers the signal we're ready to negotiate. The embassy flag's been flying at half-mast all day. Did it myself this morning, soon as I had confirmation you were on your way. So they're expecting you. Expecting someone, anyway.'

'And we still don't know who they are?'

Jenkinson grimaced. 'Could be anyone. This place is in total chaos. We don't know where the Vizier is, or even if he's still alive. We're not sure where the rebels are and we can't even say for certain *who* they are. There's a suggestion that the ringleader is a Sheikh Yusuf, who's one of the Vizier's many cousins, but that's no more than a guess, really.'

'Groping in the dark,' growled Carstairs in evident disgust. The balm hadn't worked, then.

George ignored him. 'Didn't you report that this was all started by the collapse of the arms deal?'

Jenkinson shrugged. 'It's one theory. You've got to remember, Mr Gulliver, there's no such thing as politics here. Not in the Western sense. It's all personal rivalries and family feuds. These aren't the kind of people you're used to dealing with. They might be slaughtering each other on a whim, for all we know.'

George wasn't quite certain what to make of this. Sure, he felt a certain relief that moral responsibility for the mayhem might not after all be laid at his door. On the other hand, he didn't much care for the concept of trigger-happy riffraff knocking each other off for the fun of it. Such folk might not be best pleased if he turned up in their tents minus the required bag of gold. 'Not the sort we can expect to do business with, then?' he asked.

'Huh!' sneered Carstairs.

'Oh, they have their own sense of honour.' In spite of his fatigue, Jenkinson was still capable of putting military oafishness in its place. 'Only it's not necessarily the same as ours. See, they're not really like anyone else. Suspicious of outsiders. Christians. Moslems. Everybody. Treat their enemies like dogs.' He touched George's arm, in what was presumably intended as a gesture of reassurance. 'Tend to be strict in their idea of hospitality though. Once you've established yourself as a guest.'

'I see.' The knot in George's stomach was tighter than ever. 'And to become their guest, I just drive out of the embassy in the morning, take the desert road and keep on going. Yes?' He managed to outline this appalling proposition in the matter-of-fact tones of a motorist asking directions in a harmless English lane.

Jenkinson wasn't about to be outdone in sang froid. 'That's it. Their instructions are pretty clear. I've left the ambassador's Land Rover for you. Tank's filled up. Spare cans of petrol in the back.' Foreign Office training, his tone suggested, always told in the end.

'Fine,' said George, ignoring the way his stomach kept clenching in protest. 'Seems we're all set, then.'

'One thing.' Carstairs chipped in. 'You must be back here by dawn the day after tomorrow. We can't wait.'

'Absolutely.' George was beginning to understand how Captain Oates must have felt when he sacrificed himself to the howling wilderness. 'That's the deal. You absolutely mustn't take any additional risks for me.' He found it hard to believe that he was sitting in a cold, uncomfortable aircraft in the middle of nowhere calmly agreeing that he might be abandoned; but Carstairs seemed to think it OK and Jenkinson too. Wasn't this the spirit that built the Empire?

'Only we can't hold the airport if there's any serious resistance,' Carstairs plodded on. 'There's just my battalion, plus the support elements who flew in with you. In and out, that's the plan.'

'So.' George was beginning to feel strangely detached. 'You'd better tell me your intentions.'

Carstairs was all business now. 'Airport perimeter's secured. Embassy personnel are here already, plus a few civilians from the town. The real problem's with the oil people. Their camp's due east of here. About eighty clicks. We'll be taking a patrol out at first light to convoy them back. Otherwise . . .' He shrugged. 'There's a couple of dozen other Brits scattered around out in the sticks. A few French. Some Americans. They'll have to get here under their own steam, that's all. As best they can.'

'Let's just pray they get through,' said George.

'Hm.' Carstairs didn't seem to place much trust in the power of prayer. 'I'm afraid you'll have to stay on board, out of sight. Till we're ready to pick you up.' He looked at his watch. 'Two hours.'

'I'll be ready.'

'Right.' Carstairs stood. 'Things to do. I'll send some rations over. And a first-aid kit.' For the first time, a spark of friendliness flickered. After a brief hesitation, he thrust out a hand. 'I want to wish you the very best of luck, sir.'

The gesture almost unmanned George. He shook hands and mumbled a thanks. There seemed to be a slight quaver in his voice this time. He wanted to swallow, but repressed the need. Keep a stiff upper lip, Gulliver. He watched as Carstairs saluted and strode off. A proper salute, this time. Jenkinson was saying something about a background briefing on Sahelian customs, but George hardly heard. He was thinking of Carstairs' handshake. It had been a compliment, right enough. Exactly of the kind, in fact, that any military commander might offer a volunteer setting off on a mission from which he probably wouldn't return.

As Jenkinson had warned, the oil-drum markers ran out a couple of miles from the embassy. George braked the Land Rover to a standstill and mopped his forehead. The road, if such it could be called, stretched indistinctly ahead for twenty yards or so, before seeming to merge with the grit-grey of the desert. The trick now, he'd been assured, was to proceed with the utmost caution, keep a sharp eye on the terrain and check his compass every couple of minutes. You shouldn't get lost, Jenkinson promised. Not if you're careful. Anyway, you can bet the kidnappers will have you tagged the minute you drive out of the embassy gates.

George peered nervously through the windscreen. In every direction, as far as the eye could see, there were several kinds of bugger-all: grey sand, occasional rocks, a few bits of brownish vegetation in scrubby clumps. Off to the left, on the far horizon, there was a fat and improbably ugly tree which might or might not be a baobab. There was no sign whatever of human life, no evidence that man had ever set foot in this ghastly land. Apart of course from the road, or rather track, which only existed at all if one had the eyesight of a frontier scout. George shifted sweatily in his seat. Unless some burnous-festooned assassin was lurking behind that distant baobab, there wasn't the slightest possibility that he was under observation. He couldn't decide whether to feel disappointed or relieved.

A whiffle of wind scraped across his face. Though Sahelia couldn't quite match the eyeball-frying, skin-stripping glare of first-division hellholes like the deep Sahara, one wouldn't wish to linger. Ignoring Jenkinson's warning about the importance of rationing, George poured himself a mouthful of water. It was warm, tasting of polystyrene from the jerrican, but eased the scratchiness in his throat. The relief didn't last. Within a minute, his mouth was as dry as ever. He thought briefly of frosted beer and cold showers. Time to move on.

He put the Land Rover into gear and set off again. Keeping to the track wasn't as difficult as he'd feared, provided he was careful and kept his speed down to not much more than walking pace. The necessity now was to ignore the heat and the jolting, keep one's eyes fixed on a stone up ahead, on the next rut in the track, on a piece of lonely scrub. After a mile or two he began to feel more confident and pushed the speed up a little. Only a little. The track unwound beneath his wheels, grey on dismal grey. He glanced at his watch. Ten-forty-five. He'd stop at eleven for another mouthful of water, then press on until midday, before turning back. God knows, that should be enough. He'd done his best. Made the effort. Only . . .

Only what, George?

Only this. To return in bathos with nothing accomplished was inconceivable, wasn't it? There must be reason in his presence here. Had to be. Or there was no—.

He slammed on his brakes, jolting forward in his seat. The man was clad from head to foot in robes of black. Mounted on a camel. Motionless by the side of the track. George felt his heart beginning to thump. He was reminded, absurdly, of that scene in *Lawrence of Arabia*, when Omar Sharif rides into view like the wrath of Hell across the shimmering sands. He got out of the Land Rover, knees weak, and waved a tentative hand. The man in black just stared, every inch the Western image of a desert warrior. Perhaps he'd seen the film too. Then, without any apparent instruction from its master, the camel turned and began to shamble off untidily into the desert.

George watched, nonplussed. He didn't care for the idea of leaving the track. On the other hand . . . This is what you've come for, matey. This has all been arranged. Obviously. You can almost hear the pieces falling into place. The fancy made him feel a little better. He got back into his vehicle and turned it off the track. By now the guide was several hundred yards away, heading easterly, seemingly indifferent to whether he was followed. George halted again. The line of the track was already indistinguishable from the surrounding terrain. He'd have to keep checking his compass. He set off again, careful to keep his distance. As though somehow it mattered. His four-wheel drive bounced and swayed along a surface only marginally rougher than the track. The camel, he noticed, was keeping up a fair old pace, for all its ungainly appearance. He had to keep his speed rather too high for comfort in order to stay in contact. Perhaps it was just as well. The strain of driving in such conditions might help keep his mind off whatever lay ahead.

It seemed to work. After an hour or so, he no longer had the energy to be fearful. His mouth was dust-dry and he couldn't swallow. His hands clenched aching on the wheel. His eyes were prickly with tiredness and the sun. Up ahead, the camel shambled on regardless, its rider not once troubling to look back. Presumably his intention was to demonstrate the magnificent indifference of the desert warrior, the turd.

George ran a leathery tongue over cracked lips. First rule of negotiation, he thought. Don't let the other side take the initiative. *Nil carborundum.* Weren't these bastards supposed to be solicitous of their guests? Well, then. The hell with it. He halted the Land Rover and sat there panting. There was water in the container by his feet. He unscrewed the cap with shaking hands and poured himself a warm mugful. Then another. He gasped with the pleasure of it, moistened a handkerchief and ran it over his face. Better. Justifiable, too. He needed to arrive in good order.

He set his vehicle in motion once more. By now his guide was only a dot in the distance, but in this flat and featureless landscape it hardly mattered. The man was probably bluffing anyway; he'd surely never dare turn up at wherever it was without his British visitor safely in tow. George felt some satisfaction at that insight. He was beginning to think as a politician should, when representing the interests of Her Majesty's Government.

He peered ahead. This couldn't be right. The horizon was empty. He blinked. Still empty. No sign of a camel or a nomad in black. Impossible. He depressed the accelerator a fraction more. The vehicle lurched alarmingly. He slowed down. No need for panic. He'd just keep heading due east. It would be all right. Nobody in his right mind could leave an emissary from Whitehall stumbling hopelessly around these waterless wastes. Could they? He recalled Jenkinson's observation that the locals had no idea of what constituted proper behaviour. Damn. He checked his compass again. Still travelling in the right direction. Concentrate, he told himself. Think of the ambassador and his wife and an injured little girl. You're here for a purpose. And with a Guide rather more reliable than some shitehawk on a camel.

As though to reward this affirmation of faith, the ground dropped away suddenly and sharply beneath his wheels. He jerked to a halt. In front of him the slope plunged steeply to a vast, circular hollow in the earth, a crater gouged cleanly in sand and rock, as though scooped by some giant's spoon. At the bottom, a couple of hundred feet below, there were patches of incongruous green speckling the dun, date palms, a scatter of mud dwellings. One building in the centre, larger than the others, gleamed in improbable white. Somewhere in George's soul a memory stirred.

He took a deep breath and edged his vehicle carefully forward. The path twisted down from the lip of the crater, a thin ribbon of packed soil that spiralled down, leaving no room for error. George kept his eyes fixed rigidly on the ground. If the earth crumbled, or his offside wheels slipped over the path's edge ... Well. Nothing could prevent a long, screaming roll to destruction. Yard by yard he crept down, endlessly stabbing his brakes.

He was shuddering by the time he reached the bottom. Tension. He halted the Land Rover and sat for a long moment, until he felt calmer. He drank a mug of water. Behind him, the path snaked upwards. From this angle it didn't look especially formidable. Perhaps it would be easier to drive back up. He hoped so.

The settlement or oasis, or whatever it was, seemed to be about half a mile away across the crater floor. There was no sign of his guide. No movement at all. Well, there wouldn't be, he supposed. Not in this suntrap. The heat down here was relentless, sweltering off the rocks, quivering in the air. Even your authentic desert desperado might think twice before venturing out of the shade. George resisted the temptation to pour himself another drink. It would have been a callous indulgence. Somewhere over there, in one of those scrofulous huts, the ambassador and his family might very well be dying of thirst.

He drove forward in low gear. The buildings were rather more distant than he'd imagined, but he made fair progress across the rocky ground. As he approached, he began to make out definite signs of human habitation. There were camels tethered next to what appeared to be a well, a flicker of movement inside one of the shadowed doorways, a whiff, faint but unmistakable, of excrement. All that was missing was a welcoming committee. He slowed to a crawl. There seemed no centre to the place, except possibly the well and the low, whitewashed building beyond. He pulled up and climbed stiffly out of the Land Rover. The searing metal was too hot to touch. He stood with what he hoped was an appearance of confidence, well aware of unseen eyes. Somewhere a child began to cry, a noise quickly hushed but startling in its suddenness.

'The Right Honourable George Gulliver, I presume,' said the unmistakable accent of the Home Counties.

George stepped back, startled. Unable to help himself. He was dimly aware of figures emerging from a dozen doorways, but he couldn't turn to look at them. He stared at the man who had spoken, took in the robes of dazzling white which stood out even against the walls of the whitewashed house and for a wild moment imagined . . .

But the moment passed. Perhaps because of some subtle change in the light, perhaps because such flights of fancy never last. George blinked. The speaker's robes were of course not dazzling at all, but in need of a wash; and his features weren't in the least angelic. Cold blue eyes, a nose like an axe-blade, thin lips, no beard. George guessed his age at about thirty-five. He gathered his wits. 'I'm George Gulliver,' he confirmed, loudly enough for everyone to hear. 'I come here to represent the Government of the United Kingdom.'

The apparition in off-white inclined his head with the kind of grave dignity that in theory anyway tends to go with the job of desert chieftain. 'We have been expecting you, Mr Gulliver,' he said in a voice that would have gone unremarked in a BBC newsreader. 'I am Sheikh Yusuf.' The announcement was clearly intended to impress, so George performed a stiff little bow. 'I am honoured to have you as my guest,' the Sheikh continued. 'My home is your home. Please.' He gestured for George to enter and barked an incomprehensible command at his black-clad followers, who seemed to have overcome their initial shyness. They dutifully scuttled off, about their business.

Not a bad performance, George thought, for a murderous thug who probably enjoys making love to his camel. He bowed again, to show that he wouldn't be outdone and allowed himself to be ushered inside.

SEEING THE LIGHT   285

The room seemed dim after the glare of sun. There was a carpet on the earthen floor, a scatter of fat cushions, an urn in the corner, filled with water. Against it stood a sword, with silver hilt. A kalashnikov rifle was propped beside it.

'I regret the poverty of the hospitality I can offer,' murmured the Sheikh, settling himself down on the biggest cushion. 'Please.' He waited until George had taken the other. 'You must understand that it is only temporary. Because of the circumstances.' He clapped his hands. From an inner room two women appeared, bearing glasses of tea and a bowl of small round globs which were presumably the Sahelian version of fairy cakes. The women set out the food and drink and departed as silently as they'd come. Though both were dressed in what looked like shrouds, their faces remained uncovered. Odd, that, since all the men – the Sheikh excepted – seemed reluctant to let anything show but their eyes.

'Yes,' sighed the Sheikh in his disconcertingly correct diction. 'Unfortunate circumstances.'

'Nevertheless, I'm honoured to be here.' George thought there could be no harm in bowing again.

'Of course,' said the Sheikh.

George sipped his tea. It was minty, lukewarm and oversweet. Anywhere other than in this wilderness, it would be downright disgusting. He drained his glass and performed a little pantomime of gratitude, inclining his head in the Sheikh's direction and smacking his lips as Jenkinson had instructed. It seemed to do the trick. The Sheikh clapped his hands again and more tea was produced. Apparently, these buggers insisted on forcing at least three glasses down one's throat before they'd condescend to talk business. Desert hospitality.

'I must compliment you, Sheikh Yusuf, on your excellent command of English,' George ventured. Jenkinson had advised that you couldn't go far wrong if you slathered it on with a trowel.

'Ah.' The Sheikh waved a deprecatory hand, while managing to look well pleased with himself. 'My family employed an English tutor for many years. He taught us about the empire on which the sun never sets.' A brief smirk. 'He came from Cheltenham.'

'Oh, yes. I know Cheltenham well.' This ought to have been an encouraging beginning, but George felt deeply uneasy. It might have been something to do with the Sheikh's stone-cold eyes. Or perhaps it was just that he couldn't, offhand, remember anything remotely good that had ever come out of Cheltenham. 'It's obvious your tutor had an apt pupil,' he ploughed on. He was aware that two or three men had entered the room behind him, but didn't turn. He drained his glass of tea, hoping to get the niceties out of the way as quickly as possible. The Sheikh seemed not to notice the empty glass. His eyes were fixed unblinking on George's face. To hell with it, he thought. Never mind Jenkinson's advice. 'I must ask about the safety of our ambassador, his wife and his daughter, Sheikh Yusuf,' he said firmly.

The Sheikh frowned. He muttered something to one of the gangsters in the background and received an incomprehensible jabber in reply. Then he clapped his hands. The women reappeared with more tea. Throughout this performance, George kept his expression neutral, wishing he could whistle up a platoon of paras. He sipped his tea.

'You seem impatient, Mr Gulliver,' observed the Sheikh after a long moment, his voice chill. The eyes seemed reptilian now. Disturbing.

'I'm grateful for the refreshments. Sahelia's generosity to guests is well known.' George stressed the word 'guests.' He was uncomfortably aware that he was sitting with his back to an unknown number of cut-throats. 'However, I'm sure you understand that I have travelled a long way.' He picked up his glass and drained the liquid within. There. Three servings of the ghastly stuff out of the way. 'I really do need to know.'

The Sheikh stared at him in the lengthening silence. 'Your ambassador is safe,' he said at last.

George kept his face impassive. 'And his wife and daughter?'

'Them?' A flicker of disdain. 'Still alive.'

George couldn't quite analyse his feelings at that instant. They went beyond relief. He felt a surge of something quite incongruous in this murderous company, this squalid hovel.

Happiness, perhaps? No, more than happiness. It felt rather like joy. A validation of everything. 'I would like to see them, please,' he said.

The Sheikh's expression froze. 'I have told you. They are safe.'

'Nevertheless.' George stared straight back. It was going to be all right. He knew it. Wasn't this a script written by an Author who knew precisely what He was doing? 'It is necessary,' he said, serious.

The Sheikh did some more muttering. There was a stir in the background. In spite of himself, George felt an anticipatory twinge between his shoulderblades. Still he didn't look round. Then the Sheikh lifted a hand. The edges of his lips curved upwards. It wasn't quite a smile. 'You are a great man in your country,' he announced. 'The leader.'

'I hope to be.' This was the kind of stuff that, according to Jenkinson, should appeal no end to these cockchafers. 'I expect to be,' George firmly amended. 'My colleagues decide in three days. Then I shall be in command.'

It seemed to work. The Sheikh's features softened into something that might have been mistaken for friendliness. 'I have heard this,' he said. 'On your BBC World Service. You see?' He reached behind his cushion and held up a small portable radio. 'All-band capacity,' he boasted. 'We keep in touch. But . . .' A sudden frown. 'There is nothing on the news about your visit to Sahelia, Mr Gulliver.'

'I should hope not.' George leaned forward, urgent. 'I must stress, this meeting is highly confidential. Any agreement between us must remain secret. For the time being.' It was a curious fact, he thought, that the mere mention of secrecy always added a certain plausibility to events; half the intelligence agencies in the world made a fat living out of the human propensity to place more faith in classified information than in the usually more reliable stuff to be found in the newspapers. 'Her Majesty's Government,' George continued solemnly, 'believes it can trust in your discretion.'

The assurance seemed to impress the Sheikh. He inclined his head with what might have been an attempt at graciousness. 'It is right that we should speak as equals,' he said. 'I shall take you to the prisoners.' He rose to his feet. 'Come. We shall see.'

George stood too, nodding in belated acknowledgment at the three desert types lounging blackly by the door. None of them responded. Outside, the sun was as fierce as ever, but now the place had come to life, shrouded figures in every doorway, a knot of men jabbering around the well. Small boys were clambering over the Land Rover, shouting. One sat in the driving-seat, sawing at the wheel. George patted his pocket to reassure himself the keys were safe. 'Come,' said the Sheikh impatiently. He strode off. George followed, wincing at the heat and the pace. Behind him, the three shrouded gangsters followed as close as jailers. Which perhaps they were.

The Sheikh halted by an adobe shed indistinguishable from the others. In the opening that served as a doorway, an oaf stood clutching a rifle. George ducked past, squinting as his eyes adjusted to the gloom. The place stank like a privy. The place was full of armed men, but at a command from the Sheikh they shuffled out into the afternoon. In the half-light, George could see a scrap of curtain partially concealing what seemed to be an alcove in the far wall. He pulled the material aside. The stench was more noticeable now. It seemed to come from a bucket. One hardly needed light to guess its contents.

'Ambassador?' It was difficult to make out anything in the darkness.

A shadow stirred. 'Who's there?' it said. The voice was hoarse.

'I've come to get you out of here. It's George Gulliver.' Somewhere in the room there was a whimper. A girl's voice. George stepped forward. 'It's all right,' he said. 'It's all over. You're going home.'

The whimpering stopped abruptly. George could just about see the ambassador now. The man had struggled to his feet and stood unsteadily. In the outer room, the Sheikh was saying something in a tone of sharp command. George stepped forward to clasp the ambassador's arm, wordless. An oil-lamp glowed suddenly.

'My God,' whispered the ambassador. 'It really is you.' He swayed. 'It really is.'

'It's me.' He pulled the man towards him, in a very un-British hug, reaching his other hand for the woman who stood to one side, blinking in the light, her lip trembling. She seemed dazed. 'Mrs Dalton,' he said. 'You're all right now.' She stumbled forward then and they all clung together, incoherent.

'You see?' said the Sheikh. 'Safe.'

George ignored him. The whimpering had started again. He could see the girl lying in the corner, unconscious in her nest of rags. 'Jacqueline?' he said.

The ambassador was trembling. 'Infection,' he said. 'Getting worse.' His wife gave a little sob on George's shoulder, then pulled away and knelt beside her daughter. George reached down and touched the child's cheek. The side of her head was covered in a grubby bandage and caked in blood. He could feel the fever. She whimpered again, then lapsed into comatose silence.

'Been like this for I don't know how long,' muttered the ambassador. He sagged. 'Would you mind awfully if I sat down?' he asked. 'I don't seem . . .' He sank to the floor without waiting for an answer.

A tide of red rage surged in George's blood. He didn't stop to think. He rounded on the Sheikh, snarling. 'Safe?' he shouted. 'You said—' He staggered and almost fell as a black-clad thug jumped from nowhere and pushed him in the chest. 'None of that!' George roared. 'Stop there!' The thug halted, uncertain of whether to give another shove. The room was suddenly still. George glowered at the Sheikh. 'This is intolerable.' He spoke more quietly now, carefully enunciating every word. 'I want these people moved at once. I want the medicine chest from my vehicle. I want food prepared. Fresh water.' He stared the Sheikh straight in the eye. 'Is this your hospitality to guests?'

One of the men in black half drew a sword. Yusuf stopped him with a gesture. 'You can be punished for this,' he said. His voice was soft.

'You would be foolish to offend the representative of Her Majesty's Government,' retorted George, managing to stay in control. 'You have enemies enough. And we have things to discuss.' By now the room was filled with the Sheikh's men, all of them armed, their eyes threatening. They're like a pack of dogs, George thought. Held back by the thinnest leash. 'The girl may die if she doesn't get treatment,' he went on, insistent. 'If that happens there can be no negotiation. You will be condemned by my country.' He dropped his voice, almost whispering now. 'You know we have troops at the airfield.'

Yusuf glared, then turned his back and began talking in an undertone to his followers. Whatever the drift of it was, they didn't seem to like it. They kept looking at George with the gleam of murder in their eyes. He folded his arms and waited. Please God, he thought. Let it work. He felt weak at the knees. His plan, if such it could be called, seemed more implausible than ever. But then, it wasn't in his hands, was it? It never had been.

'Very well.' Yusuf swung round. 'The prisoners will be moved. You can give them medicine. They will be fed.' His lips curled in one of his non-smiles. 'Then we shall hear what your Government has to offer.' He said something to his men and they burst into what seemed to be the Sahelian version of a cheer. 'We have great hopes, Mr Gulliver.'

But something was happening to George. 'There will be no talks,' he heard himself saying. His rage had dissolved now. All gone. There was a tingling in his body instead, as though his whole being had been plugged into some cosmic socket. His words seemed to be coming from a great distance, tumbling from his lips apparently without thought or calculation. 'Her Majesty's Government will not negotiate under duress,' he pronounced. This is madness, he thought. A disgrace to diplomacy. But he couldn't stop himself. He was aware that Yusuf was trying to say something, but the meaning didn't register. 'I have a proposition to put before you,' he interrupted, his voice firm. 'But not until these prisoners are set free. Then we shall talk. Only then.' And abruptly he was back to himself, back in control, as though a switch had been clicked off. Something drained out of him. He would have slumped then, but for the necessity of keeping up appearances.

Yusuf snarled something to his men and stepped in close, his expression savage. 'You are a prisoner too,' he hissed. 'You should remember.'

George drew on his last reserves. 'I have a serious offer to make on behalf of my Government,' he said coldly. 'If you accept the terms, it will be to your great advantage. Otherwise, I promise, you will get nothing at all.'

Yusuf drew back, stared at him for a long moment, then turned and walked out without a word. Silently, his men followed, taking their venom with them. George's stomach dissolved. The ambassador was saying something, his voice shaking, but George's mind was elsewhere. He was wondering how violently that pack of murderers outside would react when they discovered he had nothing of substance to offer them. Nothing at all.

'They're proud of their swordsmanship.' The ambassador's bitterness rasped in his throat. 'Did it with one slash. Some sort of party-piece. Like a sideshow at the circus.' He brushed away the beginnings of a tear. 'At first I thought she was . . . You know. She just collapsed.'

'All right, James. She'll be fine now. She will.' George knew beyond a doubt that this was the case, wished he could reassure the girl's parents that she was under a special protection. Impossible, of course.

'She needs a doctor.' The ambassador took a long, shuddering breath. 'Just look at her. Poor little lass.' He was close to breakdown. 'She's only fourteen.'

Beside the makeshift bed underneath the window, Mrs Dalton went on sponging her daughter's face. A strong woman, George thought. Practical. No time to waste on tears. He patted the ambassador's shoulder. 'Give the antibiotics a chance. Come on, man. We'll have her at the airfield by morning.' He hoped his encouragement wasn't coming out like just another piece of politician's patter. Jacqueline's condition had undeniably improved since the injection. Though the fever was still running high, her breathing sounded easier.

The ambassador gave George a look in which hope struggled to overcome doubt. 'You really think they'll let us go?'

Oh, yes. George had become quite confident about that. It was all in the plan. 'No reason not to,' he said. 'They got me here. It's what they wanted.' He wouldn't think about what came afterwards. Perhaps there was a plan for that too.

'After the way you stood up to Yusuf . . .' The ambassador dropped his voice, presumably in case of eavesdroppers. 'What you've got to understand is, the man's mad. Seriously off his rocker. Came close to killing an English doctor once, believe it or not. Raped one of her patients. She made the mistake of kicking up a fuss. Had to get the Vizier to kick her out of the country quick. For her own safety.'

George thought of a conversation long ago, at the Easthampton Conservative Club. Another part of the pattern dropped into place. 'Obviously a nasty piece of work,' he observed.

'Just about as nasty as they come. Won't take kindly to the way you showed him up in front of his men.' He leaned forward. 'Killed his own brother for passing some remark about his failure to produce sons. Can you believe it? Wounded pride, see? That's the kind of character we're dealing with.' He hesitated. 'Don't take this amiss, but I think you should handle him with kid gloves.'

George shrugged. 'I've got something he wants.'

'Probably the only reason you're still in the land of the living.' A spark of shrewdness flickered. 'You've got one advantage, though. You gave him tremendous status by turning up out of the blue. You can bet he never really expected it. If you want the truth, neither did I.' He turned to look at his daughter, lying on her pallet. 'I'm thankful you did, though,' he said. 'More than.' He blinked several times, as though troubled by a piece of grit.

'Well.' George affected not to notice. 'Let's just hope for the best, eh?'

'Hmm.' In spite of his distress, the ambassador was still a professional. He lowered his voice so that George had to strain for the words. 'What have you been authorised to offer?'

'I'm not offering them a damned thing, unless they let you go.'

'And then?'

But George was spared the necessity of an answer. A rifle-toting guard entered the room and barked something. The ambassador nodded. 'It seems the Sheikh is anxious to see you at your earliest possible convenience,' he translated.

George stood. He desperately wanted to swallow, but wouldn't betray his apprehension. You're not to worry, he wanted to say. But now that his moment had come, he found he was quite unable to utter a sound.

This time, the Sheikh was not alone. He was hunkered down on his cushion of state, a sword gleaming across his knees. Behind him stood half a dozen followers, watchful as vultures. Incongruously, one of them clutched a camera with a bulky flash attachment and long-snouted lens. George strode in and settled himself down on a cushion of his own, without waiting to be asked. Now it begins, he thought. He blinked in the sudden glare of flashbulb.

'You see. We keep a record of our struggle. For the sake of history.' The Sheikh waved the photographer away.

Mad as a March hare, thought George. Wouldn't be surprised if there's no film in the damned thing. He inclined his head. 'Most commendable.'

'So.' The Sheikh's fingers caressed the hilt of his sword. 'You have seen the prisoners are safe. Now we can talk.'

Here it comes, thought George. Let's see how you manage without a platoon of civil servants to back you up. He allowed the expectant silence to drag on for a bit, then slowly shook his head. 'No,' he said. 'There can be no talks yet. First I must express the outrage of my Government at the way you make war on children.' He curled a disdainful lip. 'On little girls.'

One or two of the thugs in the background, presumably other beneficiaries of the tutor from Cheltenham, began muttering then. The Sheikh quelled them with a gesture. His eyes never left George's face. 'It was necessary,' he said softly.

George stared back, determined to keep the initiative. 'It was an intolerable piece of brutality,' he contradicted, coldly. 'I must tell you that, if the girl dies, my Government will hold you personally responsible.' There. It was done. He watched the shock leap into the Sheik's eyes. Perhaps the bugger had been given lessons on the War of Jenkins' Ear.

'You have not come to negotiate?' The man was hissing, incredulous. His knuckles whitened as he clutched his sword hilt. His dismay seemed to have been succeeded in short order by what looked very much like a glower of rage.

'That's not what I said, Your Excellency.' George was sweating. If ever there was a time for a bucket of bullshit it was surely now. 'In spite of this incident, Her Majesty's Government believes you to be a man of honour. That is why I have come. To deal with you face to face. As leaders. Together.'

'Hah!' growled the Sheikh. Was his glare a little less rabid? Hard to tell. But there was no doubting the restlessness in the background. The sheep-shaggers didn't like any of this one bit.

'Yes, together. As leaders,' George hurried on. 'We can settle this business as statesmen should. Build a new relationship between the United Kingdom and Sahelia.' God, this was thin stuff. Time to show the carrot to the donkey. 'I've discussed your demands with the Prime Minister. At length. We do have a proposition for you.' He paused while the Sheikh muttered something to his followers. It seemed to cheer them up. 'I must stress however that it is politically impossible for me to make an offer under duress.'

The Sheikh's expression was bleak. 'You say we must trust you?'

George summoned up all the sincerity of a political lifetime. 'I can negotiate substantially when the ambassador and his family are released,' he promised. 'I have come here in good faith. Now it is for you to respond with equal good faith.' He looked the Sheikh straight in the eye. 'You'll know from your studies of my country that an Englishman's word is his bond,' he added, alert for the slightest sign of incredulity.

But, miraculously, the man was nodding as if he'd never heard of Perfidious Albion. Well done, Cheltenham. The Sheikh barked something to his vultures, who began chattering excitedly, as though pots of British gold were already theirs for the spending. The brute with the camera stepped forward and popped another flashbulb. George put on a genial expression. He could almost see the tensions in the room evaporate. 'Very well,' said the Sheikh at last. 'We have been discussing this in your absence. My people are agreed. Now that we have your assurances, the prisoners will be released.' He stood in one flowing movement. 'Come. We shall see to it.'

George scrambled to his feet, his throat constricted, his mouth suddenly dry. He found it difficult to catch his breath, hardly knew whether to exult for his achievement or cringe at the ordeal still to come. He knew of course, knew beyond doubt or the possibility of doubt, that he was an instrument in some greater purpose. All would be well. Surely. And yet . . . 'On behalf of Her Majesty's Government, I thank Your Excellency,' he managed. Somewhere in his mind a shadow moved, a half memory which slid from his grasp and vanished. 'I very much appreciate this gesture of goodwill,' he went on, working on autopilot.

'Ah, yes,' murmured the Sheikh. 'Goodwill.' An odd expression stole across his face. 'But of course we no longer have need of the British ambassador. Now we have you.' The man's mouth twisted into the shape of a smile, but as far as George could tell, there wasn't a scrap of humour in it. Not a trace.

By the time of departure, shadows were lengthening across the crater, the first stars already in a scatter across the sky. George shivered in the dusk.

'Below freezing in a few hours,' warned the ambassador. 'This is the damnedest climate you ever saw. From the frying pan into the ice bucket, eh?'

'I'll be all right. I've got a woolly pully.' At least, George thought, there was a plausible excuse for his fit of the trembles. 'I came prepared.'

The ambassador looked round. None of the Sheikh's men were within earshot. 'For God's sake, man. I hope you did. What have you got to offer?'

'You're not to worry.' George's gaze was on the Land Rover. The injured girl was being made comfortable on a bed of cushions in the back, her mother kneeling beside her. 'Just make sure you get Jacqueline safely home. And your wife.' He summoned up what he hoped was a confident smile. 'You'll be able to find your way in the dark, I suppose?'

'Been in this bloody country long enough,' the ambassador growled. 'Been in the service long enough too. I know the policy. You haven't got anything to give these buggers, have you?'

George shrugged. 'I can dress it up a bit. We politicians are good at that.' Out of the corner of his eye he could see Sheikh Yusuf and a gaggle of henchmen sauntering across.

The ambassador flushed. 'Listen to me,' he muttered urgently. 'These people may be mad, but they're not daft. Soon as we leave, they'll up sticks and get out. You can forget the cavalry coming to the rescue. By the time I've got to the airfield, they'll be long gone. And you with them.'

'I'm not expecting a rescue.' Yusuf and his gang were inconveniently close now. He dropped his voice. 'Troops are under orders to pull out in the morning. You should get there in time. I'll be OK. Promise.' Somewhere in George's mind a doubt stirred and was squashed. He tried a smile. 'I'll follow on as best I can. All right?'

The ambassador looked stricken. But by now the Sheikh was at his shoulder and it was too late for protest.

All right?' insisted George, grinning hard, looking the ambassador straight in the eye.

'You are ready to go?' asked the Sheikh.

The ambassador's shoulders slumped. 'Yes,' he said. 'We're ready.'

'We must have a picture,' the Sheikh declared grandly. 'To mark this special occasion.' He clapped his hands and the photographer stepped forward, gesturing for the incongruous little group to take up an appropriate pose. They stood in front of the Land Rover, George next to the Sheikh, the ambassador and his wife on the other side, while the camera flashed and flashed again.

'God bless you, Mr Gulliver,' the ambassador's wife said shakily, kissing him on the cheek.

'I'll tell them in London,' murmured her husband, squeezing George's hand. 'Thank you.' A whisper. 'Be very careful.'

Then they were in the Land Rover, starting the engine, moving slowly off to the raucous shouts of the mob, not once looking back. Some of the children scampered after the vehicle but finally lost interest. George watched as the sound of the motor faded to silence, watched until the tail-lights diminished and disappeared.

All would be well for the family now. They were going home. Home to England and safety and the welcome of friends. A miracle, he thought. Tangible proof of . . . ? Well. Perhaps not. Indicative evidence, let's say, of things inherently unprovable. George swallowed. There ought to be exhilaration in this moment, a sense of achievement; but of course he was only an instrument. The pen, not the Author. He felt merely drained, as though the chapter was finished and all his usefulness ended.

It's possible to control a fit of the shakes. A matter of concentration, that's all. He had to clamp his teeth together to prevent them chattering. The cold, of course. These damned desert nights. He'd been warned. Everything would be fine in a moment, when he'd found his pullover. It was over there, in his rucksack, just a few yards away. He'd walk over there in a minute. When he was ready. Once he could get his legs to do as they were told.

'It is time,' said Sheikh Yusuf.

In one respect at least, the ambassador turned out to be quite wrong. Yusuf and his friends clearly had no intention of decamping to a more secure hideout. George entered the Sheikh's quarters to find at least a dozen of them lounging idly, listening through the hiss of static to some interminable wailing on the radio. A few were drinking tea. Others smoked or scratched themselves. Cosy. Not so very different from an evening at a local Conservative Club, in fact, apart from the smell of cooking that drifted from the rear of the shack. Lamb? Goat? Something meaty and succulent anyway. George's stomach whimpered. He hadn't eaten a bite all day.

'We have prepared a celebration.' The Sheikh managed to make it sound almost like a threat, his tone cold. 'For when our business is done.' There was some chattering among his followers then. A stir of anticipation. He gestured for George to sit. 'Tonight we eat together.'

'As friends I hope, Your Excellency.' George summoned up one of his electioneering smiles but got no response. He didn't much care for any of this. Someone pressed a glass of tea into his hand and he raised it in a toast. 'May there always be cooperation between our two countries,' he ploughed on.

The Sheikh grunted, hard-eyed.

'We have already made a beginning.' Somehow George was managing to keep his voice steady. No mean feat, given the circumstances. He had the uneasiest feeling that he understood exactly why the whole ghastly crew were sitting around as though they hadn't a care in the world. Presumably they had serious expectations. An Englishman's word is his bond, isn't it? That fellow from Cheltenham must have been one hell of a storyteller. George sipped his tea, hardly tasting it. Thank God the ambassador and his family were further away with every passing minute. Probably already too far for pursuit.

All I have to do now, thought George, is talk myself out of this. A test of ingenuity, eh?

The Sheikh made a gesture and the radio was switched off. The thugs settled down in the silence, expectant. One of them brought the Sheikh's sword forward and laid it across his knees. The conference, presumably, was now in session.

George carefully set his glass down. 'Your Excellency—' A flashbulb popped, startling him. Where did these buggers get their batteries? He began again. Sonorous. 'Your Excellency, I must say first that Her Majesty's Government is anxious to rebuild good relations with Sahelia and all its peoples. We believe it will be to our mutual advantage if we now come to an informal agreement which we for our part are ready to ratify formally at a more appropriate moment.'

The Sheikh seemed puzzled, as well he might. 'An informal agreement,' he muttered.

'Absolutely.' It seemed an appropriate moment for a few judicious nods. 'Until the situation in your country is resolved, it's of course essential to keep these negotiations confidential.

Her Majesty's Government cannot be seen taking sides in this dispute.' Chew on that one, he thought. You bastard.

There was a certain restlessness among the assembled thugs. The Sheikh held up a commanding hand. 'Continue,' he said, his expression unreadable.

'We have studied your note.' George's mouth was dry. 'And we're ready to respond. What I now propose comes from the highest possible level.' The trick now, he thought, is to make this look like the most intriguing parcel under the Christmas tree. Complete with a great big ribbon on top. 'The very highest,' he pressed on. 'It is our belief that Sahelia not only has strategic importance, but has the potential to become a prosperous and stable nation in the years to come.'

But the Sheikh seemed to have had his fill of all this waffle. He leaned forward. 'When may we expect delivery?'

'Delivery?' George frowned. 'I'm not sure—'

'You say your Government is ready to respond.' A note of impatience. 'Very well. When will you deliver the gold?'

'Ah. Gold.' This is it, chum, he thought. For a wild, lunatic moment, he felt tempted to say something about the cheque being in the post. He recovered himself, made a little moue of disdain. 'I don't think so. What Her Majesty's Government has in mind goes far beyond a few bags of gold.'

The Sheikh's expression darkened. His followers sighed. Somewhere at the back of the room there was a metallic click. A rifle bolt? George stared apprehensively into the shadows. 'In the context of a developing bilateral relationship, Her Majesty's Government is prepared to offer aid and assistance to promote mutually agreed projects,' he hurried on.

It wasn't working. The thugs were growing restive. Growling. 'Projects?' snarled the Sheikh.

'Most would be associated with the development of your oil industry.' George was struggling to stay in control. 'The sums involved would be substantial. Millions of pounds sterling. Millions.' The growls subsided quite encouragingly. 'Millions,' he repeated.

'Aah.' The Sheikh sighed in obvious relief. 'Millions, you say. For a moment, Mr Gulliver . . .' He turned and said something to

his followers. It must have been amusing, since they all laughed.
He swung back and stared George straight in the eye. 'When will
we see these millions?' he asked.

'When?' George's shirt was clammy on his back. 'I'd say that's
entirely up to you.' He was desperate not to blink. 'It's in your
hands.'

The Sheikh frowned.

George breathed deeply. 'You must understand, this is all
part of a package. Her Majesty's Government is ready to recognise you as leader of Sahelia . . .' He wanted to swallow. This
was impossible. But it had to be said. 'When you have defeated
the Vizier and established your Government, of course.'

The room was still. The Sheikh's expression froze. George
could feel his own heartbeat. 'We would then be ready to
resume aid. And of course provide technical assistance in the
oilfields.' Any minute now, he thought, he'd start babbling.
'We're ready to consider joint ventures, of course. Then we'd
support your application to join the United Nations . . .'

'The United Nations?' Cold incredulity.

'We'd use our influence in the World Bank . . .'

But he had to tail off. Someone was shouting at him. There
was a confusion of angry movement. Then the Sheikh was
rearing up on his feet, hefting his sword, his face working.
'Nothing,' he hissed. 'You give us nothing.' He took a pace
forward, murderous.

'Wrong. We can give you everything.' George heaved himself
up too, yelling. Terrified. 'Don't you understand? You can be
rich. All of you. Rich beyond your wildest dreams.' He urgently
wanted to back away. Stood his ground. 'All you have to do is
fight for it.' Damn. He was beginning to stumble over his words.
'Establish control of your country. Then you can have anything
you want. Anything.'

But someone grabbed him then. There was an explosion
of raised voices, men milling around, gesticulating, arguing.
He pulled himself free. 'Nothing,' repeated the Sheikh. Was
there a flicker of uncertainty in his rage? In a sudden spark
of insight it struck George then that the man was in fear of his
own followers.

'Let me make it clear.' Thank God his voice was back under control. 'What Her Majesty's Government offers—' Then he was grabbed from behind, forced viciously to his knees. Something banged the back of his head and he pitched forward.

'You have cheated us.' The Sheikh was almost incoherent now. He leaned down and slapped George very hard across the face. 'You must pay for that. Your country must pay.' He slapped him again.

'How dare you!' George's head was splitting. He felt sick with pain and humiliation, wasn't able to move. 'My Government doesn't deal with savages,' he snarled. 'This has to stop. Now!'

The Sheikh made a gesture. The hands gripping George's arms were released. 'You cheated us.'

'I made you an offer. If you turn it down, you'll get nothing. I promise you. Nothing.'

There was more shouting. The Sheikh sneered. 'You forget. We have you, Mr Gulliver.'

George got unsteadily to his feet. There's still a chance, he thought. Must be. There has to be some sense in this. 'My Government will never pay a ransom,' he managed. His voice seemed to be coming from far away. 'If you hold me here, British troops will hunt you down. You should accept my offer.' His ears were ringing uncomfortably. 'It's still possible.'

'Enough!' The sneer was more pronounced. 'Your troops leave in the morning. We heard this on the radio.'

George gaped. Security. Bloody security again. God above, couldn't anybody these days keep their mouths shut? 'No ransom,' he said. 'You will make an enemy of my country and get nothing. Look.' He reached for an inside pocket. There was an intake of breath somewhere in the room. One of the mob raised a rifle, pointing it at his head. George stood stock-still. 'It's a document,' he gabbled. 'That's all. Something you ought to see.' Slowly, slowly, he withdrew his hand and passed over a folded sheet of paper. 'That's a copy of a letter I sent to the Prime Minister.' He was sweating. The rifle was still pointing at him. 'It makes it clear that whatever happens, no money is to be paid for my release. No gold. Nothing. You'll see that the Prime Minister has countersigned it.'

The Sheikh hardly bothered to look. He threw the letter to one of his subordinates and it was passed round from hand to hand in the uncomprehending mob. 'No matter,' he said, indifferent.

George sensed that his last chance was receding. 'Please listen to me.' His voice was quavering but he didn't care. 'If you accept my offer and let me go, you can look forward to great rewards. Huge. But if you keep me here . . .' He swallowed hard. It seemed impossible that he was standing here discussing this. 'If I'm kept here it can't . . . It's pointless. Can't do you any good. You must see.' He could detect an edge of terror in his words.

The Sheikh's lip curled. 'Did you not tell us you were shortly to become leader of your country?' He muttered an aside and his followers began stamping and banging their rifle butts on the floor in what might equally well have been delight or outrage. 'Your Government will pay,' he shouted, playing to the gallery.

But George's stomach was knotted, the ringing in his ears becoming unbearable. He swayed. 'It won't make any difference. It won't.' He shouldn't disgrace himself. Wouldn't. Even though his bowels seemed to be dissolving. 'I may not win. Quite possibly won't.' It would be fatal to plead, he thought. A terrible mistake in this homicidal company. 'If I'm out of the country I don't stand a chance of winning. You'll just be stuck with a useless prisoner.'

'Stuck?' The Sheikh muttered something to his gang. Someone pushed George and he staggered but managed to keep his feet.

The Sheikh stepped in very close, his expression bleak. 'We will not be stuck, as you put it,' he remarked, almost conversationally. He raised a hand and struck George very deliberately on his left cheek. 'If you become Prime Minister, your Government has no choice but to pay for your return.' The corners of his lips turned upwards in a parody of amusement. 'You must pray you win your election. For if you do not, we shall certainly execute you.'

*   *   *

De profundis clamavi ad te, Domine . . . George crouches in his prison darkness, shivering. Out of the depths . . . he can't quite remember what comes next, but perhaps it doesn't matter. He can't think why it should. In fact he can hardly think properly at all. Old Doctor Johnson got it wrong, didn't he? The prospect of being hanged doesn't concentrate the mind wonderfully. It just shrivels the stomach, curdles the bowels; the mind hardly functions, except in the endless permutations of dread. George might weep, were he not too parched for tears.

Something scuttles in the corner, some creature scrabbling, loud in the stone silence. His flesh crawls. He strains his eyes uselessly against the blackness. Scorpions live in the desert, shiny-shelled and poisonous. Lizards too, hungry for the taste of blood. Spiders with jointed, clicking legs. He shrinks into himself, ropes chafing raw on his wrists and ankles. 'No,' he whispers, his voice hoarse and scratched, barely audible. The scrabbling stops anyway.

And then begins again, a stealthy rustle of legs, pincers and probosces. Coming closer.

George cringes. Struggles to control himself. Nameless horrors live only in the imagination. Think. If the ambassador and his family could survive this pit for days and nights on end, he'll cope too. Somehow. Smother the hysteria. There's nothing to fear in what might well be a cockroach or some blind, timid beetle. He tries to swallow, but can't manage; it's hard when your mouth is dust. He shivers again. Perhaps he should try another prayer. Is anybody there? said the traveller.

George's heart turns. The line has just slipped into his head, arrived from nowhere. It's from a poem, he thinks. Something he must have learned in school years ago. Decades. Is anybody there? said the traveller. Something about a moonlit door. And silence. Who wrote the bloody thing? Quite inappropriate anyway. There is Someone here, Someone entitled to a capital S. Must be. Anyway, isn't it a little late for doubt?

Only . . .

Only he's been here before, hasn't he? A new apprehension grips him by the throat.

Yes, he has. It's hard to think coherently, but he's been here all right. Here in this dark and numbing cold. This is the core of his nightmare. The wasteland. The fate he's struggled so fearfully to avoid. Now there's an irony, though he's in no mood to appreciate it. He thrashes against his bonds, shocked. The ropes bite into his flesh and he subsides, defeated. The scuttling has stopped again. In the blackness nothing moves. There's only silence. And memories.

The pieces are falling into place, or seem to be: there's a Sheikh in the dazzle of sun; a building gleaming white; splashes of green across the barren rock; at the last, a cold and terrible emptiness. Echoes, every one. George is finding it hard to breathe. His chest feels constricted. He recalls every detail in visions long ago: lawns and flowers, a shining apparition; and afterwards a dissolve into the despair of an empty dark. What do you call all that, if not déjà vu? He can't grasp what it means. If indeed it means anything at all. Isn't the phenomenon something to do with a hiccup between the hemispheres of the brain? Or – who knows? – perhaps in some mysterious recess of the skull there's a bundle of neurons somehow capable of precognition. It could be his experiences aren't remotely the stuff of revelation, but a warning shrieked by a faculty long dormant yet frantic for its own survival.

But George can't cope with any of this. It isn't the least like a paper in the finals of the Moral Sciences Tripos. He's cold and thirsty, his stomach aching for food. The ropes have wrenched his muscles, rubbed wrists and ankles raw. And of course he's frightened. More terrified than ever. If he's been led to this dreadful place by some tumult in the brain, he can expect no miraculous rescue. This is what comes of indulging your fancies. He'll be taken out and . . .

There's a scrabbling once again. Close by. More than one creature, almost certainly. The sort of creatures who slither and rustle and hide from the sun. George hugs himself close. In a strange way, he finds their presence almost a relief. It's something to take his mind off the unthinkable. He grunts as the ropes bite into his flesh. There! The creatures seem to have halted their advance. Noise is the answer, obviously. The little crawlers must have fears of their own. It's a kind of comfort. He grunts again.

How long has he been here? There's no way of telling, no way of measuring time but by his growing discomfort and the numbness in hands and feet. Perhaps it's nearly dawn; back at the airfield they might even now be embarking the last stragglers, testing their engines, preparing the flight for home. Perhaps the ambassador's daughter is receiving proper medical attention at last. There's comfort in that thought too. This hasn't been a self-regarding madness then, or not altogether. Though God only knows what they'll make of it back in London.

London. He blinks, gritty-eyed. Home. Perhaps Rosemary might think kindly of him. In spite of. And Monica? Probably not. Too much water under the bridge. He licks dry lips with leathery tongue, drags his mind away from images of rivers and ripples and the plop of dripping taps. Thinks instead of how Sam Ruddock, Peter Coleman and the rest might be coping. Poor bastards. They'll be in an agony of frustration by now, with the election campaign in its final stages and a candidate inexplicably absent. He hardly dares guess what they're thinking about him. Well, it can't be helped. They'll know all about it soon enough. Might even forgive him. If the news reaches Westminster in time to affect the result.

It isn't much of a hope, but George tries clinging to it anyway. What else can he do? The evacuees from Sahelia will surely arrive home before the ballot for the Conservative leadership. In which case, surely . . .

But at this precise moment, when a touch of optimism is exactly what's needed, George discovers that his brain has at last managed to slip into gear. All at once, for no reason he can begin to fathom, he's thinking with a certain bleak clarity. Of course his presence in Sahelia won't leak, or not immediately. That's painfully obvious. To begin with, his agreement with the Prime Minister rules it out; and Michael Poultney will certainly stick to the deal, both for his own sake and to preserve official policy. The ambassador and his family? They'll be whisked away for a lengthy Foreign Office debriefing, their gratitude channelled safely into the sober paragraphs of an official report. To be published, no doubt, in the fullness of time. Meanwhile the army will do as it's told, and for the moment at least keep its collective mouth shut. There. The prospect of a hero's reputation and an election triumph on the back of it is undeniably remote.

George heaves a long, shuddering sigh. Is this how it must end, then? To be dragged out and slaughtered like a bullock? He wants to vomit. He never believed it would come to this. Never. He curls in his own wretchedness, beginning to understand. He hasn't been brought here by madness or vanity or an eruption in the brain. There's no such thing as precognition, no human faculty capable of cracking the laws of the universe. God might have a stab at it though. Give or take a few difficulties inherent in predicting the consequences of free will. So. Shouldn't he take his visions at face value rather than suppose they're the product of an overexcited brain? And if some of those visions seem accurately to have prefigured the future, doesn't that establish the validity of the rest?

This is heady stuff, though for the moment George isn't quite sure what to make of it. He feels like a pawn in some incomprehensible game. If the Almighty has somehow managed to overturn quantum physics in allowing him a glimpse of the fate awaiting him, it suggests that He knew all along how the adventure would turn out. This seems to be taking ineffability rather too far, though George has an uncomfortable feeling that he's been given fair warning: he has after all speculated more than once – been encouraged to speculate? – on the sticky end suffered by the multitude of martyrs.

'The Listeners'. All at once he has the name of the poem. Walter de la bloody Mare. 'Is there anybody there?' said the Traveller,/Knocking on the moonlit door;/And his horse in the tum tum, tum te tum, on the forest's ferny floor. English literature. Form 4A. Mr Matchet in charge. Damn. In the mind's eye he sees himself at the front of the class, reciting the whole thing off pat. A gold star for that one. Well deserved. No. He's not wandering. This is important. Somehow. He feels on the verge of . . . he can't say what. 'The Listeners'. How does the thing go?

And all at once he grasps a meaning. It's in the title. 'The Listeners'. There was someone in the old house after all. They simply weren't answering. That's it! George tries to sit up but can't manage. He lies there, breathing heavily. It's dark and cold and dangerous, but that's not so bad, is it? He's received the message. He's not alone.

But even as the glow of understanding warms his blood, there's a stirring somewhere down by his trouser turn-up. He jerks his leg, shakes his foot, frantic; but whatever it is seems to be dug in, clinging to the fibres of his sock. It's moving now. He wriggles and thrashes, bangs his heels on the earthen floor. There's the faintest scratching on flesh, perhaps a flicker of antennae searching through the fine hairs on his calf. He cringes. His body goes into spasm. It's no good. The comfort of rediscovered meaning is for the moment forgotten. Some questing, crawling creature with stealthy legs is creeping with deliberate intent towards his knee, towards the inviting warmth beyond. And he can only shrivel, sobbing. Unable even to scream.

'Scenes of extraordinary . . .' the reporter's voice spluttered into a crackle of static. The Sheikh frowned, twiddled a knob. The radio howled and burbled. Then the reporter was on again. Too loud this time. 'The most bizarre leadership contest of modern times,' he bawled. The Sheikh turned down the volume. '. . . Still no word on the baffling disappearance of the man who until the events of the last few days was certainly the favourite to win.'

'Hah!' The Sheikh thumped George triumphantly on the chest. 'You see?'

George staggered, almost losing his balance. His toes and feet were still cramped, his hands painful from the rush of returning circulation. The rough handling he'd suffered while being frogmarched to the Sheik's quarters hadn't helped. 'Do you think I could have some water?' he muttered hoarsely. His tongue felt thick and rough, his throat scratchy. It was hard to get the words out.

The Sheikh waved indifferently, still fiddling with the radio.

Someone thrust a bowl into George's hands. He was shaking so badly that he could hardly hold it. Some of the water slopped over the rim. Eagerly, too eagerly, he bent his head and slurped, messy as a dog. Shuddered with the pleasure of it. After a moment, the feeling returned to his lips. He was able to drink normally. Gulped and gulped, feeling the coolness slide sweet into his gullet. Gulped again, then upended the bowl, draining the last drop down. For a blissful moment he forgot his damaged hands and protesting joints, forgot the crunched mess on his thigh where he'd finally managed to trap the crawling creature, bearing clumsily down on it with bound wrists while it scrabbled under the cloth of his trousers, wriggling until it exploded in a gush of stickiness and a thrumming of tiny legs. He still didn't know what it was. What it had been. It didn't matter. He felt better now. Much.

'Pah!' The Sheikh picked up the radio and shook it. The man on the microphone seemed to be saying something about sensational developments, though given the way his voice kept breaking up, it was hard to be sure. Evidently desert gangsters didn't have an endless supply of batteries after all.

George closed his eyes. Back at Westminster, in Committee Room 14, the election was all but over. The tellers would be going through the ballot forms one last time, members of the Parliamentary Conservative Party straining impatiently for the result. In the corridor outside, the media would be in uproar. In a matter of minutes they'd broadcast the outcome all round the world. And then . . . ?

'Everything in this election contest has been spectacularly out of the ordinary.' The sudden, loud clarity of reception was startling. The Sheikh and a dozen of his privileged advisers huddled down, concentrating on the broadcast. 'Last week it seemed Mr George Gulliver had the contest in the bag,' asserted the reporter. 'Then came the crisis in Sahelia and the brilliant operation to pluck British citizens to safety.'

One or two of the black-clad thugs turned cold eyes on George. Someone spat an uncomplimentary remark, but was swiftly hushed to silence.

'In a quite unprecedented development, the Gulliver campaign was thrown into complete confusion with the disappearance of its candidate, a disappearance which is still unexplained.' The cheeky bugger managed to sound aggrieved, as though he regarded the lack of explanation as a personal slight. 'The mystery deepened further with suggestions that Mr Gulliver is undertaking a diplomatic mission at his own request. Downing Street refuses either to confirm or deny . . . Wait a minute. I think we may have . . .'

The Sheikh sat up. George licked his lips. Curious what a little drop of water can do, he thought, light-headed.

'I think a result may be imminent.' The voice faded, then came back through the background hiss. 'Fascinating to see the impact of this morning's report in the *Daily Despatch*. I think it's no exaggeration to say that those quite astonishing claims have thrown the entire Conservative Party into turmoil. Certainly the evidence of a tape recording studied by the BBC suggests that Mr Gulliver has undergone a deep religious experience and genuinely believes he has been given a personal spiritual revelation, direct from . . .' The incredulity in the man's tone sank below a sea of warbling interference.

A chasm opened at George's feet. He swayed. Mr Gulliver genuinely what? Genuinely thinks? Is genuinely off his head? Jack Cartwright's betrayal cut him to the heart. It must have happened that night. In the restaurant. When he was at the end of his tether, bewildered. When Jack offered a receptive ear and bags of sympathy. Only he wasn't sympathetic at all. Clearly. A tape recording studied by the BBC. A bloody tape. Every last whispered confidence taken down and used in evidence. No doubt of the verdict now, is there? Guilty. As sin. He might have burst into tears, but the Sheikh was staring at him with a curious expression. Instead he swallowed hard.

'. . . One of his most senior supporters, Sir Peter Coleman, dramatically withdrew from the Gulliver campaign this morning after listening to the tape. He claimed his colleague must sadly have suffered some kind of breakdown, and in the best interests of the country . . . Ah! I think we may . . . Yes', we have a . . .' There was some confused shouting in the background. The reporter came back on, breathless. 'Mr Michael Poultney has conceded defeat. That's an unconfirmed report. I repeat, the Prime Minister has been defeated.' Off microphone there was an exited, incoherent babble. Some distant cheering. 'This is unconfirmed. Mr Michael Poultney . . .' The man seemed beside himself. 'Quite extraordinary scenes here. Absolute confusion. Nobody quite knows . . . I can see the Chief Whip. Not looking very happy. There's the Home Secretary. Nobody seems sure what . . .' A blanket of static smothered his words.

The Sheikh was smirking. 'You have become valuable property,' he said.

George couldn't take it in. Found it hard to stand. He sank to the floor. If Poultney was out, this truly was the age of miracles. But even as the thought crept into his head, he knew. This wasn't right. All around, the gangsters were chattering like starlings, but they'd got it wrong too.

'My Government will not pay a ransom,' George said. 'It's out of the question.' At least he managed a firm tone. It was something. 'However, if you release me now, my original offer still stands.'

But even as the Sheikh was sneering in refusal, the static on the radio subsided. The reporter's voice was faint but quite audible. 'Final result,' he was saying. 'These figures haven't been officially confirmed, but we think they're accurate. Michael Poultney has lost, with just a hundred and twenty-five votes. The new leader of the party and the man who will tonight kiss hands as Prime Minister is Lucas Brotherton, the Foreign Secretary who swept from nowhere to take a remarkable two hundred and sixty votes. And perhaps even more remarkably—'

The Sheikh's roar drowned the rest. He rose to his feet, mouth working.

George cowered on the floor. The figures made no sense. Lucas Brotherton? The man must have announced his candidacy only at the last minute. But 260 votes? That must mean . . .

The room was seething. Men were shouting. Someone spat. A gob of phlegm landed on George's shoulder.

'. . . A mere seventeen votes for Mr George Gulliver,' said the radio. 'That's an astonishing reversal—'

A hand grabbed George's hair, hauling him up. He was struck in the face. Once. Twice. Fingers pinched his arms, prodded his chest. There was more spitting. Voices raging.

'Paying the price, it seems, for disappearing in the middle of the campaign,' the reporter ploughed on, unheeded. 'And of course the suggestion of hallucinations and a possible breakdown must have been the last straw for many MPs.'

But George was being dragged out of the room now, dragged into the open where children scampered and laughed and where suddenly there were crowds. Jeering. A stone flew threw the air, striking his knee. He stumbled in the dust. Lay there, gasping.

'Seventeen votes,' snarled the Sheik. 'More lies.'

George couldn't speak. There was a tang of blood in his mouth, an immense pressure in his skull. The Sheikh was saying something about making an example. Punishment for those who tried to cheat the revolution. Hard to grasp his words. The mob was pressing closer. Circling. Like vultures.

This is insane. Can't do you any possible good. But George couldn't articulate his thoughts. Then there were hands clutching his shirt, twisting his arms, hauling and shoving him helpless across the parched earth, forcing him back to the stench of his filthy cell. He collapsed retching in the darkness.

'Tomorrow,' promised the Sheikh. 'It will be tomorrow.'

Surprisingly, George dozed. He bolted awake, shivering. This time, there were no ropes tying him down. He struggled painfully to his feet. Stood in darkness, wondering. How could he possibly have slept? Perhaps, he thought, this is what happens when hope has gone. Resignation. The mind's way of coping with absolute terror. With the certainty of imminent extinction.

Only that wasn't it at all. Nothing like.

He took a long, steady breath. It was all right. He was in control. Frightened, to be sure. His belly was cramped, his knees like jelly. But he was capable of thought still. He wouldn't allow himself to disintegrate. More to the point, he couldn't entirely regret the impulse that had brought him here. Bizarre. The sheer bloody recklessness of the venture was beyond doubt; but it would have been unimaginable to do otherwise.

Not resignation, then. Something else.

He shuffled forward, counting the steps until his hands touched the rough wall. Twelve careful paces. He turned and made his way back. It was something to do. A spot of exercise in the blackness. Keeping the circulation going. How many heartbeats did he have left? At eighty to the minute, it added up to nearly five thousand an hour. Say another four hours until . . . Well. He shouldn't think of that now. Essential to keep the mind on other things. Twenty thousand beats though. Perhaps fewer. Thump. Thump. Thump. Then a spasm. And stillness. Stillness. Or would there be light in the darkness afterwards?

He couldn't allow himself to become unmanned. Even your bona fide martyrs didn't look forward with enthusiasm to the end. Thomas More used every device of the law to avoid his fate. Archbishop Cranmer wriggled and recanted. But in the end, More managed to joke on the scaffold, didn't he? Yes, and Cranmer swallowed his fear to face the flames like a hero. There was an unbreakable strength there, at the last.

George wished some of it would flow in his direction. Because he wasn't certain. He only believed. It wasn't the same thing at all.

He shuffled back and forth, back and forth. The only thing he could do now was stick to his instincts. Some good had come of this. The little girl was saved. And her parents. He held on to that. Examined it. Three lives for one. Not a bad bargain, unless you happened to be the one.

Somewhere in the distance a camel snorted. Perhaps the dawn was coming up. My last day, he thought. His stomach clenched. God help me. He couldn't be sure whether he'd uttered the words or not.

All shall be well and all manner of things shall be well . . . Perhaps the lines from Julian of Norwich came in answer to his prayer. Or perhaps not. He had, after all, made a point of reading about the English mystics following his accident. Searching for clues. The quotation might simply be a trick of memory. Still, there was something encouraging there. All shall be well ... No quibbles or caveats. It came down to a question of trust in the end. It struck George then that in fretting over his experiences he might have blundered into a blind alley. Did it matter much whether they were the creation of an electrical spasm inside the skull, a surge of endorphins, some chemical imbalance in the blood? Why should a greater purpose be excluded in any of that?

The test, he thought, should be in the consequences. He'd changed, hadn't he? Wouldn't be here otherwise. Somewhere along the way the old George Gulliver had vanished, to be transformed into ... Well, into this shuffling, frightened creature counting his own heartbeats. Yes, but a creature who'd tried. Someone who'd rendered a service. A man. The Greeks had a word for it. Metanoia. A rebirth of the spirit.

All right. This was clutching at straws. The final prerogative of the condemned. The Greeks were a notoriously unreliable bunch anyway. *Timeo Danaos et dona ferentes*. But as he heard the camels grunting outside, sensed the stirrings of a new day, he clung to his wisp as though it were a lifebelt. Somewhere in all this, there was meaning. Why else would a member of Her Majesty's Privy Council eke out his last hours in a noisome desert shack? It was necessary to believe. And, though belief wasn't quite as reassuring as proof, it would have to do.

It was long past noon when they came for George. He stumbled blinking into the blaze of sun, shook off a restraining hand. The crowd stood silent. There were no jeers or stones. Even the children seemed on their best behaviour.

He held himself straight. Took a deep breath. His guard gestured and he began walking. Grit crunched soft beneath his feet. One step. Then another. Don't look round. Don't think. Don't allow the knees to buckle. Crunch. Crunch. Crunch. This is how an Englishman behaves. Keeping up appearances. All shall be well. All manner of things shall be well. All manner of things.

He halted at the front of the Sheikh's quarters. The mob pressed in close. Waiting. In the aching silence, George heard the whir and click of a camera. His skin crawled. In God's name, they couldn't. Not that. Have some decency, he wanted to shout, but then Yusuf was emerging, his henchmen clustering behind. He stared at George for a long moment, unspeaking. A long sword glinted in his hands. The crowd oohed.

'This is a mistake.' George's voice seemed to be echoing from a distance, as though he was yelling across some vast canyon. 'This is an act of murder which brings disgrace on you.' There might have been a murmur from the mob, but he was only dimly aware of it. Blood roared in his ears.

Yusuf was speaking. Something about the penalty for treachery. George couldn't take it in. He was trying to drag his eyes away from the sword. All shall be well. All. Only there was something . . . It was hard to concentrate. He could feel a pulse leaping in his neck, feel his legs beginning to give way. May God forgive you, he wanted to say, but couldn't make a sound. The blade winked in the sun. Love your enemies. The final, impossible duty. Play your part to the bitter end. What else is there? He tried again, managing to croak something appropriate. He couldn't tell whether anyone heard. Then it didn't matter. He felt hands on his shoulders, forcing him to his knees.

His breath was coming in sobs. He was staring at a patch of earth. Every grain of sand seemed to stand out like a boulder. Sharp-edged. A hand grasped his hair, forcing his head down. He might have whimpered. Caught himself.

He sensed the movement behind him. The earth darkened. He could see the long shadow in the glare, Yusuf's arms raised, a thin sliver of blade. Somewhere the camera whirred. He swallowed, perhaps for the last time. Why should redemption demand such a fearful price? His neck ached in anticipation. But this was only a moment in the darkness, wasn't it? A short step into the light. All manner of things would be well. He had a promise.

He closed his eyes, hoping for the mercy of God. Around him the crowd grew very still. The sword began to descend.

*   *   *

'"Greater love hath no man than this," Mr Speaker Tobin's rolling cadences, weighty with the accents of his native Yorkshire, boomed through the nave, "that a man lay down his life for his friends."' He paused, like the old ham he was, a one-time pigeon-fancier transformed now by wig and gown and snowy linen into the living embodiment of Parliament, into the voice of the nation itself. Westminster Abbey was stone-silent in his presence. Not a cough or a rustle in all the vast congregation.

'"Henceforth I shall call you not servants; for the servant knoweth not what his lord doeth; but I have called you friends, for all things that I have heard of my Father I have made known unto you."' The words of St John's Gospel hung in the air, every one of them touched with just the right degree of power and significance. No doubt about it, thought the new editor of the *Daily Despatch*: if you want a proper turn at your memorial service, Joe Tobin's your man. Accept no substitutes.

'"Ye have not chosen me, but I have chosen you ..."' Jack Cartwright cast a covert glance across the aisle as the reading continued. Rapt expressions. Sombre eyes. Lumps in the throat too, if he was any judge. Even the Chief Whip seemed to be enjoying a wallow in the sentiment of the moment. Jack subsided gently in his seat. We're all here, George, he thought. Every last one of us. The good, the great, the royal and the riffraff, all here in tribute to the last authentic British hero. It must have been something like this when Nelson was buried, or Churchill lay in state. A supreme moment of national catharsis. You'd have loved it, you poor, sad, silly old sod.

'". . . Whatsoever ye shall ask of the Father in my name, he may give it to you,"' Mr Speaker Tobin concluded. He bowed gravely to the altar, giving the unmistakable impression of one equal taking leave of another, and paced slowly back to his pew. The ruffs and surplices of the choir rose smoothly for 'Jesu, Joy of Man's Desiring'. George's favourite, apparently; if there were some in Parliament who suspected that the man's musical tastes had never progressed much further than 'Rule Britannia', they took care these days to keep their own counsel. *De mortuis nil nisi bonum*. In death, George Gulliver had achieved the status no living politician could possibly have dreamed of: the exemplar of all human good. An icon. A model for us all, beyond the reach of petty truth.

Jack closed his eyes as the music soared. Nothing like a drop of Johann Sebastian, was there? All the passion of belief, all the longings of mortal man in one short hymn. Almost made you want to take things seriously. Pity the buggers insisted on doing it in German, though. '*Wenn ich krank, und traurig bin, Jesum habich, der mich liebet*,' the choristers exulted. Rosemary's doing, no doubt. She was a stickler for authenticity; and unlike George, always had a soft spot for our Continental cousins.

Well, no matter. Never mind what language we're using. This is one up to us. Oh, yes. Us. The Brits. The Anglo-Saxons. Naturally the nation felt entitled to bask in a little vicarious glory. By the manner of his sacrifice, George Gulliver had shown the world a thing or two about good old British grit. Taught the buggers what was what. Nowadays even the French felt obliged to join in the respectful obsequies. Through gritted teeth.

Wasn't it extraordinary what a spot of publicity could do? In Nottingham, according to reliable reports, some Catholic priest was seriously suggesting that George should be canonised. In London there was talk of a posthumous medal. Newspaper editorials from Capetown to Cape Cod shone with admiration for a deed well done and a nation still capable of producing the right stuff. For once, the United Kingdom appeared at the top of nobody's shit-list. Amazing.

Jack couldn't repress a modest glow of self-satisfaction. This was his doing, most of it. One stroke of luck – no, let's say one touch of sheer fucking brilliance – had propelled a good story into a moment of unforgettable history. You don't get Westminster Abbey packed to the doors, with royal personages in attendance and live coverage on television, unless there's a bloody good reason. No, sir. To qualify for the full monte, you need something truly remarkable. Something spectacular. Like the kind of magic provided so cleverly by Cartwright, J., creator of a legend.

It hadn't been easy, mind. For a few days there, when news

of George's astonishing endeavour first came out, the Great British Public hadn't quite known what to do with itself. Understandably. All those saloon-bar sniggers about religious mania and a private line to God suddenly hadn't seemed so clever any more, especially after that ambassador fellow James Dalton went on TV to describe how George stood up to the appalling Yusuf. 'The bravest man I ever met' was how the *Mail* headline treated the story next day. 'A modern martyr,' agreed the *Telegraph*. 'Carve his name with pride,' instructed the *Sun*. It was as though the whole country was indulging in a fit of self-reproach for ever doubting George's sanity; and of course it hadn't taken five minutes before everyone was blaming the *Daily Despatch* for raising such doubts in the first place.

Jack closed his eyes as the last notes of Bach throbbed to silence. Thank Christ nobody can ever find out, he thought. If the circumstances of that last interview became known . . . Well, it couldn't happen now, could it? One less worry in the world. Be grateful. Not that he wasn't as shocked as anyone else about George's death. He was. Truly. But it was wonderfully convenient all the same.

He blinked, not entirely comfortable with the memory of the dark times. Such a damned close-run thing . . .

He'd been skulking in the editor's chair at the *Despatch*, blinds drawn and door firmly shut, brooding on his abysmal boob and concentrating on not throwing up over Prudence Willow's hand-woven, deep-pile, soft-cushioned carpet. Well, *his* carpet, to be precise. His for the time being, anyway. Until he too was escorted from the building in disgrace. Might not take more than a day or two, the way things were going. His stomach clenched again. Had any national newspaper ever fired two editors in one week? He doubted it. No wonder he wanted to be sick. Perhaps Willow felt the same when she was taken away, white-faced, by two burly detectives from the Fraud Squad.

'We are assembled here, all of us, in memory of a remarkable human being . . .' The familiar tones of Michael Poultney pulled Jack into the comfortable present. He sat up straight. This part of the service had always promised to be particularly entertaining; rumour had it that the former Prime Minister was still steaming with rage over the leadership contest and might well be the only citizen in the land to remain resolutely unimpressed by George's endeavour. The mystery was how he'd ever been persuaded to deliver the eulogy in the first place.

Jack watched, expectant. Poultney was standing at the lectern before the High Altar, no trace of malice on his face. Well, of course there wouldn't be. He was a politician after all, one of nature's dissemblers. Not a bit like the rest of us. This was a man who could wield the knife or administer an assassin's poison with such grace that his victim would never notice until the onset of necrosis. Important to concentrate, then. Essential to examine every nuance. The old fraud was talking without a blush of a valued colleague, an old friend, a devoted servant of Her Majesty. Strange. No hint of acid, not the suggestion of a concealed barb. It was as though the disappointment and bitterness of defeat had simply been wiped away. So much for rumour. It was beginning to dawn on Jack that Poultney might – just possibly – mean every word. Had he too been overwhelmed by that shattering glimpse of George's last moments on earth?

The picture. It all came back to that unforgettable picture, didn't it? Jack could see it still, as clearly as the day it landed on his desk. It was the moment everything changed. He'd never known such a surge of relief. Better than sex. Better even than a pat on the back from the company chairman.

He'd been moping in his office as per usual, wondering why in the name of Christ he'd ever wanted to be editor. He almost found himself regretting Prudence Willow's arrest for dipping her fingers in the corporate till. One lousy week in the job and he was learning a bitter truth about his readers: the ungrateful bastards had no loyalty, no stamina, no inclination to go on buying the *Daily Despatch*. After the Willow fiasco, they'd prissily cancelled their orders by the truckload. News of the desert rescue and Ambassador Dalton's emotional interview on TV pushed circulation even lower. Nobody wanted to touch the paper that had painted George Gulliver in fool's clothes.

And then the miracle. That's what it was. A solid-gold, bona fide, damn-your-britches miracle. As soon as he saw it, he knew his problems were over. He stared at the photograph wide-eyed, while his pictures editor spluttered some tale of how a camera-toting rebel had managed to meet up with an Italian freelance journalist in a remote town called Bardai, somewhere in Chad. Jack had never heard of the place. Didn't care. It hardly mattered how the evidence had crossed the desert to some flyblown North African market-place. What mattered was that he possessed it now.

'Got this to ourselves?' It was hard to keep the excitement out of his voice. If he'd been a believing man, he'd have ventured a silent prayer.

'If we're prepared to pay.' The pictures editor swallowed nervously. 'He wants fifty thousand.'

'Give it to him. All of it. Don't haggle. Just make sure we keep the exclusive.' Jack wasn't concerned by the startled look in the other man's eyes, or by the vast hole about to be torn in the editorial budget. This was unmissable. The opportunity of a lifetime. He was looking at a new beginning, right enough. Jesus. Feel the adrenalin. Poor old George, eh? They'd never found his body, not so much as a bone to remember him by. But this was better. So much better.

The picture was diamond-sharp, every detail clear. George was kneeling on the sand, his head bowed. Above him the executioner glared in a swirl of black robes, his sword raised. Pitiless. Sun glinted on the blade. Jack couldn't stop looking. Christ, what must George have been thinking in those last seconds? Now there's a question. That's what made the picture so compelling. There was horror in the scene, sure. It would be a dull reader who didn't feel it crackling off the page in the morning. But it wasn't horror or the evil of the act that drew Jack's eye. It was the expression on George's face. This wasn't some terrified victim cringing in the dust. This was a man facing the end . . . Jack couldn't immediately think of the appropriate words. Then they came to him. Facing the end nobly. Serenely. It wasn't fanciful. The readers would see it too. The whole world would see it. In his moment of death, George Gulliver looked like a champion, triumphant after a desperate fight; or like some traveller who ventured far across a bleak terrain to stand comforted at last in the lights of home.

Bloody hell, Jack thought. If this doesn't get them crying into their cornflakes, nothing will.

And so it had proved. No front page in the history of modern journalism, in his humble opinion, had ever made quite such an impact. He'd run the picture across all six columns, giving it the full drop. Just three words in the headline: THE FINAL SACRIFICE. Powerful? You bet. Even with a quarter of a million extra copies printed, the *Despatch* had sold out by 10 a.m., with the punters screaming for more. The rest of Fleet Street was reduced to chaos, on its knees, forced to beg for the right to publish the photograph next day. Hah! In the end, there wasn't a newspaper or television station in the world that wasn't pathetically grateful to stump up the asking-price; and of course it meant a fat bonus in the Cartwright bank account at the end of the month. Well deserved, too.

Not that the money really mattered. Jack had discovered a far greater prize. For the first time in his life, he'd tasted influence. Real, kiss-my-arse influence. The kind that changes people's lives. The kind that makes a difference. With one front page, he'd touched the emotions of the nation and the wider world. He'd turned George from a mere martyr into a superstar, a universal emblem of chivalry. And, by the way, he'd altered the course of the British General Election. Decisively.

Delicious.

He glanced across the aisle at the Prime Minister, Lucas Brotherton, who as usual since polling day was looking uncommonly pleased with himself. Huh, thought Jack. You'd never be in office but for me, matey. Me and George, you smug bastard. George and me. Remember the state the Tories were in, do you, before we did our stuff? Twenty points down in the polls and heading for a wipeout? Embarrassing. Pitiful. But we gave you the green light for your snap election, didn't we, old chum? Sure we did. Changed the national mood in the twinkling of an eye. Gulliver and Cartwright, architects of a political sensation. Worth a little gesture of appreciation, wouldn't you say? A knighthood, perhaps? Come on, Brotherton, why not? You know it makes sense. Remember how Margaret Thatcher used to dish them out like jellybeans to her friends in the press? Smart lady. In those days you'd seldom find editors especially anxious to criticise the Government. It would have been like a bunch of down-and-outs attacking a Salvation Army soup kitchen.

Jack realised he was glowering. He turned away before Brotherton could catch his eye. No point in antagonising the man. He was still Prime Minister after all, still worth cultivating. Even if he *had* managed to scrape home by only two seats. A second General Election couldn't be long delayed; and this time no miracle could save the Tories. Well, then. There would be a dissolution honours list in the aftermath, a chance for the defeated administration to reward its more deserving supporters. Something to hope for, eh? Sir Jack. No, Sir John sounded better. Sir John and Lady Cartwright. Might even restore a little enthusiasm to the marital bed.

Up at the lectern, Michael Poultney was beginning his peroration. George Gulliver, he was saying, had the stamp of greatness on him. He was one of those rare beings who transcend the limitations that bind the rest of us. We shall never forget how he illuminated our lives. And we will miss him. In our quiet moments, we will.

Jack surreptitiously looked at his watch. Nearly done. One more hymn and they'd be out of it. Not before time. He'd heard quite enough about George Gulliver for one day, thank you very much. The caravan moves on. Foolish to pretend otherwise. It's the way of the world.

Who, when you came right down to it, would really miss George? Nobody who mattered. Nobody in Cabinet. There's nothing cheers a government minister quite so much as the removal of a political rival. His constituency wouldn't pine either; the local Association in Mowsbury hadn't wasted any time before picking that young sprog Simon Fishlock as its new candidate. Even the girlfriend, Monica something, was apparently planning to marry her boss. Off with the old, on with the new, hey? Happens all the time. As for Rosemary . . .

Jack caught a glimpse of her up at the front, with the rest of her family. What a star she'd turned out to be. The dignified widow. Keeper of the flame. Shortly to be ennobled, so word had it, as Baroness Gulliver. A chance at last to move out of George's shadow and beat her own drum. Would she really want to turn back the clock?

The great organ of Westminster Abbey burst into the introductory notes of a final hymn. The congregation rose, drew collective breath, launched itself heartfelt into the opening verse.

> He who would valiant be
> 'Gainst all disaster,
> Let him in constancy
> Follow the Master . . .

Jack joined in enthusiastically with the rest. He liked a good tune. And it hadn't been a bad send-off, had it? No, indeed. A grateful nation says farewell. So long, George. But it's all for the best. Better a dead hero than a live embarrassment, eh? Better for everybody. Let's leave it at that, shall we?

> Since Lord thou dost defend
> Us with thy Spirit . . .

Jack sang at the top of his voice. Sang with vim. Brio. Sang like a trouper. It was an excellent way of sharpening the appetite; and he was looking forward enormously to his lunch.

The vultures flapped heavily to earth and folded their wings. Two of the creatures, pink-necked and watchful. Anxious for their supper, no doubt. It would be the juicy bits first. The eyes. The goolies. The tongue. Followed in short order by an entrée of steaming entrails. Yum, yum. They edged closer. Silently.

Major John Carstairs, 2nd Battalion, the Parachute Regiment, watched them come. Not long now. A couple of hours maybe. No longer. The scavengers would just have to wait. Or were they capable of tucking in before their meal was actually laid out? That was one thing they didn't tell you on the desert survival course. 'Fuck off!' he screamed. The words came out as a painful croak. The birds simply stood there, unimpressed.

Never be without your rifle. That's the lesson, Carstairs. Keep it with you at all times. Love it like a woman. Caress the stock, fondle the barrel, stroke the trigger. Gently, now. Gentle. Slow and soft, with the tips of the fingers. Feel the oilslick slither. Sense the power. God, he wished he had his rifle. One bullet to end it all. Clean as a whistle. Or maybe he could have picked off his two uninvited guests instead and had vulture blood for tea. No. Don't think about drink. Don't think of the rifle either. Dumped days ago, wasn't it? Maybe weeks. Hard to keep track of time.

Carstairs closed his eyes against the glare of the sun. No use regretting the rifle. No use regretting anything. This is where you die, my friend. Flattered to death, that's the truth of it.

And he had been flattered. Shit, no point beating about the bush. He'd been ecstatic. Like a schoolboy on his first date. The Prime Minister wants to see you. Privately. Tell nobody. Come to Downing Street by the back door, understand?

Sure he'd understood. It had to be work of national significance. An affair of state. When Her Majesty's First Minister takes you by the arm and presses a whisky into your hand and murmurs confidentially in your ear, it's impossible to repress a little thrill of self-importance. Keep an eye on Mr Gulliver, Prime Minister? Certainly I will. Follow him at a discreet distance? Watch and listen and report back? But of course, sir. Consider it done. No explanations necessary. Queen and country, sir. Tickety-boo.

He groaned. Opened his eyes. The vultures seemed closer now. At least he still had his knife. He'd give one of the creatures something to think about when the time came. If he had the strength. What an end though. What a bloody stupid end.

The sheer oddness of the enterprise had begun to sink in while he was secreting a transponder on George Gulliver's Land Rover. Useful little gadgets, he'd always thought. Very handy for tracking Provo vehicles in the back lanes of Northern Ireland's bandit country. Which is what inspired his first twinge of unease. The Sahelian desert seemed an awful long way from Crossmaglen; and the former Secretary of State for Defence was hardly a terrorist, was he?

Well, ours not to wonder why. Simple soldiers do as they're told. As indeed do simpletons. Duty's the thing. Stick to your orders, Carstairs. Track your man across the desert. Coast quietly down the slope towards the village. Lights off, naturally. Never mind the risk. You're a para. *Utrinque paratus*. Ready for anything.

He'd been lying in cover behind a clump of rocks when they brought Gulliver out. Once again, a worm of doubt wriggled in his mind. Observe and report, that was the task. That's what the Prime Minister wanted. The assumption had to be that George was up to no good. But it was becoming clearer by the second that the man wasn't engaged in any scallywaggery. He looked very much like a prisoner. Like a condemned man. In fact . . . Damn. Sweat smeared his binoculars. He wiped them clean. He could see George on his knees now. Some bugger in black was hoisting a sword. Measuring him for the chop. Lord, there'd be something to report to the Prime Minister now. Wouldn't there just?

At that moment, something strange overcame Major John Carstairs. Something not at all in character. For once in a military lifetime, he forgot his orders. Simply threw them aside. He couldn't help himself. It was as though all his training, all the disciplines of a hard regiment, all his instincts of self-preservation were suddenly snatched away by an unseen hand. Spooky. He'd reached for his rifle, hardly able to believe what he was doing. Aimed in one smooth movement. This was crazy. Unforgivably stupid. But his finger was on the trigger. Squeezing.

He was running to his vehicle before the black-clad executioner hit the ground. He gunned the engine, cursing his own folly. Raging at himself. Impossible to go back the way he came; he'd be caught before he was halfway up the slope. Very well then. Forward. Into the village. Out the other side. Why in God's name was he doing this? Damn. He crouched low behind the wheel as his vehicle bucketed across the ground. A body thumped against the side. God, there were dozens of the swine. He clicked his rifle onto automatic and gave them a wild, one-handed burst. Plenty of yells. Plenty of shrieks. Some of the rebels were firing. He hunched lower in his seat. He had a couple of grenades in his pouch. Pull the pins. Don't bother counting to three. Hurl the pineapples anywhere. Doesn't matter. Keep the pot boiling. A bullet whanged off his dashboard, smashing his one and only compass. Brilliant. Have to navigate by the stars now. In the unlikely event of getting out alive. Still breathing though. Not a scratch so far. More than you deserve, you reckless clown. Somewhere behind him, the grenades exploded. He was in the village square, then. Skidding to a brief halt. Doing the one thing that still had to be done. Still operating under this crazy compulsion to get himself killed. Arsing around like a lunatic. Don't think. Head down. Foot hard on the accelerator. Something whupped into his flak-jacket. But he was through the village by then, driving as though his life depended on it. Which of course it did.

Crazy. Absolutely. Beyond all understanding.

Something was hurting. Probably the hit he'd taken. Would have been nasty but for the jacket. Good old Kevlar. Only a bruise. So why . . . ?

He opened his eyes. Shrieked. One of the vultures was scrabbling at his chest, pecking. Stinking with the rottenness of decay. He jerked his arm across, knocking the creature away. It retreated a few yards and stopped, glaring coldly. Its accomplice sidled closer. Carstairs scrabbled to pick up a handful of sand and threw it weakly in their direction. They retreated a few inches more. Settled down to wait.

It was the stench he couldn't stand. The stink and the scratch of talons. He struggled feebly to his knees. The birds stared. He was choking with fear and disgust. Hating them. Despising himself. With a final effort of will, he managed somehow to climb to his feet. He stood there, swaying. One last hill. One last climb before surrendering. Maybe the vultures would give up and call it a day. Maybe . . . But he couldn't kid himself. There had been so many hills. So many frustrations. Days and endless days skulking in caves as Yusuf's men raged across the desert in search of vengeance. Long nights crawling in low gear by the light of the stars. No compass. No radio. He'd been almost certain there was a road a couple of hundred clicks North of the rebel village, but he'd failed to find it. Perhaps he'd driven across the damn thing in the dark without realising. Or maybe it had been wiped out in a sandstorm. The reason hardly mattered. He'd known he was lost long before the petrol ran out. And then the painful weeks eking out the last dribbles of water, emptying the jerricans one by one, digging for roots and desert grubs, discovering a rockface where in the chill of night a few beads of moisture would appear, weeping through crevices, collecting in the tiniest droplets. If a man licked the rough stone, licked and sucked for hours on end, it was possible to take enough liquid on board to survive the following day. Just.

Carstairs almost wished he'd never done that desert survival course. All those hard-earned skills only served to prolong the agony. How many weeks stuck in this awful wilderness? Eight? More? It was becoming impossible to think much beyond his thirst and pain. God, but he was tempted to give up. Just sink to the ground and wait for the end. If it wasn't for those bloody vultures . . .

He prodded his companion with the toe of his boot. 'Up,' he croaked. 'Get up.' He kicked, harder this time. 'Get the fuck up!'

George Gulliver moved his blackened lips. No sound emerged. Carstairs kicked him again.

'Can't,' whimpered George. 'You go on. Leave me be. I'm sorry.'

Carstairs bent and grabbed George's collar. 'You get to your feet, you soft bastard. That's an order.' His head was spinning, but he kept on pulling. 'Up! Up! Get up! Don't give me any fucking sorry.' He was shouting, ignoring the barbed wire in his throat. Ignoring the pain. He was thinking of the vultures.

Yet it was beginning to work. George was stirring. Slowly. A millimetre at a time. Leaning. Almost pulling Carstairs down. Until at last he stood. Haggard, obviously unready for a final effort, but at least capable of movement.

Good man, Carstairs tried to say. The words wouldn't come

out. He pointed up the hill. This way. This is where we're going. This is what we've got to do. George just looked disbelievingly at him through red-gummed eyes. Then he turned and began walking. Staggering rather, one foot dragging after the other. Carstairs trudged after him. One step at a time. Thinking of exercises on the Brecons, when the muscles screamed and the lungs caught fire and you'd die rather than give up. One step. Another. Another. He was alongside George now. Giving him silent encouragement. Shuffling forward. Bit by bit. They'd rest soon. When they reached the top. Rest and never get up. Let the scavengers have our flesh. We'll have given it our best shot. Done the best we can. Can't say fairer than that.

They reached the top at last, two shrivelled men in scarecrow rags, shuddering in the extremity of exhaustion. Before them, the desert stretched to the horizon, miles of baking dun. Miles. They clung together, gasping. Blinking in the harshness of the sun.

For a long moment they couldn't move. Couldn't believe. The spell was broken only when the growl of a distant engine reached their ears. They stared at each other wordless, too tired to summon up a smile. Then arm in arm, they began stumbling towards the road.